Fakers

A Licking Thicket Novel

Lucy Lennox

May Archer

Fakers

Brooks Johnson's Words To Live By:

When returning to Licking Thicket, TN, for the first time in ten years to reunite with your nosy neighbors, heartbroken ex-girlfriend, and matchmaking mama who never quite believed you were gay, it's best to bring a fake boyfriend as backup...

Just don't be surprised when your ex-girlfriend does the same.

And when her incredibly hot fake boyfriend becomes the one island of calm in a sea of bovine-based insanity, it's best to exercise caution... especially when he pushes you up against the rough barn wall to check you very thoroughly for splinters...

Just don't be surprised if you fall head-over-hooves in love with him.

Chapter One

Brooks

Have you ever seen a train wreck happen in real time?

Yeah, no, me neither.

But then I watched Kale Storms, heir apparent to Storms Marketing, LLC, lean across the glass table in our Midtown Manhattan conference room and fucking *purr* at our potential client, General Beauregard T. Partridge—the octogenarian founder and CEO of Partridge Pit BBQ, with its ninety-seven dining locations across the South and a brand-new line of specialty sauces—like it was leather night at the club and the General had been a naughty boy.

"So I think you'll find that what we've designed for you here, Mr. Partridge, is something really *sleek* but also *raw*. Something *fresh* but also *classic*. Something *sexy* that also encapsulates the inherent *impotence* and *mortality* in all of us. Something that's going to *elevate* your barbecue sauce from a humble condiment people slap on grilled flesh into something *better*." Kale's lips pouted and his eyes smoldered. "I think you know what I mean by that, Mr. Partridge. I think you're *ready* for the sexy. *And I think you want it.*"

As I sat in my chair, momentarily paralyzed, I suddenly had the distinct impression I was watching that train wreck from *inside* the fucking train.

Putting Kale in the lead on this project had been a shit idea from the get-go, and I'd told Pamela so. "He's twenty-three," I'd reminded her. "Enthusiastic and full of potential but *green*. You know? And Storms Marketing has a reputation to uphold."

This was Brooks Johnson speak for "Holy fucking shit-balls, Pamela! What were you thinking, giving this ginormous opportunity to your idiot nephew, who has approximately the same IQ as the leafy green he was named after? And *furthermore*, how could you do this without talking to *me*, the guy who's spent the last five years as your right-hand man, helping you build the solid reputation Kale's about to toss in a dumpster and set on fire?"

But Pamela had brushed an imaginary fleck of lint from her fitted blouse and smiled her Botox smile. "We all have to start somewhere, Brooks, darling. *You* were an absolute *prodigy* at twenty-three, remember? Besides, Kale has you for a mentor, so I'm *confident* nothing will go wrong."

Which, I happened to know, was Pam Storms speak for "Yes, I know he's a total fuckup, but I gave you a chance once upon a time, Brooks, so you owe me. You'd better *make damn sure* nothing goes wrong."

And I'd tried. I'd really, *really* tried.

I'd offered Kale help brainstorming concepts. He'd given me a patronizing smile and said brainstorming stifled his creativity.

I'd suggested he loop in Paul Siegel, the senior marketing communications director and my second-in-command. Kale had informed me he'd "hired his own team, Brooks. Fresh blood. People who really *know* advertising"—

which was infuriating on many levels, but primarily the financial one, since I happened to know Storms Marketing didn't have anywhere *near* the kind of budget "fresh blood" cost.

I'd insisted on seeing his mock-ups. He'd refused.

I'd threatened to go to his aunt. He'd ignored me.

I'd been ready to hack Kale's laptop to get the info, when Paul reminded me that I had no clue how to do that. "Besides," he'd said reasonably, pushing his glasses up his nose, "how bad could his presentation really be, Brooks?"

Watching Beauregard Partridge's eyes widen and his cheeks flush pink beneath his white-white hair as Kale reminded him of his *impotence and mortality*, I could confidently say it was pretty fucking bad.

I lifted one eyebrow at Paul across the table. He winced and rubbed his forehead below his receding hairline, and I knew we were thinking the same thing: *How the hell is Brooks going to fix this?*

But I would. It was what I did. I smiled and I was polite, I never argued or let anyone down, I tap-danced like a fucking champion, and I made shit happen.

It was how I'd gotten the scholarship that had gotten me out of my tiny, ridiculous town. It was how I'd landed a job right out of college and worked my way through grad school. It was how I'd become Pamela's VP before I'd turned twenty-five. It was how I was going to save up enough money to start my own agency within the next seven years. Once I had a goal, there wasn't much I wouldn't sacrifice to make it happen, so somehow I was going to fix this too.

I cleared my throat and moved to hijack the meeting when Kale turned off the lights and hit Play on the ultra-modern wall projector. The room was suddenly filled with a terrible screeching of birds, and glowing, stylized letters on the screen spelled out *Plate of Bones... Flavor is Coming.*

Oh. My. God.

Scratch pretty fucking bad. Try epically terrible.

I slumped back in my seat, and the next three minutes passed by like a sort of black-and-white Stanley Kubrick fever dream. I had vague impressions of a Throne of Iron made out of forks and knives, of a tablecloth saying *House Partridge* with a stylized chicken logo in the center, and of a psychopathic-looking guy slurping reddish sauce—which *did not look like sauce*—off his fingers.

I glanced around the table. Kale looked smugly satisfied, and so did the three members of his "team." Meanwhile, General Partridge and his entourage—two granddaughters and a nephew—stared at the screen in slack-jawed horror even after the montage ended. Paul's pale eyes were wide behind his glasses. He fumbled in his pocket and pressed his asthma inhaler to his lips.

And me? Weirdly enough, I was *angry.*

I didn't get angry often. Emotions twisted me up, so I usually tried to keep things calm and logical. But watching that travesty, I remembered sitting in my parents' living room back in Licking Thicket, Tennessee, on football Sundays, singing the Partridge Pit jingle with my brother and sister at the top of our lungs, just to drive my mama crazy. It was one of my happiest memories from home, one of those times I'd actually felt like I belonged.

I felt vaguely like Kale Storms had just gone and crapped all over my childhood.

Kale brought the lights back up, and we all blinked like prisoners emerging from a dungeon.

"Well," he said, rubbing his hands together with a happy sigh. "Have you seen enough, Mr. Partridge?"

"More than." Beauregard T. Partridge sat straight as a rod in his chair and slicked his hair down with a trembling hand. His shoulders looked a bit frail beneath his dark gray suit, but his eyes positively *burned* as he gripped the polished wood of his walking stick and stared at Kale like he wanted to cosh him over the head with it.

I was just about ready to help him.

"You know—" General Partridge's cute, twinky nephew tried to summon a polite smile. "I think what Uncle Beau is trying to say is that we're not quite sure—"

"Hold it right there, Parrish. I'll handle this," the General told the younger man gently. He turned back to Kale with no trace of that gentleness. "I have never in my entire life been so insulted. When my Pattie"—he pointed at a young brunette who looked remarkably like him, but for the fact that she'd hung her head in shame—"told me we needed to come to New York City to get newfangled *branding*, I admit I was skeptical. But after this?" He shook his head, and it made his jowls quiver. "Under no circumstances will my company ever pay one cent of our hard-earned money for this... this... *horseshit*, or my name isn't Beauregard T. Partridge!"

Paul's eyes pleaded with me across the table to *do* something. The Partridge Pit BBQ Sauce line would be a huge coup for Storms Marketing. Securing this account would guarantee our annual bonus, and I knew Paul had approximately ten billion nieces and nephews to spoil and a younger sister getting married this year. So I did something I'd sworn I wouldn't do the day I'd left Tennessee.

"Why, General Partridge!" I said, rising to my feet. "Sir, I am just so, *so* sorry for this misunderstanding." I let the no-nonsense, unaccented voice I'd worked so hard to achieve soften back into its natural lilt, let the flat vowels and consonants go round like I had *alllll* the time in the world to craft the syllables before I released them. I flattened my tie to my chest with my left hand and extended my right as I moved around the table. "You might not remember me. Brooks Johnson? I have to apologize on behalf of my colleague here."

General Partridge's instinctive good manners meant he couldn't fail to stand and shake my hand, just as I'd anticipated, so I was sure to shake once, firmly, look him in the eye, and smile, the way my daddy had taught me.

"I don't know about a misunderstanding," the General began. "I think I understood very well. The throne was made of forks and knives, Mr. Johnson. You don't eat barbecue with forks and knives! It falls off the *bone*."

"I know. I do know." I clapped Kale on the shoulder so firmly he stumbled into his chair looking shell-shocked and uncertain. "But you remember how it is with young folks, don't you, General? Eager to impress, but not always sure how?"

Kale looked about as eager to impress as he was to learn ballet, so I carried on quickly.

"I was just *thrilled* when I heard we'd have the opportunity to speak to y'all. My family've all been... big, big fans for years," I lied, crossing my fingers behind my back and hoping my mother never heard about this.

My family was pretty fine with folks loving who they loved and worshipping whatever entity they worshipped, but Cindy Ann Johnson had been devoted to Susie Dupree's Deluxe Barbecue since they'd had a single storefront back in my hometown, and she'd rather give my grandmother's secret sweet tea recipe to all the ladies on the town beautification committee than darken the door of a Partridge Pit.

General Partridge did not look convinced, and I could see I was going to have to pull out the big guns.

Paul had better fucking build a shrine to me after this.

"We've fired up the grill to give your family a thrill..." I began to sing.

Seven pairs of eyes stared at me. I liked to think my singing wasn't quite as horrifying as Kale's Game of Thrones: Barbecue Edition, but it was clearly close. There was a reason choir was the one extracurricular my mother had never made me stick with.

Think about that bonus, Brooks.

"With tender, tasty meat that's ready to eat..." I added spirit fingers and a little box-step dance move my junior cotillion instructor would facepalm over. "And sauce with flavor everyone will savor. So come on down, we're right in your town! You'll always fit at Partridge's... *Pit!*" I concluded with a flourish.

For a second, General Partridge looked at me and wheezed, and I worried I'd not only humiliated myself, but I'd caused a nice old man to stroke out with my singing.

But then I realized the wheezing was laughter, and that General Partridge wasn't dying, he was getting to his feet and extending his hand to me out of something that wasn't just ingrained politeness.

"Good Lord, I haven't heard that jingle in *years*! My oh my, that was a *classic*. You, Brooks Johnson, have *gumption*. Alright, son. You want another shot at my business? You've got it." He nodded his white head. "One week. You can come see me at my place in Nashville." He side-eyed Kale, who still looked stunned. "And leave your young friend *here.*"

———

"Brooks Johnson," Paul said as we walked back to my office that afternoon after Pamela treated us to a celebratory lunch at my favorite sushi restaurant. "You... are *magic.*"

I snorted and dropped tiredly into my chair, tossing my phone on my desk. "And don't you forget it, buddy. When my magic self wants your ass here tomorrow, and Sunday, and *alllll* night and day next week so we can work on this fucking thing, no complaining."

Paul slumped in his usual seat on the opposite side of my desk and grabbed the stress ball he left there for our planning meetings. "No complaining," he agreed. "Even if my mother storms the office Sunday and tries to drag me out to Cedarhurst for Romi's baby sprinkle by force, I'll refuse! I'll tell her I have six sisters, but only *one* magic boss who gives Uncle Paul the money to spoil them with presents."

I smirked as I folded my hands behind my head and leaned back to prop my feet on the desk. "Please. You'll fold like a cheap card table the second she starts talking. You always do."

"Yeah, well. Easy for you to judge when you live seven hundred miles away from *your* mother."

"On purpose." I loved my family, but those hundreds of miles were in everyone's best interest. I'd never really belonged in the Thicket, though I'd spent the first eighteen years of my life trying very hard to pretend I did. I was a gay man with no interest in farming, fishing, or raising children, which meant there wasn't a lot for me to talk about over beers at the town's single bar. Video chatting every week and regular visits meant we stayed in touch and I got to be cool "Uncle B" to my nieces, but distance from my hometown meant not reliving painful memories and not letting anyone down.

And, *God*, since when did I spend time thinking about Tennessee when I had a major project due in a week's time?

"Alright. Let's get this done." I put my feet back on the floor and opened my laptop to a blank screen. "First things first..." I turned my ideas notebook to a fresh page, got ready for brainstorming... and distracted myself again. "What's a *sprinkle*?"

Paul frowned.

So did I. That was *not* what I'd intended to ask.

"Ah. Well. It's like a baby shower, but smaller? Like, when the first baby is a girl—or, in Romi and Noam's case, the first *three* are girls—and then you have a boy, or vice versa, people *sprinkle* you with gendered clothing and toys for the new baby. It's seriously old-fashioned, but nobody turns down free gifts, so." He shrugged. "In my opinion, it's mostly an excuse for Romi to get some much-needed attention. She can talk about her sciatica and how she was a slave to her morning sickness just like Princess Kate for an hour and people just nod sympathetically."

I grabbed a pencil off the desk and tapped it against my notebook. My little sister Gracie had two older girls and was pregnant with her third baby. I wondered idly if she'd had a sprinkle. No one had mentioned it to me, but then... maybe they wouldn't.

Paul ducked his head slightly to meet my eyes. "You okay?"

"Huh? Oh, yeah. *Pfft*. Totally. Why wouldn't I be?" *Get it together, Brooks.* But thinking about Licking Thicket and my crazy family had opened a doorway in my mind that I usually kept firmly shut.

"You literally sang and danced today," Paul agreed. "I've occasionally wondered if there's a line you *won't* cross to get the job done, and it looks like the answer's *no*."

I narrowed my eyes. "You'd better believe it, buddy. But frankly, I'm also sitting here *mystified* that a single, straight man has absorbed so much about the ins and outs of pregnancy. Sciatica and morning sickness?"

Paul shrugged, totally unconcerned. "Four of my sisters have kids, a minimum of three kids each, and my mom likes me to be present for every family event, just in case there's a single woman around I haven't been introduced to." He rolled his eyes. "At least being gay means your mom isn't trying to set you up all the time."

"She probably would," I said darkly. "If she really believed I was gay."

I definitely hadn't meant to say that either. My mouth seemed to be disconnected from my brain suddenly.

"Does she think you're lying?" Paul wrinkled his nose. "Why would you do that? I mean, it's none of my business, probably. It's just... you never talk about your family, and you never go home to visit. I've always kinda wondered why."

"It's not really a secret," I hedged. "My family is great." But I didn't elaborate.

Paul was maybe my closest friend in the city—the guy I'd call if I ended up in the hospital, and the one who'd feed my cat when my boyfriend and I were away on vacation...

If I'd ever had a cat.

Or a boyfriend.

Or took vacations.

But "magical" Brooks Johnson, VP of Storms Marketing, was a completely different creature from Brooks Johnson, former high school quarterback and once-upon-a-time winner of Mr. Licking Thicket. The Venn diagram of those lives had no overlap, and I'd made that decision consciously. I'd never wavered... until now.

"So, are they, like, super conservative, or—?"

"Not at all. My dad's sister Birdie's a lesbian, and everyone in town *adores* her." I tapped my pen on the desk some more, pondering how to explain the whirlwind called Cindy Ann Johnson to a person who'd never met her. "Mama can be a bit dramatic. Even though her accuracy rate is less than zero, she likes to think she has her finger on the pulse of every situation in town—"

Like I'd summoned her with my thoughts, my phone began to dance and twitch across the desk, playing her ringtone and flashing her smiling face on the screen.

"Whoa. Maybe she *does*," Paul joked, looking down at the phone.

I didn't laugh.

A phone call, not a video chat. On a weekday, not a Sunday. In the middle of the day, not the evening. When *everyone* in Licking Thicket, Tennessee, knew Fridays were for Luncheon Club.

This could not be good.

I slid to accept the call on speaker without hesitating. "Mama? Are you okay?"

"Oh, Brooks, honey!" she cried. "I'm so glad you answered! I need you to come home, baby. It's your daddy. His heart."

My chest seized, my limbs went numb. Somehow, I was on my feet without even realizing it.

Then my dad's voice called from the background, "I'm *fine*, Brooks!"

I struggled to fill my lungs with oxygen as my mom chided, "Honestly, Redmond. Settle down. You're *not* fine. You heard what Dr. Yates said."

"He said," my dad insisted, "that I'm gonna be *fine*, Brooks."

My mother sighed gustily. "As fine as a man *can* be when he has a stent where his heart once was, I suppose, Red."

"That's not how arterial stents work, and you know it, Cindy Ann." But my dad's voice sounded... threadier than usual. Tired. Not his usual deep, gruff tone. It worried me.

I slumped back down in my seat.

Paul motioned between himself and the door, but I shook my head. I needed one sane person in the room, and it wasn't gonna be me after a few minutes on the phone with my family.

"Mama," I interrupted. "Please explain to me very precisely what's happening."

"*Welllllllll*," she began, and I closed my eyes, mentally settling in for a very long and *imprecise* story. "You know it's August, Brooks."

"Yes, it is."

"And you know what *that* means here in Licking Thicket."

Paul mouthed the words "Licking Thicket?" like he wasn't sure he'd heard correctly, but he had. *Oh, he had.*

"Yes, ma'am," I admitted with a wince. "I guess I know."

"It's time for the Great Lickin' Festival," she said unnecessarily, "to celebrate our glorious agricultural heritage." She sighed again. "And I don't need to tell you how excited your daddy and the other men in the Thicket get at Lickin' time."

I squeezed my eyes shut, wishing I hadn't put the phone on speaker, but it was too late now. "No, ma'am."

Paul made a strangled, coughing noise, and my eyes popped open. "Ignore me," he whispered, waving a hand. "Just dying softly."

"He ran up the steps to the hayloft to get the buckets for

the Lickin' Lope," my mother continued in her deep drawl, "then down to the basement to get the cattle prods for the bachelor auction. All that up and down was just... too much stimulation, I guess."

Paul started shaking his head, like this *conversation* was too much stimulation. I shot him a glare.

"Next thing I knew, he was calling *your brother* to come take him to the hospital because he was having chest pains."

"Only 'cause I didn't wanna worry you, honey bunch!" my dad yelled.

My mother didn't dignify this statement by acknowledging it. "*Anyway.* D came over and took both of us to the emergency room. Turned out your father's arteries were clogged, so they put a stent in there, and they already sent him home this morning, if you can believe that!" From her voice, it was clear that *she* couldn't, but I for one was massively relieved.

"Well, that's great, though! I'm so glad everything's okay! You just let me know what you need, Mama, alright? I'll have some dinners catered out to the house for you. Is another lawyer taking over Dad's clients? I'm gonna hire you some help with any heavy labor you need done, too, while Dad recovers." I opened up my email program and started typing up a list of instructions for my assistant, Carlin. "Two guys? Or three? What do you think?"

The silence on the other end of the line was deafening.

"Mama?" I poked the screen to make sure the call hadn't dropped.

"Brooks," she said. "I wasn't kidding before. We need you to come to the Thicket. To come *home*."

Paul began nodding fervently and mouthing, "Go! Go! Go!"

I ignored him.

Instead, I swallowed hard. "Well, I would. I mean, I *will*! Sometime soon. Soonish." Or not. "But right now I just—"

"The Lickin' is next week."

"Yes, ma'am, I know, but I have—"

"And it's not just any Lickin', Brooks. This is the Great Centennial Lickin'."

I closed my eyes. "Shit." I'd forgotten the invitation I'd gotten earlier in the summer.

It was a sign of the seriousness of this that she ignored my language. "You know your daddy's Head Licker on the Lickin' Committee, and has been since Pop-pop stepped down thirty years ago. A Johnson's been Head Licker for as long as there's been a Johnson in the Thicket."

"Head Licker!" Paul whispered. He wasn't bothering to hide his glee anymore. He was *crying* with laughter.

Bastard.

And he wondered why I never talked about this.

"There are other Johnsons, Mama. You have three children. Gracie could do it. Or Dunn. Or Aunt Birdie."

"Dunn's got late calves coming this week. Dairy business doesn't stop for the festival. And Gracie's always gonna be my darling girl, but she's a Mawbry now. No, Brooks, if my Red Johnson can't be standing tall and proud in front of the Thicket, it's gotta be you, son. "

I wondered if she heard herself say these things and understood how horrible they sounded.

"If you can't come..." She sighed. "He'll overtax himself and his stents will fall out."

I was fairly certain *that* wasn't how stents worked either.

"Mama, I am absolutely swamped. I have a presentation for a potential client to put together by next week. It could be *the* make-or-break presentation of my career. It's important. And I—"

"More important than your family?" My mother's voice went quiet. Deadly quiet. "You've been gone *ten whole years*, Brooks Johnson. You know how I know?"

It was my turn to sigh. *Of course* I knew how she knew. She was my mother, and she loved me. But she wouldn't be my mother if she didn't draw it out as dramatically as possible.

"You left town right after the *Ninetieth* Great Lickin', the night you broke poor Ava's heart." She choked off a sob that I knew was half-exaggerated... but also half-real. "The night you broke the whole *town's* heart."

Christ alive.

I stared at the ceiling and shook my head. "Mama, how many times do I have to explain? It's not that I didn't care for Ava. Or you. Or Licking Thicket. It's just that—"

"I know, I *know*. You had other plans. First it was college, then graduate school, then internships. Now it's work, work, work, work, work. And *being gay*." I could practically hear the air quotes and the eye roll. "It's always something with you, Brooks."

Paul had one hand over his mouth now, his eyes comically wide behind his glasses.

"I'm being very serious," I informed her. "About the presentation *and* about being gay."

"Oh, really? So, who's your client, Brooks?"

"It's—" I stopped cold. *Fuck.* I couldn't tell her I was consorting with the enemy! *Lie, idiot, lie!* "I... can't tell you. It's a secret."

Paul drew a hatch mark on an imaginary scoreboard with one finger. I had a feeling that point was not being awarded to me.

I rolled my chair back so I could bang my head against my desk repeatedly.

"Uh-*huh*. So your client is the CIA?" My mother's drawl made each of those initials ten syllables long.

"No. Obviously not, Mama. They don't advertise—"

"And can we expect to meet your boyfriend when you come home?" she continued.

Paul sketched a second hatch mark.

He was dead to me. He really was.

"I... Look, it's not that I don't... It's just that I..." No matter which way I approached this, I could not figure out a way to explain to my mother that having lots of really enjoyable, really casual sex with guys was a viable life choice. "Not every gay man has a boyfriend!" I insisted.

"*Mmm hmm*. You know, Ava's coming home," my mother said coyly.

I sighed. "No, Mama. How would I know? I haven't talked to Ava in a decade." And God knew, Ava wouldn't have accepted my call if I'd tried. Even at eighteen, she'd been five hundred pounds of sass in a one-hundred-pound human, which was part of why I'd liked her so much... and why I'd stayed with her way longer than I should have.

"All the way from California too! *Which is further than New York.*"

Paul's shoulders shook, and he bit his lip as he made a third hatch mark.

"We're having a *special* parade this year for the centennial. Almost every living Mr. and Ms. Licking Thicket is coming back to participate, all the way back to Emma Stevens, Ms. Licking Thicket 1950! There's been only *one* person who sent regrets. Do you know who that one person is, Brooks?"

I shook my head. By process of elimination, it seemed safe to say, "Is it me, Mama?"

Paul lifted his finger to mark another point.

"Yes, Brooks," she said sadly. "And since we've already established that you don't *really* have any work to do or any boyfriend to worry about, I truly don't see why you can't come home, just this once, to help your daddy out. We'd *love* to see you, baby. I'll make your favorite desserts every single night."

And this was why I didn't go home. I could already feel myself sliding backward with every "Yes, ma'am," morphing into the Brooks Johnson I used to be. I hated it.

It was on the tip of my tongue to say *no* one final time *and mean it*, when my dad spoke up again. "Brooks, if you could see your way to coming home and fixing this for us... for *me*... Well. I'd really appreciate it, son, that's all."

Ugh. I hated letting them down, especially since my dad wasn't the kind of guy to ask for help *ever*... especially when fixing shit was what I did. But how could I fix two problems at once?

I thought about Beauregard Partridge and looked at my blank idea notebook.

Then I thought about singing the Partridge Pit jingle on my parents' old sectional, and how genuinely scared I'd been when I thought my dad was sick... or worse.

Paul grabbed a cube of sticky notes from my desk, scribbled something, and stuck it to the front of the placard on my desk, snort-giggling all the while. He turned it to face me. Instead of my name and Vice President, it now read:

Brooks Johnson, Mr. Licking Thicket 2010

I rolled my eyes. I was glad Paul seemed to be enjoying himself, because revenge was gonna be swift, and he'd better have his asthma inhaler ready when I thought of a suitable punishm—

Oh. Oh, hot damn. The idea came to me the way the perfect hook for an ad campaign sometimes did—a brilliant flash I'd learned not to question—and I suddenly knew exactly how Paul and I could craft a flawless presentation for the General *and* I could help my family... and maybe, while I was at it, finally convince my parents once and for all that I was really, actually *gay*.

I gave my very straight coworker my most angelic smile, and he frowned in response.

"You know what, Mama? You're right. I'll come home tomorrow. After all, I'll have plenty of time to do my work while I'm there. Being Head Licker is mostly ceremonial." Cut a ribbon here, start a race there, announce the new Mr. and Ms. Licking Thicket when the festival was all said and done. How hard could it be?

"Well, there are a lot of ceremonies, but... yes! Oh, Brooks! Oh, thank you, honey! We..."

"But make sure you have room for me *and* my boyfriend."

Paul's head went back. "What boyfriend?" he mouthed.

"W-what boyfriend?" my mother stammered.

"Oh, Mama, you're going to *love* him," I said gleefully. "His name is Paul."

Chapter Two

Mal

I was struggling to attach the final metal spring onto a saw blade when Ava Ivey came storming into my studio.

Okay, fine. It wasn't so much an art studio as a shitty-ass garage behind my landlord's house. Well, half of a garage anyway. The other half was a shrine to Neil's 1956 Ford Fairlane Sunliner convertible that was shrouded in a pristine hot pink cover underneath an additional protective layer of thick canvas dust blanket. I hadn't seen the car itself in five years despite it being the reason I'd met the guy in the first place. I knew how to source old car parts. It was one of my many underappreciated talents.

"Put that crap down. Can't you see I'm in crisis?" Ava said before flopping dramatically in the overstuffed and over-duct-taped recliner in the corner.

I wiped my sweaty forehead on my shoulder. "Can't you see I'm in the middle of making an angsty octopus?"

"Mal, this is serious. I need some help."

I finally got the spring threaded through the tiny metal ring I'd welded to the saw blade earlier this afternoon. It still needed something... I wasn't sure what... but it could wait. I knew from experience that an Ava crisis meant the end of my focused creativity for the night.

I sighed and climbed down from the ladder, careful not to catch my work coveralls on the sharp edge of the barrel sponge I'd fashioned out of an old Stromberg carburetor. After I finished the octopus, I had plans to start working on the fish. The giant reef piece had originally been commissioned for the lobby of the Auto Club Speedway in San Bernardino, but they'd had a change of heart when one of their marketing directors claimed that lobby "real estate" was too valuable for an art piece and needed to be used for sponsorship displays.

I wasn't quite sure what I was going to do with a twelve-foot-square reef sculpture made from auto parts, but it wasn't in my nature to leave a piece unfinished. Just like it wasn't in Ava's nature to knock before entering a premises in a snit.

"Spill." I walked over to the shop sink and washed my hands, fully expecting her to tell me more about the workplace drama at the day spa where she worked. Those ladies were both terrifying and incredibly fascinating from a sociological and entertainment perspective. I kind of wanted an update on the whole "Kolby broke up with Logan and asked out his sister" drama from last week.

"I'm pregnant."

I tilted my head like a dog who wasn't sure what that sound was. "Say again?" As far as I knew, my best friend hadn't gotten a hot beef injection since the Halloween party at Tori and Jen's house last year. The one where everyone but me seemed to have gotten spooky action.

"Don't make me repeat it. Here." Her hand shot out and damned near impaled me with a white plastic stick. The minute my brain realized what it was, I jumped back and shrieked, proving Ava may not have been quite the biggest drama queen in this relationship.

"Get it away from me!" I flapped my hands wildly. "Ew. Ewwww. Gross. Why? Why would you..." The reality of what she was saying sank in. "But... but you have the Licking next week."

She looked at me like I was crazy, which was pretty funny since she was the one from a place that had such an event. I was from a place that had a much more respectable event called the Homer Harvest Festival. It was different.

"It's called the Lickin', and don't you think I know that? Brooks Goddamned Johnson is coming, and supposedly, he's bringing a *boyfriend*. I'll be damned if he's going to make me look bad again in front of the entire effin' town. It was hard enough when he dumped me with that bullshit 'gay' business after we were crowned—"

I cut her off. I could not, would not, listen to any more wailing about the Great Dumping that had happened ten years ago, crushing her plans for being Mrs. Perfect Small-Town Wife and leading her down the path of ruin. At least, according to her mother and all the other biddies in the Thicket.

"Yeah, yeah, I know. But back to this baby thing. What... I mean who... who did you sleep with? What the fuck? I thought you were on the pill."

I'll admit I knew too much about her uterus, but we'd been each other's everything for a good seven years. She also knew too much about certain pierced parts of my own private anatomy. And if that was because I was a crybaby around piercing and tattoo needles, well, that wasn't anyone else's business.

Except for Ava's. Of course.

"I don't remember his name. It was... um..." She narrowed her eyes at me. "Don't judge."

I rolled mine. "As if."

"You're judging me already."

Duh.

I squeezed into the big recliner next to her since we were both small enough to share. Ava's head landed on my shoulder. "Just tell me. You know you're going to anyway."

"It was at Beyond Wonderland. Remember when that EDM band played that I liked and I decided to take shots every time there was a beat drop?"

I remembered. The beat hadn't been the only thing that had dropped that night. I'd had to borrow a friend's stroller to get Ava home.

"When? We were together the whole time." I racked my brain to think of any part of that weekend we weren't joined at the hip. Sure, she'd flirted with some guys and even shared a blanket with one of them on the lawn one night. "Wait. Wait. Jesus, Ava. Fuck. You seriously fucked a guy while sitting right next to me?"

She let out a big sigh. "He told me he was a yoga instructor, but I think he was just really bendy. Do you think that means the baby will be flexible? I hope so."

I still couldn't wrap my head around what she was telling me. "That was only six weeks ago."

"Yeah. That means I missed my period twice. The first time was two weeks after the concert, and I was just grateful I could take those surfing lessons without being in a mood all weekend. Then I finally realized it never showed up, so I took a test."

Her voice had finally broken, and the real Ava came out. "I'm so scared, Mal. What am I going to do?"

I wrapped my arm around her shoulders. "Do you want to keep it?"

She reeled back with a gasp. "Of course I want to keep it!"

"Shh, simmer down. Just making sure. You know I'm here for you. You won't be alone. I promise I'll help however I can." I tried not looking at the lethal metal sculpture right in front of us. My life was hardly kid-friendly. But I could change. Since the day we'd met at the Eyebrow Waxing Appointment We No Longer Speak Of, Ava had been there for me. She'd held me while I cried over the end of my favorite television shows and yelled at me to get my head out of my ass when I'd accidentally started dating the world's douchiest canoe. She'd accompanied me back to Homer when my mom had died two years ago and held me back from beating the shit out of my father when he'd called me names right there at the gravesite.

So, yes. I would be there for Ava and her baby no matter what. I'd do anything for this girl.

She sniffled and snuggled back into my shoulder. "I need you to come to the Lickin' with me."

But not that.

"No."

She opened her mouth to say more, but I cut her off. "Absolutely not. You know I'm allergic to stupid small towns, and that goes quadruple for small towns in Tennessee."

"I went to Homer for you."

"You're a sucker."

She smacked my chest, but I barely felt it through my coveralls. "You owe me."

"I'll change diapers for a solid year. I'm not going to

your crazy-ass town to meet your crazy-ass family after everything you've told me about it."

"It's not that bad," she promised.

"It's called Licking Thicket. The mayor's name is Red, and his wife's name is probably hyphenated. Her first name, I mean. And I'll bet you my next Friday night's tips at the club that she's on a steering committee of some kind."

"Ha!" she said triumphantly, sitting up in victory. "Not hyphenated."

I narrowed my eyes at her until she looked away and admitted, "It's Cindy Ann. No hyphen."

I poked her in the ribs. "And the steering committee?"

She sighed, blowing her bangs up in the process. "She's the chairwoman of the Thicket Beautification Corps."

"Corpse? Like, dead person?"

"No. Corps, like... like corps. I don't know what corps means. The thing with lots of soldiers. Corps."

I snickered. She was proving my point. She came from a more ridiculous town than I did, and mine had been premium pecan level on the nutty scale. "I believe that's pronounced corps," I corrected, leaving out the *ps*. "Like an apple core."

"Oh, she's also on the Apple Festival committee too." Ava's skin turned pink. "Um. The Lickin' Pickin'."

"No," I said again, shoving her to the side so I could get up and put some distance between us. "Not happening. I will not ever again set foot in a place with an orchard-based festival, a harvest-based festival, a holiday-based festival, or a mascot-based festival."

Her eyes darted away. That was her lame attempt at hiding something.

"Out with it."

"No, I was just..."

"Out of curiosity," I said, holding up an index finger, "what is the high school mascot of Licking Thicket?"

She pushed herself up from the chair and headed toward the door. "Never mind. It's not important. Be ready to go tomorrow at nine. I found us cheap tickets online, but you're only allowed to bring what fits in a backpack and your pockets or you have to pay extra."

"Ava," I said in my best attempt at a serious commanding voice. Let's face it, I didn't have one of those. "I'm seriously not coming. I love you, but I just can't."

She looked back at me over her shoulder, glancing between me and the reef sculpture behind me. "Did I forget to mention that I can get you a vendor booth in the art festival for free and the CEO of the tech company that just built its headquarters in the Thicket is both a scuba diver and a classic car enthusiast? And their brand-new building doesn't have any art in the lobby yet?"

Then she flashed me her widest smile, the one she knew I couldn't resist. "And he's gay?"

Fuck me.

"I couldn't possibly get my stuff shipped out in time."

"If you think for one minute I'm returning home an unwed mother after leaving the Thicket in utter disgrace because of Brooks Fucking Johnson, and I'm doing it all without the support of the one person who actually gives a shit about me, you're mistaken." Her voice was back to shrill. "Malachi Forrester, the flight is at nine tomorrow *night*. You have twenty-four hours to get your shit together because you are coming with me and you are not leaving my side. And pack a suit. I won't have my date wearing oily coveralls to the Lickin' Dinner Dance." She turned around and walked out into the summer night.

"I don't own a suit," I yelled after her. "And I usually wear my birthday suit to any lickings thank you very much!"

I turned back to the almost-finished sculpture, the one I'd spent the better part of the past four months painstakingly perfecting to the detriment of my other work. I couldn't afford to pass up the chance to find a good home for it. If her connections back home could possibly help me find a place for this installation... it would save me hours and hours of pounding the pavement and trying to sell an already-made giant custom sculpture. I'd sent a few inquiries to local galleries, but since I'd never been selected for a showing, I didn't hold out much hope.

Sales were the worst part of being an artist. I'd rather stick my finger in an electrical socket than try to convince some corporate automaton the value of a custom piece of art for their office building. Corporate drones and I were like pastel beige and neon pink—we didn't go together. The last time I'd tried to sell something already commissioned for someone else, it had been a disaster.

And Ava was right. I wasn't about to let her go home to face her family alone, especially considering her news. She'd been there for me during the disastrous trip to Homer, so I'd be there for her in the Thicket.

Besides, it was just a week, and it wasn't even my own hometown. How bad could it possibly be?

Chapter Three

Brooks

It was funny how fast things changed.

Two days ago, I'd been in New York wearing a tailored suit in my air-conditioned office. My assistant had gotten me a sugar-free latte with a half-pump of caramel and gone over my schedule before I'd started my day as the VP of an up-and-coming marketing firm. People had listened to me and respected me because I knew what I was talking about.

Today, I was at the Lickin' Homecoming Barbecue in my parents' backyard, sporting a sleeveless brown shirt that read *Licking Thicket* across the front above a giant Holstein cow head and *Head Licker* across the back above a picture of a cow's rump—one of many identical shirts I'd be wearing this week and then burning in a cleansing ritual the minute I got home to New York. I'd started sweating through this shirt the second I'd stepped outside, because Tennessee on an August afternoon had the same climate as hell's seventh layer. My mother was trotting me around, proudly reintroducing me to the entire town, and having me fetch sweet tea and potato salad while she had the same conversation over and over with nearly every person we encountered.

"Cindy Ann, this brisket is amazing! Better than Susie Dupree's!" some nice older lady would exclaim, which was about the highest compliment a person could pay my mother. "And this sweet tea! You've *got* to tell me your secret!"

"Now, you know I would, Barb, but I'm afraid you have to marry into the family for that kind of information! Red's mama passed it down to me the day we got married," Mama would laugh.

The nice lady would pretend to look me over. "If I were a few years younger, Brooks, I'd give you a run for your money," she'd joke, wagging a finger at me, and I'd smile politely.

I loved my parents, and I was committed to taking on the Head Licker title so my dad, who looked genuinely exhausted, could recover from his heart procedure stress-free. But by the tenth repetition of this conversation, it became clear that I was severely out of practice at the nodding-and-smiling thing. I was also hungry, hot, stressed about work, and insanely tired.

See, in my moment of vindictive brilliance Friday, I'd forgotten Paul's fear of flying was so bad he needed his inhaler when he *thought* too hard about airplanes hurtling through the sky. I could hardly leave my beloved boyfriend after telling my mom he was coming, though, could I? So we'd ended up driving. For thirteen fucking hours.

When we'd arrived, I'd been ready to fall into bed and sleep for a year, but my mother had kissed my cheek, handed me a two-page itinerary of my appearances as Head Licker for the week ahead, and informed me that I'd be sleeping on the lumpy pullout in the den while Paul took the guest bed, since there would be "no canoodling of unmarried persons under her roof, gay or not."

Canoodling. Honestly. Who even said *canoodle* anymore, anyway?

I hadn't read through my itinerary of appearances yet, but I could already tell it would put a serious damper on the amount of *real* work I could get done in the next few days, and Pamela had already started calling to demand updates. It also seemed like whatever free time I did have, my family was determined to make sure I didn't spend with Paul...

Not that my one true love seemed to mind this overly much.

Paul clearly had not understood that being my fake boyfriend wasn't just about being nearby so we could work on the campaign, it was about being my fucking *wingman*, damn it. Instead of standing by my side like a good fake boyfriend should, he'd let himself get carted off by my sister the minute she'd introduced herself and given us each a big hug. Gracie had told me to relax because she'd protect Paul from Mama... which unfortunately meant there was no one around to protect *me*.

Sure enough, when I glanced over at my sugar bear, he was sitting in the shade of a giant oak tree snuggling a baby against his chest, happy as a proverbial clam, while regaling the ladies with his knowledge of red raspberry tea leaves and which diapers stopped leaks best. It would have been creepy if it weren't so perfectly Paul. Ask the man to run a meeting and he'd panic, ask him to ride in a plane and he'd have an asthma attack, but ask him to deal with a cavalcade of fussy babies and women discussing lactation, and he was cool as a cucumber.

Probably *literally* cool as a cucumber, since he was in the freakin' *shade*. Asshole.

Paul looked up and saw me glaring daggers at him. He

pressed his fingertips to his mouth and blew an extravagant kiss in my direction, then drew a heart in the air.

I gave him a bright smile in case anyone was looking... and flipped him off by rubbing my middle finger against my nose.

I was totally fake-breaking-up with him when we got back to New York.

"'Scuse me, Ms. Cosway," I said, breaking into my mom's conversation. I slapped at my ankle, where another damn mosquito was sucking away a pint of my blood, and wiped the sweat from my damp forehead. "Mama, I'm gonna go inside for a bit. Looks like Payton and the rest of the kids have demolished most of the brownies already. I'll go see if the second batch is cool." By which I meant I would stand in front of the window air conditioner and *hold the brownies* while they cooled.

"Nonsense, Brooks, honey! You'll miss all the fun! Oh, look! Lurleen's here. Come on!"

I gritted my teeth and let her tow me across the yard again, like I wasn't a foot taller and at least fifty pounds heavier than she was.

In point of fact, I had *never* found parties fun. My whole childhood had been spent devising hideouts at get-togethers so I didn't have to make small talk, and you'd think my mom would remember that since she'd seemed equally devoted to finding me and forcing me out. But I was *not* here to start fights or correct assumptions. I was here to help my family, and then I was getting the hell out of the Thicket.

"Lurleen!" my mom exclaimed. She dropped my arm so she could exchange cheek kisses with our across-the-road neighbor like it'd been a hundred years since they'd seen each other instead of a day at most. "You look wonderful! Brooks, honey, you remember Ms. Jackson?"

"Yes, ma'am. Nice to see you." I nodded politely at the woman with the familiar helmet of black curls, electric-blue eyeliner, and bright red dress.

Lurleen Jackson was everything I loved and hated about Licking Thicket. I remembered her making dinner for my family for weeks on end when my mom broke her arm back in the day. I remembered her giving me strawberry Popsicles because she knew they were my favorite. I *also* remembered her ratting me out when she found me holed up in her pantry reading books when I was ten and I was supposed to be down in her rec room, socializing with her daughter Alana and the other kids.

She was the sort of person who *loved you* if she loved you, and would flay the flesh from your body with her acid tongue if she didn't. I used to be decidedly in the first camp, but judging by the way she looked me up and down, she wasn't sure where I fit anymore.

Join the club.

"Nice to see *you* again, Brooks. In person, I mean. We missed you at the Thicket Christmas last year. And the year before. And at Dunn's surprise party. And Gracie's daughter's preschool graduation." Lurleen lifted one drawn-on black eyebrow.

Ah. Camp Flaying. *Delightful.*

I smiled harder. "It's really hard to get time off when you're working your way up the corporate ladder. I missed being here for those things, but I like to think I have my daddy's work ethic."

I nodded toward the smoky area on the far corner of the patio, where my dad's salt-and-pepper head and pink cheeks were barely visible over the top of his grill. He'd literally set up a barstool in front of the cooker so he could turn the chicken and brats, while also keeping my mother more or less appeased that he was "resting." When I'd suggested that I should maybe handle cooking duties as Head Licker, he'd been downright *offended*.

"A Johnson mans his own grill, Brooks. You can take these tongs when I'm *dead*, you hear?"

Message received.

Lurleen lifted her chin, neither agreeing nor disagreeing, and let her gaze wander around the yard. "Real nice turnout this year, Cindy, honey. I think this is the biggest crowd I can remember."

My mom grinned and ducked her head modestly. "Just about everyone on the Beautification Corps said they'd stop by, and Monette and Brad are bringing Ava over any minute now."

Jesus. That comment, delivered with a coy little smile and a head tilt in my direction, made it hard not to roll my eyes.

Figured that I'd come back to town after ten years away, bringing a boyfriend no less, and my mom was still utterly convinced that one look at Ava Ivey was gonna make me pick up stakes in New York and start building a picket fence here in the Thicket instead.

Not. Happening.

I opened my mouth to say something to that effect, when my mother spied someone new to speak to. She gave Lurleen a distracted goodbye, yanked my wrist like a leash, and yelled, "Come on, Brooks!"

I felt like a tall, blond sheepdog and wondered what she'd do if I started panting.

"Pastor Mitchell!" my mom said, rocking us to a halt a few seconds later. "This is my son Brooks. You remember me telling you about him? Brooks, this is Chester Mitchell. He's been pastor of our community church for five or six years now."

Pastor Mitchell was a middle-aged man with close-cropped curls, expressive, dark eyes behind wire-rimmed glasses, and a bright, white smile. "Oh, yes! Brooks from New York City. You know, I once thought of getting my degree at NYU, but I ended up staying in Tennessee. I've often wondered what I missed. It's much different from here, I'm imagining?"

I laughed a little. Sum up the differences between the Thicket and New York? Impossible. Where would I even begin? I could say that my entire Williamsburg apartment would fit in my parents' living room, and I had no outdoor space to my name, but on my block alone, I could get authentic cuisine from three countries I hadn't even *heard* of growing up in the Thicket. I could tell him that the noise and traffic were terrible, but there were museums and performance art on every street corner—culture you could never find around here. I could try to describe the manic energy of the city, which was only tolerable because I also had the sense that I could do anything—*be* anything—there. But how could I make someone from around here under-stand that, amid all the bustle and congestion, New York was wide enough to handle the real Brooks Johnson... while in Licking Thicket, despite the endless open space, my entire life had had to fit in someone else's teeny box?

"It's, ah... great," I said shortly. "Loads to see and do." If a person had time and money. "I have a great job." Even if it meant working with the likes of Kale Storms. "Lots of friends." More like acquaintances for now, but there was plenty of time for friends when my career was further down the track.

"Well, you won't be bored here in the Thicket, that's for sure!" Pastor Mitchell said.

Won't I? I once again willed back my eyeroll.

"That's right! Plenty's changed since you were last home!" My mother beamed. "You know, Pastor, my Brooks is seventh in a proud line of Johnson Head Lickers that dates back a century. Head Licking is a way of life in our family."

I really wished she wouldn't put it that way.

"Is that right?" Pastor Mitchell said kindly. "Well. Nice of you to come home and take that on, Brooks."

I smiled. "Oh, it's not—"

"And, of course, this means Brooks will be competing in the Lope on Tuesday," Mama continued, patting my shoulder proudly.

Wait, was I? *Fuck.* I needed to read that itinerary. The Lickin' Lope was a four-mile run through the woods carrying a metal pail filled with milk. I couldn't remember what it was supposed to commemorate, or if I'd ever known in the first place. What I did know was that folks here trained for this event like it was the Olympics, and rivalry was cutthroat, even though the only prize was a tiny metal plaque and bragging rights.

"That right, Brooks?" Pastor Mitchell grinned. "My son Theo's in the Lope. You'll have some competition."

"No doubt." Considering I hadn't run a trail in a decade, let alone carrying a pail of dairy product—that sort of thing was frowned on at my gym—it was going to be a bloodbath.

"Nonsense," Mama said. "Brooks won the Lope for the first time when he was fifteen. Youngest Lope winner *ever*. And then he won it *three years in a row*. I'm confident he'll win again."

She nodded once, like that was the end of it, and I felt a stirring of that same feeling I'd had when I was a kid and my parents said stuff like that. Like I wanted to win, just to show them I could.

This whole week was going to be a shitshow.

Pastor Mitchell smiled. "And will you be in the charity bachelor auction Friday? Highest-earning bachelor gets to pick which charity gets the money."

"Me? *No!* Nope. My brother will be there." Assuming Dunn showed up, which a quick glance around the yard showed he hadn't bothered to do today. My brother had a good heart, but was shit at follow-through, and it looked like *that* hadn't changed any more than anything else in the Thicket. "But I'm not a bachelor. I have a boyfriend. Paul. And he's very jealous." I pointed toward the oak tree, and we all turned to look at Paul, who was crouching down, playing peekaboo with someone's toddler. "Ah... you wouldn't know it to look at him. Clearly. But he's a real tiger. *Grrr.* Besides, I've got plenty of excitement this week already, trying to do my work while making appearances at some of the events on that itinerary."

"Some?" My mother narrowed her eyes. "You did read the whole itinerary, right?"

"Oh. Uh. Sure! I just didn't *memorize* it," I lied, wondering where I'd even put the papers. She'd said it was mostly ceremonial, hadn't she? There was a committee meeting Monday, the dinner dance Saturday. Apparently running through the woods and auctioning bachelors in between?

She frowned. "Lickins' don't just *happen*, Brooks! They're a lot of work behind the scenes, and that means the Head Licker has to— Oh, good heavens! It's Monette and Brad!" She waved an arm in the air like she was directing air traffic. "This means Ava's got to be with them! Calm down, Brooks!" She seized my wrist again and started to tug.

"I'm perfectly calm." But there was no way on God's green earth I was letting myself be led over there like a dog on a leash or—I glanced down at my shirt—like a cow to the slaughter either.

"Gamma!" Gracie's oldest daughter, Payton, said, appearing at our sides with fingers absolutely *covered* in the remains of chocolate brownie. "I need to wash my hands, and Mama said you'd open the door for me."

"Oh, Payton..." My mother glanced down at her granddaughter and then over at Ava's parents, who'd stopped to exchange greetings with some other folks. Her indecision was clear.

"I'll take her," I volunteered.

"Nonsense!" my mother argued. "You'll—"

"Yes!" Payton cried. "Uncle B! Please, Uncle B?"

I gave my mother an exaggerated shrug. I mean, I could hardly disappoint the poor girl. I made a mental note to upgrade her Christmas present.

"Come on, Payton," I called, already retreating toward the house.

I made sure Payton did the most thorough handwashing job ever in the upstairs bathroom—the CDC could take tips from me—and when she was done, I told her she could go back out to play.

She hesitated. "I'd rather stay inside and draw pictures."

I smiled down at her. A girl after my own heart. "Do you have art supplies here at Gamma's?"

She nodded. "In the den."

"Perfect. That's where I'm staying while I'm here, so if anyone asks, you can tell them you're guarding my room because I asked you to."

Payton threw her arms around my legs. "You're the best, Uncle B."

I totally was. And I figured a "best uncle" would probably spend a minute in the kitchen by the air conditioner, just in case his niece needed him, right?

I slunk down the hall like *I* was a kid again, afraid of being caught, and I snuck glances at the backyard out the window to make sure my mother and Ava weren't coming... which was how I nearly ran into a person standing in the hall by the kitchen.

"Oh my God!" I said, grabbing the person—a man, definitely a man, though much less bulky than me—by the shoulders. "I'm so sorry. I was, ah... distracted."

And if I hadn't been before, I certainly was once I got a look at him. *Holy shit.*

"No, sorry, my bad," the guy said. He straightened his black T-shirt and brushed an unruly mop of wavy, brown-gold hair away from his magnetic blue eyes. "I was distracted too."

He motioned toward the pictures on the hallway wall— a collection of bovine-inspired artwork my mother had begun before I was born—and shook his head wordlessly. I felt my face heat.

"Ah. Yeah, it's quite a theme, isn't it?" I said. "Cows in flower crowns?"

"I can't tell if it's horrible, or wonderful, or both."

"Both," I decided. "Most things are."

He turned to give me a quick, startled smile, and I realized belatedly that while he'd been staring at the wall, I'd been staring at him.

Honestly, there was a lot to look at. Besides the sexy, untamed hair, the man had sharp, intelligent eyes that looked like they missed nothing, high, rounded cheekbones, a scruffy jaw, and plush, pink lips, like a master sculptor had perfectly softened all his other features to balance the intensity of his eyes. His body was lithe, leanly muscled, and delightfully warm. He had a little silver hoop in his left ear, a freckle in the hollow of his throat, and a stack of bracelets up one wrist. He could've been anywhere from fifteen to thirty years old. I felt a pulse of awareness in my gut.

Please don't be fifteen, please don't be fifteen.

"Are you okay?" he asked, frowning at me in concern.

Damn it all, I was *still* staring.

"Yeah, no, totally. Just, um." I cleared my throat. My mother's art display was the last place on earth I'd expected to meet someone as striking as this. Why did this have to happen while I was a giant, sweaty mess? "Making sure *you* are."

"Oh." His expression cleared, and his lips twitched. Apparently, I was still staring at his lips. "I'm fine. Except that I stepped out of the bathroom down here and this cow started staring into my soul."

I had to force myself to look away from him and focus on the cow painting, but when I did...

I laughed out loud. "It really *is.* That cow knows exactly what you're thinking right now."

The man gasped, and the sound went straight to my balls. "You think? In that case, that cow needs to mind her fucking business before she gets corrupted." He looked me up and down, from my messy, sweaty hair to my sneakers, and I'd swear the smile he gave me was pure flirtation.

The smile I gave him in return sure as hell was.

This kind of thing never happened to me. *Ever.*

"Have you ever seen a real cow?" I asked, because I was the fucking king of suave conversation.

Jesus Christ, how had I ever managed to have sex with anyone?

"A real cow? Obviously," the guy said, folding his arms over his chest. I couldn't help but notice the defined muscles in his chest and arms. He was shorter than I was but definitely not scrawny. Fuck he was sexy. He smirked. "Don't I look like a country boy?"

I laughed, feeling all the stress from the day start to fall away.

The guy was wearing black boots, black jeans so tight they showed every delicious bulge, a black T-shirt, and those bracelets, which were not the kind you swapped at a Boy Scout Jamboree. He was the hottest thing I'd ever seen, and my stomach was suddenly swooping a little... make that *a lot*.

Maybe Mama had been right about there being all kinds of new things in the Thicket if this was the kind of guy I could find here now.

"About as much as I do," I said, forgetting for a moment that I was decked out like a Dairy Association billboard. The guy didn't seem to mind.

Keep him talking. Keep talking forever. Come on, Brooks! Talking is your specialty. Making people like you is what you do.

But of course, my mind flatlined when I needed it most, and I had the sudden, terrible fear that panic might cause me to break into the Partridge Pit song and dance like I'd done the other day.

Fortunately, one of us still had a functioning brain.

"So, what brings you here to Thicky Ticky?" he asked archly.

I snorted. "Licking Thicket," I corrected. "Show a little respect, if you please."

He grinned up at me—*thank you, sweet baby angels*—and I felt that grin flip my stomach back the right way round... and then burn lower.

"I'm here for the Lickin', obviously," I continued. "Where the townspeople honor their agricultural heritage, and the natural mineral licks in the area that give the town its name."

His jaw dropped. "Wait, are you serious? *That's* what the name is about?"

I ran my tongue along the inside of my cheek, trying not to laugh. "*Licking*, as in a mineral lick. You know, the kind sheep and cows like? *Thicket*, as in plentiful grass for grazing. Why, what were *you* thinking the name was about?"

He shook his head slowly, and his wavy hair fell into his eyes again. "You don't wanna know."

Oh, I was damn sure I did.

"Thank you for educating me," the guy said solemnly. "I'm a Lickin' virgin, obviously, and I'd hate to appear naive."

"I'm a veteran of many a Lickin'... though none recently," I admitted, and that was true in all senses of the word. "If you want, I could... Um..."

The guy leaned toward me, like he was dying to know how I was going to end that sentence.

So was I.

"*Maaaal!* Mal! How long does it take for you to—" Ava Ivey came around the corner from the kitchen, blonde curls bouncing, and stopped short when she saw me. She looked back and forth from me to the guy beside me, and I felt the weird urge to step in front of him.

Mine.

But I didn't move a muscle, obviously. Clearly, he and Ava knew each other.

"Oh. *Brooks*," Ava said, in much the same tone one might say, "Oh. *Explosive diarrhea*."

I rubbed at the back of my neck. "Ava. Hey." My tone probably sounded like that of a guy who'd broken up with a girl on the night she'd expected him to give her a promise ring... because I was.

"You're *Brooks*?" my guy—who was clearly not *my* guy and never would be—said as his face seemed to shutter closed with a snap. "The asshole who broke her heart?"

I sighed deeply and recited my mantra. I was *not* here to start fights. I was not here to correct assumptions. I was most definitely not here on a Brooks Johnson apology tour... even if I really, really wanted to explain myself to this guy.

Ava and I would never have worked—what eighteen-year-olds were ready for a lifetime commitment, even if they were both straight?—and I'd broken up with her because I'd cared about her too much to keep pretending. Hell, I still loved her in a way... just not a way that would ever lead us to make babies together.

"Oh, Brooks!" my mom called from right behind me, which was really the only thing that could make this situation better. "There you are! See, Monette? I told you he hadn't left town!" She and her friend came around to join our little group. "Brooks, did you say hello to Ava? Did you tell her how beautiful she looks?"

Read the room, Mama, I thought, but what I said was, "Sure did! And you *do* look amazing, Ava. Really. Positively glowing."

The guy winced. "Oh, damn—"

Ava's face crumpled and her pretty blue eyes filled with tears. "Fuck you, Brooks! I am *not* glowing!"

Mrs. Ivey gasped. "Ava Marie! Remember you're a *lady*."

Ava wrapped both of her arms around my guy's waist and leaned her head against his shoulder. "This is my *boyfriend*," she sniffled. "Mal Forrester. And we are very, *very* happy together."

"Your *boyfriend*," I repeated, a little stunned.

How was that possible? The guy had been flirting with me... hadn't he? I ran through our earlier conversation, suddenly unsure.

Ava's arms visibly tightened around the man's waist, and he gave a strangled cough. "Oh! Ah, yup. Yes. I'm her boyfriend, alright. Indeed I am. I've been head over heels for my little honey nugget for years! *Many* years."

"But, Ava." Mrs. Ivey frowned. "Sweetie, you never said a word! And I thought you were with that other man, that dentist, just last summer—"

"Ha ha!" Mal interrupted. "Did I say many years? I meant... I meant... I've *pined* for her for many years. But we only made it official recently. At the Beyond Wonderland concert. Under the stars. And a really thin blanket—"

"Malachi," Ava said sweetly.

"Yes, pumpkin pie?"

"Shut up now."

"Yes, love monkey. See how patient she is?" he said confidingly. "Is it any wonder I was too shy to tell her my feelings?"

"Too shy?" I repeated. "You? Really?"

"I can be *shy*, Brooks," Mal said with no shyness whatsoever, and a glint in his bright eyes that made me want to... made me want to...

"It's alright, Brooks, honey," my mom said softly, patting my arm. "Calm down."

I inhaled sharply. "I'm *perfectly* calm," I insisted, but

unlike earlier, I felt not a shred of calm. One brief conversation had destroyed my equilibrium, and I didn't like it.

"Heya, Brooks." Paul came up behind Ava with somebody's baby draped over his chest and a worried frown on his face. "Everything cool?"

Oh, thank God.

"Yes! Yes, it's all fine." I waved him over, and he walked toward me, only somewhat reluctantly. I hauled him up against my side, and he gave a little grunt. "Everything's perfect now that *you're* here, my little... my little..." Fuck my absentee brain. "Paul."

"Your little Paul?" Mal said suspiciously.

"Yes. *My little Paul.* We can't all use every pet name in the bakery case, *Mal*. So I call him my little Paul, and he calls me..."

I looked down at Paul expectantly. We were a *team*. We brainstormed constantly and could finish each other's sentences. I knew he wouldn't let me dow—

"Big Daddy Brooks," Paul said, staring up at me with a wide, adoring smile.

I was going to kill him slowly.

"Hello," Paul said, holding the baby on his shoulder expertly while extending the other hand to Ava. "We haven't been properly introduced. I'm Paul Siegel. Brooks's ah... main squeeze."

She took his hand reluctantly. "Ava Ivey. Brooks's *ex-*main squeeze."

"Ava. A radiant name for a radiant woman," Paul said, smoothly ignoring the second half of her statement. The baby on his chest started fussing, and Paul did a little bob-and-weave dance that got it to be quiet.

Ava stared at him in open fascination.

So did Mal.

So did I.

Frankly, I think all of us did.

Fortunately, he didn't notice.

After a moment Ava sniffed. "Mal! I need *tea*." She turned toward the kitchen.

"Oh, I can get you some," Paul said, instantly coming to attention and putting one hand at the small of her back to guide her down the hall, while still holding the squirming baby in the other. "Come sit down, if you want, and I can make it for you—"

"Nonsense! *I* can make it for her!" Mrs. Ivey said shrilly, hurrying after them.

Mal shot me a murderous look before turning on his heel and following the Ava parade too.

I blew out a breath and rubbed a hand over my forehead.

"Don't worry, honey," my mother said. She patted my shoulder consolingly. "Maybe they're not serious."

"Pardon?" I stared down at her.

She shrugged. "You just looked... real upset at seeing Ava and her boyfriend, that's all."

"What? No. If anything, I was upset because he's not much of a boyfriend. I'm pretty sure he's gay. Or bisexual. Or... a total flirt, if nothing else."

"Uh-huh," she drawled.

"I'm being serious," I insisted.

She snickered. "I believe that you believe that, Brooks. But honey, not everyone has to be gay, you know?"

"Yeah, I know, but *he*—"

She tilted her head toward me knowingly. "What's more likely, sweetie? That Ava hooked herself a second guy who's 'gay'"—she added the air quotes, and it was every bit as annoying as I'd imagined when we were on the phone—

"or that her first love is jealous of her new relationship and wants to get her back?"

She winked and slipped down the hall to join the rest of the group in her kitchen, but as I watched her walk away, I couldn't help thinking glumly that I kinda *was* jealous of Ava's new relationship.

Only it wasn't Ava that I wanted.

It figured that the only guy I'd had such a strong, instant connection with in... well, *ever*... was tied at the hip to someone I could never bring myself to hurt again. It *also* figured he was a total asshole who, despite his ridiculous pet names, clearly didn't realize what an amazing woman he had on his arm.

That part, at least, I could fix...and I damn well would.

Chapter Four

Mal

WELL, that was unexpected. I'd been knee-deep in ridiculous bovine paraphernalia when I'd finally met Brooks Johnson. *The* Brooks Johnson. Arbiter of all the pain a head cheerleader and homecoming queen could possibly be expected to endure.

"He's taller than you made him sound," I muttered, climbing up the rope ladder to the "guest suite" I'd been assigned for the week. For some reason I couldn't stop thinking about the asshole in the cow T-shirt. How was it even possible to look sexy in a shirt with a screen-printed cow butt on it?

The man was six feet of pure Ken doll perfection—blond, fit, and model-gorgeous. Exactly the kind of guy I wished was not my type, but *was*. He was even sexier in person than he was in the photos I'd seen of him in Ava's scrapbook. In high school, he'd been the quintessential hunky jock, but now... now he was definitely more grown-up with broader shoulders and a thicker five-o'clock shadow.

If I'd had a three-ring binder, I might have had to doodle his name in it simply because he was that pretty. And also sweet. And kind of goofy. I sighed. Leave it to me to think Ava's ex was all that. I felt like a traitor and had to remind myself he was the enemy.

"He's a jackass, is what he is. Did you see that poor, sweet man he somehow roped into dating him? If that man's gay, I'm the queen of Sheba."

Ava plonked down next to me once we were through the hatch and into the open-plan tree house. And by "open-plan" I meant it was just one room about as you'd expect for a tree house. I was just grateful it had screens on the windows and was big enough to fit a full-sized futon.

"Jesus, Ava. Your childhood tree house was nicer than my childhood real house." I tossed my duffle down and blew out a breath. I'd spent last night on the sofa in their den, but today more family had come in from out of town and Mrs. Ivey had sweetly but firmly declared Ava's "city friend" would be moving out to the "guest suite." I'd gotten excited for a minute until I'd remembered we weren't in Beverly Hills and Ava's family lived on a dairy farm. "If I see one spider, I'm catching the first flight out."

Ava blew her bangs off her forehead. "Good luck getting a ride out of town during the Lickin'. Traffic comes in, Mal. It doesn't go out."

I shot her a look and tried not to shudder. This town had great potential for becoming the setting for a horror movie.

After kicking off my shoes, I set my backpack on the small wooden table next to the futon and began unpacking my stash.

"Oh my God, gimme those," Ava hissed, pointing to the pouch of Dove chocolate pieces I pulled out of the bag.

I clutched it to my chest. "Hell no. I only brought

enough for a carefully distributed four pieces a day. I can't get through this week of insanity without my Dove bites."

Her eyes narrowed, and my skin prickled. Was this how the horror movie began?

"Fine. You can have *one*," I said with a sniff. "But then you have to procure your own coping mechanisms, m'kay?" I reached into the bag and pulled out a single foil-wrapped square before passing it over.

She continued to stare at me until I placed a second square in her hand. She didn't stop the freaky stare-down until she finally had five squares.

"Any more than that and the baby will get diabetes," I warned, hugging the remaining chocolates to my chest. "And everyone will hate you for being a chocolate stealer."

She popped a piece into her mouth and shoved the crumpled-up foil in my pocket. "He didn't look very good, did he?"

If we hadn't been such close friends, I might not have known who she was talking about. But I'd spent years hearing about Brooks Johnson in excruciating detail.

"Uh... I feel like there's no good way to answer that." He'd looked damned good to me. Until I'd realized who he was, of course. Then he'd looked like the wretched warted *monster* that he so obviously was.

I just hadn't realized wretched warted monsters could be so damned sexy. My bad.

"His hair was all..."

"Golden?" I suggested without thinking. Since I was busy putting my clothes away amongst the binoculars and other secret agent gadgets in the little wooden chest opposite the futon, I wasn't paying much attention to her babbling.

"Dull and lifeless. He needs a conditioning treatment,

honestly. And I don't say that easily. Also... his body was like..."

"Cut? Ripped? Chiseled?" I tried not to drool since there wasn't a bathroom in the "guest suite" for me to use to wash my face.

"Kind of pudgy." She said the last word in a whisper as if she'd been talking about a neighbor's chlamydia.

I snapped my head up to glare at her. "Listen, babe. I love you. You know that. But I will not condone lying in this..." I looked around at the cobwebby space. "House."

She rolled her eyes and lay back on the cushion with a huff. I sent up a silent prayer of thanks that a big cloud of dust didn't come out with the impact. Lord only knew how long that futon had been out here. I'd convinced Ava to steal three sets of sheets for it to create a thick barrier between me and whatever mites had made a sweet home in the thing over the years, but it still gave me the heebie-jeebies.

I glanced at her. "Why do you even care? I thought we were over him."

"We were. We *are*." She didn't sound convinced. "It's just..."

I lifted a brow at her, and she threw up her hands. "It's just... being in the Thicket—with him—is bringing it all back. We had our whole future ahead of us, you know? It was going to be perfect. He was the most popular boy at school, the football quarterback, the head of the honor society. I was voted most likely to win Miss Tennessee one day, and Brooks was gonna go to UT and then take over his daddy's law business, and it was like... we had it all. When we were crowned Mr. and Ms. Licking Thicket that year..." She sighed. "I just thought it meant something."

I moved over to sit next to her and put my arm around her shoulders. "It did mean something, sweetie. It meant you had a big future ahead of you. That doesn't mean it had to be a future together. The man is gay. Even if he hadn't come out, you would have been miserable if the two of you had gotten married."

She rolled her eyes again. It was a favorite reaction of hers. "He's not gay. Give me a break, Mal. We dated for years. I'd know. Plus, the man's never brought a boy home before, and when he does, the guy is clearly straight."

I laughed at her. "He's gay, Ava. I promise."

"Oh, so now you think your gaydar is functioning? What about last weekend at the Twisted Sister? I pointed out the man in the blue shirt, and you swore he was straight. Then he came over and asked you to dance."

I pet her hair. "Sweetie, he didn't ask me to dance. He asked me to suck him off in the men's room while his girlfriend was pulling the car around."

She blinked at me. "Oh. Well, what about that time—"

I held my hand out to stop her. "I'm going to stop you right there. My gaydar is not perfect, but your Brooks Johnson? He *gay.* Super gay. Like really very gay." Maybe I needed to stop thinking about how gay he was because it made me remember how intense his gaze had felt on mine. It wasn't healthy.

"Pfft. The man he's dating mentioned wanting to run to Walmart to buy some blue jeans."

I tilted my head at her. "Come again?"

She moved away from me to lean against the opposite arm of the futon so she could put her feet in my lap. I began rubbing them automatically. She had me trained well.

"Paul said he didn't have any blue jeans. And Brooks had told him he needed blue jeans for the Great Lickening Thursday."

I opened my mouth to say that it was perfectly understandable for a man not to have packed blue jeans to come to Tennessee in August, but she opened her mouth before I could.

"He only brought Dockers."

Dockers.

I stared at her. "Shit. You might be right."

She closed her eyes and groaned when I pressed my thumb into her arch. "He was cute, though, right?"

I thought of Brooks and his tall, wide-shouldered presence. Even if I hadn't seen the framed homecoming photo of him and Ava on the front hall table at the Johnsons' house tonight, it was easy to picture him as the most popular boy in school growing up. He had shiny blond hair cut shorter than he'd worn it in high school which made him look ten times more professional and a thousand times more boring.

"So cute," I said absently. Before I'd learned who he was, I'd noticed green eyes with flecks of blue in them. His lips had curved up in a self-deprecating grin that had revealed the tiniest little crease next to one of his eyes. He had a single eyebrow hair that seemed to be fighting against traffic like it was trying to go up the down escalator. Was there such a thing as an eyebrow cowlick?

"He said they work for the same ad agency. That's how they met," Ava continued. "Did you see how sweet he was with the baby?"

I didn't remember seeing Brooks with a baby, but I nodded anyway. "So sweet." And he was. As much as I hated him on principle because I was Ava's best friend and Brooks Johnson was enemy number one, I hadn't been able to help noticing him running around fetching things for his mom all evening and offering to help several of the older ladies at the barbecue find comfortable places to sit. I'd even overheard a lady giving him hell for staying away from the Thicket for several years, and Brooks had simply stood there politely nodding and saying how much he'd missed everyone.

"It's not like they're going to last. Even if the man is gay, Brooks is going to leave him. It's what he does. He leaves."

She said it with a sniff and a hair toss, but I could see the hurt in her eyes. Brooks Johnson had been the one who'd gotten away, and I'd known from the get-go coming back here was going to poke at that old wound until it bled like a stuck pig.

"Honey, the man is gay. What would you have had him do?" I asked softly, rubbing my way up her calves.

She met my eyes and seemed to deflate. "It was the way it all happened, Mal. Not... not the fact that it happened."

I narrowed my eyes at her until she huffed. "Fine. So I wanted to marry him. Is that so bad? Did you see him? The man's a dish."

"Such a dish," I groaned. "A hotttt dish."

I may have been a little too enthusiastic with my support because she flared her nostrils at me. "Simmer down, horndog," she muttered. "Besides, you wouldn't like him. He's..."

Sexy? Sweet? Possibly dating a straight dude?

"Mercurial."

We locked eyes at her unexpected word choice and immediately burst into laughter. "Say what now?" I asked.

Her eyes were shining, and her cheeks were pink. She looked more relaxed than she'd been all night. "Isn't that the word for constantly changing? Kind of like fickle?"

I nodded. "He seemed steady to me. What do you mean?"

She looked up at the dusty tree house rafters. Thankfully, the cool night air was blowing through the space through open windows on opposite ends. One faced the house, and one faced the acres and acres of grazing land Ava's family owned.

"He's the kind of guy who always fits in with whoever he's with. At an honor society meeting? He's teacher's pet and super smart. At a pep rally for the football season opener? He's a dumb jock. At church with his family on Sunday? He's passing the collection plate with polite murmurs of peace be with you."

I shot her a look. "God, you're right. The man sounds like a total dick."

She glared at me. "That's not what I said. He's just... it's hard to figure out who he is since he's constantly changing to be whoever people expect him to be. He's like a well-intentioned faker. I used to think it was a good thing, because he made friends wherever he went. Now, I don't think it's possible to trust a person who isn't one thing or the other." She sighed. "Maybe I'm not making any sense."

I thought back to the man I'd watched tonight at the barbecue. He'd done everything asked of him and had catered to every guest the way he'd obviously been taught by his parents. They'd looked at him with such pride. From the outside, it looked like he was exactly the man Ava had always described: Mr. Perfect. But then... then I'd remembered the snarky guy interpreting cow art with me and the awkward goofball who'd asked me if I'd ever seen a real live cow. He'd seemed his real self for those few minutes in his family's darkened hallway, especially the split second of insecurity when it seemed like he was going to offer to show me around.

But the minute he'd heard Ava's voice, his big, broad-shouldered frame had seemed to shrink in on itself, and his polite "perfect host" mask had reappeared. He was Mr. Licking Thicket again, the town's Best In Show and pride of the Johnson clan.

"Ava, have you ever thought that maybe... maybe the Brooks you knew was simply a teenager who was trying to figure out who he was? That he was trying on different parts of his persona to see which one fit best? You were eighteen for God's sake. He probably didn't even know who he was at the time."

"Maybe so. But the night we were crowned Mr. and Ms. Licking Thicket, I thought he was going to give me his class ring as a promise. Everyone had said so. Megan Dayton had heard from Enji Ishida who'd overheard Brooks's sister Gracie talking at the food trucks the night before about how Brooks was going to give me a ring at the dance."

"And he didn't." Honestly, hearing this story was a little bit like watching Groundhog's Day for the fiftieth time. I just had to grin and bear it even though I'd rather scratch my eyeballs out. But there was a tiny part of me a smidge more interested in hearing the details now that I'd actually met the villain of the tale in person.

"No. He gave me a trophy he'd won to remember him by. A little plaque that had *his* name on it." She yanked her feet off my lap and stood to root around in my bags, presumably for more snacks. "And a fucking cow horn attached. As if I needed any more cow merchandise for fuck's sake."

"Okay, I wasn't going to say anything, but the cattle themes around here are a bit too—"

"And did it have a key on it or a special meaning?" she asked, interrupting with her usual rhetorical question. I'd learned years ago not to interfere with the natural pace of the retelling. "No. Nothing. He just thought I'd like a little something to remember him by. And then he said he was sorry he'd led me on, and he was going to Columbia instead of UT, and he wished me all the best, but he was gay."

I mouthed the next words along with her. "Onstage. Right when the curtain opened and the mic went live for us to accept our crowns."

She wandered over to the little window facing the fields. "The words *I'm gay* reverberated around that barn like a shotgun had gone off. The whole fucking town heard it. Everyone gasped. Little old ladies fainted. Children cried. It was a whole scene, Mal."

"And you call me dramatic," I muttered, reaching for an emergency chocolate from the secret stash in my bathroom kit.

"Worst day of my life. Still. And that's saying something after the whole unplanned pregnancy thing. I was a laughingstock."

I stood up and stretched, wondering how much more of this I could take before I could sink into the musty lumps of my palatial sleeping situation. "So what's our plan?"

She turned to look at me with a confused expression on her face. "How do you mean?"

"You've been stewing about that moment for ten years now, and now you're both finally back in town at the same time. Are we seeking revenge? Are we taking the high road? Because I really think—"

Her face lit up when I said the word "revenge," and my stomach dropped. I really hadn't meant it. The last thing I wanted to see was Brooks Johnson get even more pressure from this town to be someone he wasn't. I knew what it was like to grow up in a tiny town as a gay man. I knew how stifling and lonely it felt. Even if Brooks hadn't had the addition of poverty and ignorant parents on top of it like I had, I could still imagine things hadn't been as easy for him as they'd appeared.

"I want to break him and Paul up."

I blew out a breath. "Babe."

She held up a hand. "No, listen. Hear me out about Paul. That man's no more gay than I am. So I think maybe he's somehow gotten roped into dating Brooks under false pretenses. Like maybe he's experimenting with his sexuality."

I sighed, but she kept going. "Mal, damn it. If that man's gay, I'll eat my..." She looked around the tree house until her eyes lit on my candy stash.

"Don't even think about it," I growled.

"Just let me poke the bear a little, okay? Will you do that for me?"

I leaned over to pull the futon out into the sleeping position so I could put the sheets on it. "How do you mean, exactly?"

"Remember when we watched that episode of Gaybee where one of the contestants was flirting with a guy at a bar, and the contestant made a bottoms-up joke and the guy didn't get it?"

Sometimes Ava made no sense whatsoever. I looked at her like she was speaking a foreign language.

She put her hands on her hips. "You said that if that man was actually gay he would have gotten the joke?"

"Oh, right. Yeah. It was actually... never mind. What does that have to do with Paul?"

She grinned her pageant-winning smile, the one with Vaseline teeth and sparkling—devious—eyes. "Let's do that. But with Paul."

"Out him as straight?"

She shook her head. "No, God no. I just... I just want to

know for me. Like maybe he's really straight, and somehow Brooks has manipulated him into—"

"Hon, Paul's an adult..." I began. "If he's straight, he's probably helping Brooks out the same way I'm helping you out. He wouldn't have wanted to come home single and deal with all this matchmaking-mother bullshit. Which, by the way, I totally see now and understand why you threw me under the bus."

Ava headed toward the escape hatch and lifted it before tossing down the rope ladder. "Either way, Paul's going to need a friend. I'm going to talk to him and figure out why he would agree to help Brooks out. And if he's by some chance gay, and he thinks he's in love with Brooks, I need to save the poor man from the same fate I experienced ten years ago. You didn't see the way Brooks looked at Paul, like he was nothing more than a study partner. It's like Lickin' 2010 all over again. Brooks is no more in love with that man than he was with me, and Paul deserves better."

She began climbing down but looked back up at me when only her head and her wild blonde curls were still visible. "And I'll be damned if I'm going to be the only one of us single and miserable at this damned Lickin'."

I thought back to her blurted confession at the Johnson house earlier tonight.

"Who says you're single?" I called down to her. "I thought I was your honey nugget!"

She snorted and shot me the bird over her shoulder. "Damned straight. And don't you forget it."

"I didn't sign up for this," I warned.

She spun around and peered up at me, the familiar bravado and determination clear as day on her face. "Join the fucking club, Malachi." Then she turned to continue her trek to the main house.

Ava Ivey was the mercurial one. I'd always told her she was like two sides of a rare coin. On one side was the sassy, confident esthetician who worked hard and was beloved by her clients. The woman who dropped everything to come running when I needed her. The brass-balled tiger who'd once told my landlord that if he didn't replace the shoddy flooring in my apartment, she'd report him to the housing authority.

Then there was the other side of the coin. The vulnerable woman who was terrified of ending up alone. The timid Southerner who was reluctant to speak up to her own boss when her paycheck was a couple of hundred dollars short. The scaredy-cat who crawled into bed with me every Halloween night "just in case" ghosts were real.

I loved both sides of her, but I also knew how unpredictable she was. You never knew which side the coin would land on next.

The following day the tiger came out with claws extended. It seemed she'd had the entire night to stew about it, and she'd dragged me to Monday's Lickin' planning meeting with a storm cloud of laser-focused revenge thundering over her head. I was still half-asleep and hugging my coffee from the local cafe when we approached the town hall building.

"I'm going to expose him if it's the last thing I do," she said under her breath.

I grabbed her elbow and yanked her into the vestibule just off the entryway of the small community center.

"Say what now?" I hissed.

"You heard me. While I was trying not to puke my guts out this morning, it occurred to me why this is bugging me so much. Brooks shouldn't just get to come back here and lead the Lickin' Committee like he did nothing wrong, Mal! He didn't just leave *me*, he left the whole town, and my mom says he's only seen his family in person, like, six times in ten years, when *they* visit *him*. This is bullshit. What if you're wrong and everyone else was right? What if Brooks isn't even gay? What if that was just an excuse for Mr. Perfect Ad Executive to leave Licking Thicket because he thought he was better than the rest of us? The Thicket deserves the truth."

Now I was pissed, but I tried to keep my voice down so no one could overhear us as other people began filtering into the building for the meeting. "He *is* gay. Stop that nonsense and trust me when I say I know what I'm talking about."

"But, Mal—"

"No! You listen to me and listen good. Get your shit together, princess. You got me? I'll be damned if you're going to be the one making a scene in this little fucking—"

Suddenly my T-shirt was choking me, and I was forcibly removed from the vestibule and tossed out into the morning sunshine. A very angry Brooks Johnson stared daggers at me.

I swallowed the sudden lump in my throat and tried not to strip off my clothes and throw myself at his feet. Why the hell did I have to find asshole alpha-male bullshit so sexy?

"What the fuck do you think you're doing?" he demanded.

Chapter Five

Brooks

"WHAT ABOUT A CELEBRITY ENDORSEMENT?" I mused as we drove down Walnut Street bright and early Monday morning. "Some up-and-coming country star, maybe? Or someone from NASCAR?"

Paul said nothing, clearly stunned by the brilliance of my idea... or simply not paying attention to me at all.

I smacked his arm lightly. "Focus."

He glanced up from the papers in his hand and pushed his glasses up his nose. "Brooks, you're not just *on* the Lickin' Committee, you're the *head* of the committee. You get that, right?"

I stifled a sigh. We were on our way to the final Lickin' Committee meeting before the festivities kicked off at the Lickin' Lope the next day, and while I was really glad Paul had managed to unearth my Lickin' itinerary from whatever corner it had landed in Saturday night, I really wished he'd concentrate on our *actual* work. Pamela was less than thrilled by how little we'd gotten done over the weekend, and I needed to step things up if I wanted my bonus. I was glad to be here to stand in for my dad and help my family, but I was not going to let it derail my career or my future, either.

"I'm literally wearing a shirt that says Head Licker," I reminded Paul. "I'm aware. But it's all ceremonial. So maybe get out the ideas notebook, and we can spend a few minutes brainstorming so we're in a better position to work flat out all afternoon, okay? General Partridge wants us in Nashville Friday, and we still haven't come up with a tagline *or* a theme."

Paul wanted to build off the old-fashioned jingle the General had liked the other day, but I felt like we needed to do something different. Something fresher. I was having trouble thinking of anything *fresh* here in Licking Thicket, though.

"Yeah, about that," Paul said. He tapped the pages in front of him. "Friday you're judging a football throw, emceeing a bachelor auction, and doing a bunch of stuff in between. How are you gonna be everywhere at once?"

"I'll just have to skip some stuff, I guess." I remembered my dad really enjoying being Head Licker when I was a kid, so he couldn't have been running around doing *everything*, right? "I'll emcee the auction, but that's at night. We'll just have to see if we can have the meeting with the General first thing, then get back early. It's two hours each way, give or take, plus maybe an hour for the presentation... It's doable." It had to be.

"We could ask General Partridge for more time—?"

"No way," I said, swinging the car into a parking space about a block down from where we needed to be. "You don't get clients by asking for extensions, Paul. Remember you said there's no line I won't cross to get ahead?"

Paul sighed and reached for the door handle. "If you say

so. Don't forget your dad's binder of stuff. You promised him you wouldn't forget it."

I rolled my eyes but collected the overstuffed folder from the back seat just in case. The Lickin' Committee met all year round, so I couldn't imagine there was much left to iron out. This would be more of a pep rally thing, where we'd all stand in a circle and yell "*Go team!*"... or possibly moo, which was the Thicket's version of an encouraging cheer.

"So," Paul said when I joined him on the sidewalk. "What's the deal with you and, ah... Ava?"

I shot him a side-eyed look. "I think we covered that in-depth yesterday. She's my ex-girlfriend. We dated in high school."

"And you broke her heart."

I stopped outside the Melt, the Thicket's burger joint, and stared at him. "Who told you that?" I didn't think he'd been in the hallway for that part of the conversation yesterday.

"Gracie. I-wen. Maureen. Penelope. Ladli." He ticked the names off on his fingers. "Everyone at the barbecue, basically. They all pity her." He wrinkled his nose and had to fix his glasses. "Which is stupid because she's fucking gorgeous, and smart as hell, and has great taste in tea, and is a licensed esthetician. And she's clearly leveled up in the boyfriend department since you, too, but whatever."

Leveled up. *Pfft.* Leveling up would involve a boyfriend who didn't come to his girlfriend's hometown and flirt with other people, a reality I planned to make clear to Malachi the next time I saw him.

"Ava has every reason to be mad at me," I told Paul. "I didn't break her heart, not really, but I bruised her pride for sure. I'd suspected I was gay for a while, but I didn't know how to tell anyone, you know? I was convinced folks would turn on me, and it was easier to just… smile and nod and not make waves. But that meant Ava had expectations for us. Hell, the whole town did."

I felt the same fiery-hot tingle of anxiety crawl up my spine that I'd felt back then, and I rubbed at the back of my neck to get rid of it. Even years later, the sinking knowledge that I would disappoint someone just by being who I was killed me.

"I knew I needed to leave the Thicket if I was ever going to become comfortable with myself, but every time I tried to bring it up, Ava would tell me some great plan she had for our future, and I'd tell myself the timing was wrong. Then somehow it was just a few days before I was supposed to be in New York for school, and I panicked. I blurted out the truth at the worst possible time, in front of the whole town at the Lickin' Dinner Dance that Saturday night."

"*Damn*, Brooks."

"I know." Just telling the story made me cringe. "But that boyfriend of hers is worse than I ever was." My free hand clenched into a fist, and I shook my head and resumed walking. "I might not have been in love with Ava, but at least I didn't cheat on her."

Mal had no right being all warm and funny and intelligent and sexy when he was *taken*, damn it.

I stepped around an older couple coming out of the Feed and Seed.

"I dunno. I thought he seemed nice," Paul said glumly. "In the kitchen last night, I mean. He was really attentive to Ava."

"You think everyone's nice, Paul. I told you, he flirted with me in the hall ten minutes before! He'd damn well better—"

I stopped dead and stared at the vestibule in front of the community center, where Mal, that asshole, was *looming* over a wide-eyed Ava, who looked unusually tired and fragile this morning.

"No!" Mal said sharply, and Ava's blue eyes widened. "You listen to me and listen good. Get your shit together, princess. You got me? I'll be damned if you're going to be the one making a scene in this little fucking—"

I didn't wait to hear more. I was gonna kill him.

I shoved my binder into Paul's hands. "Attentive, my ass."

I stalked toward them and grabbed Mal by the back of his T-shirt.

"What the fuck do you think you're doing?"

"What the hell?" he yelled as I dragged him down the sidewalk to the front of the original Susie Dupree's Deluxe Barbecue, which fortunately hadn't opened for the day yet, and hauled him up against the brick wall. I heard Ava squawk in protest, but Paul murmured something in response. I honestly didn't care. I was too busy trying to figure out how to get this asshole to show her some respect.

"Answer me."

The guy swallowed, managing to look defiant and sexy and nervous and sexy and guilty and *sexy* all at the same time. "I *thought* I was having a private conversation with my honey nugget, if that's okay with you?" he snapped, brown waves falling in his face. "Take your jealous caveman shit elsewhere. It's... it's not sexy."

I gritted my teeth. "It's not jealousy, for fuck's sake. I'm gay. *As you know.*"

I let that last bit with all its possible interpretations hang in the air, because Mal had been flirting with me, damn it, even if my mother and Paul refused to believe it.

Sure enough, Mal's cheeks flushed and he looked away for a brief second. He licked his gorgeous lips—I mean, his cheaty, *flirtatious* lips—and tried to stand up straight, which was kinda tricky because I was standing quite close to him.

As in, really close to him.

As in, my entire forearm was braced across his chest and my face was just a couple inches from his.

"You can back up anytime now, asshole." He sounded snarky and a little breathless, possibly because I was cutting off his air supply. The man wasn't small, but he wasn't nearly as large as I was, and I had the uncomfortable realization that I was the one doing the looming in this scenario.

I eased off just slightly but still held him in place.

"I'll let go when you promise me that you're gonna do right by Ava. Not cheat on her *or* verbally abuse her."

"Verbally..." Mal's bright blue eyes narrowed. "Fuck *you*. I'd *never* hurt her. You're the one who's done a kick-ass job of that."

I set my jaw. "I know it. And that's exactly why I'm not going to let you ruin this Lickin' by being unkind to her." I stepped away from him.

He rolled his shoulders and shot me a glare. "Ava is the most important person in my life, dumbass." His voice held the unmistakable ring of truth. "I love her. I dropped everything to be here for her, and I will take care of her. You should stay away from her and from *me*."

Honestly. He made it sound like I *wanted* to be near him, and I didn't.

Like, hardly at all.

I folded my arms over my chest. "Fine. Treat her right and we won't have an issue."

Mal nodded once, then I nodded once. All the while,

we stared at each other like a pair of Old West gunslingers at high noon.

Then Mal rolled his eyes and turned on his heel, leaving me behind.

"Hey!" I demanded, jogging after him.

We started walking toward the entrance of the building side by side and stopped simultaneously when we realized we were heading in the same direction.

"I'm going to the Lickin' Committee meeting," I informed him. "I'm the..." I would not say Head Licker. Not to Mal. "I'm in charge."

"Yeah? *Fucking awesome.* Because I have questions. Ava needs to know where to get a cheerleader uniform for the parade Saturday. Mrs. Ivey volunteered me to do some running race thing tomorrow, but I don't know where to go or what to do. And I'm setting up a vendor booth with my sculptures on Wednesday for the Licking Artists' Fair on Thursday. I have no idea who to contact about those things." He raised his chin stubbornly. "That's why I'm *also* going to the Lickin' Committee meeting."

I frowned. I obviously had no answers for any of those questions either, except the first. "There aren't uniforms for the parade." Were there?

Mal's glare turned withering. "*Of course there are.* Mrs. Ivey literally talked about nothing else all morning at break-fast. It's the Big Huge Hundredth Lick-Off, or whatever the fuck you people call it. Everyone in the parade is dressing in decade-appropriate clothing from the year they won."

I glanced down at my shorts and boat shoes in relief. "Awesome. Done."

He sighed. "*You* are supposed to wear your football uniform. Jesus. How do I know this and you don't?"

Good fucking question. Where was this meeting? And where was Paul with my itinerary?

I shouldered past Mal into the building... and entered utter chaos.

Well. Apparently I didn't have to wonder where the meeting was, since folks had decided to hold it right in the lobby. At the top of their lungs.

"Holy shit," Mal whispered under his breath from beside me. "They've gone feral."

This basically summed up my initial impression, as well.

"Brooks!" Coach Cosway, standing near the entrance, caught sight of me first. "Thank goodness you're here. Tell *this woman* that the Friday Morning Football Throw is a family-favorite Thicket tradition, and we won't be postponing it for any dang kiddie craft fair!" His blue eyes gleamed zealously in his round, pink face. "As Head Licker, you'll obviously be throwing the first football and awarding the prizes for the kids when it's over!"

That woman, who happened to be Mrs. Cosway, set her hands on her hips. "Brooks, honey, please remind this idiot that his own son is participating in the craft fair this year, and it's about time we had a more inclusive family activity for Friday morning anyway!"

I didn't realize I'd leaned over a little until the warmth of Mal's shoulder made its way through my shirtsleeve. For some reason, just knowing he was there made me feel a little less harried. It was strange since the man had just annoyed the shit out of me two seconds earlier. Why was I drawn to someone who bugged the shit out of me so easily?

He's beautiful, sexy, intriguing, mischievous, confident...

I shook my head. None of that had anything to do with my mission right now. I tried to focus.

"Inclusive? Football's plenty inclusive, Charlotte! Just ask your *daughter*! She's got the best arm in town for her age group!" He sounded proud and exasperated in equal measure.

"George and Charlotte, nobody cares about football *or* crafts if they don't have *food*." A woman in a hijab I only vaguely recalled from the day before pushed her way through the crowd. "Brooks, you might not remember me. I'm Salma Alvi? Your father put me in charge of coordinating the food trucks, but he was supposed to get back to me about the final placement. Everyone wants to be closest to the pavilion, obviously—"

"And some of us have been here for years and deserve first choice!" John Timms, who owned the Thicket Tavern, piped up from the back.

The warm scent of sandalwood reached my nose, and I realized Mal was still there at my elbow. I wondered why he hadn't bolted out of there while he still could.

"Or maybe some of us who are newer but more popular should get some consideration?" a guy about my age I'd never met before argued. "Veg Out has been doing a steady business for nearly three years now."

"Mario, sweetie, you know I'm a slave for your veggie wraps," my aunt Dot said, "but y'all can sort this later. The bachelor auction brings this whole town together, and I don't have the final list of names with their selected charities. We vet all the charities in advance," she added as an aside to me, "to make sure there's no funny business."

Mal snorted softly. "Funny business, heh. As if the concept of auctioning men off isn't funny enough. Jesus."

I ignored him, mostly because if I turned to look at him, I'd probably make a goofy face in front of the entire town.

Besides, he wasn't my priority here. And also, he was still on my shit list for being a jerk to Ava.

"All those decisions can happen in good time," said old Bert Cobb, whose farm ran along the far side of the road across from my parents. "The Lickin' Lope is tomorrow, and I told Red I couldn't collect the milk to fill the pails on my own this year. My bursitis is flaring up something terrible. *Somebody'd* better decide who's helpin' by milkin' time." He stroked his quivering mustache like he was calming a wild animal.

I ran a hand through my hair as two things simultaneously became very clear.

First, my dad was absolutely not up to the job of being Head Licker. Not in his current condition. And second... neither was I, for a vastly different reason.

"Brooks, honey, my question's real quick." Mrs. Jepsen, my old piano teacher, waved a hand from the back of the crowd. "I just need to know which piece you picked for your piano solo at the recital Thursday morning."

"My..." I hadn't played the piano in a dozen years. "But the Head Licker doesn't have to play piano."

I knew that for a *fact*, since my dad couldn't play a piano if you put a gun to his head and threatened to take away his grilling tongs.

"Oh, of course not! But we had a last-minute cancellation, and your mama said you'd step in. Any old piece would be fine, Brooks. Doesn't have to be anything fancy. You always did such a good job with 'Clair de Lune'!"

Yeah, back when I was six.

"I don't—" I began.

"Brooks, honey, my question's even faster," Lurleen said importantly. "What was the total number of tickets sold for the dinner dance Saturday, so I can tell Miss Susie?"

"Miss Susie?" I repeated.

"Well, yes! Miss Susie of Susie Dupree's Deluxe Barbecue agreed to cater the event *for free* as a gift to the town for our support. Susie is a *saint*." Lurleen patted her jet-black hair and added modestly, "We're second cousins."

I nearly whimpered. I could maybe fix most of this, but I couldn't fix *all* of it. Not all at once. Still, I felt compelled to try... I just wasn't sure where to begin.

For a second, I sort of forgot how to breathe. But then I felt Mal's arm shift along mine, and it almost felt deliberate, like a sign of solidarity or support. Surely I was imagining it.

"If you end up playing a piano solo," he said in a sly voice too soft for anyone else to hear, "be warned that I'm taking a video and posting it online. I will make *sure* it goes viral."

My gaze darted to the right to collide with Mal's, and the force left me lurching mentally. His eyes held challenge... and maybe even a little sympathy? Or possibly I was reading him wrong again.

Either way, his comment was enough to break through my moment of panic and remind me that an enormous world existed outside of Licking Thicket, and it wasn't my job to please these folks. Not anymore.

"Mrs. Jepsen, I am *so* sorry, but I'm not going to be able to do the solo. That recital should be for your current students, anyway, so let's keep it about the kids." I winked and she smiled, just a little.

"As for the final totals for Saturday..." I looked around for Paul and found him off to one side of the lobby, standing protectively next to a wooden bench where Ava sat like a very tired, unwell princess. He had my dad's binder in one hand and held up a paper with the other.

"Sixteen hundred fourteen, as of last Tuesday," he

called, because we really *did* have an amazing connection, when he wasn't impersonating my boyfriend.

"Who's that?" Lurleen asked no one in particular.

"That's Brooks's Little Paul," Mal said sweetly.

I shot him a baleful look.

"And who are *you*?" Lurleen demanded.

"Oh, I'm—"

"He's Second Licker," I interrupted, before Mal could call himself Ava's honey nugget or something equally annoying. "He's kind of my assistant."

Everyone stopped talking and stared.

"What?" Mal kind of squeaked. Then in a softer voice he muttered, "I've never been second in any kind of licking situation."

"Don't be ashamed, Mal. It's an important role. If you focus and work hard, you'll be Head Licking in no time." I patted him on the shoulder supportively.

My ears heated up as I tried my hardest not to picture Mal licking *anything*. "Is that all you needed, Lurleen?"

She shrugged and nodded. "I suppose."

I clapped my hands once. "Excellent! Now, I'm gonna have to think about the food trucks." The room exploded into yelling, and I held my two hands up palm-down, like I was patting the air in front of me, the universal sign for *calm the fuck down*. "I know, I know. But clearly this requires some serious diplomacy." I shot Salma Alvi a commiserating look. "I'm gonna let Ms. Alvi make recommendations, and I'll approve them. So you can all go kiss her ass today and kiss mine tomorrow."

That got a reluctant chuckle from the crowd, and I felt... competent. Capable. I often felt that way when I was in charge of a meeting at work, but I'd never felt it around here.

"Mr. and Mrs. Cosway, I think we need to work out a way for the craft fair and the football toss to happen at different times. No one should have to choose which to participate in, right? I mean—" I pressed a hand to my chest. "—I know I certainly couldn't choose."

"Does that mean you'll be at both?" Ms. Cosway asked suspiciously. "You'll give out the blue ribbon for the craft fair *and* the football toss?"

"Of course," I agreed smoothly, conveniently ignoring my meeting in Nashville. Both of them shrugged, looking mollified. "Or Second Licker will, right, Mal? Now, what else?" I was on a roll and did my best to ignore the death lasers shooting into me from the man at my side.

"The milk," Bert Cobb reminded me. "We got all the farms lined up to donate some, and I can drive the truck, but somebody's gotta go door to door to do the ceremonial collection in the old milk truck. You remember, Brooks! The ceremonial milk collection?"

I didn't remember this *at all*. In fact, I'd think I was being punked, if not for the dozens of other town residents nodding sagely. Then again, I'd never been involved with any of the behind-the-scenes before. I'd taken part in the Lope, but I was starting to realize that with most things in Licking Thicket, I'd only worried about the *what*, not the how or the why.

"Of course," I lied. "I remember perfectly. So all I'd have to do is grab the buckets of milk?"

Bert scratched his head. "I mean, I guess. If you wanna take all the magic out of the thing."

"No," I assured him gravely. "I promise to feel very appropriately magical." At this point, I'd whisper incantations under the full moon just to check something off my list.

Bert looked well pleased.

"Now, who's in charge of uniforms for the parade?"

Mal shot me a homicidal warning look.

"I believe that falls into the Second Licker's responsibilities."

This was turning out to be more fun than I'd expected.

"THANKS FOR THE RIDE, LURLEEN!" I called as the woman drove down the street in her ancient Buick. Then I sighed as I traipsed out to the milking parlor at the Ivey Family Dairy.

It had taken three and a half hours to sort out the mess at the community center, even without finalizing the placement of the vendor booths and the food trucks. That was two hundred and ten individual minutes of my life I would never get back—an entire morning and early afternoon when I should have been doing *real* work.

And it wasn't over yet.

Paul had taken my keys and left halfway through because Ava hadn't been feeling well and needed to rest. On his way out, he'd reminded me that I'd just *triple-*booked myself for Friday morning, which meant someone was gonna have to call General Partridge to reschedule, unless I could convince Mal that being Second Licker was a real thing... I didn't even want to imagine what that would look like.

Mal had already left by that point—I'd watched Mr. Ivey walk him out with an arm over his shoulder, not that I'd been subconsciously aware of him all morning or whatever. I'd only noticed because my *own* dad had called around the same time, probably to make sure I wasn't blowing up his town while he was sitting on the sofa watching television and buying commemorative silver coins.

"I've got things under control, Dad," I'd soothed.

"But the week of the Lickin' is always a mess. People *say* they're fine with the way I've organized shit, but when it comes time to execute, they wanna reinvent the wheel. Don't let 'em take advantage, Brooks. Not even your mama," he'd added in a whisper.

"Oh yeah, no, that hasn't been a problem at all." Was there a word that meant something worse and more egregious than lying? Because that was what I was doing. "Maybe folks are feeling merciful since they know you're recovering and I haven't been back in a while."

"You sure?"

"Positive," I'd enthused. "I've got this. Remember, Head Licking is in my blood!"

I'd immediately looked around to make sure no one had heard me.

Bert Cobb had instructed me to meet him at Ava's family farm to make my first milk pickup of the afternoon, but when I stepped into the big, circular milking parlor at one o'clock sharp, there was no one there, human or animal. When I thought about it for a minute, this made sense. The milking parlor was designed to milk a whole herd efficiently, but no dairy farmer was milking his entire herd at midafternoon. Not when milking usually occurred every twelve hours.

Maybe I'd gotten the time wrong?

"Hello?" I called, but there was no answer. I stepped outside and called louder, but there didn't seem to be a soul around.

I was ready to go up to the house to check on Ava—and

yeah, fine, see Mal—when I heard a crash in one of the little, old-fashioned lean-tos near the tractor garage, followed by a cow's mournful bellow.

"Mr. Ivey? That you?" I called, trying to moderate my voice so as not to startle any people or bovines.

There was still no answer, so I headed back there to investigate, taking care where I stepped since the ground was about 80 percent straw and mud, and 20 percent something that looked like mud but wasn't. I rounded the side of the lean-to and froze in place.

"Annabelle, I thought we were friends. I thought we'd established a real connection," Mal said. He blew out a breath and brushed the golden-brown hair out of his eyes with the back of one hand, while picking up a five-gallon bucket lying on its side in a milk puddle with the other. He sat back down on his stool and awkwardly patted the cow's flank while she rolled her eyes and shied away. "Alright, fine, maybe not *friends*, per se, but *friendly*. I just washed your teats for half a fucking hour, didn't I? And all I'm asking is for you to be still and let me finish you off so I can go back to the death futon in the tree house and cry my self-loathing into a rapidly diminishing supply of Dove chocolates while the spiders in the rafters make plans to eat my flesh. Okay?"

I leaned against the doorframe and whistled low, feeling lighter than I had in hours. "A plus plus. Your seduction technique is on point."

Mal shut his eyes, leaned his head back to the ceiling, and shook his head. "Of course you walked in right now," he moaned softly. "Of course you did."

"No, no, don't be embarrassed. This is highly educational. I don't have a lot of experience with females, you understand. So, first you get 'em all excited with the teat-washing—"

"I hate you."

"—then you bring it on home with the tears and the chocolate."

"Did you want something here?" Mal demanded.

I definitely wanted something here. But nothing I could have.

"I thought you said you'd seen a cow before," I said instead.

"Seen, yes. Milked, hell no. But apparently, this is some archaic test a man has to pass in order to date an Ivey woman, according to Ava's father. Like, if we're ever on a deserted island, just me, Ava, and a milk cow, I'll be able to provide for her?" He threw his hands in the air in frustration, and Annabelle side-eyed him. "Did you know her father has seventy-five head of cattle? Jesus Christ, how does he find time to do anything else all day?"

Holy fuck, I wanted to kiss him. Just looking at his tired blue eyes and his mulish expression and his lips—those fucking *lips*—was a unique kind of torture that made my legs shake with the desire to get closer to him and my hands tremble with the need to touch him. But I would not. *Not not not.*

"He has automatic milkers, Mal."

"Huh?"

"Giant metal building down that way? It's a milking parlor. He hooks a whole bunch of cows up at once. The milking part takes just a few minutes."

"But then...?" He looked from Annabelle to the empty bucket. "Was this just a joke?"

I pushed off the wall and walked toward him. He sounded genuinely upset, and that didn't sit right with me.

"Nah, Mr. Ivey's not like that. I mean, the part where he didn't tell you Annabelle was a kicker was probably his idea of a joke. There's a kick bar over there by the wall by those old buckets and the stanchion, but he had to know you didn't know what it was."

I nudged Mal gently in the side with my knee and he scowled but stood, letting me take his place on the stool. I steadied the pail and started milking Annabelle with no fuss whatsoever.

Apparently cow milking was one of those riding-a-bike life skills. Who knew?

"Anyway, Mr. Ivey probably just wanted to learn more about you, you know? Like, how you handle adversity or some shit. When Ava and I dated, he did almost the same thing to me. I mean, I knew how to milk, obviously, so he—" Mal wandered over to the wall, distracting me because my eyes naturally wanted to follow him. He picked up the stanchion. "Oh, that's not the kick bar, that's the—"

"Stanchion," he said crankily. "Yes, I know. I'm looking at it for its sculptural aesthetic, not its function, okay?"

"Chill out, I was just trying to—"

"Be perfect at absolutely everything? Yeah, no, I've seen that in action today plenty, thanks."

I blinked up at him. "The what now?"

"Oh, I could totally do your piano concert, Mrs. Whoever, but I'd hate to upstage the children! Sure, I'll collect milk with magic! I'll throw footballs! I love yarn crafts! Pick me, pick me!" He rolled his eyes. "Tell the truth, Brooks, are you a really clever robot? Or are you so used to wearing polite masks you don't even notice them anymore?"

I felt my jaw drop. "That is *not*..." I began. But all I could think was, I definitely noticed the polite masks. I just didn't think anyone else ever had. Not my parents, or my siblings, or the girl I'd dated for a year in high school, or the people I worked with now.

So how the fuck had this guy?

"Stand aside and let *me* milk your cow," Mal continued. "Let *me* save Ava. Let *me* rescue the town from having a no good, very bad Lick-fest. Brooks Johnson is all things to all people. He fixes everything!" He folded his arms over his chest. "You know, it's okay not to be perfectly perfect all the time, right? That it's actually really fucking off-putting?"

I swallowed hard. Wow. Okay, then. I'd thought we'd shared a moment earlier in the day. I'd thought we were about to sign some kind of peace treaty here. Apparently I'd misread his feelings the way he'd misread the cow's.

I stood up. "Gosh, that's so helpful to know. Thank you, Mal," I whispered fervently. "I guess I'll leave you to it." I swept my arm toward the stool and the half-full bucket like a magician's assistant. "Good luck."

He raised his chin—which should *not* have inspired a Pavlovian lust response in my gut, for God's sake—and took a step toward me. "I am perfectly capable of doing it."

"Absolutely, you are," I agreed brightly. Then under my breath added, "Despite all evidence to the contrary."

"You can leave now," he said imperiously, pausing directly in front of me. "Surely there are a hundred things that require your attention as Head Licker..." He leaned forward and whispered, "*Boss.*"

My cheeks went hot, but at least now I could see why he was being so snippy with me. "I'm sorry about that. Second Licker's not really a thing. But... I was just so... You make me so..." I took a breath. "Anyway, this *is* the thing that requires my attention, Mal. I'm here collecting milk, remember? Old Bert will be along any minute, and I'm sure you wouldn't want him waiting, what with his bursitis and all. Or is politeness a sign of being a robot too?"

He narrowed his eyes, but I could still see the blue fire in their depths. "You're infuriating. Has anyone ever told you that? And don't blame me for you being 'so.'" He used air quotes and sarcasm which reminded me so much of Ava, it almost made me smile.

I resisted the urge to laugh. Literally no one had ever called me infuriating. And no one provoked me this much. I didn't *let* anyone provoke me this much. I felt out of control, and I didn't like it one bit. But also... I kind of liked it. A lot.

"You know—" I began.

"Brooks? Mal? What the heck's going on?"

Ava walked around the side of the shed, her face flushed and sleep-creased, and Mal and I sprang apart like we'd been doing something a lot more fun than fighting about milking a cow.

"Ava, babe," Mal said, belatedly striding over to her side. "How are you feeling?"

"Fine. Tired." Her eyes flicked back and forth between us suspiciously. "I asked what's going on."

"Your dad gave Mal the Brad Ivey Dating Test," I explained. "I offered to help, but Mal got cranky."

Ava's mouth dropped open in horror as she stared at Mal. "Oh, damn! He made you palpate a cow?"

I snorted. "No, he only made Mal *milk* Annabelle, to provide your family's contribution to the Lope tomorrow. I was the poor sap who had to stick my entire gloved forearm up the business end of Moonpie just for the privilege of taking you to prom."

Ava's eyes met mine. She snorted, then I did, and soon we were both laughing out loud.

"God, I can't believe you went through with it," she giggled.

"You were a good friend, Ava. I would have done worse." I shot Mal a glare. "And that's *not* just me being polite."

Mal's nostrils flared.

"Anyway. Turns out Mal doesn't need help with milking after all. He's perfectly capable. So, I'll just wait out in the yard for Bert to come along with his truck." I forced a smile. "For what it's worth, Mal, I owe you an apology for earlier today. I accept your resignation as Second Licker."

"Mr. Perfect strikes again," Mal mocked.

But as I walked away from the shed, I knew I wasn't perfect. Not even fucking close. Because if I were anywhere close to perfect, I wouldn't have wanted to grab Mal Forrester and kiss that mocking smile off his face.

Chapter Six

Mal

I couldn't decide if I was annoyed at Brooks or sort of felt sorry for the guy. It must have been exhausting always trying to be so infallible all the time. And boring. Boring as fuck. It was like a little look into the inner workings of a small-town crown prince, except I had to begrudgingly admit this one wasn't as awful as the one I'd known in Homer. That guy had taken the stereotype a hundred percent too far by literally stealing my lunch money each day, knocking up not one but two girlfriends, and unsuccessfully attempting to blackmail me into sucking him off under the bleachers all the while spewing homophobic bullshit.

Cliché, thy name is Kevin Odom. Good riddance. At least I wasn't back in Homer, and while Brooks Johnson was clearly the town's golden child and annoying as fuck, he didn't seem like a bully or a user. He was more of an over-pleaser. Earlier today at the planning meeting, it had been a bit like watching a cartoon superhero point his bright-white smile at the townsfolk just in time for a tooth to glint and bestow solutions to the world's problems upon them.

"Brooks sure does look good, doesn't he, honey?" Mrs. Ivey asked serenely from the foot of the dining table.

I blinked at her and wondered if she was some kind of mind-reading savant dressed as the head of the Licking Welcome Wagon.

"'Course he does, Mama," Ava muttered. "Personally, I'm more attracted to a less showy type."

"Thank you, honey nugget," I said wryly.

"Not *you*, Mal. I meant Paul, for example. I love a man in glasses."

I almost choked on my chicken. While Paul was definitely attractive, there wasn't a human alive who could think he held a candle to Brooks. It was a bit like saying a Bernzomatic welding torch from Home Depot was nicer than a Victor Journeyman setup from a true welding supply outfit. Pfft. It may get the job done, but it wasn't the same thing at all. And once you held the Journeyman in your hands...

"Paul seems like a perfectly nice man," Mrs. Ivey said with a sniff. "But, darling, he's gay."

I snorted and quickly tried turning it into a cough behind my napkin.

Ava's lips quirked into a small grin. "Oh, so he's gay, but Brooks himself isn't?"

Ava's brother, Elliott, chuckled. "Score one for little sis."

"No offense intended, Mrs. Ivey, but I'm not sure your gaydar is calibrated very well," I added politely. Ava elbowed me in the gut.

After this lovely dinner with the family—and by lovely, I obviously meant horrific—I was counting down the minutes until I could give my excuses and scurry back to the blessed solitude of my arboreal guest house. Before the last ear of corn had been gnawed to the quick, however, Ava's dad put me under the interrogation lights.

"You're going to win this race for her tomorrow, right, son?"

I snuck a glance at Ava in hopes she'd be holding up a cue card with a little guidance on what the heck he was talking about. Instead, she was happily stripping a drumstick like a starving teenager biting into a turkey leg at a medieval festival.

"Do you mean metaphorically, or...?"

Mr. Ivey's eyes narrowed. "The Lope. We need this. The Ivey family has won every Lope that's been run without a Johnson. Just because Brooks is back this year and Elliot's not competing doesn't mean they get to take the title away from us." He sat forward, pushing his dinner plate off to the side where Mrs. Ivey scrambled to clear it to the kitchen. "It's one thing for that boy to win the race when he was in top shape as the QB for the Bovines, but I'll be damned if some pencil pusher from New York City is going to embarrass the Iveys. Do you understand what I'm saying, son?"

I was pretty sure he was saying the Thicket's high school mascot was a cow, but that should have been obvious. It certainly explained the random *moo* shouts I'd heard earlier today when Brooks had walked into the planning meeting. At first I'd thought they were heckling the poor guy, and then I'd assumed they were making a comment about his "pencil pushing" physique. Which, honestly, was pretty damned fine if you asked m—

"Malachi!"

I jumped at Mr. Ivey's bark. "Yes, sir. I mean, I can try. I do run fairly regularly." I glanced at Ava again, who, if I was keeping track properly, was enjoying her sixth ear of buttery corn.

She nodded. "Yes, Daddy. It's like I told you. Mal runs when he's upset which means he's in really good shape."

She made me sound like I had an anger management problem. "That's not—"

"Good," Mr. Ivey said, sitting back and clasping his fingers over his belly. "That's real good, son. I knew we could count on you for something."

How was it possible to feel like I'd both impressed and disappointed him at the same time?

"You're... welcome?" I glanced toward the kitchen, both hoping there might be dessert to soothe my hurt feelings and hoping there wasn't dessert so I could leg it the fuck out of there.

Mrs. Ivey came in carrying a cake with lit candles. "Mal, dear, why don't you lead us?"

I glanced around the table hoping someone, somewhere would tell me what the hell was happening. Was it someone's birthday?

"Um... I don't..." Several expectant faces beamed at me, and it was worse than the interrogation lights. "Happy Birthday," I began singing and thankfully everyone else joined in immediately. I found out from the final stanza that it was, indeed, the Thicket's own birthday cake.

Because the Lickin' was born out of a celebration of the town's founding. Which made sense if you thought about it. Singing the birthday song to a town, however, did not make sense, especially in a private residential celebration.

I leaned over to Ava once the song was over. "Are you a founding family or something?"

"Don't be ridiculous," she said with a scoff. "The town was founded by a big cluster of Johnsons and a whole passel of Mawbrys. It wasn't until Enid Mawbry married Randall Ivey in the 1920s that the Iveys really established themselves."

"1913 actually, sweetie," Mrs. Ivey said, handing me a tiny sliver of cake and one undersized ball of ice cream. I assumed this meager offering was a result of the intense fitness expectations on me the following day. "He lost his first wife on the *Titanic*, so the date is important. It's why he came wife-hunting in the Thicket in the first place."

"The *Titanic*? Wow," I said before thanking her for dessert.

Elliott snickered. "Pretty sure he lost his first wife in a bet down at the Feed and Seed, Mama. At least that's what Grandpa told me once."

"Hush your mouth," she hissed. "Anyway," she said sweetly back at me, "once Gracie Johnson married into the Mawbry family... well, let's just say it was almost as exciting and long-time-coming as our Ava here finally marrying Brooks."

She blinked happily at Ava as if she hadn't just struck a prison shank into my fictional love match.

"Mom, that's never going to happen," Ava said for what had to be the millionth time. "Besides, I have Mal now." She shot me a smile, and it took all of my self-control not to roll my eyes.

Mrs. Ivey swallowed. "Yes, well, be that as it may, you have to admit an Ivey/Johnson wedding sure would be something to see. I don't think I'm the only one in town who thinks—"

"What's that?" I asked loudly, cupping my ear. "Lassie says someone's fallen into the well. I'd better go check."

I raced out of the room by way of the sink to deposit my

dirty dishes before hoofing it out to the guest house and climbing up the rope ladder to freedom.

It was short-lived, however, because sunrise comes quick during Lickin' week, and before I'd even settled into a particularly agriculture-themed dreamscape, Ava's father was honking the air horn and shouting up at me about early birds.

"Yeah," I grumbled back. "Yeah, got it. I'm, ah, doing my pre-run meditation. Need a few minutes to wrap it up, m'kay?"

Before I could even roll over and bury my head under the pillow, much less fall back asleep, the air horn honked again and two dozen birds went screaming past my open window.

"Coming!" I singsonged through gritted teeth.

Thankfully, Ava had procured some kind of miracle elixir from the café, and by the time I dragged my ass to the starting area of the race, I was fully caffeinated and ready to give it my best. After the frustrations leading up to my being in the Thicket, I figured I had plenty of emotional energy to burn off on the run. I could knock out a 5K in my sleep, so this little fun run wasn't going to be a problem.

"Here's your bucket," Ava said, handing me a metal pail of...

"Milk?" I glanced up at her in confusion. "I'm not thirsty, but thanks?"

"No, idiot. You have to carry this on the run. It's a reminder of the way the original Thicketeers used to hand-deliver milk to the townsfolk."

I heard some young men snickering behind me, and I turned to shoot them a glare. Despite not giving a shit what some dumbasses thought of me, I still felt the familiar nerves wobble in my gut. Apparently you could take the scrawny gay boy out of Homer, but you couldn't make him forget.

"Don't be ridiculous. I'm not carrying a pail of milk on a run." I faced forward and took a deep breath, trying to let go of old memories.

"Mal, everyone carries a pail of milk. That's the whole point of the Lope. The person who comes in fastest without losing their load."

This couldn't be real. I looked around us to see that it was, in fact, real. All of the runners were accepting their milk pails with a smile.

Ava continued. "It's calibrated. You can't lose a drop or you get points deducted. Dude, you're the one who collected the milk for this. Didn't you know what it was for?"

I threw up my hands. "Are you asking me why I was milking cows on a dairy farm? Really?"

"Stop being a drama queen and take it. We need this win, Mal. You have no idea what a bad mood my dad will be in if an Ivey doesn't win this year."

I thought maybe my back teeth might break before the week was out, and I wasn't in a financial position to replace them. "Fine. But if I win this fucking race, you're going to stop stalling and take me to meet your CEO friend so I can sell my damned reef piece."

She grinned and handed me the bucket. "Absolutely. Good luck!"

Once she'd blended into the crowd, I turned back toward the front of the starting group. The town assholes were still goofing off, and I secretly hoped they spilled their milk and cried about it. Hard.

"This is what my life has come to," I muttered under my breath. "I need to get back to California."

"Dude, there's something wrong with your pail handle."

I glanced over to see one of the guys from the asshole group pointing at my bucket. There was no way I was falling for his prank. Been there, done that.

"Mpfh. Thanks," I said before mentally rolling my eyes. "It's fine."

"No, for real. It looks like it's about to—"

I ignored the rest of his bullshit as soon as I spotted Brooks at the front of the pack. He was wearing tiny running shorts that were 92 percent bubble butt and 8 percent drool-worthy bulge. I wondered if I could use his body like the rabbit lure on a dog track. There was a good chance I could win this race by following that muscular butt as long as I saved enough in the tank for the final kick past him at the end.

He must have felt me mentally stripping him down because he turned to look over his shoulder and caught me mid-stare.

Then he winked one green eye at me.

Cocky fucker. As soon as the ceremonial pistol was literally shot into the air (and I subsequently jumped high enough to almost grace everyone around me with a lovely milk bath before even crossing the starting line), we were off.

It turned out that running with a heavy pail of sloshy milk wasn't easy or fun in any way. I found it hard to believe anyone had ever delivered milk this way, and if they had, it was a practice that should have died out a long time ago when Randall Ivey made his bad bet at the Feed and Seed.

Still, I'd guessed right. All of the built-up frustration over this unexpected trip and the cancellation of my recent art commission served to pump my legs even faster than normal. I followed the spray-painted arrows through town and into the shaded woods of the nature preserve behind the elementary school. The trail was quiet, with only the soft pounding sounds of Brooks's shoes hitting the ground ahead of me. For a pencil pusher, the man could still run, and pretty soon we'd outstripped all of the other runners.

The trail through the nature preserve went steeply uphill before giving out onto an empty field where the painted arrows led us alongside the highway for a few yards. There wasn't another soul in sight, except the cows watching us from the pasture across the road. They were probably wondering what the fool humans were up to. I couldn't blame them.

And then suddenly, apropos of nothing, Brooks stopped and stared at a couple of posts sticking out of the ground in the cow pasture, his breath heaving.

"Out of breath already, Mr. Perfect?"

He shot me a scathing look, then turned his attention back to the empty posts. "This is our town sign. *Was* our town sign. I'm not sure what happened to it."

The little frown between his eyebrows did weird things to my stomach, and though I'd never admit it, I preferred him looking cocky.

"Probably the same thing that happened to your stamina," I said sadly. "Lost to the sands of time."

His eyes lit with competitive fire. "I'll show you stamina." He took off, following the arrows back into the woods with a burst of speed that would have left me in the dust if I hadn't been so committed to winning this thing for Ava... and to keeping the man's ass in my field of vision for as long as possible.

I watched in awe as his shorts crept higher with every muscled push of his strong legs. My brain fell into this haze of imagining what it would feel like to have those hairy legs wrapped around mine as he frotted against me. I wondered if his stomach had that sexy V to it or if he had a lickable happy trail leading down to—

"Aghhh!" The weight of the pail suddenly shifted, causing me to trip over a tree root and go careening into the thicket of shrubs next to the dirt trail. The handle of my pail had broken off in my hand, and milk went absolutely everywhere which only added insult to injury and made me both sticky and more attractive to the entire bug population of middle Tennessee.

Suddenly, strong arms grabbed me around the chest and lifted me up and out of the brambles before setting me back on the trail. "Let's go," Brooks grumbled. "Ava will never forgive you if you don't at least finish."

I ran behind him without thinking. "But I have to win," I said stupidly.

Brooks shot me a smirky grin. "Can't win the Lope with an empty pail." He tossed the broken pail back to me as his own full pail sparkled perfectly in the dappled sun.

I looked down at the offending object. "Motherfucker. Those assholes were right. The handle was broken."

"I saw Ollie Nutter trying to warn you, but you didn't seem to want to listen."

I glanced at Brooks with a scowl. "I thought he was fucking with me. I know guys like him."

"Guys who work two after-school jobs to pay for their little brother's soccer camp?"

His words almost made me stumble again. "What? How the hell do you know that? You haven't been back here for years."

An awkward silence descended between us. Nothing but the thumps of our footfalls broke the odd hush.

"You been spying on me, Mal?"

"Pfft. I can't help it if the Head Licker is the center of all the town gossip," I said with a sniff.

"I know about Ollie because I talk to my mother every Sunday evening and get way more information than any one person needs about the Thicketeers."

Huh. I could have sworn the townsfolk would've been called Lickers. It didn't matter. There were bigger fish to fry, and right now he was carrying one of them.

I side-eyed his perfect pail of milk. "Listen... um... I'm going to need that pail of milk."

Brooks didn't break stride. "I'm going to pretend I didn't hear that. Johnsons don't cheat."

"It's not cheating for you to pour your milk into my pail." Why did that sound so dirty?

Brooks kept stride like a pro. Clearly the years hadn't fucked with his ability to nail the Lope. "Not gonna happen, city boy."

"You're calling me a city boy? I thought you were the one who lived in Manhattan?"

"I actually live in Brooklyn."

"And I actually don't give a shit. I need that milk. Give me your load."

I had a serious problem. Nothing I said sounded remotely sane or decent.

Brooks snorted. "Baby, that's a whole 'nother conversation. One that a *straight* boy like you wouldn't understand."

"I'm not..." I caught myself just in time. "Interested in you calling me baby." Okay, that was a lie. There were many, many situations in which I would be quite alright with it, especially the ones in which everyone was naked. I swallowed and started again. "But Ava's really counting on this win, and her family nearly threatened my life if I don't bring home the gold, okay? Help a fellow city boy out."

"It's a golden horn."

I tilted my head at him and almost missed the three stone steps up to the parking lot at the end of the trail. "The what?"

"The winner of the Lope gets an engraved metal horn. It's a little plaque-like thing, but it's in the shape of cow horns."

"Of course it is." I bit back a laugh. This place wouldn't be believed outside of a bad fever dream or EDM concert high. "Doesn't matter. I need the horn. And your milk." I groaned. "Goddamn it, why does that have to sound so perverted?"

Brooks laughed, deep and clear. It was the most relaxed I'd seen him since that first night in his parents' hallway. Something about being the only person here to see and hear it made me feel special, like I was witnessing a rare sighting of the real Brooks Johnson.

"Fine. Here." He held out his pail.

I came to a stop and almost skidded across the paved parking lot. "Wait, what?"

He shrugged. "Take it. If it'll make Ava happy, it's a no-brainer."

There had to be a catch. I looked around the empty lot for a hidden camera crew. "Why would you—"

Three runners burst out of the trail behind us, suddenly reminding me that this was a race, and in order to win it, I needed to actually cross the finish line first. I shoved my empty pail at him and grabbed the handle of his full one.

"Thanks!" And then I sped onward to victory, beating out Brooks by only half a stride.

The look on Ava's face when I crossed the finish line first was worth the scraped knees and bramble scratches. She looked bright and happy, hopping up and down and clapping while Paul stood next to her, dutifully holding her purse and water bottle. For a split second, it looked like the two of them were a couple, but then Ava ran toward me and jumped into my arms excitedly.

"You did it! Oh, Mal! You're the best."

I tried not to care that Ava's mom and Brooks's mom were giving me funny looks. Was this too much PDA for the Thicket?

For a single second, Paul looked more dejected than Brooks. Then he stepped away from Ava with a smile and murmured congrats, walked up to Brooks, and kissed the man full on the lips.

Even though I stood there swimming in glorious victory, I still somehow managed to feel like I had lost.

Chapter Seven

Brooks

I've never experienced a more awkward car ride than the one home from the Lope, and that *included* the ride home from the Lickin' Dinner Dance after I'd publicly outed myself, broken up with Ava, and crushed my mom's dreams, *and* one memorable Uber ride last summer where my driver had obviously been watching porn on his way to pick me up and couldn't figure out how to shut it off when I got in the car. At least no one was high-pitched moaning as Paul and I climbed in the back seat of my dad's truck—"a Johnson keeps two hands on his own rig, Brooks"—but I would *maybe* have preferred that to the ringing, disappointed silence.

When I'd made the split-second decision to give my milk pail to Mal back in the woods, it had seemed *right* somehow, like I was paying a debt. A win for Mal was a win for Ava, and I owed Ava a win, right?

It should have been as simple as that, and I tried to tell myself it was... but a win for Mal was also a win *for Mal*, and I'd be lying if I didn't admit that was my real motive. Mal seemed to hate taking help, whether it was me milking Annabelle for him or Ollie Nutter pointing out his pail handle was loose before the Lope. He had more prickles than a burdock bur, as evidenced by the way he'd shut me down yesterday afternoon, but every once in a while, when we forgot all the reasons we disliked each other, I got this feeling that his bright blue eyes *saw* me, and it made me want to get past his spikes just to know for sure.

I rolled my eyes.

Knowing he got me on a deep, fundamental level wouldn't change the fact that he was Ava's boyfriend, or that I lived in New York and had a life to get back to. And finding out he *didn't* would mean I'd upset my parents for nothing.

I cleared my throat and pulled my sweat-damp T-shirt away from my body. "Race today was tough. Guess I'm more out of shape than I realized."

My dad's eyes met mine in the rearview mirror, and I thought he was going to say something, but then he glanced at Paul, frowned, and kept his mouth shut.

What was that about?

"You know, I haven't been trail running in years," I said, calling on all my reserves of charm. "And I didn't remember how steep that hill was, where the trail comes out of the woods right by the Welcome to Licking Thicket sign... I mean, where the sign used to be."

My mother made a noncommittal noise.

I glanced at Paul, who shrugged unhelpfully. They seemed determined to stay quiet, and that made me more determined to draw them out, damn it.

"So, why'd you decide to take the sign down?" I asked no one in particular.

"We didn't," Dad said tightly. "It was stolen. *Again.*"

My mom leaned over to pat his arm. "Stay calm, Red. Remember what Dr. Yates said—"

"The dang doctor isn't mayor of a town that's missing its dang sign, two days before the biggest dang festival of the year," Dad exploded. He caught my eye again and sighed. "Few years ago, Amos Nutter had an idea to change the sign and add a motto to increase tourism. So, they took down the old sign that just said, 'Welcome to Licking Thicket'—you remember?"

I nodded.

"And put up a new one that had a big ol' salt lick stickin' out of the ground, and a cow with a giant tongue licking at it."

I shut my eyes, just picturing a giant, phallic salt lick. *Jesus.*

"And the motto said... what was it again, Cindy Ann?"

"You'll Have the Lickin' of Your Life in Licking Thicket," she recited proudly. "I thought it was pretty catchy."

Paul and I exchanged a look. I hoped mine conveyed, "If you laugh, your life's forfeit." He seemed to become fascinated by the trees flashing by as we drove down the road, so I was pretty sure it did.

"That's... a heck of a motto," I agreed.

Dad grunted. "You're not the only one who thought so. Sign only lasted a couple weeks. Ended up on the—whatja-macallit, Cindy Ann?"

"Ebay," Mom supplied. "Sold for a pretty penny too!"

"So Amos decided to make the cow *meaner* on the next sign. He looked ready to *eat* that salt lick—"

Paul coughed into his arm.

"—but it didn't seem to matter none, 'cause that sign got sold too, same's the first."

"And sold for even more." Mom shook her head, clearly befuddled.

"We went back to the old sign after that… but it was too late," he said darkly.

"Turned out there was a real market for those signs even without the motto," Mom explained. "Folks had gotten a taste for the Thicket. And since then, we can't seem to keep them around for more than a couple months at a time."

"Sheriff Nutter can't get a handle on it, nor can old Amos with all his contacts, and neither can I. And if two Nutters and a Johnson can't get the job done, I don't know who can."

I bit my lip against a whimper. *Did they not hear themselves?*

But Dad sounded genuinely upset, so my mom patted his arm again and said lovingly, "It's gonna be alright, Red. It *will*. Folks will still find us, even if we have to get some volunteers to stand out in the field and hold up the sign, honey. Even if *I* have to stand out in that field myself. Promise."

Dad shot her a grateful smile, and my stomach clenched as something sorta clicked into place for me.

It wasn't that the dick jokes and the double entendres weren't funny, because they *were*. But growing up, they hadn't been a source of embarrassment for me either. I'd sort of accepted that I lived in a place with a weird name and a weird annual celebration, and it hadn't been until I left that I'd started making fun of it instead of being *part* of the fun. In the Us vs. Them of life, I'd wanted so badly to be something bigger than a Johnson from Licking Thicket that I'd started laughing *at* the town instead of *with* them, cringing at how silly they sounded.

I wondered if that made me no better than Kale Storms,

trying to pitch barbecue sauce while misunderstanding everything General Partridge stood for.

"Maybe we need to find a sign that can't be removed," I suggested. "Something really permanent."

Dad nodded and gave me a little smile too. "Well, if you think of something, Brooks, you let me know." He pulled the car into the driveway next to my little car, and we all climbed out. "If I haven't told you already, good job today, son," he said. He came around the truck, wrapped an arm around my mom's waist, and looked from Paul to me. "You'll get 'em next year, yeah?"

I blinked. Next year? "Maybe so," I said, surprised to find I wasn't opposed to coming back. "I can train."

"Sure you can. You boys comin' to the Melt? Dunn was complaining he's hardly gotten to see you since you've been back," Dad said.

I winced. The Melt was where the little horn-shaped winner's trophy would be presented to Mal this evening, and where the whole rest of the Thicket, including all my old high school friends, would likely be hanging out with their families, having milkshakes and burgers, and celebrating another great Lope. "I would, but I've got so much work to do..."

"Sure," Dad said, disappointed. "Well, you know where we'll be if you change your mind."

"Your parents are adorable," Paul said wistfully as my dad led my mom away. "I want a relationship like theirs someday."

"Listen to you. We've been boyfriends for less than a week, and you're already talking about marriage?" I opened my car to retrieve my ideas notebook from the trunk. "Too much too soon, boo."

"Yeah, well. Maybe not." Paul rolled his pale eyes and

adjusted his glasses. "Turns out, you're not meeting my needs, Big Daddy. We just want different things. It's not you, it's... Okay, yeah, no, it's totally you."

I leaned back against the car bumper. "Could've fooled me, judging by the way you planted one on me after the race. You did more to convince this town I'm gay in ten seconds than I've been able to do in ten years."

Paul flushed crimson and stared at his shoes. "I got into the spirit of the thing, okay?"

"No shit. I was starting to wonder if you'd push me down *right there* in front of the town and have your wicked way with me—"

"*Gag.*"

"—until you pulled out your inhaler. Kinda ruined the moment, Siegel. Or maybe my kisses are so potent, they take your breath away." I wiggled my eyebrows.

He gave me a scathing look. "That was a pity kiss, Brooks. You looked *so sad*, coming in second and then watching Mal slobber all over Ava."

"First of all, I'll have you know I didn't actually come in second. I let Mal win," I corrected.

Paul snorted. "Sure you did, buddy. You let your ex-girlfriend's hot boyfriend win the race? I totally believe that."

"Well, it's *true*. And he didn't slobber on Ava." I mean, not like I'd actually *watched closely* or whatever. Except I had. "They hugged."

"Same difference."

I slammed the trunk and started toward the house. "Not remotely, My Little Paul. Kiss me again and I'll show you."

"I'd rather eat a cow patty, and if you call me that name again, I'll make sure *you* do too," he said without heat. His shoulders slumped. "You know, I'm starting to think you're right about Mal."

"That he's gay or bi, you mean? *Thank you.* I'm glad you see it too."

Paul stopped on the front porch and scowled. "No, Brooks. He's probably straight as an arrow, he's just a shit boyfriend. *In fact...* I think he's even shittier than either of us initially thought."

"Shittier." Now I frowned too. "How? He was nice to her today, wasn't he? I spoke to him yesterday and I thought—"

"Ava wasn't feeling well earlier," Paul said, more vehement than I'd ever heard him sound about anything. "She should *never* have been standing out in that parking lot in the heat in her condition."

"Really? She seemed okay to me."

He shook his head like he couldn't believe my obliviousness. "That poor woman has the worst taste in men *ever*."

"Yeah, well, she and I have that in common." I smacked him lightly on the head with my notebook. "Now let's get to work on this fucking campaign, boyfriend."

Though it hurt my heart to do it, I'd finally given in to the inevitable and called General Partridge that morning for an extension on our presentation. I'd expected I'd have to beg a little, but the second I'd mentioned a family emergency, he'd cut me off.

"You don't have to explain. Nothing more important than family, Brooks," he'd said. Then he'd added sincerely, "Let me know if there's any way I can help."

He was the kind of client I'd always wanted to work with.

Pamela, on the other hand, hadn't been so understanding.

"Since when do you go traipsing off to Kentucky—"

"Tennessee."

"Whichever, Brooks. The flyover states all blend together. We are in the middle of producing a campaign here."

I found myself gritting my teeth against the urge to argue that *we* weren't producing anything and if *she* had supervised her nephew in the first place, none of this would have happened.

"But I told you, my dad—"

"Is not in the hospital or in any imminent danger, right? Meanwhile, we are in very imminent danger of losing this client entirely. Remember your priorities, Brooks."

As annoying as it was to admit, Pamela had been right. I'd been distracted for days, but I was back on track and determined to make this the best campaign I'd ever put together for Storms Marketing.

Paul pulled open the front door. "Let's print out the branding stuff Carlin sent over for a visual reference, and we can order some pizza. Or maybe barbecue, to get us in the mood?"

"Nah. The only barbecue in this town is Susie Dupree's Deluxe, and eating the competition will jinx us. Pizza it is." I led him down the hall to the kitchen. "But we can— Oh, hey, Mama. We were just talking about Susie Dupree's barbecue. I'm really excited for Paul to try it Saturday night."

My mother stood by the kitchen counter in her Bermuda shorts and sleeveless polo and smiled lightly. "Dupree's Deluxe is the best you'll ever have," she assured him, but then she looked at *me* and I got the same feeling I used to get when I got a C on an English test, only I wasn't sure how I'd messed up.

"I'll grab the laptop," Paul said, touching my arm before

he headed upstairs. I nodded. "Where's your printer, Mrs. Johnson?"

"Oh, honey, we don't have one, I'm afraid," she admitted. "Mr. Johnson believes—"

I groaned and threw my head back to the ceiling. I'd heard this rationale before, I just hadn't known they'd bought into it so completely.

"—printer ink is a corporate scam. They lure you in with a cheap printer, then charge you the same again for the ink."

"I will personally pay for Dad's cartridges," I told her.

"You can't, baby. Your father donated it to some politician he hated. Sort of a white elephant, you know? Let *him* pay for the ink. But you could go to the Iveys' place. Monette and Brad have a printer in the basement. And since we'll all be at the Melt for the presentation, I'm sure the house'll be free. I'll just call Monette and let her know."

I hesitated. Ava's house now felt like Mal's territory, and I wasn't sure where I stood with him. But if they weren't home, it didn't matter, right? I nodded.

"Dibs on first shower!" Paul said happily, running for the stairs.

I wasn't sure why *he* felt the need to clean up when I was the one who'd gotten all sweaty. "Leave me hot water!" I demanded.

After he left, my mother stared at the spot where he'd been standing for a long minute.

Better get this over with. "Everything okay, Mama?"

"Of course." She forced a smile, then got a tall glass from the cupboard and poured me some sweet tea from the pitcher on the counter. "Your boyfriend seems real nice, Brooks."

That was maybe the last thing I'd expected her to say. "He is. Very." When he wasn't an asshole.

She pushed the tea in my direction, and I grabbed it, thankful for something to do, but the first sip was like stepping back in time to my childhood. It was way too sweet and way too strong and completely perfect. It was home.

"He helped Mrs. Rabinowitz across the parking lot to the viewing area today, and he fanned Ava with Mamie Luther's fan when it looked like she was getting overheated."

"Paul did?" I grinned. "I'm not surprised. He's a good guy."

Mama hesitated. "You know, you've been gone a while, but I still like to think I know when my son's got his eye on someone. There was a tension in the room there last Sunday"—she nodded toward the front hall by the bathroom—"and it had nothing to do with Paul, did it?"

I blinked stupidly and my palms started to sweat. "I don't—"

She held up a hand. "You don't have to say anything, baby. Remember, a mother knows things. And then today, when you came out of those woods carrying Malachi's broken bucket, and he had yours, that just confirmed it."

"Wait, what?" My face burned. "How did you—I mean, what made you think we swapped?"

"You're so unobservant, Brooks. Didn't you notice the buckets have different colored plastic on the handles? You left with a yellow handle, and Ava's boyfriend came back with it."

I thought back to the Lope and literally could not recall the handle of my pail or anyone else's. I shook my head, stunned.

"Well, trust me when I tell you, I'm not the only one

who noticed and started getting ideas. Your father mentioned it to me before we left the parking lot, and Monette Ivey's eyes were liable to bug out of her head when the two of you appeared."

Damn. No wonder my dad had been giving me weird looks. I'd never dreamed...

"I know it's none of my business, Brooks, but... that boy is sweet, and it's clear he has real affection for you. Just don't lead him on."

My heart beat faster, thinking about prickly Malachi and wondering when my mom had decided he was sweet. "Real affection? For me? You think?"

"Of course, honey. The way he looked at Ava when she was kissing her boyfriend told the tale! He figured out you threw the race for Ava, and he's jealous."

I blinked at her blankly for a full half minute before I cottoned on. She was talking about Paul. Paul, *my boyfriend,* was the sweet boy. Of course.

"Ava and her boyfriend weren't kissing," I said dully, wondering how everyone's eyes had suddenly stopped working at the same time. "And Paul's not jealous. Paul and I both know exactly where we stand, Mama." He might have been the one person in town I could say that about. "But thanks for the sweet tea."

Later that night, though, after I'd thrown on jeans and an old Licking Thicket Bovines T-shirt, and Paul and I had parked outside the Iveys' house, I started to wonder if maybe I was wrong about Paul, too, because he was acting decidedly odd.

"Your hair looks fine, schnookie lumps," I said as he tweaked it in the passenger's side fold-down mirror for the four-hundredth time on our drive over.

Paul shot me a glare, adjusted his glasses, and flipped

the visor up. "Some of us just want to look half-decent, showing up to a virtual stranger's house, okay?"

"Why do you care?" I demanded. "All the Iveys are at the Melt, so we're using my mom's spare key and running into an empty house for five minutes to use the printer. And you've already hooked me, My Little Paul. I don't need to be seduced."

"Didn't I warn you what would happen if you called me that again?" He got out of the car and slammed the door shut way harder than necessary.

"Okay, what's got you all upset?" I demanded. I grabbed the messenger bag with my laptop inside it and followed him toward the front porch. "My mom's in love with you, you took most of the hot water for your shower, and I told you we could get whatever you wanted on the pizza later. I'm the best boyfriend you've *never* had."

Paul ignored me. He straightened his shirt and knocked on the door, running his hand over his hair one more time.

I ran up the steps behind him. "I told you, Mom said there's no one—" But the door opened suddenly and Malachi was there, looking hotter than ever in tight-fitting black jeans, a Ramones shirt, and bare feet.

Fuck.

My very first thought was that I probably looked like a blond scarecrow with my threadbare shirt and product-free hair. I started doing the same awkward combing thing Paul had done.

My second thought was that Paul, that motherfucker, had psychically *known* somehow.

"Evening," Paul said. He looked over Mal's shoulder. "How's Ava?"

"Sick," Mal said shortly, but his blue eyes locked on me, and I would swear his cheeks flushed slightly. "She was vomiting rainbows a few minutes ago, but she's resting now."

"Poor thing. Have you tried giving her mint tea?" Paul shouldered past Mal, stalking into the Iveys' entryway like he owned the place.

"Uh." Mal blinked, trying to keep an eye on Paul and me at the same time. "No?"

"Opened a window for fresh air? Done acupressure? *Nothing?*" Paul shook his head derisively while Mal stared at him blankly.

"Paul?" Ava called weakly from the couch, her surprise evident. "Is that you?"

"Yeah. Hey, you." Paul stepped into the living room and immediately switched to a soothing tone that was just as bizarrely un-Paul-like as his snappy one. He moved a half-full mug of milky tea aside with a disgusted look and perched his ass on the coffee table directly across from Ava. "I kinda wondered if you'd be up to the awards thing tonight. You seemed a little tired at the Lope this afternoon, and I hoped you'd get some rest."

Mal and I stared at each other for half a second, shocked by this strange realignment, then both of us moved at once. Mal plunked down on the sofa by Ava's feet like a guard dog, and I moved to stand at Paul's side like the faithful faux-boyfriend I was.

Ava really did look a little pale. Her blonde hair was pulled back in a messy tail, and her eyes looked bleary. I resisted the urge to pull my T-shirt over my mouth so I didn't catch whatever she had.

"Sorry to bother you, Ava, but my parents have strange opinions about office supplies, and my mom called your mom to see—"

"I know. It's fine, Brooks," she said wearily. "Printer's in the basement. You know where you're going." She waved a hand toward the back hall and whimpered slightly.

"Right. Come on, Paul."

But Paul didn't move from his spot except to grab Ava's hand—or, more accurately, her wrist. It looked like he was taking her pulse or something.

"Paul, um... *honey bunch*... did you take a first aid class? How did I not know this?" I laughed nervously.

Paul ignored me and pushed his glasses up higher. "What you need is ginger ale and cranberry juice, Ava. Best thing to settle your stomach. Do you have any?" He looked to Malachi for the answer, and Mal's eyes went wide.

"Dude, I don't know. I think there's some soda in the basement? But it's warm."

"Duh. You *want* it to be room temperature," Paul scoffed, like this was something everyone should know.

Mal shot me a look, and I frowned. I had no clue what had gotten into my "boyfriend" either. I'd entered an alternate dimension where *Paul* fixed things, instead of me. I wasn't sure how I felt about that.

Ava moaned slightly and put a hand to her stomach.

Correction. I felt pretty damn fine with this alternate dimension, because I was clueless about how to help.

"Well?" Paul demanded, making a shooing motion with his free hand. "Go print the things and fetch the ginger ale!"

"Going." I stood and slapped Mal on the shoulder. He scowled up at me. "Come on."

"No way. I'm not—" Mal protested.

"For fuck's sake, get your girlfriend her soda," I insisted, prodding him slightly.

"Go, Mal," Ava said, sounding drunk. "Fetch the things, print the ginger ale." To Paul, she added, "Damn, whatever you're doing with my wrist is *amazing*."

I headed for the basement, and Mal reluctantly followed.

The Iveys' basement was divided in half by a long wall that ran along the right side of the stairs. To the right was what they called the "dirty" basement, where they kept the washing machine and their overflow refrigerator. To the left was the "clean" basement, which used to be the Ivey kids' rec room. I'd played Spin the Bottle on that linoleum floor, back before I'd had any idea what kissing was supposed to feel like, and I'd wondered why the hell I was so underwhelmed. Walking down those stairs was a little like entering a time warp.

"Hey. I don't know what your boyfriend thinks he's doing, but move it along so we can get back up there," Mal said from behind me. "I'm grabbing the soda."

I rolled my eyes. "Hey, Mal? Why don't you grab the soda? Just because I told you to."

"You're an ass," Mal said predictably before he headed left and I headed right, flipping on the light as I went.

The rec room was Mrs. Ivey's exercise studio now, judging by the pink yoga mat on the floor and the giant mirror along the wall. But there was also a desk filled with color-coded office supplies, a newish printer, and a computer that had to be ten years old at least.

I set my bag on the desk, removed my laptop, brought up my email, and tried to connect to the Wi-Fi... and that was when I encountered a big problem.

When Mal came back in, I was bent over with my ass sticking up in the air, trying to pry the desk away from the wall.

"Oh, damn," Mal said blandly from behind me. "Brooks, do you need me to explain how printers work? 'Cause twerking isn't usually required."

The look I shot over my shoulder probably would have been more scathing if the man didn't look so goddamn delectable with his arms folded over his chest and his lean biceps on display. "Har har. The printer's not hooked up to Wi-Fi, so I had to connect the fucking cable, but your future mother-in-law has all the cables stapled to the damn wall and it's not fitting in the slot on my laptop fully or something, so it won't print. It says Connection Not Established."

Mal flopped in the desk chair and spun around, cradling a bottle of ginger ale in his lap. "Hmmm. Sounds like a personal problem. But don't be embarrassed. I bet lots of guys have 'connectivity problems' because their cable's too short. I mean, not *me*, obviously. But I think they sell supplements for that. I read it in *Men's Health*."

"You're so helpful. 'Oh, no,'" I said in a high-pitched voice. "'I *love* Ava! I'm there for Ava. I'll take care of Ava.'"

He skidded to a stop, and I could feel his eyes on my back. "I *do* take care of Ava."

"Sure. That's why Paul is up there with her now giving her a wrist massage and you're here making size jokes about my printer issues." I yanked on the desk and muttered, "Come the fuck *on*. Is this thing lined with lead?"

Mal put the soda bottle on the ground. "Hey, it's not my fault your boyfriend likes to stick his nose in other people's business, asshole. And if your man's got enough free time to wanna play nursemaid to my best friend and enough pent-up frustration to suck your face off in public, that says something about *you*."

"Suck my face off?" The kiss Paul gave me had zero tongue, thank fuck. "You're insane."

Mal made a filthy, wet slurping noise. It was disgusting... and also made my cock twitch. It wasn't lost on me that he'd called Ava his best friend... *not* his girlfriend.

I straightened to face him. "What are you implying exactly?"

He stood putting himself right in my space. "I'm not *implying* anything. I'm saying flat out that if *you* were a better boyfriend, your boyfriend wouldn't be so worried about my... girlfriend."

Too little too late. I lifted an eyebrow at him. "Girl-friend? Or best friend? You seem to be confused."

Mal's tan skin was bright pink over his cheeks, and his blue eyes flashed like a warning for someone smart enough to take it: *Back off.*

Clearly, I was not that smart. "Relationship advice is pretty rich coming from you. I handed you that win today—"

"You did it for Ava."

"—*and* I tried to help you yesterday—"

"I never asked you to, Mr. Perfect!"

"—so what exactly is your problem with me?"

Mal's nostrils flared, and the way he stared at me made my spine prickle with the need to fight or flee, fight or flee, or maybe...

Mal lunged forward—or, hell, maybe I did?—and we found a third option, one that involved his two hands latching onto my hair like an anchor in a storm and his open mouth pressed to mine.

Holy shit.

Mal's kiss wasn't anything like I'd expected. It started out confident, defiant, almost like a punishment, but the second our tongues touched, the battle became a dance, and the clash a smooth glide. The kiss softened from an excla-mation point to a question mark, and I could nearly taste his surprise, an echo of my own, in the tangy, sweet flavor of his mouth and the way he rubbed his body against me.

It felt so good, so fucking right and *necessary*, that I wrapped both of my arms around him to hold him in place, one hand landing low on his back just above the curve of his ass, while the other went higher, keeping our chests pressed together. This was the only kind of win I wanted, in that moment. The only prize worth having.

"Oh, fuck, you're good at that," he muttered, breaking away. His hot breath gusted against my cheek in ragged pants, and his fingers pulled at my hair, tilting my head back so he could scrape his teeth over my chin. "I fucking *knew* it would be like this. Fuck, fuck, fuck. You are so fucking hot."

Every *fuck* hit me on a subconscious level, amping up my need, even before my brain had a chance to parse them and figure out what he was saying. But a second later it didn't matter—nothing else mattered—because his lips were back on mine, and Mal—who was a goddamn genius and true hero—rolled his hips so our hard cocks rubbed against each other.

I groaned and he did it again, pushing me back into the desk. *Again* and something behind me clattered, sending paper clips flying as my hand gripped at his ass cheek like the safety bar on a Tilt-A-Whirl. *Again* and the damn printer started humming and whirring.

Connection Established.

And then some.

"Holy shit, Mal," I breathed, not caring about where we were or *who* we were or who was waiting on us. "Don't stop. Please—"

"Jesus fucking Christ!" Paul called from the top of the stairs. "How long does it take to get some fucking ginger ale? Are you brewing it?"

Mal jumped away like I was a live wire, and for a single second, we stared at each other, shocked and appalled and *wanting*.

"Brooks?" Paul yelled again.

I swallowed. "Yeah! No, we're coming. We... I... The printer wouldn't connect, and Mal, uh... helped me fix it." I gave Mal a helpless shrug. It wasn't a lie.

A sheet of paper fell out of the printer and drifted to the floor beside me.

Mal pushed both hands through his hair and gave a huff of disbelieving laughter, but his eyes were dazed, and I wanted so badly to wrap my arms around him before we had to go upstairs. To my "boyfriend." And his... Ava.

Shit. This was the part where I was supposed to feel guilty. Where I *did* feel guilty, damn it.

Mal's eyes took on a panicked look. He adjusted his jeans and bent to get the soda off the floor.

"Wait!" I said softly after he stood. I grabbed the shoulders of his T-shirt and smoothed it down, then tucked his rumpled hair behind his ear. "Okay. You're good."

"Mr. Perfect," Mal said, except it didn't sound like an insult this time. Or not entirely. And that made the breath I'd only just caught stutter in my chest.

He hurried up the stairs while I breathed deeply and waited for my papers, trying very hard not to think about what we'd just done.

Chapter Eight

Mal

IT WAS surreal to go from kissing Brooks to getting a lecture from his boyfriend about what a shit partner I was to Ava. If he only knew. I felt awful. I'd truly thought the man was straight and just pretending to be with Brooks for whatever reason, but when he'd kissed Brooks in front of the entire town earlier today, I'd had to admit I could be wrong.

And then I'd gone and eaten his boyfriend's face off.

It had tasted so damned good. Brooks had been passionate and receptive, so unexpectedly *present* in a way I wouldn't have imagined before. So far this week he'd seemed like he'd had one foot out the door, one half of his brain back in New York sorting through work problems or anticipating a return to his "real" life. But for those brief moments in the basement, I'd felt like I'd had him all there with me.

He'd been mine. Just for a while.

But then I'd had to face his irate boyfriend, and his lecture had surprised me.

"She deserves better!" Paul ranted, pacing back and forth in front of the kitchen table while he waited for the ginger ale to stop fizzing. "You... and she... there's... I think maybe you don't understand that she doesn't *feel well*."

"I do understand," I said, starting to actually like the guy. Anyone who'd stand up for Ava like this had my respect and approval. "But maybe you should be more concerned about your own partner rather than mine."

He stopped and blinked at me, flushing deep red and fumbling in his pocket for his inhaler. "That's not... I mean... I am. I do. Brooks is... fine."

I snorted. "I hope someday my one true love calls me fine."

Paul looked flustered, and it was kind of cute. "I kissed him. In front of everyone."

"And?" I squinted at him. "You think kissing your boyfriend deserves some kind of medal?" My stomach lurched as I remembered kissing his own boyfriend minutes before and thinking the man kissed like a champion. Maybe kissing him *was* like earning a medal. It felt like it anyway.

"No, that's not what I..."

Ava shuffled into the kitchen. "I think I want corn again. Is that weird?"

Paul's entire face softened like a damned Snapchat filter with bunny ears and hearts for eyes. "Not weird at all. It's totally normal in your... um..." His pale eyes flicked at me. "World," he finished lamely.

It hit me fully then. Despite the kiss at the Lope, this man was no more gay than Red Johnson or Brad Ivey. He was into my best friend in a big way. And somehow he knew she was pregnant. Had she told him?

At least I could let go of my guilt over attacking his boyfriend, not that it was something I ever should have done or even consider doing again. No way. Brooks Johnson was off-limits. He was still the man who'd broken Ava's heart, and I was a shit friend for even looking at him with lusty thoughts.

"I'll find some corn," I said, moving to the fridge.

Ava sniffed. "Um, actually, now that I'm here, I wonder if there are any frozen french fries? Or corn dogs?"

"Corn dogs?" I mouthed at Paul just as I heard a snort from behind me. Brooks had finished his printing and sauntered into the kitchen like he hadn't just been dry humping me in my fake-girlfriend's basement.

"You always did love those things. Does your mom still keep a stash of them?" he asked, joining me at the fridge before opening the freezer door. He pulled out a box without even sparing me a single glance. "Fifty-three seconds, right?"

Brooks pulled a corn dog out of the box and put it on a paper towel, clearly completely at home in the Iveys' kitchen. I hated seeing his familiarity with their home since it reinforced the fact he'd been Ava's high school boyfriend and had known her long before I had.

I opened the fridge door and stuck my head in. Hopefully the cool air would calm my racing thoughts.

Paul sounded worried. "Make sure it's steaming. Hot dogs need to reach at least one hundred and sixty-five degrees inside to avoid listeria."

I laughed. Meanwhile, Brooks was oblivious. I wondered what he'd think when he found out she was pregnant with no partner. Would he judge her the same way she worried her parents would? I hoped not.

"Come on, Paul," Brooks said. "I still owe you that pizza. If we don't order soon, the Pizza Palace will close."

Ava sucked in a breath. "Ohhhh, pizza. Mal, can we do pizza too?"

I closed the fridge in time to see a few more bubble

hearts float out of Paul's eyes. "Let's all do pizza together," he said.

Brooks and I locked eyes long enough for me to know that would be a really bad idea. But before either of us could say anything, Ava clapped her hands and grinned. "Perfect!"

Perfect.

And there followed the most excruciating two hours of my life. The only part of the conversation that wasn't incredibly awkward was when Paul and Brooks told us about the ad campaign they were working on. We all laughed when Paul explained how the meeting with General Partridge and the blowhard from their agency had gone. Ava had given them a few good ideas when they'd tried brainstorming new concepts, but so far nothing had seemed quite right. It was interesting to watch their process regardless.

The only other good thing to come out of the dinner was a strange kind of peace that seemed to appear between Brooks and Ava. Afterward, when Paul and Brooks had finally, blessedly, left, I asked her about it.

"You and Brooks seemed to get along well."

She lay back on the brown corduroy sofa in the family room and groaned, patting her stomach. "That was so good. I don't remember the Pizza Palace ever tasting that great before."

"You and Brooks," I said, trying to bring us back around to the topic at hand. "How are you feeling about him these days?"

She sighed. "You know... I kind of feel sorry for him. I used to think he had the world in the palm of his hand, you know? He was smart, cute, successful at everything he tried... but now I realize he's just some corporate schmo living in a big city where he's nothing special at all."

I stared at her. "That's... really shitty."

"No," she said with a sigh, sitting up a little. "I don't mean it like that. But he always seemed larger than life, like he was going to grab the world by the balls and really make something of himself. But he doesn't seem happy, so what's the point? It makes me realize I kind of did the same thing."

"What do you mean?"

She shrugged and picked at her fingernail polish. "I liked being Miss Licking Thicket. I liked knowing everyone in town and waving hello everywhere I went and... feeling like I belonged. Being back here makes me feel at home in a way I just don't get in LA. I miss it. I feel special here... loved and protected. Even though my parents might throw a hissy fit when they find out about the baby, I still feel like they'll be there for me. Back in California, it's just you and me. Doesn't that bother you at all?"

Before I could answer, she continued. "I wonder if it bothers Brooks or if he has people in the city who care about him."

"He has Paul," I spat like a bratty teen.

She flapped her hand. "No. Not really. Paul's temporary. Someone as sweet as Paul isn't going to put up with Brooks's crap for very long. He deserves better, and I told Brooks that tonight while you and Paul were paying the pizza guy."

I cracked a smile. "You did what?"

She huffed. "It's true. Brooks doesn't realize what he has and—"

I cut her off. "You know Paul gave me the same lecture about you, right?"

Her face softened, and she got all dreamy. "He did? He's so sweet."

"Uh-huh. I thought he was your mortal enemy?"

She flapped her hand in the air. "Oh, I'm over it. Brooks's fine. I was kind of expecting to come home and want to jump his bones, but I really don't. And honestly, he's going back to New York and I have no desire to…"

Her voice faded out as I went through the roller coaster of emotions of first feeling free to actually admit my crush on him to being crushed at the reminder he lived on the opposite coast. There was no point in having a fling with a guy who was leaving Sunday. Especially when the days between now and then were full of bovine activities.

"Well," I said, squeezing her leg and standing up. "I'm glad you're at peace with it anyway. The man's gay after all, and at the very least you deserve someone who's bi." I winked at her and leaned in to kiss the top of her head. "I'm headed to bed. Can I get you anything before I go?"

She tapped her chin. "Another corn dog?"

———

THE FOLLOWING morning I awoke refreshed and somewhat excited. Wednesday was the setup for the vendor fair in the town square, and I was grateful to be able to forget about Ava, Paul, and Brooks for a little while and concentrate on putting my art on display. My boxes had arrived and been stashed in the Iveys' garage, and Ava's mom was arranging for someone with a pickup truck to give me a ride to town for the setup.

I should have known it wouldn't be a well-meaning stranger.

"You ready?" Brooks asked, peering at his feet.

I looked past his slumped form on Ava's front porch and saw a big-ass pickup truck. "You're my ride?"

"Apparently."

He didn't seem all that thrilled about it which pissed me off more than it should have. "Surprised you didn't get the Thicket's Early Riser medallion," I snapped. "Or a position on the welcome wagon committee with how chipper and friendly you are in the morning."

His head shot up, and his green eyes widened. After a second of studying me, his lips twisted into a smirk. "I did, in fact, earn the Thicket's Early Bird award at school back in the day, but the prize was a cheap alarm clock from Walmart, not a medallion."

I hated his adorable face.

"Mpfh," I said, stepping around him and heading to the garage to retrieve my boxes. "Figures."

We loaded up the truck in silence, but when we finally began to bump down the Iveys' long driveway, Brooks spoke up.

"Listen, I owe you an apology. I should have never kissed you like that last night. You're, um, here with Ava, and I shouldn't have done anything to put your relationship in jeopardy, much less betrayed her myself by disrespecting her that way."

Even though he was right to feel bad for what we'd done behind Ava's back, it still stung to hear him regret that incredible kiss.

I sighed. "I'm sorry too. Paul deserves better than that."

Brooks glanced over at me for a beat before both of us burst out laughing. Paul was no more dating Brooks Johnson than I was dating Ava Ivey.

"What gave it away?" Brooks asked.

"I said something to him about poppers, and he told me they sell the best ones at Party City."

Brooks laughed even harder. "Tell me you're lying."

"I'm lying," I admitted with a grin. "But I did make a comment at the barbecue the other night that your brother was a hot daddy, and Paul quickly corrected me. Said Dunn didn't have kids yet."

Brooks groaned through his laughter. "Don't call my brother a hot daddy. That's disgusting."

"How can Paul not know what a hot daddy is? Aren't there daddies in the het world?"

He shrugged. "He does, but his vanilla, picket-fence world is more likely to be filled with nice girls and good girls."

"Daddies like good girls," I teased. "Maybe Paul would make a good daddy one day."

Brooks shuddered. "Can we not?"

"You don't want to imagine your boyfriend as a hot daddy?" I batted my eyelashes at him. "Maybe he wields that inhaler like—"

Brooks reached over and put his hand over my mouth. "Shut it. That's my coworker you're talking about. I have to be able to look at him across the conference table with our clients without picturing him in bed."

"How the hell did you convince that straight boy to go gay for you?" I truly wanted to know.

He sighed. "It's a long story, but basically we have a work project that has to get done, and he knew I didn't want to show up back here single. The whole town thinks this 'gay thing' is a phase, and I'm sick and tired of it. I knew if I didn't bring home a boyfriend, my family would do their best to get Ava and me back together."

"Your family seems to have taken it in stride, though," I

said lightly, looking out the window at a young father teaching his daughter to ride a bike in their driveway.

"Yeah. Actually, my mom's afraid I'm going to break poor Paul's heart."

I looked back at him. "How so?"

Brooks flicked on the turn signal before heading into an empty parking spot across the street from the town square. "She's convinced I threw the Lope on purpose. For Ava."

"Well, you did."

After putting the truck in park, Brooks turned to lock eyes with me. "No I didn't," he said softly. Before I could open my mouth to ask him what he'd meant—if what he was implying was true—there was a loud knock on the window behind me.

I jumped in my seat, nearly strangling myself with the seat belt. "What the fuck?"

"It's my brother," Brooks murmured.

I turned to see Dunn's big smile shining from under a John Deer ball cap. He waved at us like a clown while Brooks lowered the window.

"Hi, Daddy," I said breathlessly, patting my chest like I was having palpitations. Brooks made a growling sound and rolled the window right back up. The surprised look on Dunn's face was priceless.

"No," Brooks said to me.

"But—"

"*No*. If you care about me at all, you will refrain from implying my brother has a sex bone in his body."

"Mmm, Dunn's sex bone..."

Brooks slammed out of the truck while I cackled. He was so fun to rile up. I scrambled out of the truck and made a big deal of hugging Dunn hello while he was still frozen in shock.

"Hey, bro," I said. "You come to help us set up?"

"Um, no? I'm here to tell you where to go? My mom made me get here early to save you a good spot. She seemed to think it was important, which makes no sense since Mr. Ivey said you sell stuff from a junkyard."

That stopped me in my tracks. I ignored the junkyard jab for a minute. Why in the world would Cindy Ann Johnson care about a stranger from California getting a prime spot in the Thicket vendor fair?

"While technically it's stuff from the junkyard, it's actually considered found-object art or mixed-media art," I said, sounding way snootier than I intended. "I take junk and turn it into art."

"Dunn, knock it off," Brooks warned.

"Oh, sorry. I didn't know you *made* something with it. I thought... Never mind. Shit, Mal. I didn't mean to offend, really." He looked sincere. His goofy face suddenly fell to a worried grimace. "Let me help. I'm really sorry. I didn't think before I spoke. It's... kind of a bad habit of mine."

I let out a breath. When was I going to stop assuming the worst of people? "It's fine. Yes, you can help. Some of these boxes are heavy."

Brooks made sure Dunn carried the worst of the boxes, but by the time we schlepped everything to my booth, we were all pouring sweat. "I'd forgotten how muggy the South was in the summer," I grumbled, pulling my T-shirt up to wipe off my face.

Brooks's eyes tracked the trail from my waistband up to my chest, his gaze lighting my skin on fire even more and threatening to plump up my dick in front of all the other vendors busy setting up around us.

Dunn took off to help some other people while Brooks

cleared his throat. "Want me to find us some cold water? I think they have coolers full at the service booth."

I nodded. "Yeah, thanks. I'll start unpacking."

It was several degrees cooler under the tent, and I was happy to see the fair had provided each booth with a long table and two folding chairs. I sank into a chair and began ripping open boxes. By the time Brooks got back with dripping wet bottles of water, I'd set up the portable display wall for the back of the booth and hung up several items.

"Holy shit, Mal," Brooks said, handing me a bottle. "This is what you make? It looks like a rabbit..."

I cracked open the water and took a huge gulp before wiping my mouth with the back of my hand. "Yeah, Ava loves that one too. There's a series of meadow animals. See the fox and the vole? Then there's a mouse and a dragonfly. Over here are the wildflowers that go with this series."

My mouth was getting away from me, so I shut it and turned back to another box to continue unpacking. I felt Brooks move behind me to look at more of the items on the display wall.

"That's an old wrench," he said like he was discovering hidden treasure. "And the wings are made out of..."

"It's a vintage hand rake," I said over my shoulder.

"And his neck... is this some kind of faucet or valve?"

"A vacuum breaker. It's a kind of valve that stops back-flow." I tried concentrating on what I was doing rather than preening under Brooks's kind words.

"Mal, this is amazing."

I bit my lip to keep from begging for more. "Thanks."

He finally took a seat in the chair next to mine and sipped some more of his water while I set out some of the smaller handheld items on the table.

"How did you get into this?" he asked, running the pad

of his index finger along the bolt legs of a little robot. "Look at this detail."

I didn't answer him at first; I couldn't. It was too... personal, too raw. But then the edge of his pinky finger brushed mine, and he whispered, "Hey. I'd really like to know more."

I glanced up at him. His face was sincere and open, the Brooks I felt like no one else noticed for some reason. So I opened my mouth and began telling him a story I'd never told another man since leaving Homer.

"My dad ran the local junkyard," I said, before shifting nervously in my chair. It had taken me several years to get over the shame of it, and old thought patterns died hard. "And we lived in a trailer on the property. I shared a room with my brothers, which sucked, so I stayed outside as much as I could."

I unwrapped a collection of superhero figures to lay out. These always sold well at fairs, and the look on little kids' faces when they began recognizing some of the components was always fun to watch. "Anyway, I'd spend hours rooting around among the crap in the junkyard. Sometimes my dad would send me to fetch a certain part from a certain car or appliance. I got to know what everything was at a pretty young age, and then I just started... putting things together. It's embarrassing, but it was kind of like this stuff was my toy box, you know? We didn't have money for real action figures and racetrack sets. So I made my own."

I cleared my throat. "Kind of pathetic really," I added.

"Kind of amazing," Brooks said forcefully. "And creative, and inventive. These are incredible, Mal. People are going to go crazy for them tomorrow."

The temperature under the tent must have risen because my face was hot and sweating again. "Thanks."

"Where do you source your supplies in LA?" He carefully lifted up a giraffe from the open box and began peeling back the bubble wrap.

"I usually take day trips to places like San Bernardino, Bakersfield, or even Tijuana. But I'm always on the lookout for cool new places to get stuff. Sometimes thrift stores or flea markets have cool and different stuff, but it's a crapshoot."

He set the giraffe next to a lion with a bicycle gear mane. "The Thicket actually has a unique junkyard because of all the farm equipment around here. People come from all over to get replacement parts there." He glanced at me before digging into the box for the next item. "Um... I could take you there on the way back to Ava's if you want."

I wasn't sure how I felt about all these emotions bubbling up and Brooks being so supportive of my art. He didn't fit into any of the boxes I was dead set on shoving him into which meant he was a wild card. I didn't do well with wild cards.

"Yeah, that... that would be nice. Thank you." I stood and shook off the feels. "So, did you and Paul come up with any other ideas for the ad campaign after you left last night?"

"Not really. I'm starting to stress about it. I didn't realize how demanding this Head Licker position would be when my mom roped me into it." Brooks gently straightened some of the little metal insects I'd set out on a rock I'd swiped from the Iveys' farm to use in the display. "It's okay, though. I don't want my dad overdoing it."

Oh how I wished Brooks Johnson in real life had turned out to be the villain Ava had painted him as for all those years. But in reality he was kind and considerate. A good son and a generous helper.

I busied myself with some more sips of my water before I spied the brown paper bag he'd set down with the drinks. "What's this?"

"Oh, Lou Klein was giving away some of her apple muffins. I grabbed us a couple. She has an orchard out past the old..." He chuckled. "I guess you don't know where the old Yancy place is. Anyway, Lou makes all kinds of incredible bakery items and sells them at her orchard shop. She'll have a booth at the fair tomorrow too."

I took out a muffin and bit into it. It was one of the best things I'd ever tasted, and I couldn't help the groan that escaped me. "Dear God. This tastes good. Like, family recipe good. Secret ingredient good. Small-town good."

Brooks stared at me.

"Wha?" I mumbled with my mouth full of another bite.

"That's it." His grin grew wide, and he hopped up and grabbed me, spinning me around in a circle with a whoop. "Holy shit, Mal, you did it! That's the slogan! Partridge Pit is Small-Town Good!"

I forgot myself for a moment and basked in the feel of him. He smelled like coffee and apple bread mixed with clean sweat and faint hints of fresh spring-scented soap. The strong bands of his arms held me tight, and for just a brief moment, I rubbed my nose against his jumping pulse point.

When he set me down and pulled out his phone to text Paul, I busied myself with whatever the hell was on my table while I tried to get my shit together.

Brooks Johnson was not at all the man I'd thought he was, and the man he was turning out to be might as well have been a salvage yard magnetic handler while I was a helpless old junker waiting to be snapped up and crushed.

Chapter Nine

Brooks

Me: SMALL. TOWN. GOOD!!!
Paul: Uh...BIG CITY BAD???
Paul: We talk caveman talk? Make Brooks feel better?

I ROLLED my eyes down at my phone.

Me: No, idiot. It's the tagline we've been searching for.
Paul: Hmm?
Me: For Partridge Pit! Get this—no celebrity endorsements, just testimonials from real people who really use and love the sauce in their recipes! Think block parties, Fourth of July BBQs, Christmas potlucks.
Me: We don't need to ELEVATE barbecue, we need to connect with people and remind them Partridge Pit is already an authentic part of their daily lives!
Me: Partridge Pit is Small-Town Good!
Paul: Ohhh.
Paul: Ohhhhhhh.
Paul: Brooks Johnson, you have never been sexier to me than you are right this minute. Fuck. That's perfect.

Me: *Right???*
Paul: *I'm calling Carlin now to get the graphics folks started with look and feel.*
Paul: *Pamela is going to pee herself with excitement.*
Paul: *Kale might cry.*
Paul: *How'd you come up with it, anyway?*

I glanced over at the man currently setting up a display of incredible artwork he'd created out of things no one else valued. He'd already smiled and chatted with a bunch of other folks setting up their booths, and was gabbing with Pastor Mitchell and his family like he'd known them for years when even *I* had only met them last weekend. When Brianna Mitchell exclaimed over a little pink robot made out of a popcorn tin, with wrenches for arms and golf balls for feet, Mal picked it up and handed it to her, waving off Pastor Mitchell when he reached for his wallet.

Damn, but I liked that guy.

Me: *I didn't come up with it. Mal did.*
Paul: *Mal? WTF? The short, skinny dude who's incapable of safely heating a corn dog for his girlfriend is a marketing savant now? I don't believe it.*

I tamped down a flare of annoyance at what I was starting to realize was Paul's ridiculous jealousy.

Me: *Wait, are we still PRETENDING to talk like cavemen, or is that just who you are now?*

Predictably, Paul didn't reply.
Mal waved goodbye to the Mitchells and bent down to retrieve something from a box on the ground. His dark

green T-shirt pulled tight across a pair of broad shoulders and a leanly muscled back I now knew had been honed by hard, physical labor, welding his sculptures together. When he straightened, he cocked his head at his display, intelligent eyes narrowed with a level of concentration that made me full-on *shiver*, despite the bone-singeing heat of the sun, wondering what it would be like to have that concentration focused on *me*.

Yeah, no, short, skinny, and incapable were not how anyone should describe this man.

The chemistry between us had been undeniable from the second I'd laid eyes on him, a crazy-intense attraction like magnets aligning that I would have told you couldn't be real since I'd never felt anything like it before. But whereas most of the guys I hooked up with back in the city got *less* attractive the second they opened their mouths—legit, there were only so many times I could hear about a guy's six degrees of separation from someone famous, or "*the* hottest new club in Billyburg, Brooks!" without rolling my eyes so far back they'd stick—with Mal, every damn thing I learned about the man made me want to learn more, despite how fucking impossible the whole situation was.

I rubbed a hand over my mouth, low-key checking to make sure I wasn't literally drooling over him, and Mal's curious gaze met mine.

"You about ready?" I asked.

"Oh." He turned in a circle and nodded, stacking the boxes filled with packing material under the table. "I guess so. What happens now?"

"Now you close up your tent and lock it with that padlock."

Mal surveyed these cutting-edge security measures with a raised eyebrow. "That's it? No armed guard, no nothing?"

I shook my head. "Not in the Thicket. Sheriff Nutter and his crew will keep an eye on the square overnight, but there's not much crime here. Except for the people who keep stealing the Welcome to Licking Thicket sign," I added sourly.

"Wait, you mean the sign we saw on the Lope?" Mal asked, bending down to fasten the tent closed. "Or, the empty spot where the sign used to be, I mean?"

I sighed and briefly explained everything my parents had told me. By the time I was finished, Mal was laughing so hard he was almost in tears... and *I* was nearly hard just from watching him laugh, which made me wanna cry for a different reason. The longing I felt for him was becoming seriously annoying.

"Who *wouldn't* want that sign?" Mal demanded, wiping his eyes. "This town is a parody of itself, and every single person here is in on the joke." He delivered this truth bomb in a tone of frank admiration that made me want to kiss the shit out of him for articulating something I hadn't been able to say.

Instead, I reminded myself that I was heading north in exactly four more days, while he was heading west, and he was *Ava's boyfriend*, at least as far as the town was concerned.

I took a step backward. "Come on. I need AC before I melt."

Mal nodded.

When we were in the truck a little while later with the AC cranking and some country song on the radio, I gave him a sideways glance. "So, thanks for your help. With the campaign, I mean."

"Sure." Mal grinned at me across the cab. "Do I get royalties?"

"If by royalties you mean my endless admiration and thanks, then yes."

His grin spread. "And if I meant dollar bills?"

I smirked. "Then no."

"How about a favor?" He wiggled his eyebrows, and it was the cutest goddamn thing. "Like, one favor to be redeemed at the time and place of my choosing."

"Hell no," I said automatically. "Do you not read fairy tales? This is how people lose their firstborn child."

"The fuck would I want with your child, Brooks?" Mal's cheeks went pink. "I mean, just thinking about being an uncle is..." He cleared his throat. "I'm the only dependent I can handle, thanks."

Fair point. "Fine, then. I owe you one favor." I paused at the four-way stop sign on Orchard Street. The air shimmered with summer heat. "You sure you still wanna go to that junkyard?"

"Is that my favor?"

I barked out a laugh. "So suspicious. No, Mal, this is a separate thing."

"Then, yes. Definitely. Mr. Ivey told me the first day we got here that I could use his workshop, but I haven't really had any materials to work with." His hands twitched like he was fighting off a compulsion to weld something right this minute.

I felt one corner of my mouth go up. "And you can't go a week without sculpting?"

He shrugged. "Sometimes. It's kind of an emotional release for me. When I'm stressed or... whatever, I pour it all into the work."

I was almost sad that we pulled up in front of Thicket Salvage two seconds later, because I had so many follow-up questions, like what had made him "stressed *or what-*

ever" here in the Thicket, and whether it maybe involved me.

From the street, the junkyard looked like the entrance to most any other farm in the area; it just so happened that this farm grew a crop of rusted-out tractor parts. The property had a white clapboard house with a green lawn and a wide front porch to the left. Off to the right was a driveway that led to a heavy orange fence.

A sign on the fence read "Honk for Service," so I did, and a few minutes later, the world's tallest man stepped out of the house, wiping his hands on a dish towel. His longish dark hair was slicked back, and every visible inch of the skin on his hands, arms, and neck was covered in black tattoos.

"Help you?" he asked in a deep growl.

"Yeah, hey. I'm Brooks Johnson. This is Mal Forrester. I grew up around here back when Mr. Yancey ran this place, and I wondered if we could poke around?"

The guy leaned his hands on the open window frame and eyed me up and down, his gaze catching on the *Licking Thicket* emblazoned on the front of my shirt. He didn't seem impressed.

"You need a specific replacement part?" His mocking tone indicated how unlikely he thought that was.

"No. We—"

"I do metal sculpture with found objects," Mal piped up. "I really won't know what I'm looking for until I find it and inspiration hits."

The man's gaze sharpened, and he gave Mal the same up-and-down look he'd given me, but somehow with Mal, he managed to make it *smolder*. "You're the artist from LA who's staying at the Ivey place and has a booth at the fair tomorrow." It wasn't a question.

Mal's surprise was palpable. "I... yeah. That's me."

"My aunt was telling me all about it, 'cause she knows I find that shit fascinating. I'll be in town tomorrow. Maybe you can show me some of your stuff?"

"Oh. I. Wow. Thanks. That's..." Mal blushed—fucking *blushed*—a deep pink. "Cool. Definitely."

"I'm Diesel Church." The guy gave us... but mostly Mal... a chin-lift. "Let me know if I can help you in there, okay?"

He pushed a button that made the gate retract, and I drove through without saying a word.

"Diesel Church," I scoffed under my breath. "Fucking porn star name."

Mal whacked my arm. "The hell is wrong with you? He was nice!"

"He wasn't nice, he was flirting. It's different."

Aaaaand apparently I was ready to give Paul lessons in acting like a caveman. *Fuck.*

"Since when is flirting a crime? I'm not *doing* anything with him. I'm with Ava. Obviously."

Ava. Obviously. Right.

I parked the truck in the dubious shade of a garage and jumped down. Further back in the yard, there were rows upon rows of cars in neat lines. To the left was the farm equipment.

I grabbed my dad's tool kit from the back of the truck. "Unless someone got the notion to move a field of tractors in the last decade, you might wanna head that way." I pointed left. "But I'll follow wherever you go. If we see something big, we can get the truck. Or if you see something really big, Diesel can get the wrecker. You know, there's a kind of order to—"

"Brooks." Mal put a hand on my arm and tucked his tongue into his cheek, his blue eyes dancing. "I appreciate how perfectly, *perfectly* knowledgeable you are about junk-yards, but you remember the part where I told you I grew up on one, right? They all kinda work the same way."

I felt my own cheeks flame and stood straighter. "Right. Well, I can wait here, then, if you—"

But Mal just grabbed my wrist and towed me toward the farm equipment, cutting off whatever bullshit I was about to spout. Just being around the man was like riding a Tilt-A-Whirl, horrible and exhilarating and wonderful.

We strolled down a John Deere graveyard in compan-ionable silence for a little while. Every few paces, Mal would inspect a piece of equipment older than the two of us put together. At one point, after he'd climbed up on a riding mower and spent a little longer than usual examining the seat, he gestured toward the tool bag wordlessly. I knew enough about tractors to hand him a screwdriver. When he'd gone to town on some radiator parts, I'd gotten out the channel lock. It fascinated me how confident and capable he was in this environment, and it was hot as fuck being his assistant.

"So, how'd you end up in Los Angeles?" I asked as he worked. I figured this was a fairly innocuous question. I *hadn't* figured that Mal would be on the defensive again suddenly.

"Why is it always *me* who has to talk? How'd *you* end up in New York?"

Fine. I could show him how to answer a casual question politely.

"The usual way, I guess?" I felt the back of my neck turning red under the hot sun, and I was sweating through my T-shirt. "Columbia and UT were the places that gave me scholarships. University of Tennessee was really close to home, and I wanted to get a little further away..."

"To *find yourself* in the big city?" Mal said fake-dramatically.

"Honestly? Yeah. Kinda. So Columbia was the only real choice." I shrugged. "I studied business and found I liked advertising. To me, it's not about selling people shit they don't need, it's about helping to connect people with products they can use. Or at least, that's how it's supposed to work."

I had serious doubts about whether it would continue to work that way when people like Kale Storms were in charge. All the more reason to start my own business sooner rather than later.

Mal finished detaching the seat and tossed the tools back in the bag at my feet. His hair was plastered to the back of his neck, and it didn't make him look a whit less attractive, damn it. "That's very Hallmark of you. Country boy learns important lessons in the city, then comes home. Isn't that how it goes?"

I blinked. "Uh, no. I'm not about to take over my dad's farm or whatever. And I don't have a true love I left behind here. And eating Lou Klein's apple muffins is the closest I wanna get to owning a bakery *or* an orchard, so..."

"Damn." Mal jumped down from the tractor, and his eyes pinned me in place. "You know an awful lot about those movies."

"I... I work in advertising," I said with a sniff. "It's important that I have an understanding of what is, um... appealing to middle America. As a, um... target demographic."

Mal tilted his head to one side. "Aw, bless. That was almost believable. *But not quite.* You watch them daily, don't you?"

"No! Weekly. At *most*." I sighed. "Shut up."

But of course he didn't.

"Deep inside you—" Mal clutched a hand to his chest and spun in a circle. "—there's a country girl longing to return to her roots. Maybe you could take over this very junkyard, Brooks Johnson, and..."

I grabbed his free hand and spun him again, right into my arms, with his wrist held at the small of his back and our torsos pressed together. For a second, we stared at each other, breath mingling, without a sound but the distant *whoosh* of the traffic on the highway. "What's your role in this story, then?" I asked gruffly. "Prince in disguise?"

Mal swallowed hard and pushed at me with his other hand. "Yeah, right. Prince of the junkyard, you mean? I'm a metal artist from Homer, Tennessee, by way of Los Angeles. I'm a background character in your movie."

"A really prickly prince who likes to ask questions but not answer them." The urge to kiss him was way too strong, so I let him go abruptly, grabbed the tool bag off the ground, and kept strolling down the aisle. "How'd you get to be a guy who fears cows and cow art?"

"*Pfft.* The only thing I fear about cow art is how epic it is," he deadpanned, catching up to me with the tractor seat clutched in his hand. "Only the truly enlightened among us can really understand it."

"Yep. You and my mom," I agreed. "So what about—"

"Holy shit, look at that auger!" Mal said, cutting me off as he ran toward the corkscrew-shaped implement.

I rolled my eyes at the sky. If Mal thought I'd be put off by his deflection, he was dead wrong. I hadn't gotten where I was by quitting, damn it.

We'd taken two loads of stuff to the truck, and Mal had knelt to dismantle the exhaust pipes from a couple of newer tractors by the time I tried again. "So, why Los Angeles? Was it a beach thing, or...?"

Mal sighed, clearly irritated. He paused his work but didn't turn around. "If you must know, Los Angeles seemed like an open-minded place where I could live in my car for a while without hypothermia, and I had just enough gas money to get me there. And I pulled myself up by my bootstraps, whatever those are, and now I'm happier and *sexier* than ever. Can we stop with the twenty questions now? It's getting boring."

Learning about Mal was anything but boring.

I stepped up behind him and put a hand on the small of his back, not to crowd him, but to let him know I was there. "Was it that bad at home?"

He shook his head once, silently, but I was almost sure he leaned back into my touch. "Not really, I don't— I mean, I guess you need to define *bad*? It was civil. I was eighteen and my dad suggested Homer wasn't the best place for me to choose to live my homosexual lifestyle. I agreed. Wasn't like I'd been dying to live in a junkyard anyway, right? Or in a town with a bunch of assholes? The really bad shit didn't come until later, when he spewed homophobic slurs at my mom's funeral." He said this flatly, with the total emotionlessness of a guy whose grief was not fully healed. He looked over his shoulder. "Not everyone has parents like yours, Brooks."

I had a vision of myself driving to the other end of the state just to punch his dad, not that this would help Mal in any way.

"Yeah, well," I said, taking a step back and trying to lighten the mood. "If you'd had *my* mom, she wouldn't've believed you were gay for a solid ten years, until you brought a fake boyfriend home, and even then, she might've warned you about breaking his heart." I chuckled. "Can't win whichever way I go."

Mal snorted and moved on to the next exhaust pipe. "Yes, it's very hard when you can't be perfect, isn't it?"

I scowled and stepped away from him. "Stop saying shit like that. I'm not perfect. I know I'm not."

"Yeah, but you still want to be." Mal turned to face me. "Ava told me once that you change your personality depending on who you're with. A jock with the athletes, a mathlete with the nerds."

"I get along with a variety of people," I said defensively. "All of those are part of my personality."

"Sure. But there has to be a core of you that doesn't change and doesn't feel bad about it either, no matter what anyone thinks. You don't have to be perfect. Just be... Brooks."

I snorted. The guy had no idea what he was talking about. "*Be Brooks.* Who the hell else would I be?"

Mal shook his head and turned back to his work, but I'd swear there was a smile hidden in the curve of his cheek.

"So, why a fake boyfriend, anyway?" Mal demanded.

I shrugged. "Why not?"

He flicked a glance back at me. "I meant why not a *real* one, but that's a solid answer. I'd like it noted that I'm letting that stand, because I recognize when shit is none of my business, unlike some peop—"

"I dunno. *Jesus.*" I rolled my eyes. "I haven't found the right guy yet. I haven't been looking, because I'm definitely not where I wanna be in my career before I get serious with someone, so casual things work well for me." I shrugged, then challenged, "Why don't *you* have a boyfriend?"

"Uh, because I'm deeply in love with Ava? Duh."

"Uh-huh."

"Relationships are hard in LA," he said, stacking a second pipe on the ground next to the first. "Anyway, we were talking about *you*."

"I don't think—"

"Licking Thicket is..." Mal hesitated, eyes roaming the junkyard. "I don't know what it was like ten years ago, but right now it's cool, Brooks."

"Small-town good?" I teased.

"No, just... *good*. Full stop. Look around you. There's a pho restaurant in this town right next to the burger place, which is, like, symbolism or whatever. And they have amazing taste in metal sculpture. And your local junkyard owner wore a shirt with a pride flag."

Wait... "Did he?"

Mal snickered. "Oh, didn't notice *that*, but you noticed him flirting?" He rolled his eyes. "I'm just saying, maybe you can make your peace now. Maybe you don't have to stay away for ten years next time. Be glad you have a home to come back to."

I frowned. I'd been thinking that exact thing, which made it even odder that Mal said it. Once again, I felt *seen*, and the feeling went to my head like my mom's peach moonshine. It made me reckless.

I took a step forward, backing Mal against the giant tire of a bright green cultivator. He hadn't been expecting it, clearly, because his eyes were wide as a startled calf's.

"You're getting a sunburn," I said softly, running a finger down the center of his nose.

What the fuck? I kicked myself mentally for being the same smooth bastard I'd been earlier in the week and the shit that flew out of my mouth around this guy.

But Mal swallowed hard, and his eyes glazed like I'd said something filthy or flirty. "W-what are you doing?"

"I was thinking I might kiss you," I said conversationally. "Since we've identified that you're not actually with Ava and I'm not actually with Paul, maybe if we kept things very, *very* private we could—"

"Hey, guys?" Diesel called from somewhere down the row, his voice getting closer. "How's it going?

Mal pushed at my chest with both hands, one of which was still clamped around a wrench, and I took a giant step back. "I don't think that kind of privacy exists in Licking Thicket," he murmured.

Diesel paused next to the tool bag in the center of the aisle. "Hey. I wondered if you needed help, Mal?"

"It'd really help if he'd go the fuck away," I said under my breath, turning to inspect the dusty tire like it was suddenly fascinating.

Mal pushed his lips together like he wanted to laugh, but he shook his head politely at Diesel. "Not really. I've already gotten more than I came for." He darted a look at me. "More than that would be greedy since I'm going home Sunday night, right?"

I pushed out a breath. *Right.*

Mal stepped around me to collect the rest of his haul, and I squeezed my eyes shut for a second.

Sunday night I'd be back in the city. I could hit up a bar or open an app, select from a plethora of really hot, really willing, really *uncomplicated* guys, and get rid of this jumpy, nervous energy in my gut almost immediately, the way I'd done a hundred times in the past.

I wondered why that option wasn't remotely appealing at the moment.

Then I opened my eyes just in time to see Mal give Diesel a friendly smile, and I thought I knew the answer.

Chapter Ten

Mal

When I woke up the following day, I was shocked to realize it was already Thursday. My crazy week in Licking Thicket was more than halfway over. Soon, I'd be returning to the real world where coffee didn't come in a cup with a cartoon salt lick on it and no one in the general vicinity bore the nickname Plutie, Sonny, or Skeets.

I had to admit to being excited for the vendor fair, though. So far, everyone had been very supportive of my work, and I always loved selling at the small-town fairs. People usually had great stories of oddball junk that had been repurposed, and sometimes they even offered to go home and collect their junk to donate to "the cause." I'd gotten very good at saying no thank you to sincere offerings of other people's garbage, but I still appreciated the kind gestures. And it was especially fun to see families out together or couples holding hands while strolling through the booths and munching on local fair food.

After climbing out of the guest house and dropping into the yard, I made my way into the kitchen in time to over-hear Mrs. Ivey lecturing Ava about her outfit.

"What happened to the ensemble I laid out on your bed, honey?" Mrs. Ivey asked from her position in front of the pancake griddle. "I picked it up for you at Deb's Closet just last week. It's darling."

"It's a pinafore, Mama," Ava said calmly. "And Deb's Closet isn't gently used so much as rode hard and put away wet."

"Don't be ridiculous," Mrs. Ivey said, waving the pancake flipper through the air. "I have it on good authority Missy Stonewall herself owned that top before Deb got a hold of it."

"Be that as it may, it looks like something you'd lay across the dining room table on Thanksgiving before placing a gravy boat on top of it." Ava grabbed a dry pancake from the stack next to the griddle and took a bite out of it. "Besides, it doesn't fit. I'm wearing this."

Mrs. Ivey gave Ava an up-down that made it very clear what the older woman thought of Ava's white sleeveless shirt and teal-colored shorts. "Your..." She turned to me before lowering her voice at Ava. "Bosoms are... indecent in that blouse."

"They're like ten times bigger than normal," Ava said before catching herself. Her eyes widened in horror. "I mean, this bra makes them *look* bigger. Maybe you're right. Maybe I'll change." She turned and bolted out of the room.

I tried to pretend I was invisible, but it didn't work. Ava's mom shot me a big Welcome Wagon smile. "Malachi, good morning, dear. Are you ready for some pancakes?"

After an awkward pancake breakfast slash fashion show, I finally told Ava if she changed into one more shirt with a Peter Pan collar or an inset lace panel of any kind, we were going to have words. When we left the house, she was back in the original white sleeveless top which, admittedly, now seemed a little porny in hindsight.

When we got to the vendor fair and saw Brooks and Paul helping set up, Paul caught sight of the unfortunate mammary situation and ran right into a trash barrel, damned near tipping inside.

"Jesus Christ," Brooks scoffed, rubbing the center of his forehead with his fingers.

"Straight," I muttered to Ava out of the corner of my mouth. "And a shit actor to boot."

"Oh my God, are you okay? Oh you poor thing!" Ava scurried over to help Paul which included brushing debris off his front, which only served to mortify him more.

"No, *no*. I'm okay! I swear!"

And he was, if by "okay" he meant sporting an Ava boner. I glanced at Brooks with a raised eyebrow. "Your boyfriend—"

"Don't say it," he growled, barely suppressing a grin.

"I think he might be bisexual," I whispered.

"Shut up," he said with a laugh.

I left the three of them and made my way over to my vendor booth before opening it up and adding the two new pieces I'd made in Mr. Ivey's workshop last night. Ava had fallen asleep right after dinner, and I'd spent the next several hours enjoying the quiet solitude of work with nothing but Mr. Ivey's tools and my own music blasting through headphones.

There were obviously more people here than yesterday, and the excitement was palpable. Crafters and artists were putting the final touches on their displays while the food booths began setting out incredible-smelling treats on their tables. After a few minutes, Brooks's voice came over the speakers set all around the town square.

"Welcome to the Lickin' Artists' Fair," he said. I could just see a sliver of him standing on a stage at the center of the booths. "If you're feeling peckish, remember there's a whole host of food trucks with offerings from our local restaurants, including Miss Susie Dupree's Deluxe Barbecue, home of Dupree's Deluxe Dipping Sauce. Miss Susie has graciously sponsored the Lickin' for thirty-three years now, and we thank her for her generous contribution." It sounded like he was reading off a paper, and I chuckled at the lack of enthusiasm in his voice.

He sounded much more sincere when he continued. "Be sure to pick up a map from one of our volunteers so you can find your way through all of the incredible offerings we have here today. You'll enjoy everything from Minerva Warren's colorful hand-knit sweaters to Jayden Polk's delicious salted-caramel ice cream to Mal Forrester's unique found-object sculptures to Kevin Lee's handmade dollhouses and Sam Trammel's meat pies. Today is the only day to grab the best these artisans have to offer, so don't let those special items pass you by. As my mama would say, don't forget Christmas is just around the corner and Aunt Brenda isn't easy to buy for."

The people around me chuckled, and I realized that they probably knew Brooks's Aunt Brenda personally.

My gut felt warmed by his kind words. There had to be over a hundred vendor booths set up around the square, most of which were probably local Thicket businesses, but he'd mentioned mine by name. It was sweet of him, but not nearly as sweet as what he proceeded to do on and off throughout the fair.

"Dr. Dalton, come over and see these," Brooks said while I was finishing up a sale to a young mother. He led an older white-haired man over to the booth and pointed to one of the sculptures on the display wall behind me. "Mal here makes animals and whatnot from items in the junkyard. Isn't this amazing? This Shakespeare quote is made out of—"

"Well, look at that," the older man said with a grin, squinting at the sculpture. "Old typewriter keys. And... are those vintage dental tools in this piece here? Where in the world did you find those?"

Brooks sounded pleased. "That's the one that made me think of you. Isn't it amazing?"

"I'll be damned," he said, putting his hands on his hips. "It's a crocodile. Made from extraction forceps."

I finished saying goodbye to the customer and turned toward the doctor. "I accidentally ended up with a box of old dental tools when I bought a junk lot at an auction. My friend Ava had the idea for making a toothy croc out of it."

I wondered if this was the doctor Ava had told me about, the one who might be interested in my reef sculpture for the clinic. But before I could ask, Brooks winked at me and said, "Dr. Dalton is our dentist here in the Thicket."

It wasn't lost on me that Brooks was claiming ownership of the Thicket, something he hadn't done much of so far this week.

"Oh, right," I said, stepping over to pick up another piece from the table and hold it out to Dr. Dalton. "You might like this one too. It's a soap box derby car. These side-view mirrors are mouth mirrors from that same lot of tools."

He took the car gently from my hand to examine it more closely. "So clever. However did you think of all this?" As he continued to exclaim about the various elements of the little car, Brooks pulled me away to ask if I needed anything.

"Cold drink? Or a snack? Are you hungry? I can—"

Two guys I sort of recognized from the Lope came up, interrupting Brooks's questions with a shout.

"There he is! Dude, where have you been all week? And don't get me started on that shirt, bro," the first one laughed.

Brooks's shirt proclaimed him *Head Licker*, of course, but this time, for some reason, I wanted to murder anyone who thought it was funny.

"Look at you, all dressed up to oversee the kids in the Great Ice Cream Lickening!" the second dude-bro said, punching Brooks in the arm. "Sometimes it feels like just last year when the three of us were in that contest—you, me, and Len. Remember, Brooks?"

Brooks smiled and nodded like he was ready to start reminiscing, but the first guy interrupted. "Ethan, buddy, it *was* just last year when you were in the contest. You're why Mayor Johnson had to institute an age limit on the participants." He rolled his eyes and looked at me. "Ethan's two favorite things are ice cream and contests, you know? It wasn't fair to the little ones for him to win all the time."

"Screw that." Ethan folded his arms over his chest and scowled. "Rosetti almost beat me last year."

"Gino Rosetti? The guy who was a year ahead of us in school?" Brooks looked confused.

Len shook his head. "Nah. Gino's daughter Gabby. She's eight. Big brown eyes and brown pigtails."

"But with the ice-cream-eating power of someone three times her size!" Ethan said defensively.

"Sure, bud," Len soothed. To Brooks, he said, "You gonna be at the *unofficial* Lickening tonight? We're planning a shot contest, and you and Ava have to come. It'll be like old times."

Brooks's gaze flicked to me before he looked back at the

two men. "Yeah, uh, sure. Of course. You'll have to ask Ava, though. This is, uh... her boyfriend, Mal."

Len crinkled his brow and gave me a judgy up-down. "No shit?"

I stuck out my hand. "Mal Forrester. Nice to meet you."

He shook my hand, making sure to prove his masculinity with a tight grip. I wanted to roll my eyes, but I retained my manners instead.

"I'm Len Dixon, and this here's Ethan Howe. We're friends of Ava and Brooks from high school. Come on by the Tavern tonight and hang out with us, alright? We'd love to catch up with Ava, and you can hear all kinds of stories of what these two got up to back then." He winked and slapped me on the shoulder before fist-bumping Brooks and leading his friend to another booth.

"Mpfh," I muttered under my breath. Brooks furrowed his brow at me, but before he could accuse me of being a dick, another group of people walked up calling out his name.

"Oh Brooks, darling! Look at you. So much like your daddy. See, Vera, I told you he was the spitting image of Red. That time in the big city didn't change anything, now did it?"

Brooks's jaw tightened the barest amount, enough to tell me what he was thinking, that he sure hoped his time in New York had changed him at least some.

"Hi, Mrs. Little. Miss Viv. Are you enjoying the fair?" Brooks put on his bland politeness mask, all Vaseline teeth and Southern-fried platitudes. Gone was the genuine insecurity of the boy who'd stumbled over why he hadn't found love yet. As far as anyone around would know from looking at him right now, Brooks Johnson had the world in his teeth.

Everything was under control and just the way he wanted it.

But as soon as those ladies wandered off, forty bucks lighter in the purse and weighed down with metal woodland creatures, his mask fell.

"Can I take over here for a little bit so you can catch a break?" he asked. A sliver of concern wrinkled his forehead. "It's awfully hot, and I don't want you to—"

Dr. Dalton finally made his decision. "Son, I think I'm going to have to take this croc off your hands, if you don't mind. I was wondering if you might be interested in making a few other pieces to go with it. There's no rush, mind you, but we have a big wall space in the office that could use a few more pieces, and these are just perfect."

I turned to help him with both his purchase and talking through the commission. I was grateful to discuss any commission with someone since Ava had discovered the tech CEO she'd promised me was out of town on business this week.

Despite tuning in to what my customer wanted, I was also very aware of where Brooks was in the booth. He answered questions for a few people and even helped ring up another one, wrapping the little superhero figure carefully in newspaper before handing it over for the customer to place into her canvas shopping bag. After that, he was called away, presumably to put out some kind of fire.

I wasn't surprised at all, but when he came back over to the booth twenty minutes later with a huge slushy lemonade and a takeaway box full of a gorgeous gourmet salad topped with grilled chicken, my heart nearly flapped out of my chest like a drunken pelican.

"For me?" I squeaked.

He nodded, his ears turning pink at the top. "Yeah, it's no big deal. I just thought you'd be—"

"Thank you," I said breathlessly. "That's so thoughtful of you. How much do I owe you?" I reached for my wallet, but he snapped his head up to glare at me.

"Nothing. It's... no. Nothing. Jesus. I bought you lunch because..." He clamped his lips closed and shook his head. "Because." Brooks looked everywhere but at me. "Anyway... I should probably go. But here's my cell number if you need anything. Just text me, okay?"

He shoved a scrap of paper into my hand and disappeared back into the crowd. I stared after him, sipping the blessedly cold lemonade and wondering how in the world I'd managed to fall for my best friend's ex-boyfriend.

"He's the sweetest thing ever," Ava sighed. She stepped behind my table and dropped down onto one of the chairs. I felt the pinch of betrayal in my gut.

"Yeah. Uh, yeah. He... brought me lunch. He's probably bringing it around to all the vendors."

Ava looked up at me in confusion. "Paul brought you lunch? But I just finished eating with him at the Holly's Kebabs stand, and he said he had to go back to the Johnsons' to get some more work done on their barbecue sauce presentation."

We stared at each other for a minute while the crossed wires sorted themselves out, and then we both laughed. "Oh my gosh," Ava said, clapping a hand over her mouth. "Do you think Brooks would be very mad at me for thinking his boyfriend was sweet?"

I thought back to the night Brooks tasted my tonsils in Ava's own basement. "No, I don't think so. But I think... I'm pretty sure..." I was torn about confessing Brooks's secret that Paul was faking it for the sake of Brooks's reputation in town. It wasn't my secret to tell, but at the same time, I didn't want Ava to feel the least bit guilty for developing a crush on Paul. "You were right when we first got here. Paul's not gay," I finally said.

"You say that, but..." She trailed off as she spied the subject of our conversation running across the crowd toward the booth. Paul thrust something in his hand toward Ava.

"Your ChapStick," he said through heaving breaths. He pulled out his inhaler and took a few puffs, then pushed his glasses up his sweaty nose. "I forgot I was carrying it for you."

The three of us stared down at Ava's generic drugstore lip balm with its torn label and *Buy 3 Get 1* sticker.

Ava looked up at him like he'd just scaled Mt. Kilimanjaro for her. "Thank you so much. That's so sweet of you, Paul."

"Dude," I couldn't help but ask, "how far did you get before you remembered you had that in your pocket?"

"Oh," he said, still sucking in oxygen. "Just to the end of the Johnsons' driveway, so not all the way back."

While Ava fussed over him and offered him some of my lemon slushy, I couldn't help but blurt, "Paul, do you ever watch Drag Race?"

Paul blinked at me and tilted his head. "Like, with the cars?"

I lifted an eyebrow at Ava. "Yeah. Like that," I muttered in time to hear a snort behind me. It was Brooks, carrying a drinks tray full of colorful icy concoctions. "Oooh! What do you have here? Ava gave my last drink away to someone more deserving."

He set the tray down and began handing the first one to Ava. "Fuzzy Thickets. They're nothing at all like Fuzzy

Navels, but for some reason are named after them. They have vodka and—"

Before he could say another word, Paul and I both shouted, "No!" and flailed toward the drink as if it was a bomb waiting to go off. Bright orange liquid splashed from the clear plastic cup all over Paul's short-sleeved button-down and onto his pristine white dress shorts.

Brooks stood frozen with his empty hand still outstretched. "Mind telling me what's going on?" he asked calmly.

Paul was busy tutting over Ava as if she'd been the one to get doused in a Fuzzy Thicket instead of him. Brooks turned to me for an answer, and I winced. "It's... just that..." I glanced at Ava.

"Oh for God's sake," she hissed. "I'm pregnant. Now hand me some napkins."

Brooks reached back to the drinks tray to pull out the stack of napkins shoved under one of the drinks and handed it to her. "Are you sure?" He glanced worriedly at me. "Is... I mean... are you two..."

I clapped a hand over my mouth to try and hold back the snort. "No, honey," I said. "Not mine. Not by a long shot."

Was I just imagining his sigh of relief?

He nodded and turned back to Ava. "Are you okay? I mean... I don't want to pry, but... do you need anything, or...?"

Paul stopped fussing with the napkins and glanced up at Brooks. "She's fine. More than fine. She's gorgeous. Look at her. She's strong, and healthy, and—" He seemed to realize what he was saying because he stopped suddenly with a slight gasp. "It's none of our business."

Ava softened like butter left in the summer sun. "I'm

good, actually. I was scared at first, but now... now I think it's going to be okay." She took a deep breath. "I haven't told my family yet, though, so you can't say anything."

Brooks shook his head. "No, no. Of course not. Never. It's your story to tell. And Paul is right. It's none of my business anyway. But, you know you can come to me for anything, don't you? If you need help, or... anything at all."

She smiled at him. "Well, if you truly mean it... I was hoping you might be willing to marry me and help out, just... just until the baby turns five and starts school."

We all stared at her like *she* was now the bomb and it had suddenly, terribly detonated all over us.

"What?" Paul squawked. "*Him?*"

Ava started giggling before pointing at Brooks. "Your face. Oh my God, you should have seen your face. Why didn't I think to grab my camera? Priceless."

My heart almost skittered out of my chest and landed in a splat on the vodka-soaked ground.

I turned to Brooks. "By any chance do you have one of those Fuzzy things that's nothing but straight vodka?"

Chapter Eleven

Brooks

"Tell me again why we had to come tonight?" Paul asked as he parked my car in the little lot beside Henson's Grocery and walked across the street. "Because I have some concerns."

"Because it's tradition," I replied, categorically refusing to be concerned about anything. "It's gonna be great."

This day had *already* been great, one of the best I'd ever had in Licking Thicket, and I was already a little bit drunk on good feelings and a couple of Fuzzy Thickets. I'd come to the Thicket expecting all the things I'd hated about this town to be exactly the same, but I'd been wrong. Seeing folks appreciate Mal and the other artisans and craftspeople at the fair had been eye-opening, and judging the ice cream eating contest—a Head Licker task I'd been *dreading*—had proved beyond a doubt this place had changed in the years I'd been gone, just like I had.

There had been ninety-seven kids lined up at two long tables to take part, and I'd been pleasantly surprised —*shocked*—by the diversity they represented. Turned out, according to my mom's whispered explanation, a giant tech company had bought a big plot of land that used to be the old Easton farm and had built a campus there, drawing people from all over the world.

"Why didn't you tell me?" I'd asked her.

She'd shrugged. "Well, honey, I suppose I figured if it mattered to you one way or the other, you'd've come home to see for yourself."

I'd had no reply to that, so she'd patted me on the arm and walked away to make sure all ninety-seven kids had plenty of ice cream—including dairy-free varieties, for those who didn't drink milk—proving that the shit I *had* actually missed about this place, the community spirit and the feeling of being a part of something bigger, hadn't changed at all.

I took a deep breath of the sweet evening air, smoothed down my Head Licker T-shirt, and twitched my shorts so the hem hung straight. I'd insisted on going home to shower before coming out, telling Paul I was covered in melted ice cream, but that was only part of the reason. I'd also been covered in layers of dried sweat after an afternoon in the sun, and if I was gonna be with Mal at the bar tonight, I wanted to smell more like Creed Aventus and less like Essence of Brooks.

I mean, not that I was going to be *with* Mal, obviously. Definitely not when I had a "boyfriend" and he had Ava. But the way he'd shot me little smiles all afternoon when he didn't know I was looking had made my toes curl in my shoes, and—

"Hello? Earth to Johnson? Concerns? Which I have? And expect you to reassure me about?"

I blinked at Paul, who was waving a hand in front of my face. "Huh?"

He huffed out a breath and grabbed me by the shoulders on the sidewalk outside the bar. "Okay, I say this with love, as the sexiest, straightest, soon-to-be former-ex-boyfriend you've *never* had—"

"Debatable."

"—but you need to move your brain a good three feet north of your belt, Brooks, and pay attention. You and Ava haven't been in public together all week. And most of the people you two used to be friends with are gonna be in this bar, right? This is gonna be every high school reunion you've missed for the last ten years condensed into one night, *plus* copious amounts of alcohol. You need your head —by which I mean the one on top of your shoulders—in the game."

"I've got my—"

Paul grabbed the back of my neck—a trickier feat than you'd think, since I had several inches of height on the guy— and spoke intensely. "No puffy-heart eyes at Malachi. No longing glances. No holding hands under the table."

I stepped back and his arm fell away. "Holding hands? Are you warning me off Mal, or warning yourself off Ava? And, need I remind you, she's a very *pregnant* Ava."

Which was another surprising but cool turn of events, and I was really happy for her.

"I'm aware, yes." Paul's face turned red, and he studied the cracks in the sidewalk for clues. "She wasn't in a relationship with the father, you know. It was a... a onetime thing."

"Okay," I said slowly. He made it sound like that was the biggest potential impediment to him having a relationship with her. "But she still lives in Los Angeles, man. Just like Mal."

"She might not always, though." His gaze lifted to mine. "She might... I mean, I don't know for sure, but... she sounded like she might consider moving back here. To the Thicket. So she has family support for her and the baby."

"Yeah?" I frowned. "I guess I can see that. But it doesn't change the fact that you and I live in New York. Not a lot of ad agencies in middle Tennessee, bud. And that's a hell of a commute for a guy who doesn't fly."

"I know," Paul said glumly. "I know. But we're not talking about *me* anyway. *Pfft.* Nonsense. Ava and I are just... friendly. She'd never want... She'd never be..." He waved a hand negligently, a sure sign he was lying through his teeth. "Whatever. Point is, if she's living back here in Licking Thicket, she has to be able to hold her head up. She's not gonna be the girl who fell for a gay man *twice*. Or, worse, the girl who lost her *second* gay boyfriend to her *first* gay boyfriend. You get me? Someday, she's gonna be the head of the Licket Beauty Thing."

"The Licking Thicket Beautification Corps," I said absently, watching Mal and Ava stroll down the street toward us. Mal had a supportive arm wrapped around Ava's shoulders, but I could ignore that. The way the damp ends of his hair waved around his chin, though, and the tight-as-fuck jeans sitting low on his hips, were impossible to ignore. They made me want to plot ways to *ensure* Ava lost her second gay boyfriend to her first.

Which would be bad for many reasons. Many.

And I'd remember them any minute now.

Paul turned his head to see what had caught my attention. "She could beautify *anything*," he sighed forlornly. Then he straightened and socked me lightly in the shoulder. "She's the most important thing here, Brooks. Not you or me, since we're leaving, and sure as fuck not *Mal* since he'll probably have a new guy by next week. Just her and the baby."

I swallowed hard at the idea of Mal moving on to a new guy—which, yes, was crazy talk, considering we'd exchanged one and a half kisses, if you counted the near miss at the junkyard, and a bunch of longing looks. Paul made sense, damn him.

I forced myself to look away from the pair approaching us. "Look, I'm not a particularly possessive guy, My Little Paul, but I'm guessing you should be directing that loving look at *me*. I can maybe try to keep my hands off Mal, but you'll need to be more convincing about being my main squeeze."

Paul groaned. "I'm not kissing you again, Big Daddy."

Lurleen's daughter Alana walked past us with a group of her girlfriends, heading for the bar, and I was pretty sure she overheard his last comment, damn it. "Everything okay, Brooksy?"

"God, yes! Perfect!" I cried, flinging my arms around Paul. "So perfect! I just get insatiable around my honeybear sometimes," I added in a confiding voice, "seeing the way this pale blue shirt just brings out the, uh... the paleness of his eyes? *Rowrrrr*. But he's concerned that public displays of affection just aren't done in the Thicket, and he wants so badly to impress my friends and family!"

"I hate you," Paul muttered into my armpit.

Mal and Ava walked up, and while Mal looked amused, Ava glared at me. She looked simultaneously ready for bed and ready to claw my eyes out.

I dropped my arms, releasing Paul from our awkward embrace, and he adjusted his glasses self-consciously.

"Oh, don't be shy on our account," Alana said with a mischievous smile. "But you might wanna wait to get frisky until after the drinks start flowing." She held the door open for us and then for Mal and Ava. "I'm so excited that the gang's all here! Tonight's going to be the most fun *ever*."

I forced a smile. Suddenly the prospect of being close to Mal, the hottest creature in the universe, while having to pretend I wasn't aware of his presence, was no longer appealing. "Yay," I deadpanned, soft enough that only Paul, Mal, and Ava heard it.

"Here's how this is gonna work," Paul said, low and urgent. "Mal and Brooks, you need to take Ava's drinks. Alternate. And remember Ava's reputation is on the line."

Delightful. So I'd be *drunk*, horny, and cock-blocked. Better and better.

"You're getting bossier as our romance progresses, My Little Paul. What, pray tell, will *you* be doing?"

"Someone needs to be designated driver and to take care of Ava. Ideally someone who doesn't think fried eggs and bacon are a cure for morning sickness."

"Hey! In my defense, it works on hangovers," Mal argued.

"Fine, then," I agreed with a sigh. "Fine. You drive. Mal and I will take shots for the team."

Alana led us to the back of the bar, where a bunch of familiar faces were standing around a cluster of high-tops. The tables were already cluttered with dozens and dozens of shot glasses filled to the brim, showing the party had been ready to start without us.

"Look who I found!" she yelled. "Y'all know Brooks and Ava, and this here's Paul and this is Malachi—"

"Mal," Mal interrupted firmly.

"Right." She darted him a surprised glance. "Mal. Okay, so going around the table, that's Sonny Parvis on your left, that's Skeets and Lorna Miller, Latonya and Maureen Henson from the grocery store, Len Dixon, Penelope Kelley, Sonny Vasquez

—he's one of our local doctors who works with Doc Yates. That's Ollie and Kendra Nutter—you know Ollie's cousin Frank, Brooks? He's the sheriff now and sort of my boyfriend—"

"You've been dating for a million years, Alana, and he's been sheriff for a million and one. Not sure that's news," Ethan piped up.

"It is to *them*." Alana glared. "Frank's coming later on. Anyway, you know *that* is Ethan Howe. Then Sonny Burnett, Nora Hernandez, and um... this is Diesel Church. He's new in town. Runs the junkyard."

"Right. We met the other day," I confirmed. "Didn't realize you were new around here."

"Only been here three years." Diesel shrugged. "Means I'm still a suspicious character."

"Nah, man! Folks think you're suspicious because of all your tattoos and weird piercings, and the way you look perpetually pissed off," Ethan said earnestly. "Not 'cause you're new. But it's cool. I like you anyway."

Pen Kelley face-palmed, and a couple other people shook their heads, but Diesel's mouth twitched like he was fighting a grin before he rubbed a hand over his mouth. "Thanks, Ethan."

"Alana, I thought you'd invented some trivia game," Maureen said. "Let's play it while I can still stand. Pregnancy and breastfeeding have killed my tolerance." She winked and nudged the trio of empty shot glasses in front of her with one finger.

Alana lifted her eyes to the exposed beams. "Alrighty, then! Ava, you come stand by me and Kendra! We have so much to dish about!"

"No!" Ava said, clutching my arm suddenly. "I, um... I really want to catch up with Brooks also. Since he's, um...

leaving Sunday." She arranged us around one end of the table so Paul was next to Sonny, then Ava, then me, then Mal... then Diesel.

Mal gave Diesel a shy smile, and Diesel replied with a "Hey, Mal. Good to see you, man."

Clearly, I was not fucking consulted about this placement, but given the way Ava was clutching my arm, I couldn't figure out how to fix it without calling more attention to us.

"Okay," Alana said, unlocking her phone. "You ready? We're playing Never Have I Ever: Fighting Bovines Edition. For those who didn't go to school here... substitute your own high school experiences." She winked at Mal. "If you've done the deed, you take the shot. Ready?"

"Born ready," Maureen said. She passed around a tray of shots as Latonya laughed.

"Okay, never have I ever... gotten straight A's every semester, all four years."

Ten billion pairs of eyes turned in my direction, and I groaned. "Unfair," I said, but I tilted the clear liquid into my mouth and let it light my esophagus on fire. "Oh, motherfucker. Moonshine?" I demanded, eyes watering.

"Welcome back to Bovine country, Johnson!" Penelope said, and the entire table *moooed* in chorus.

"Not a word," I warned the sexy man at my side. "Not a single—"

"Moo," Mal said, and I had to fight my smile as Ethan came around the table to high-five him.

"I think I feel this stuff burning a hole in my stomach," I said under my breath.

"That's what you get for being Mr. Perfect," Mal whispered back.

"Okay, moving on. Never have I ever... cheated on one of Mrs. Brachtl's open-book philosophy tests!"

Alana barely had the words out of her mouth before she'd raised her glass, and since literally anyone who'd ever been in poor old Mrs. B's class had almost been *compelled* to cheat in order to pass, we all followed suit, laughing as we did.

Ava slid me her glass as soon as I'd slammed mine down, and I noticed Mal and Diesel shrug at each other and smile as they took shots too, like they were partners in crime.

I downed Ava's shot and accidentally-on-purpose stumbled into Mal as I did it.

"Whoa, my bad," I said, yanking him toward me several inches as I set him back on his feet and put a hand on his back to anchor him. "Sorry, Mal."

"Were you drinking before you left the house?" he demanded under his breath.

"Only the Fuzzy Thickets from earlier." But Mal smelled like sandalwood shampoo and fabric softener, and I thought maybe I could get drunk on that.

"Okay, next round. Never have I ever... kissed someone on school grounds!"

I hesitated and Ava did too. We'd never been that kind of couple, but there'd been one time—

Len grinned and pointed accusingly from across the table. "Bleachers count as school grounds, Brooks. Remember the time Coach Cosway caught you two making out under there when you were supposed to be in physics? *Legendary*. Drink up, buddy! You too, Ava."

Ava and I exchanged a smile that was more like a grimace. I didn't remember that experience as legendary at all. More like awkward and fumbling and embarrassing for both of us. But I drank obediently and slid Ava's shot over to

Mal, who took it with way more force than necessary after downing his own.

"Your arm is still on my back," he hissed under his breath.

Shit. I moved it away.

"Never have I ever... skipped class to make out." Alana laughed good-naturedly. "Guess we know who'll be drinking this round already, huh?" She wiggled her eyebrows at me.

I sighed and took my shot and Ava's.

"Is this whole thing going to be about sex?" Mal whispered, clearly annoyed. "'Cause if so, you're gonna be under the table in ten minutes."

"How the hell should I know?" I demanded. "I didn't make the quiz."

"You've apparently done every other damn thing, though." He grabbed another shot from the table and downed it without waiting for a question.

"No, I really didn't. It wasn't—"

"Okay, next one! Never have I ever... gotten in trouble for riding a tractor while intoxicated."

Paul shot me a questioning look.

I laughed and shook my head. "Fuck, no. I didn't grow up on a farm, remember. And not everyone who has access to a tractor does stupid—"

The table exploded into laughter as Ethan and Mal both took shots.

Mal's cheeks burned. "It's a long story, and I'm not drunk enough to tell it," he muttered loud enough for the table to hear.

"Ava, girl, you brought back a good one!" Nora yelled. "Mal, you're alright."

Mal smiled back, and it made my stomach flip. Or maybe it was the moonshine.

"Okay! Never have I ever…" Alana drummed her fingers against the table dramatically. "Lost my virginity to someone at this table!"

Oh, damn.

More than half the people around me drank. Ava pressed her lips together and didn't meet my eyes. Mal kept his gaze on the table. It suddenly occurred to me that even though he was doing his best to be a part of the group, it was clear Mal felt like an outsider similar to the way I had back in high school. Fitting in took time, and as long as he was just visiting, he'd never feel completely accepted. And neither would I.

"Okay!" I said loudly, stepping back. "This has been so fun, Alana, but I'm gonna go grab another round at the bar and then mingle for a minute. Kinda my job." I shrugged and gestured toward my Head Licker shirt. "You guys have a good night, alright?"

I wove my way through the packed room toward the bar, stumbling a little thanks to the moonshine.

It wasn't that I was precious about sex. Like, at all. I didn't even care about all the people at the table knowing what I'd done or hadn't done, since that was the way things went when you grew up in the Thicket. The problem was, they all had these cute, happy memories of those times and I… *didn't*. It was a painful reminder that I'd always felt like an outsider, even when the rest of the world thought I'd fit in just fine.

"Hey," a voice at my shoulder said a few minutes after I'd slid into the crowd at the bar. "You okay?"

I recognized the sandalwood scent and wished I didn't. "Of course. Mr. Perfect, right? Can't be anything *but* fine."

Mal's hand came to rest at the small of my back, and I shuddered out a breath, not realizing how badly I'd needed a comforting touch like that until it came.

"You wanna talk about it?"

I shook my head. "Nothing to say. I'm gonna get Ava some soda. Maybe we can covertly pour it into shot glasses for her."

"Don't bother," he said. "Ava was reading Alana the riot act when I left. 'Have you ever considered that for someone who didn't feel comfortable coming out until he left high school, the good old days weren't necessarily good?'"

"She said that?" My jaw dropped. "Ava did? Our Ava?"

Mal's hand rubbed in a small, soothing circle just above my waistband, too low for anyone else in the crowd to see. "Yep. Our Ava. And for what it's worth, Alana looked devastated and apologetic about it," he admitted grudgingly.

"Damn."

"And when I said I was going after you, Ethan got all sniffly and told me I was a great boyfriend. And Diesel had to explain that I was with Ava, not you."

"Ethan is..." I laughed, shaking my head.

"Smarter than people give him credit for?" Mal finished.

I looked down at him and swallowed. "You think?"

He pressed against my side, letting me feel the firm heat of his body, and my head swam. "Evidence would suggest."

"And Diesel is—"

"A nice guy who looks like he could use some friends?" Mal suggested.

"But not—"

"No."

"Oh."

Shit. His lips were so close, and I... I was *not* too drunk to remember we were in a crowded bar, damn it.

I forced myself to step away. "Maybe we could go—" I began.

"Brooks! How's our brand-new Head Licker doing?" Amos Nutter said, shaking both my shoulders. "Mayor Red! How proud are you to see your boy in this shirt?"

"Very proud! But then, I'm always proud of Brooks." My dad stepped up beside Amos and winced down at his half-drunk beer stein guiltily. "Evening, son. Your, ah, mother doesn't need to know about this, does she? She's been a little bit... overprotective recently."

I shook my head, feeling like I'd been plunged from a hot shower into a cold bath, and my poor drunk brain couldn't keep up. "As long as you're taking it easy?"

He looked relieved. "I am! I am. But a Johnson knows when he needs to wet his whistle, Brooks."

I nodded at this sage advice. Then I remembered my manners. "Dad, you know Mal, right? He was the artist in the show today with the amazing found-art sculptures? His table was super crowded the whole day. Best showing at the whole fair."

Mal blinked up at me.

"Sure, I know Mal! Doc Dalton wouldn't stop talking about him," my dad said enthusiastically. "And about your sculptures. Kept pointing out details to us, like we haven't got eyes of our own." He winked at Mal. "Anyway, I'm real excited you found your way to us, Malachi. Can't wait to see more of your work."

Mal nodded, kinda dazed, and I noticed he didn't correct my dad about his name.

My dad sighed. "Well. If you boys'll excuse us, I'd best be getting on home. Your mama's working on making a sign from an old bedsheet, and I need to make sure she doesn't go *too* crazy with her puffy paint and the glitter."

"A sign?" I repeated. "For what?"

"You know, to replace the Welcome to Licking Thicket sign that got *burgled*." Dad's eyes narrowed and his hands clenched into fists. "Or should I say *serial-burgled*."

"Calm down there, Red," Amos said. "No use getting all upset again. You know Frank's looking into it."

"I remember," I told my dad. "I'm so sorry. I totally meant to find you a more permanent sign." I ran a hand over my head, and the bar spun slightly. "I completely forgot."

"Don't you give it another thought," Dad said sincerely, but how could I not, especially once the rest of the conversation penetrated my brain?

"Wait, glitter?"

Dad shrugged. "We got a coupla empty signposts and no sign, son, and we need a sign before the bachelor auction tomorrow and the parade Saturday. Amos suggested painting letters on some cows and grazing them out in the field—"

"Now that was meant to be a *joke*," Amos insisted.

My dad shook his head and mouthed, "No it wasn't." In a louder voice he added, "The dang cows move around so much, you don't even wanna *know* what they ended up spelling." He shrugged. "Anyway, a glittery sign'll be eye-catching, right? Gotta make the best of what you've got."

I nodded slightly and returned the hug he gave me when he left.

"Hey, Brooks," Ava said, bouncing up behind us. She grinned from ear to ear and looked more cheerful than she had all week. "So, it turns out I'm not feeling well."

I blinked. "You're not?"

"She's not," Paul confirmed. He cleared his throat. "I'm gonna take her home. To rest."

"*You* are?"

"I am."

How drunk was I?

"Okay, then," I said cautiously. "I'm ready to leave if you all are."

Mal snorted. "He means they're abandoning us so they can be alone, Brooks."

"Alone," I repeated. Then I gasped as the penny dropped. "To *canoodle*?"

"Oh my God. Drunk Brooks might be my kryptonite," Mal told Ava in a hushed voice I wasn't sure if he knew I could hear.

"I'm not *drunk*," I protested. "I'm just a tipsy bit teeny. And I thought *you* were the one saying we needed to be careful and no one mattered but Ava," I accused Paul.

"You said that?" Ava whisper-squealed. She pressed her lips together. "Paul, I'm feeling really, *really* unrested right now."

"I think if all four of us walk out together, no one will know where we each end up," Paul said excitedly. "Come on. Brooks is in no shape to say goodbyes anyway."

"And given that he's in this shape, where do you propose that we spend the next couple hours?" Mal demanded, following in Ava's wake. "I'm not as drunk as Brooks, but I can't drive."

"Brooks could give you a scenic walking tour! Of Downtown Licking Thicket. And the high school. And the 24-Hour QuickMart at the end of the street," Ava pleaded, once we got to the sidewalk. "Please, Mal?"

Mal cast me a sideways glance and smirked. "I'm giving you shit, Ava. Go. We'll be fine."

"Oh, you're the bestest." She gave him a hug and let Paul hurry her down the street. "And I promise, we'll only dirty, like, *one* set of the sheets on your futon. Tops."

"Wait!" Mal wailed. "Wait, you're going to the tree house? Ava! Goddamn it."

Once they left, the sidewalk was almost silent. I squinted at the light outside Henson's, which seemed to break into a hundred smaller lights the longer I stared.

"Okay, so maybe I'm a little drunk," I admitted as Mal and I started walking down the sidewalk toward the school.

"Baby, you are *so* drunk," Mal said, but he fit his hand in mine and I thought if he kept calling me baby, then maybe it was fine.

"I didn't mean the night to work out like this, you know? I forgot."

"Forgot what?" Mal sounded amused. "How moonshine worked?"

"No. That it doesn't matter what it says on your T-shirt. That's why I went to New York," I confided. "The real reason."

Mal peered at me for a long moment. "Nope. You're gonna have to help me make this mental jump, Drunk Brooks. Your T-shirt? What?"

"Yeah." I paused to pull at the back of my shirt, which weirdly refused to twist itself around my body. "See? Head Licker."

"I see." Mal smoothed the shirt down my back, and I arched into his touch because it felt so good and... why the hell not?

"Used to say quarterback," I told him as we resumed walking. "But it still wasn't *me*."

Mal made a thoughtful noise and wrapped his arm around my waist. He fit perfectly under my arm with his head sort of against my chest, and in a startling burst of sobriety, I remembered I was wearing my good cologne and was thankful.

"Keep going," he prompted. "About football."

That would've been easier if I remembered what I'd been saying. "Uh. Well, I started playing football when I was six 'cause Coach Cosway told my dad I had a good arm. I practiced, and I got good at it, but I didn't like it. Not really. Not hardly at *all*."

"Why?"

"Why didn't I like it?"

"No. Why would you practice something you didn't like?"

"To get good at it," I repeated slowly. Pret-ty sure I wasn't the only drunk one around here if Mal couldn't see something that obvious. "Same reason I did math team and trained for the Lope and all the other stuff folks wanted me to do. When you're good at things, when you fix problems, people like you, see? Otherwise, if you're just *you*..."

"Yeah," Mal whispered. "I see."

I shrugged and took a deep breath. "There was one path for me in Licking Thicket. Or I thought so, anyway. And the whole thing made about as much sense to me as running through the woods with a bucket of milk, but I didn't know how to fix it. So I stepped off the path entirely."

"You *loped* off to New York." He snorted.

I laughed delightedly and stopped so I could press a kiss to the top of his head. "That's probably the least funny thing you've ever said."

"And yet you're laughing like I'm hilarious." He grimaced. "Drunk Brooks is drunk. But is he too drunk?"

"For driving? Yes," I said sadly.

"What about for kissing?"

The sizzle that went through my bloodstream sobered me up faster than three cups of coffee, and before Mal could blink, I had him plastered against the vinyl siding of Ladli Laghari's tax office.

"No," I said solemnly. "Definitely not too drunk for that. I've been thinking about kissing you again since the last time I kissed you, and I'm pretty sure you know it."

Mal bit his lip, and his eyes glittered with blue fire under the streetlights. "Take me to your school, then."

"My school? What for?"

His voice was a whisper of pure temptation. "Because I have a sudden need to see those bleachers."

Chapter Twelve

Mal

Even if I did happen to be under the influence of three too many Thicket Lickers or whatever the hell those shots had been called, I was still perfectly mentally clear about one thing: I wanted to wipe all of Brooks's stupid memories with Ava off the face of the planet. Hearing their friends talk about their time together was eye-opening. Maybe I hadn't fully realized they'd been an actual couple with... all the physical things that came along with it.

So I was being an immature ass.

Brooks practically tripped over the sidewalk as I yanked him away from the building he'd pressed me against. "Which way to the school?"

His grin was sweetly affectionate in a dopey buzzed way. "Why you wanna go to school when we can go to kissing instead?"

Brooks's forehead crinkled in confusion. "I mean go to the kissing place. The place to kiss... Oh! The tree house. We could do the kissing there."

"Nope. We're doing this under the bleachers. Which way?" I didn't want to think too hard about why I'd suddenly become so fixated on having him under the damned bleachers, but now that I'd gotten it into my head, I knew it was what I wanted to do.

"That way. Past Merv's."

Sure enough, we stumbled past a bright pink building with a yellow-painted sign declaring the place Merv's Merch. I vaguely remembered meeting a man earlier today named Mervin who'd asked me a lot of questions about my sculptures. He'd looked nothing like his name, though.

"Did you go to school with Mervin?" I asked.

"Mervin Baker?"

I snorted. "How the hell would I know Merv's last name? The Merv I met today. The one who owns the store. He seemed like he was our age. But how did he get the name Mervin?"

"Oh. Yeah. No. He was like six years ahead of me. I went to school with his sister Maureen. You met her at the bar."

"The lesbian couple, right?" I spotted the tall lights of the football field up ahead.

"What? No. What? There wasn't a lesbian couple at the bar. Maureen dated Butchie all through high school. He played cornerback."

I stepped in front of Brooks and faced him, causing him to look up at me in surprise. "You dated Ava all through high school," I reminded him gently.

"Yeah? So?"

"Maureen and Latonya have the same last name. Unless, of course, they're sisters, but that would be unexpected since Latonya's Black. And also because Latonya had her hand on Maureen's upper thigh in a very non-sisterly way."

Brooks looked even more confused than before. "Wait. What? Mo and Latonya? But that... but..."

I stepped back beside him and took his hand so I could keep leading him toward the bleachers while another piece of his small-town identity crumbled and fell away.

"But if they came out and got together... why... why doesn't anyone believe I'm fucking gay?" The anger came back in his voice as the tipsiness faded away.

"Babe, I think they do believe you're gay now, but ten years ago you were a guy who'd had a girlfriend all through high school. Maybe they couldn't believe they'd never suspected it, the same way you felt about Maureen. Maybe that's why they seemed unsure."

He scoffed. "I'm sure of myself. I'm very sure of myself!"

We arrived at the field, and I quickly ushered him into the hidden depths beneath the metal bleachers. Memories were pinging around in my head like hail on the hood of a car.

"Why didn't you realize they were together when Alana introduced them that way?" I asked absently, looking for just the right spot.

"Wha? Oh... uh... well, I mean... I was kind of busy looking at you."

I turned to face him, struck dumb by his words. "You were?"

Brooks's eyes softened. "You're so fucking beautiful. I lose all of my brain cells when you're around."

I sent up a prayer of thanks for the alcohol's effect on his loose lips. "You're a terrible liar."

He pouted which made me want to nibble on his lower lip more than I wanted to breathe. "Am not. Wait, no. I mean I'm not lying. You're sexy as fuck, and I can't think when you're around."

I stepped in close to him until our chests brushed. Brooks sucked in a breath. "So, you're saying you can't think right now?"

"Huh?"

I leaned in and brushed the tip of my nose against his cheek. A little whimper sound escaped his throat. I stuck out the tip of my tongue just to taste the edge of his ear. Just one taste. That was all I needed.

"Mal," he breathed.

He smelled like fancy cologne and woodsmoke, Fireball shots and clean summer sweat. I wanted to inhale him. I wanted to consume him. I wanted to strip him down and put my hands and mouth over every inch of his naked body.

"Please." His voice was thready and desperate in a way that went straight to my dick.

I thought about the last time I'd been under high school bleachers. Three big muscular assholes had shoved me down into a puddle of soda and mashed-up hotdogs that had spilled from a nearby trash can. They'd shouted and called me names while beating the shit out of me for daring to believe one of their teammates actually wanted to be with me.

I'd been caught staring at Carson Smith one afternoon while walking home past the practice field. When he'd come up to me the following day to flirt with me, I'd been shocked. As a horny teenager, I'd been completely unable to turn down his quiet offer to meet me under the bleachers after the game for a blow job. His dark creamy skin was going to feel amazing under my fingers, and I'd wondered how his pink tongue would taste against mine.

But when I'd made my way there, he and several of his

teammates had started laughing, screaming slurs at me and dragging me under the deep shadows of the bleachers. No permanent damage had been done, thanks to one of their girlfriends shrieking at them to cut it the fuck out, but it had still left me angry and full of bitter memories and resentment. High school had sucked for a gay kid who couldn't pass for straight even if he had overalls and a John Deere ball cap on.

After that, I'd pretty much given up on fully trusting people who offered me anything I truly wanted.

But here, now? Jesus. It was like finally being able to exorcise those demons by sucking face with the mother-fucking captain of the football team and watching him lose control. My hands shook with a combination of need and nerves. There was always a voice in the back of my head wondering if this would be another moment where I'd discover I'd been duped.

So maybe I was being stupidly immature, but I reveled in the fantasy as he stood there panting and begging for me. My dick was so hard it almost hurt, and I pressed it against his hip as I stood up on my toes to tease him.

"I'm going to go down on my knees for you," I said in a low voice right into his ear. "Going to suck your dick right here where anyone could catch us. Anyone at all could walk up and discover Mr. Perfect under the bleachers fucking another man's face."

Brooks's entire body shuddered, and his hands came down on my hips, pulling us tighter together. I felt the long, hard ridge of his erection against me, and I reached down to press the heel of my hand down the hard length. The groan that came out of him spurred me to shift until our cocks were grinding against each other.

"Fuck, that feels good," Brooks said before squeezing his

eyes closed and leaning his head back. His hands shook as he moved them up to my shoulders. I leaned in and kissed his neck, inhaling the summer scent of him and noticing the faint scritch of his beard on my skin.

I fumbled for the button of his fly before ripping his shorts open and reaching inside. Suddenly, Brooks's brain kicked into gear and he reached for my jeans, shoving at them wildly until they were halfway down my thighs, taking my briefs down with them.

He grumbled something at me before reaching up to grip my jaw in one hand so he could look me in the eye. "Can't fucking stand not kissing your mouth." And then he was.

Our mouths fused together in a hot, wet kiss as his hands moved down to pull our cocks together and stroke. All I could do was grab onto the front of his shirt and try not to fall down. His hands felt strong and sure. His tongue tasted cinnamony and sweet. The slide of our hot cocks together took my breath away until I was humping into his hand frantically.

"So good," he murmured against my lips. "So fucking good. Just let me..." He kissed me again and squeezed us together tighter until I was arching up into him in desperate hopes of coming. So much for my plan to suck him off—I couldn't even pull away from him enough to kneel down.

I needed him now. I needed to feel him come with me. I wanted him to have the best damned orgasm he'd ever felt so that he remembered this incredible moment here with me. It was everything I thought I'd always wanted, except it was light-years beyond anything I'd ever imagined because it was with him.

I didn't care where we were, only that we were together,

touching and exploring and sharing this singular moment of connection.

Brooks brought his free hand down to cup my balls, and that's when he noticed it. His entire body tensed, and his inquisitive hands felt all around my taint. The pressure of his touch on my guiche piercing was enough to speed me headlong into my release. I shouted into his mouth and arched into him as I came all over his hand.

"What the fuck?" he moaned, running his fingertips over the piercing again and again until I felt him come too. His hand was suddenly slick and wet with the combination of our releases before he let go. "Fuck. Oh God. Fuck."

Both of us were heaving in breaths, our cheeks pressed hotly together as if we weren't quite ready to actually separate.

"Mal, fuck," he said again.

"Yeah." I moved my face down to hide it in the side of his damp neck.

As reality shoved its way back in, I realized what a fool I'd been. If I'd sucked him off, maybe it wouldn't have been so intense. Maybe I wouldn't have seemed quite so desperate. Because that had only been the tip of the iceberg. What may have looked like a quick frot to anyone else was really a rare moment of me losing control.

And I never lost control with people I hooked up with. Ever since feeling so out of control growing up, I made sure I did sex on my terms. Hookups or dates, it didn't matter. There was never a moment I allowed myself to be at the mercy of another man. I'd learned early on that the benefit to living in a big city with an active hookup culture was getting to have sex the way I wanted it: predictable, enjoyable, and without any feelings of obligation or commitment. Even the few times I'd dated a man for more than a few months, I'd found it hard to fully let go. Trust wasn't something I came by easily, and it had been the cause of most of those short relationships dying early deaths.

"Mal, I'm so sorry," Brooks said.

My heart lurched. Was he going to tell me this had been a terrible mistake? I yanked myself back from him and started putting myself to rights. "Yeah, fine."

There was a moment of silence. I looked up to see confusion on his face. "No, you don't understand. I... I..." He blew out a breath and yanked off his Head Licker shirt before reaching out with it to wipe the cum off my stomach before I could pull my shirt down over it. His movements were careful and sweet.

He glanced up at me from under his lashes. He looked... embarrassed. "I'm sorry I came so fast. I wanted to make it good for you."

I stared at him, wondering if this was a trick. "What? Are you kidding?"

"No. I had all these plans to take it slow and kiss you and feel you and... well, I didn't really mean to hump your leg and then masturbate all over you."

I barked out a laugh, realizing he was being serious. He really did feel bad. I stepped back into his body and stood on my toes until we were nose to nose. "That was the hottest sexual experience of my life, and I've had some super fucking hot sex, Brooks Johnson."

His eyes widened, the whites visible in the shadows. "It was?"

I answered him with a soft kiss, taking my time teasing his lips with mine until I felt his arms tighten around my back. We stayed like that for a long time, simply enjoying the closeness and lazy aftermath of a good orgasm. When we finally pulled apart, Brooks met my eyes.

"I don't like thinking of you having hot sex with other men," he admitted. "Makes me want to punch shit."

I couldn't help but laugh. "You don't seem like the punching shit type of guy."

He narrowed his eyes. "I could punch shit if I wanted to."

Brooks was so fucking cute, I wanted to hump him again. I ran my hands up his chest and enjoyed the muscles under his bare skin. "Have you ever punched anyone in your life?"

"Yes. My brother, Dunn."

I laughed even louder. "Brothers don't count."

"Mpfh."

I cupped his neck. "I like that you're not the punching type," I confessed. "No one wants to date a puncher."

As soon as the words were out of my mouth, I clamped my teeth together in shock. What the fuck had I just said?

"Date, huh?" He gave me a teasing smirk, knowing full well how mortified I was for the slip.

"Never mind."

Brooks leaned in and dragged his lips along the shell of my ear before murmuring, "Let me walk you home, sweetheart."

I nodded since using my mouth for words would have required oxygen I didn't have at the moment.

We walked in easy silence, holding hands like high school sweethearts until we finally arrived at the end of the Iveys' driveway.

"Sleep well, Malachi," Brooks said after a long string of good-night kisses.

"Mm-hm."

But I didn't. My head was too full of him, and I had work to do.

Chapter Thirteen

Brooks

You know how some mornings you wake up to the warmth of the sun on your face and the sound of birdsong in the air, and the second your eyes open to greet the day, you feel profoundly grateful for all the beautiful things in your life that led you to this place?

Yeah, me neither. Fuck no. And especially not this day.

I woke up Friday morning, sprawled facedown on the lumpy pullout with a mouth full of cotton and a headache that pulsed in counterpoint to my heartbeat. The sun was shining, alright, and the fucking songbirds were out in full force, but I would have paid someone my entire savings to shut the blinds I'd somehow forgotten to shut and chase the birds away with a broom. I was still in my shorts from the night before, but I was naked from the waist up, and instead of my cologne, I smelled like green grass, which was fucking weird because I hadn't been around any...

Oh.

Oh, yes I *had*. The whole evening came rushing back in a single second—Mal and me playing drinking games with Alana and the others, Mal following when I left the table,

Mal leading me to the bleachers, Mal kissing me and touching me and making me beg. Mal, who had a piercing that was the hottest thing I'd ever felt and I'd give anything to see. Mal, who'd said we were *dating* and made my heart skip like Snow White through the fucking forest. Mal, who overloaded every one of my senses and made me want to realign all of my priorities...

Mal, who'd be going home to Los Angeles in two days, probably never to be seen again, unless I figured out a way to relocate New York to the West Coast or, equally impossibly, convinced the man to do something insane like move his welding kit into the Brooklyn one-bed of a guy he'd known less than a week.

In a lifetime of fixing problems, this felt like the biggest one I'd ever tried to solve, and I had exactly two days to do it, while also still working on the presentation that was going to make or break my career.

No pressure or anything.

I groaned softly and someone very close to me sighed.

My eyes flew open, and I scrambled back on the bed, making a squawking noise not unlike a violated chicken. "What the hell?" I demanded blearily.

"That's a bad word, Uncle B." Payton stood by the side of the bed and stared down at me in solemn judgment. "I didn't wake you," she informed me.

"Uh. Okay?" I closed one eye and squinted at her.

"*Technically*, Gamma said I was not to come in here and get my art supplies because I'd disturb you while you were sleeping. Only it's been two *Zhuzhus* and a *Bizzaard-vark* and you still weren't awake." Her little mouth pinched to one side, suggesting I'd failed her somehow.

"I..." My voice broke and I cleared my throat. "I have no idea what that means, kiddo."

"Baby shows Myleigh's watching." She looked distinctly unimpressed. "Mama said I have to watch 'em, too, because today's Myleigh's turn to pick shows. And Gamma said it's my job because big siblings have big responsibilities. And Mama said that's bull puckey, and didn't Gamma learn anything when Brooks moved to New York? And Gamma said, 'Oh, Gracie.' And what's bull puckey, Uncle B?"

"I don't..." I shook my head, completely mystified. I needed way more caffeine to handle this conversation.

"So, anyway, I came in here just so I could know exactly when you woke up. And also because it's, like, *super* boring out in the living room, with Gamma crying and stuff. So can I get my supplies? Since you're awake now, I mean?"

"Wait, Gamma's crying?" I repeated, sitting up and forcing both eyes open again as panic made my hangover recede. "About what?"

Payton flopped back onto the foot of the bed like she was getting ready to make a snow angel. "About the tragedy. That's why we came-d over. Gamma was sad and called Mama."

"Sh...sugar babies!" I corrected, jumping off the bed. "What tragedy? Is it Grandpa? Is he okay?"

"Duh." Payton kicked her heels against the bed leg. "'Course he's okay. He was out in the kitchen a minute ago, pouring his medicine tea into Gamma's houseplant when he thinks she's not looking. And she keeps refilling his cup when she thinks *he's* not looking. Grown-ups are so weird."

I sat back down heavily in relief. "That's the truth."

"Grandpa told Gamma, 'Calm down, Cindy Ann, or you'll wake Brooks. Plenty of time to tell him the news.' But you woke up all by yourself, didn't you, Uncle B?" She blinked at me innocently.

I snorted. "Sure, honey. All by myself."

"And," the little con artist continued, "Gamma said, 'Poor Brooks is gonna be *devastated* when he hears.' And Mama said she thought you were more likely to be tickled off 'cause it means more work for the Lickin'. What's tickled off?"

"*Ticked* off, kiddo. It means angry."

"Oh. So which are you? Devastated or tickled?"

"Neither yet." And, please God, neither *at all*. "I should probably get up and find out what happened, huh? Don't suppose you know what it was?"

I wasn't too worried. My mother could out-drama Meryl Streep any day of the week, and I figured if it were a real emergency, someone would have woken me.

Payton shrugged. "All I know is Gamma said today is a day of mourning for all of Tennessee. But doesn't Tennessee have mornings every day, Uncle B?"

I snorted, suddenly understanding why my sister sometimes looked shell-shocked. Her kid was too smart by half.

"You know what? If you let me grab my clothes and shower, you can have this room to yourself for the whole day."

Payton's face screwed up. "No Myleigh?"

"Nope."

Payton was gone before I could blink an eye, and I was left with the remnants of a headache and a still-warm bed. I looked around the room, hoping some clean clothes would fly out of my suitcase and a cup of coffee would magic itself into my hands. I felt the overwhelming desire to hear Mal's voice just to center myself. Last night seemed like a really long time ago.

I reached for my phone to call him... which was when I realized I didn't have his number. I'd given *him* a scrap of paper with my number on it the other day, but he'd never used it or given me his digits in return.

What the hell was wrong with me? I'd hooked up with the man, I was low-key dreaming up ways to see him after leaving the Thicket, but I couldn't get in touch with him? *Priorities, Brooks.*

I grabbed a pair of jeans and yet another Head Licker shirt, took a second to make sure my suit for the bachelor auction tonight was hanging crease-free in the closet, gave one last longing look to the bed, and forced myself into the shower. It was Friday, which meant I had approximately twenty-seven appearances around town on my docket that morning, a presentation to put together in the next couple of days, a really hot guy to hunt down, and some tragedy in the kitchen to manage. I didn't have time to rest.

I felt a little more human when I was clean, and I headed down the hall for coffee. The television was on in the den, and I heard Gracie in there talking to Payton and Myleigh. I expected to find my mom in the kitchen, stress-brewing vats of sweet tea, which was her usual response in a crisis, but she was nowhere to be found. Instead, the room was occupied by my ex-girlfriend, who leaned against the counter looking fresh as a daisy in a white dress, yellow shoes, and a cheerleader ponytail... and my fake boyfriend, who was all up in her personal space.

"Ava Marie!" I gasped, and Ava straightened guiltily before she realized it was me.

Her pretty eyes narrowed on me. "Brooks Johnson, don't you have some moonshine and Fuzzy Thickets to sleep off?"

I grinned as I crossed to the coffeepot. I'd always appreciated Ava's sassiness, but now I felt like I could enjoy it *more* since it wasn't tangled up in all those things I'd thought I was supposed to feel for her and *didn't*.

"Did that, mostly. I have to meet Coach Cosway on the football field by nine to judge the football throw." While trying very hard not to be distracted by memories of what had happened under the bleachers the night before. "Then I have to hand out blue ribbons at the craft fair. So, what's this big drama Payton told me about?"

Paul shrugged. "Don't look at me. I was working until Ava texted she and her mom were on their way over. You might recall that work is that thing we do on Fridays when we're *not* sleeping off moonshine—"

"Yeah, yeah." I turned to Ava. "What do *you* know?"

"Nothing." I gave her a disbelieving look, since her mother was as big a gossip as my own, and she pursed her lips. "If you must know, my mother and I aren't speaking to each other at present. I was eating a donut at Wally's this morning when she informed me that white was not a very *slimming color* on me." She sniffed and ran a hand down the front of her dress. "Do I look... fat?" she asked Paul.

"You look *beautiful*," he whispered with such sincerity that even *I* went "*Awww.*" On the inside, of course.

But when it looked like Ava was moving closer and preparing to suck his face off in gratitude, I interrupted.

"Is it possible for a person to catch morning sickness?" I asked no one in particular, pressing a hand to my stomach. "I suddenly feel queasy..."

"Hush your mouth, Brooks!" Ava hiss-whispered, stepping away from Paul, who rolled his eyes behind his glasses. "My mother just went to load a box of bidding paddles for the auction into your mother's car, and our dads ran out to do an errand. They'll all be back any minute."

"Then it's probably good if she doesn't walk in on me

watching you playing tonsil tennis with the love of my life, right?" I said mildly. "Unless you're ready to come clean about the whole thing?"

I wasn't sure *I* was, but I'd follow her lead.

"No." Ava exhaled and rubbed a hand over her forehead. "Definitely not. I don't think. Or... I dunno. Maybe? The whole thing is so complicated."

That was for damn sure. "So, um, speaking of which... where's Malachi this morning?"

Paul laughed. "Super-smooth segue, bro. Ten out of ten casual stars."

I flipped him off.

"He was asleep when my mom and I left to come over here and wouldn't wake up, even for Dove chocolates." Ava's eyes danced. "And those are his favorite. He was up pretty late, you know. I had a dozen 3:00 a.m. texts on my phone when I woke up, and half of them started with the word *Brooks*."

"Oh, yeah?" I tried for casual again, but Paul's expression said I'd failed once more. Mal had seemed fine when I dropped him off. Hadn't he? Had I been too tipsy to remember? "As it happens, I uh... might possibly have neglected to get his phone number last night at the bar? So could you maybe..."

Ava tapped her lip thoughtfully. "Mmm. Not sure I should give Mal's contact information to a man who refers to me kissing my boyfriend as *tonsil tennis*." She laid a proprietary arm on Paul's chest while his eyes widened in a euphoric daze. His hand absently searched his pocket for his inhaler.

"Boyfriend?" he breathed.

"Hey! Paul was *my* boyfriend before you took him to your tree house last night!" I reminded her, propping my forearm on Paul's shoulder. "Homewrecker."

"Oh my God, I feel so objectified!" Paul exclaimed. "Am I just a hunk of meat to you people? A bone for you to fight over?"

"Oh, honey," Ava began, frowning worriedly. "I'm so sorry—"

"Are you kidding? It's fucking awesome!" Paul said gleefully, nudging up his glasses and patting down his thinning hair. "I've been waiting my whole life for this. Don't stop now!"

Ava and I looked at each other and snickered.

Ava held out her hand. "Phone," she demanded.

I handed it over. Then I eyed Paul, who looked like breathing in Ava's exhaled air was the greatest joy of his existence. For the first time ever, I was a little jealous of him. He and Ava still had plenty of hurdles, but at least they knew they were on the same page, more or less. After what Ava had said, I was starting to wonder if Mal and I were.

"So, lover boy." I nudged Paul's arm. "Have you heard back from Carlin about the graphics?"

"I did." Paul winced and moved away from Ava just far enough to grab his own coffee mug. "Carlin also gave me an earful about Pamela. Turns out Pamela got tired of us putting her off about the presentation and went directly to Carlin to learn about what we're doing."

My heart beat double time. "And?"

Paul stretched his neck. "She's not exactly thrilled. The adjectives I heard were *childish* and *simplistic*."

"Shit. But General Partridge will love them! At least I *think* he will."

"But he won't get to see them if Pamela overrides you, buddy," he said sadly. "She didn't say it in so many words, but Carlin thinks she's giving the project back to Kale."

"What? So he can create some kind of *Walking Dead*-themed barbecue sauce campaign?" I really *did* feel queasy suddenly, and ridiculous as it sounded since I'd known the man less than a week, I wished Mal were with me. I just felt *better* when he was around. Things made sense.

Ava handed me back my phone, and I immediately typed out a message.

Me: Hey. It's Brooks. Just checking in. How are you?

That sounded casual, right? But, like, attentive? The gaps in my dating experience were so wide, I could feel a breeze blow through them.

"You don't have to look so worried. He was alive and well. Just really tired," Ava said airily. "As you'd expect."

"'Cause he was up all night texting you about me," I said dubiously. "Right."

"You... you really have no idea what I'm talking about, do you?" Her eyes were wide and excited. "He didn't tell you about the sign?"

"The signs of what?" The signs he wanted to be with me? The signs he was so freaked-out he was up all night?

"Not *signs*, silly, the—"

"Oh, Brooks, thank goodness!" My mother ran in the back door and wrapped me in a painfully tight embrace. "You'll never believe what happened."

"It's a dark day for the Thicket," Mrs. Ivey intoned, following her in more slowly.

"Never in my wildest imaginings..." Mama broke off with a wet sniffle.

"What?" I demanded. If someone didn't finish telling me *something*, I was gonna lose my mind.

"Susie Dupree," Mrs. Ivey began in a hushed tone. "Of Susie Dupree's Deluxe Barbecue. She's.... she's...."

"Dead?" I whispered.

"Out of business," my mother sobbed at the same moment.

"Wait, what?" I looked back and forth between the two women.

"Oh, for heaven's sake." Gracie appeared in the doorway from the living room, rolling her eyes. "Turns out Miss Susie's a thief, as well as a purveyor of mediocre barbecue, Brooks, that's all."

"Grace Mawbry!" Mama gasped. "I don't even know who you are right now!"

"Probably because my whole life has been a lie, Mama," Gracie said solemnly, leaning back against the doorframe. "According to the *Bovine Beacon*, Miss Susie's super-secret sauce recipe was actually Beulah Love's recipe, which was printed in a church cookbook back in 1983—"

"Allegedly!" Mrs. Ivey interjected.

"And you know what that means, right?" Grace continued without missing a beat.

"It means there's an injunction and all the restaurants are *closed*," Mama wailed. "Closed until further notice, Brooks, when they were supposed to provide us with dinner for tomorrow night!"

Oh, *damn.*

"Yeah, yeah." Grace strode across the room and laid a hand on my shoulder. "But more importantly? It means every time we thought we were eating Dupree's Deluxe..." She leaned toward me. "We were actually eating *Love Sauce.*"

I snickered and Gracie winked. I really did love my

sister. "I begin to see how Payton got so terrifying," I told her.

"Brooks," Paul breathed. He reached over and whacked me in the arm. "Partridge Pit's market share is gonna explode. You and I need to get on this! If we call Pamela now, we can—"

"Brooks *needs*," my mother corrected, "to do his job as Head Licker and figure out a new plan for dinner tomorrow night! Susie Dupree's Deluxe has provided dinner at cost for thirty-three years! Half the ticket sales are already tied up in the deposit, and all her funds have been frozen. Your father really shouldn't be upset in his condition, Brooks—"

"Brooks needs to get out to the football field," Mrs. Ivey said, checking her watch. "Coach Cosway'll be wondering where you are, honey."

I blew out a breath and ran both hands through my hair. A hundred things "Brooks needed" to do, and only one thing I *wanted* to do, namely finding Mal and kissing the shit out of him. But that was going to have to wait.

"Brooks *needs* to delegate," Gracie said in a no-nonsense tone. "And he needs some volunteers." She held up her hand.

Surprisingly, Ava held up hers too. "I'll help however I can. But you know, I think you guys are missing a pretty obvious solution," she offered.

"Ava, honey," Mrs. Ivey began dismissively.

"Let her talk. Ava has great ideas," Paul said stoutly, standing at Ava's shoulder.

Ava blushed just a little and bit her lip. "Well... General Partridge," she said. "Since y'all are working on his ad campaign, Paul, couldn't you and Brooks maybe pull in a favor? Ask him to cater this real cheap in exchange for good publicity?"

"Brooks Johnson," Mama began in a hushed voice. "You're working for… for…"

"For the guy who could save our bacon in this whole fiasco?" Gracie said excitedly. "Holy crap! Do you think he'd do it, Brooks?"

"I…" I looked at Paul, who gave me a wide-eyed shrug. "I think he might? He's a really nice guy. He was very sympathetic when I told him about Dad's heart condition. Told me to take as long as I needed."

"I'll call his office," Paul said, reaching for his phone and stepping to the far side of the kitchen.

My mother frowned. "Well. *Hmph.* I suppose he can't be all bad, then."

"Did you hear that, Brooks?" Gracie shook my shoulder. "Miracles are happening right in this kitchen. Where is Dunn when we need him?"

"Hush, Gracie," Mama chided. "I can admit when I'm wrong." She looked from me to Ava to Paul. "And I'm starting to think I've been wrong about a lot of things."

I glanced down at my phone. Still no reply from Mal.

Which was fine. Of course it was! He was *sleeping.*

And it was bizarre to feel his absence like a sore tooth, anyway.

Still, I unlocked the phone and typed.

Me: *Your fake girlfriend just saved the day and you missed it. You awake yet?*

"It's eight forty," Mrs. Ivey said worriedly. "Brooks, honey, the kids will be waiting at the field."

Shit. Right. I slid my phone away. "Okay, I'll—"

"I'll do it!" Gracie volunteered. "After all, I had a better throwing arm than Brooks once upon a time."

"Come on. We were like six and five then," I scoffed.

"So you admit it!" Gracie winked. "Give me one of your extra Head Licker shirts. Mama, can you watch the girls?"

"Well, of course I can, but tradition says—"

"And Paul and I will handle the craft fair," Ava said, grabbing Paul's forearm as he came back to the table. "Paul is a *genius* with handicrafts."

"How would you know—?" Mrs. Ivey began.

"Best balsa wood bridge construction at Surprise Lake Camp three years running," Paul confirmed, wiggling his fingers. "I'm kind of a Renaissance man. And Brooks, the General can talk to you anytime before noon, in person or by phone, just let his assistant know. It's a long drive—"

"But it'll have to be in person," I decided with a sigh. I had zero desire to drive two hours each way for this meeting, but that was the right way to do things, and what I wanted wasn't important.

I changed into my suit and brushed my hair carefully under Payton's watchful eye.

"You look nice, Uncle B," she pronounced when I was finished and she led me back to the kitchen.

I hoped so. I was about to ask for a favor from a guy my boss was going to screw over by providing him with a subpar campaign, unless I could figure out a way to fix that too.

One crisis at a time, Johnson.

"Payton's right," my mother said, looking me over critically. "You look terrific."

"You'll knock 'em dead, Big Daddy," Paul said with a wink.

"I just wish..." Mama sighed. "Tradition states that the Head Licker—"

"Gets to decide what the right traditions are, Mrs. Johnson," Ava piped up. "There's more than one right way to do almost everything."

I gave her a grateful smile. I wasn't sure I believed her, but I liked that she'd said it.

"So, what were you saying earlier?" I demanded as I walked out with her and Paul. "About, um... Mal? And me not seeing the signs?"

"Hmm? Oh, that. Never mind. I'll let it be a surprise," Ava said.

"Thanks bunches. You know, he's not replying to any of my texts. Is he upset, or..."

"I told you, he was sleeping. And if he's not sleeping, he's welding something in my dad's barn and isn't looking at his phone. It's a bad habit of his. You know, I think I kinda like this new side of you, Mr. Perfect." Ava's grin took the sting out of her words... more or less. "It's cute to see you worrying and overthinking."

"Ava, I have never *not* overthought things."

"Yes, but now you're letting people *see* it, and you didn't before. It's cute."

"Thanks again," I said wryly. "You're such a good friend."

"I really am," she singsonged. Then she threw me a wink. "I'll prove it to you tonight. Now go do what you've gotta do. You're taking Bellevue Road, right?"

"Is there another way to the highway?" I demanded. "Obviously."

"Perfect!" she chirped.

I sighed as I climbed into my blazing hot car and headed through town and out toward the highway.

Maybe I could text Mal again. Or maybe I could call him.

Or maybe I should just leave well enough alone and play it cool.

Traffic slowed to a crawl in both directions once I turned onto Bellevue. At first I rolled my eyes, thinking only *I* could manage to get caught in a traffic jam in Licking Thicket, but then I noticed that the traffic was only slow in the area by the field where the Welcome to Licking Thicket sign usually stood.

I wondered what crazy sign solution my mom had finally come up with to cause this much of a stir. I couldn't make out the sign from my angle, since it was hidden by trees, but judging by the way people hung out of their cars to take pictures, either my mom had way overdone the puff paint and glitter, or Amos Nutter's alphabet cows had rearranged themselves to spell out something pornographic.

I sighed as the guilt from last night came rushing back. I should have taken the time to find a new sign, rather than spending my days chasing after Mal. I should have fixed this. Maybe then...

My thoughts flatlined the second the sign came into view. I jammed on the brakes and veered to the side of the road, ignoring all the people who honked at me. I stared at the sign in disbelief.

As it turned out, there wasn't a single trace of glitter involved, and the sign wasn't really a *sign* at all... it was a goddamn sculpture.

The background of the piece was a rectangle of corrugated metal—the kind found on every barn roof here in town. Its blue paint had long ago started to rust, giving it dimension and permanence. The words Welcome to Licking Thicket were spelled out in a bunch of old tools—everything from hoes to hammers, barbecue tongs to marching band instruments, and even something that looked like the handle off a kids' wagon—welded to the background. And below the words was a *cow*—a cow made of ten different kinds of metal spots and an old license plate, with a familiar triangular tractor seat for a head and a kick bar forming its horns, a wire brush for a tail, and a milker for its udders.

And next to it all, like the period at the end of a sentence, was my own damn trophy from the last year I'd won the Lope—a trophy I'd given Ava as a memento a decade ago that I'd figured she'd destroyed, but which Mal had found and redeemed and made a part of the Thicket again.

In short, it was insane... and insanely beautiful.

Every component of the sculpture was necessary; everything was decorative and *nothing* was; every piece was an unlikely, integral part of the whole. It was ridiculous and over-the-top, maybe, when you looked at it from a distance, but up close, it was a melding of a whole bunch of semi-useful things into something better than any of them could ever have been on their own.

It was the embodiment of Licking Thicket. One man's pile of junk and another man's work of art.

I stared at it for a long minute with my jaw hanging open, and then I took out my phone and dialed a number.

"General Partridge?" I said a few minutes later when his assistant connected me. "Sir, I need a huge favor. Let me explain."

Ten minutes after *that*, the General had not merely given us a good deal, he'd insisted on sponsoring the entire dinner dance *for free*. And agreed to be a guest of honor in the parade, to boot.

"I respect the hell out of a man who's committed to his family and his town, Brooks. I'm happy to help out. And I'm real eager to see what you've been cookin' up for my campaign too. Don't suppose you could drop by today?"

"I'd love to, sir," I said without hesitation. "But I can't today."

For once, there was no question in my mind about what and *who* my priority was. I knew *exactly* where I needed to be. And it just so happened to be exactly where I *wanted* to be, also.

"I can give you a sneak peek tomorrow, though," I said, suddenly realizing the best way to placate the General would also help me do an end-run around Pamela. It wasn't the sort of thing fair-and-moral Brooks Johnson would usually do, but I had a feeling it would be effective. "Maybe you can give me five minutes before the parade?"

"Tomorrow," the General agreed. "I'll see you then."

I slid the phone away and swallowed, still staring at the sign.

Over and over again that week, I'd been shocked by the way Mal saw the *real* me—the responsibility and commitment I felt to the town, my need to do everything right, my frustration at not fitting in.

But looking at this piece of sculpture no one else in the world could have created, I realized it wasn't just me he saw, it was all of Licking Thicket. Everything that made it crazy. Everything that made it *home*. And in doing so, Mal had shown me and all of us what made *him* so freakin' special.

Now I needed to make sure he believed it too.

Chapter Fourteen

Mal

I'D ONLY MANAGED to catch an hour of sleep before the sun shined directly into my face through the tree house window and woke me back up. As soon as I awoke, my brain began spinning with too many thoughts, and I knew it was pointless to try and go back to sleep. Plus, I needed to clean up my mess in Mr. Ivey's workshop before he wandered in there and thought he'd been ransacked.

After helping myself to a shower, a couple of granola bars from the Iveys' pantry, and a big icy refill for my water bottle, I made my way back out into the morning sunshine. It was already hot as fuck which was another reason I knew it was pointless to try and keep sleeping in the tree house. Unfortunately for me, the guest accommodations didn't boast any air-conditioning amenities, which meant my only hope of catching a bit more sleep later today would be begging Ava to sneak me into her bedroom for a nap.

I greeted a few cows gazing through the fence at me as I made my way to the workshop and slid open the big barn doors. Everything was exactly as I'd left it a couple of hours before. The coppery tang of metal was still heavy in the air, and seeing the remnants of my work made me unusually proud.

As I began putting tools away, I thought of Brooks for the millionth time, the way he felt when he'd held me close, the way he'd sounded when he'd begged for release, and the intense way he'd looked at me when he'd told me how much he'd wanted to kiss me...

I moved through my tasks with my head firmly lost in the events of the previous night, not realizing until it was too late that someone had entered the workshop.

I jumped and let out a decidedly unmanly squawk when someone grabbed me and shoved me back against the rough wood of the wall. My heart slammed in my chest with fear before I realized it was Brooks.

And then it slammed in my chest with excitement.

Without a word, Brooks shoved a knee between my legs and clasped the front of my neck in one big hand, pinning my head to the barn wall and forcing me to look at him. It was a kind of physical aggression I'd never even considered from someone as kind as Brooks, but it was pushing all of my *yes-please* buttons and ringing all of my *take-me-now* bells. The piercing way he looked into my eyes made me instantly hard.

"Hi," I breathed. I felt my throat move against the clutch of his grip. My dick hammered against the front of my pants.

"The sign." His voice was rough and almost broken, and then he leaned in and took my mouth with his. It was harsh and possessive, commanding and unexpected. But Jesus fucking Christ was it the hottest moment of my life.

I wanted him. Desperately.

"For you," I managed to say between kisses.

"Need you," he said against my lips. "Want you so much."

"Take me. Have me. Please." I wasn't above begging. My brain wasn't even really aware of what was going on, but every instinct in my body was desperate to have Brooks inside me, around me, over and above me. I wanted him— needed him—everywhere.

He flipped me around until I faced the wall. My hands came up to keep me from scratching my face against the rough wooden planks, but I shoved my ass back at him to make sure he knew I was completely on board with what- ever the hell he had in mind.

Brooks fumbled at the front of my pants, muttering complaints about buttons, zippers, barn doors not having locks, and bubble butts that should be illegal. I wanted to laugh, but I was too busy trying to catch my breath. It was like something out of a porn scene, except I actually had feelings for him. Big feelings.

"Please," I said again, to make sure he knew I was all in.

He pressed his body against me, and the roughness of his clothes against the bare skin of my ass made me even harder. "I always imagined the first time we had sex would be in a bed. Do you—"

"Stop talking and fuck me into this wall."

He surged his hard cock into the cleft of my ass, making me whimper. "Less clothes," I begged.

I felt him step back for a brief moment, and then there were cool slick fingers seeking my hole. "Oh fuck," I breathed against my arm. "I love a man who's prepared."

"Tell me if—"

I nodded. "I will, I will, just go."

His lips brushed against the edge of my ear, his breath hot against my neck. "I've never wanted anyone as much as I want you." His words were deep and quiet, just for me, and I squeezed my eyes closed to help remember them. I wondered if I'd ever hear something like that again and if I'd ever believe it as much as I believed it now, with him.

Brooks's finger slid inside, and then two. My breathing ticked up even more, and I must have made some whimpering sounds because his free hand came up and covered my mouth. I hadn't realized how loud I was being.

"Don't want company," he murmured into my ear. "Just us. Just you and me."

His voice took on the rhythm of his fingers as they pumped in and out and stretched me open. I fell into a kind of trance, feeling him against me and inside me, listening to the cadence of his newly familiar voice followed by the soft crinkle of a condom being opened.

"Brooks," I whispered, reaching back with one arm to hold him tightly against me.

"I'm here." He pressed the side of his face against mine for a beat before turning and kissing me tenderly. "Deep breath, sweetness."

I did as he said and inhaled. As soon as I began letting out my breath, he slid the tip of his cock in and entered me in short thrusts. The stretching sensation reminded me of just how long it had been since I'd had anal sex. It wasn't something I did on a whim with a hookup, and normally I would have been a little horrified at my lack of prep. But this was Brooks, and for some reason that made it all okay. Better than okay. I needed him inside me like I needed air to breathe.

My groan added to the sounds of our panting breaths and the smack of his skin against my ass as his thrusting picked up speed. It was filthy and carnal, raw and crude, and it was a million of my fantasies wrapped up and made real.

"Fuck, fuck," I gasped as he changed the angle just right. "B-Brooks, fuck."

Once he got up a good rhythm, one of his arms wrapped around my chest like a steel band while the other hand gripped my chin and held my head at an angle so he could devour my mouth.

I kept my fists clenched against the wall, but I was pressed so hard against it, my forearms would likely have scratches and splinters from the wood. I didn't care. Every single mark on my body from this encounter would be appreciated later as a memento of this wild moment in time.

"So fucking tight, Jesus." Brooks kept his mouth on mine as he groaned. "*Malachi.*"

"Make me come," I begged.

He let go of my face and moved his hand down to grip my dick. I let out a cry as he squeezed just right and began stroking me.

"Want you to spill all over this barn wall," he said into my ear. "Want to feel you let go, but I want to keep fucking you forever. You feel so good. So fucking good."

The rumble of his voice in my ear, the scent of our combined sweat in my nose, and the feel of his tight grip on my dick all came together to get me there.

"Oh God," I cried just before coming all over his hand. I banged the barn wall with my fist to keep from screaming some more as my body clenched around him.

Brooks made a kind of choking sound as he slammed into me for the final time and held me tight through his own orgasm.

After our bodies finished shuddering, but before we'd

caught our breath, I let out a huff of laughter. "And here I thought things were going to be awkward."

Brooks laughed against the back of my neck, and his arms tightened around me as he pressed a kiss to my nape. "God, you're sexy." He gently pulled out and squeezed my shoulder with a murmured "Hold on" while he found somewhere to dispose of the condom. When he got back to me, he was carrying a clean shop rag. He wiped me down tenderly with a sweet half-smile on his lips.

"Thanks," I said. Honestly, I couldn't remember if anyone had ever been so sweet with me after sex. It left me feeling exposed and vulnerable, like I was an animal dead asleep with my belly pointing straight up to a sky infested with buzzards.

"I intended to come here and thank you," he said while he pulled my pants and underwear back up and fastened everything. "But then I saw you there, leaning over the damned workbench with your sexy ass sticking out. Jesus. Why is it that my good intentions go out the window and I lose my mind whenever I'm around you?"

I dropped my shoulders and looked down at my feet, trying hard not to think about whether or not that meant that Brooks wouldn't have wanted to have sex with me had he been in his right mind.

He tilted my chin up until I was looking at him again. "I lose my mind in the best way, Mal. The kind of way that makes me crave being near you. I couldn't stop thinking about you from the moment I left you last night until I fell asleep, and you were the first thing on my mind the moment I woke up this morning. I'm already missing you again and I haven't even left."

I ran my hands up his broad chest and around his neck, taking a big step forward until we were close enough that I could breathe again. This wasn't real, I knew it wasn't. But, God, how I wanted to pretend for just a minute.

I leaned my head against his shoulder and tucked my nose into his neck, seeking more of his expensive scent. It was mixed with coffee and now metal shavings, and it was enough to almost make my dick hard again.

"That sign," he said again, as if we hadn't just stopped long enough for a hard fuck against the wall in Mr. Ivey's workshop. Brooks cleared his throat. "Mal... I don't... I don't even know what to say. How... how..." He let out a breath and ran his fingers through my hair before tilting my head up again so I could see him. "How did you do that? Why? Why did you?"

I shrugged and tried hiding in the safety of his neck again, but he wouldn't let me.

"It's incredible. I can't even begin to tell you how amazing it is, and how..." His voice trailed off, rough with emotion. "How special you are for doing that for the people of this town."

I wanted to laugh. While I was quickly coming to appreciate and even enjoy the people of Licking Thicket, I hadn't done it for them. I'd done it for Brooks. Because seeing the stress on his face when everyone mentioned how much the missing sign upset his dad had been too much for me. He deserved an easy win. He deserved to have not another single thing more added to his plate this week.

"It's permanent. I hope that's okay. It's reinforced with rebar that's buried in cement deep in the ground. The cement takes a while to cure, but it should be fine. At least... that's what the package said. Um, that's why that ugly plastic tarp is around the base. That's part of the curing process for the concrete, but it can come off after a few days.

Five, I think is what it said." Did I sound like I was talking nonsense? It felt like it.

"How the hell did you do all of that so fast, and by yourself?"

"Well, it wasn't easy finding rebar at four in the morning, but Diesel is a light sleeper, so that helped."

I felt Brooks's body stiffen up at the mention of the junkyard owner's name. "Oh. That's good. That you had help, I mean."

His face had gone into a neutral zone, and suddenly I remembered his petty jealousy at the junkyard the other day. I grinned up at him. "Please tell me this is you being possessive. No one has ever given enough of a shit to pee around me before."

He opened his mouth to respond but then seemed to stop while he fully absorbed what I'd said. "No one has ever acted jealous about you before? How's that possible?"

I felt a little embarrassed. "I don't really date that much, so..."

"Mal. Even if I only had you in my arms for the length of one dance at a club, I think I'd growl and snap at any other man who even looked at you long enough to take your drink order."

I stared at him, my heart puffing up like some kind of cheeseball cartoon. Maybe I wasn't supposed to want someone to be snarly jealous over me, but I totally did. "I promise Diesel only helped me deliver and install the sign," I teased. "And I only touched his junk a little."

His face flushed and his eyes narrowed. It was a very new and interesting look on the usually put-together ad executive. Before smoke started coming out of his ears, I leaned up and kissed him, nipping his bottom lip between my teeth and saying, "Old metal parts, babe. What kind of junk did you think I meant?"

"Har, har." He kissed me back and held me so tightly, my feet started coming off the ground. Before I had a chance to lift my legs up and wrap them around his waist, someone behind me cleared their throat.

We jumped apart like someone had thrown a bucket of cold water on us. Thank God we had our clothes back on and all put together.

Brooks's brother, Dunn, stood in the open doorway with his thick arms crossed in front of his chest and a bewildered expression on his face. "Brooks? I thought that was your car outside. Exactly what am I looking at right now?"

I felt all the blood drain down to my toes and slither into the dusty barn floor.

"Uh. The thing is, Dunn..." Brooks began. He looked at me blankly.

"The thing is," I repeated. "Brooks was, um... assisting me."

I hated lying, but I didn't know how to tell the truth without betraying my best friend.

"Oh, he was assisting you!" Dunn said, nodding in understanding. "Right, right. No, that makes sense."

I breathed a sigh of relief.

Then Dunn tilted his head to one side. "Assisting you... with his arms wrapped around you, huh?"

Shit. "I... uh... Yes. Funny thing, actually..."

"He was choking," Brooks said with absolute conviction. "I was saving his life."

I wanted to punch him in the shoulder and tell him to shut up, but instead I nodded slowly. "It all happened so fast. It was... terrifying?"

"I bet!" Dunn's eyes widened. "Wow. That's just

incredible, Brooks. Absolutely incredible. I mean, you know I've always looked up to you, since you're my big brother and all, but now... you're kinda my hero."

"I, ah..." Brooks shuffled guiltily from one foot to the other. "I wouldn't go that far, Dunn."

"Oh, I would," Dunn said solemnly, his green eyes shining. "I'd go even further than that. I have never in my life heard such a cockamamie, bald-faced lie."

"Wait, what?" I sputtered.

"You have stones of galvanized *steel*, Brooks Johnson. I'm proud to know you." Dunn swiped a finger under his eye like he was wiping away a tear.

"But I'm not... I wasn't..." Brooks stammered, unable to go further.

"Bro, the only thing Mal was choking on was your *tongue*." His laughter filled the barn. "Now, mind you, when we saw the sign on our way back from the livestock exhibition, I was pretty close to planting one on Mal, myself, next time I saw him, and frankly so was Mr. Ivey. But I guess now he doesn't have to worry that he's been having impure thoughts about his future son-in-law, at least." He shot me a wink.

I swallowed. "The thing is, Dunn, Ava and I—"

"Are none of my business," Dunn said, his expression turning serious. "Just like Ava grinning at Brooks's boyfriend over at the football field a few minutes ago like he walked on water isn't my business. And *no*, I don't think Mr. Ivey noticed, and I'm not gonna tell him."

"Thank you," I whispered.

"Nah. Keeping my mouth shut's not something to thank me for. But that sign..." He shook his head. "I don't know how to thank you enough for that. My dad... he's a good guy, Mal. Real responsible, just like Brooks. And this town is like his fourth child. So, when shit goes wrong, like those signs being stolen, he worries like a father would." He hooked his thumbs in his pockets. "That art piece you created for us is beautiful. It's something the whole Thicket can be proud of for generations. But more than that, you took a weight off my old man's mind, and that means you took a weight off my mind too. And Brooks's. And Gracie's. And my mama's. Far as I'm concerned, that makes you one of us now. If you ever need a friend, you've got one. And if you ever need a favor, you let me know."

I stood frozen in place for a minute. I'd never had anyone express that kind of appreciation for my work before, and my throat was tight with a tangle of emotions—mostly good ones—I'd need to sort out later.

"Thank you, Dunn," I managed to choke out. "Truly."

"I owe you one," Brooks said, clapping his brother on the back. "Or maybe more than one. You're a good man."

"Yeah, well, I'm gonna collect those favors right now, I'm afraid. I gotta get back to town, and I need a ride. Besides which, there are twenty-seven kinds of peach cobbler waiting for someone to judge 'em in an hour or so."

"Right." Brooks sighed.

"But I'll give you a second just to make sure Mal's totally out of the woods." He winked. "Just in case you need to resuscitate him again."

He slapped me gently on the arm and whistled as he strode back out into the sunshine.

I barely had time to blow out a breath of relief before Brooks's mouth was on mine again.

"I'll see you tonight?" he asked, after he'd rearranged my tonsils and all of my brain cells.

"Mm-hm."

His grin was showstopping beautiful as he backed away

from me. "Maybe afterward we can spend some time together again? Alone?"

"Mm-hm."

He blew a kiss at me before turning and jogging off toward the driveway. I stood there wondering what he'd meant by "afterward," but I didn't much care as long as afterward brought more kisses and naked time with Brooks Johnson.

"There you are," Ava said after who-knew-how-long I stood there daydreaming. "I've been looking all over for you. I figured you'd be asleep."

"Oh, uh, not so much. I was hoping maybe I could sneak a nap in your room where it's a little cooler than the surface of the sun."

She waved her hand like it wasn't important. "Fine, whatever. But first we have to get you fitted for the tux."

I stared at her. "I'm sorry. What?"

"For the auction tonight. The man at the shop said as long as I get you in there in the next hour or so, he'll be able to do it."

"Ava, buttercup, this is one of those times you started a conversation a few minutes before starting to speak out loud. What auction and why do I need a tux?"

She looked at me with a crinkle in her forehead. "The bachelor auction. Brooks has to emcee and doesn't want to participate, so they need someone to fill in as a bachelor. We need to sell you to the highest bidder."

My brain was still a little fuzzy from painting Ava's dad's barn wall with my jizz earlier. "Sell me."

She rolled her eyes. "Not like, really sell you. Just, you know, for charity."

"This is such a strange town," I said.

Ava's eyes softened. "Yeah, but it's kind of also the best, you know?"

I thought about what Dunn had said about being one of them, what Brooks had said about me being special, and all the friendly faces and interesting conversations I'd had yesterday with the locals at the vendor fair.

"Yeah. It's pretty great," I admitted. "And your family... I think they're going to be okay when you tell them about the baby."

Her eyes filled and she nodded. "I think so too. They'll be disappointed because they want me to have the best of everything. But..." She sniffed. "But I have them, and I have you. And I kind of feel like I have Brooks back in a weird way, and then..." Her chin trembled a little.

"Paul?"

She nodded some more and stumbled into my arms for a big hug. "I like him so much," she admitted in a whisper, as if saying it too loudly would jinx it. "Why couldn't this have been his baby, Mal? It's not fair."

I rubbed her back. "No, baby. It's not fair at all. But I can tell that if it's in his power to make things good for you, Paul is going to try his hardest to do it. That man is over the moon for you."

"You think so?"

"Anyone with working eyeballs thinks so," I said with a soft laugh. "He seems like a keeper. But..."

She pulled back to wipe her eyes. "But he lives in New York," she finished for me. "I know. And that's okay. I... I'm going to move back to the Thicket, Mal. I want to raise my baby here, and I'm going to need Mom and Dad's help."

My heart dropped. We'd been each other's everything in LA for years. I couldn't even picture my life without her there.

"I want you to come with me," she added, biting her bottom lip and giving me Bambi eyes.

"Don't look at me with those eyes," I warned. "What you're asking is ridiculous."

"Is it, though? Think about it. You could afford to rent a place with a huge workshop all your own. You could ramp up your online and mail-order business and find space in local galleries to sell your stuff. Most of your big commissions come from online leads and relationships anyway, and Southwest flies nonstop from Nashville to LAX. You can get back there anytime you need to."

I looked around us at the dust and bits of straw everywhere, remembering what it was like growing up in a small town. "I love California," I said. "You know that. I worked my ass off to get out of my small town, Ava. How the hell am I going to be okay moving right back to one before I've even found—" I stopped myself just in time. "What I mean is, I'm single. How the hell do you expect me to find hot sex around here?"

Do not look at the cum on the wall. Do not look at the cum on the wall.

"We're two hours away from the music and club scene in Nashville. We're four hours from southern gay Mecca in Atlanta. We're—"

I cut her off. "Not the same as LA."

She gave me a look. "Of course not. But LA doesn't have me. And it doesn't have your niece or nephew. Please at least think about it, okay? I don't want to pressure you, but I also don't want to do this without you."

I stepped forward and pulled her into my arms again, holding her tight and trying not to think about having just fucked her ex-boyfriend in her father's workshop. I was a selfish jackass.

"I love you," I told her. "I want you and this baby to be happy. You know that, right?"

"I do. And I love you too. And I want the same for you. Even if that includes Brooks Goddamned Johnson." She pulled back and winked at me.

I sighed. "He lives in New York too. Remember?"

Her eyes sparkled the way they did sometimes when she had insider information or juicy gossip. "Nothing is permanent, Malachi."

"What do you know? What are you hiding?" I poked her in the side where I knew she was most ticklish.

She yelped and hopped back. Her smile was like bringing the sunshine into the barn. "I just have a good feeling about all of this, that's all. But right now, we need to get your tux fitted. I plan on selling you for top dollar. Some lucky Lickin' lady is gonna get herself a sexy California boy tonight." She swished her hips and singsonged her way out of the barn.

Great. My dreams were all coming true. Now I knew what Brooks had been referring to when he'd promised to connect with me "afterward."

After he paraded me around in front of a bunch of strangers and auctioned my gay ass off.

I wondered how much money I was willing to donate and whether or not I could convince Diesel to use it to buy me just so I could see what Mr. Perfect Brooks Johnson would do when Diesel won me and carried me off into the night.

Chapter Fifteen

Brooks

AUCTIONING BACHELORS HAD NEVER BEEN an item on my bucket list, but at least now it was something I could put on my resume. And to tell the truth, it had been a lot more fun than I'd anticipated... except that I'd only caught the barest glimpse of Mal all night, wearing a formfitting tux and looking like all my teenaged dreams rolled into one sexy package.

"Later," I'd promised him hours ago, when he'd arrived with Ava and we'd shaken hands like the near strangers we were supposed to be. He'd shivered in anticipation. "I've got plans for you."

Now, finally, it was *later*. And I couldn't wait to collect on my promise.

"Going once. Going twice... Sold!" I yelled triumphantly, banging a gavel against the podium set up under the basketball net on one side of the Licking Thicket High School gym. "Amos Nutter, you've been sold to Lurleen Jackson for thirty-seven dollars and forty-three cents."

Angela Nutter, Amos's wife, who'd been unable or

unwilling to bid thirty-seven forty-*four* for her own husband, didn't seem too upset by this development.

"Well, darn it all! Competition was just *fierce* this year, hmm? But no sore feelings, Lurleen. Amos'll love having someone new to chat to about his theories on cow insemination!" she trilled.

Lurleen, who'd looked a little smug a minute before, now seemed taken aback as she walked up to the front of the gym to claim her prize.

"I do have lotsa theories!" Amos agreed excitedly.

"Alrighty!" I said into the microphone as Lurleen reluctantly led Amos away. "Well, this has been another amazing year for the bachelor auction! Twenty-four bachelors makes this the biggest auction in history. In just a second, I'll tell you how much we've raised in total for charity, um—"

I broke off as my mother lifted a hand to get my attention and ran over, waving another bachelor bio card in the air. She leaned into my space.

"One more entry!" she told the crowd with a wide grin.

I frowned. Who the heck was left?

She handed me the card, and I read it with dawning horror, seeing all my careful plans for the evening go up in smoke.

"Are you *sure?*" I demanded, searching the crowd. "Because I don't really think..."

"Positive!" she said gleefully.

I took a deep breath and forced a smile. "Okay, then. One more entry. Uh, Malachi Forrester, come on down."

Mal pushed through the crowd, his wavy hair tamed for once and his lean muscles so perfectly encased by the lines of the tuxedo I had to grip the edges of the podium to keep myself from throwing him over my shoulder and carrying him out into the cool night air.

"Hey," he said softly. His blue eyes were warm and as full of mischief as I'd ever seen them. "So... this is possibly the weirdest experience of my entire life."

I tipped the microphone away. "Did Ava coerce you into this? Is Mr. Ivey holding one of your sculptures hostage? Blink once for yes, twice for no."

Mal laughed, sounding a little drunk, and blinked repeatedly. "In this week, I have milked a cow for sport. I ran through the woods carrying a bucket of milk while dozens of otherwise reasonable adults *mooed* at me so I could win a race—"

"Win? Oh good Lord, you're delusional. You're not of sound mind to consent—"

"Let it go, Elsa," Mal laughed. "I won. That's how history's going to remember it. And it's bad sportsmanship for you to remember the details."

I shook my head. "But I thought you and I—"

Mal shrugged. "Ava said she has a plan. She said to trust her."

"Shake a leg, Brooks!" Angela Nutter yelled, both hands cupped around her mouth. "Sell the man!"

I blinked, feeling the same urge I'd felt the first time I met Mal, the urge to push him behind me and growl, "*Mine!*"

"Uh. Okay, then," I said, waiting for Mal to reconsider. But he didn't.

I sighed.

"So, our last bachelor of the night is Malachi Forrester." I glanced down at the card. "Mal is twenty-seven years old. He's a metal sculptor from Los Angeles. He enjoys..." I glanced up at Mal, who smiled innocently. "He enjoys cows and cow art, spending time in barns, drinking moonshine, and working other men's junk. I mean, working *with* junk,"

I corrected, though I knew I'd read it right the first time. "His greatest accomplishments include..." I shook my head. "Being a finalist for the Bucksbaum Art Prize in 2017 and, more recently, being named Second Licker in the Licking Thicket Centennial Lickin' celebration. What am I offered as the starting bid?"

Ava stepped forward, looking lovely in a long, pink dress. She held up her paddle. "Fifty dollars!"

"Whoa." I nodded approvingly. She wasn't playing around. That was higher than any bid had gone all evening. If Mal had to be sold to anyone—and seriously, this whole fiasco was the low point of my week—I was glad it would be to Ava. "Once, twice—"

"Wait!" Diesel *fucking* Church yelled. "Aren't you supposed to say, 'Who'll give me fifty-five?' or something?"

Like I needed the man to tell me how to do this job? Like Head Licking wasn't in my blood?

"Yeah, fine," I agreed reluctantly. "Fifty-five? No one? Okay, then—"

"Seventy-five!" Diesel yelled, raising his paddle and earning himself a permanent place on my shit list.

Mal sucked in a breath. "Damn," he muttered.

"Eighty!" Angela Nutter screamed, and my jaw dropped.

Mal and I exchanged a look. His said he regretted his life choices. Mine said I regretted his choices too.

"One hundred," my own deceitful brother, *who fucking knew better*, said.

"One fifty!" my mother called, waving her paddle.

I glared at her. "This has gone far enough," I began.

"One sixty!" Ava said.

"Two hundred!" Diesel the tattooed asshole yelled.

"Holy shit," Mal breathed.

Meanwhile, for the first time in my life, I looked Diesel up and down and decided I could take him in a fight. Sure, he was way taller and more built than I was, but I was *motivated*.

"Two fifty *for my boyfriend*," Ava said, raising her paddle and darting a look at Diesel. "I won't give up on my honey nugget!"

Diesel didn't seem to get the message.

"Three hundred dollars," he said in his deep voice.

No one said anything for a minute. The only sound in the fucking gym was my molars grinding together. I glared at Ava, promising her the entire balance of my savings account, and she nodded.

"Five hundred dollars!" she said.

"Wow! Sold!" I grabbed my gavel and banged it down once, ignoring Diesel Church, who'd attempted to raise his paddle again. "Amazing work, you guys! Now! Who's ready for some two-stepping?"

I left the podium and headed for the bar where my mom was sitting. I needed a drink. I could hardly stand to look at Mal. My plan for a special night had evaporated before my eyes.

Of course, then Ava came bounding up a second later with her arm wrapped around Mal's waist.

"Amazing job, Brooks, honey!" my mom said, tackle-hugging me from behind. "I can't believe how much money we've raised! Isn't it thrilling, Ava?"

"Less thrilling that I had to pay for it." She smiled as she handed my mother a check.

"Be right back!" my mom trilled, scooting away with her money.

"So," Ava said, grinning at me. "I won!"

"Yep. Super," I told her. "Lucky you."

"Brooks." She gave me a mischievous smile. "Remember that year I missed your birthday?"

I snorted. "Which one?" There'd been ten.

"All of them." She nudged Mal in my direction. "Here you go. And Merry belated Christmas too."

Mal bit his lip like he was fighting laughter, probably at my jealousy, but I didn't care. I hurried him out to the parking lot before my mother, or Diesel Church, or anyone else could interrupt us again.

Five minutes later, when Mal was buckled in his seat and we were speeding out of the lot, his questions began... which was honestly a minute longer than I'd thought it would take.

"Where are we going, Mr. Johnson?"

"You don't get to ask questions, remember? You're my bachelor for the night. Bought and paid for at auction." I wiggled my eyebrows suggestively. "I can do anything I want to you. And there are so damn many things I wanna do to you, Malachi."

"Ugh." Mal rolled his eyes. "That's... that's horrifying. I'm *seriously* horrified right now. Stop talking."

I glanced over at the giant tent in the front of his tuxedo pants. "That does look serious."

"Shut up." He pressed a hand against his fly, and I gripped the steering wheel tighter.

"People bid on me, Brooks! Like, *multiple* people."

"No shit. I was there," I reminded him sourly.

"Your *brother* bid on me, Brooks."

I took a breath through my nose and tried to keep my tone casual. "I know. That was just... Dunn being Dunn. Friendly. Reinforcing what he'd said earlier at the Iveys' barn."

"Uh-huh. And then your *mother* bid on me."

I rolled my eyes. "I know. I figure she heard about the sign from Ava, like everyone else did, and wanted to thank you."

"And Mrs. Nutter bid on me."

"Yeah." I scratched at my chin. "No, that was just weird."

"And then Diesel and Ava got into a bidding war—"

"Yeah. Yes. I know. Once again, *I was there*, Mal." The steering wheel creaked under my hands. "No need to rehash—"

"And, you know, not to tell you how to do your job as bid-watcher or whatever, but I'm pretty sure Diesel raised his paddle one more time at the end."

"No, he didn't."

"No, I really think—"

"Well, I think it doesn't matter, because Ava's name was the one on the check and, as someone recently told me, that's how history will remember it."

Mal ran his tongue over his teeth, and the look he shot me was decidedly *sassy*, which had a predictable effect on the fit of my suit pants. "So then, why am I riding off in the night like the Bonnie to your Clyde, and not in Ava's air-conditioned bedroom giving her one of my patented foot rubs?"

Was it ridiculous to feel jealous that Mal had rubbed Ava's feet? Yes, I decided. It was.

I also decided I didn't care.

"You were there. Ava gave you to me as a present," I said smugly. "For my birthday." I glanced at him. "You're belated, but you'll do."

Mal burst out laughing. "And what exactly is your evil plan for innocent, little old me?" He batted his eyelashes.

"You'll find out soon," I promised. "Unless. I mean. We could just go sit and talk somewhere. The tree house? Or…"

"Brooks." Mal twisted so he was leaning against the center console of the car and laid his hand on my thigh mere *centimeters* from where my dick was throbbing. "To be clear, you can do anything you want to me short of literally taking me in the woods to kill me. Okay?"

I nodded jerkily. "Maybe move your hand, in that case? So I can get us there in one piece?"

Mal snorted, but he twisted forward in his seat. "And where is *there*?"

I shook my head. "You really don't give up, do you?"

"Nope. I never give up on a challenge. You know me better than that." He paused, and I thought what he'd said and how casually he'd said it hit both of us at the same time.

But the fact was, I *did* know him better than that, even though I'd known him for less than a week. Just like I knew he was freaking out. So I grabbed his hand and meshed our fingers together.

"I do," I agreed. "But I'm still not telling you yet."

The idea taking shape in my mind was so audacious and scary I couldn't form the words for it yet. A week ago, I'd been sure New York held all the keys to my happiness. Now I knew it couldn't possibly… if it didn't have Mal. I felt like I'd been sleepwalking for years and I could finally see the world in vivid technicolor, alive with possibilities. Tonight would be my attempt to show Mal how things could be between us with no distractions or interruptions, and no need to sneak around.

With that in mind, I turned off the main road and onto a path that was more potholes than pavement.

"Okay, so that whole taking me into the woods to kill me thing… that was actually a hard limit," Mal said.

I squeezed his hand lightly and rolled to a stop in front of a small cabin. "Killing wasn't on my mind, but taking you into the woods was. I'm hoping you'll be begging me for mercy before we're done."

Mal made a gagging noise. "Oh, sweet baby Jesus. That... was literally the cheesiest thing any man has ever said to me. Unless you're plotting to kill me by lactose overdose, hot stuff, I don't think I'll be *begging*." He unbuckled his belt and opened the door. "What the heck is this place? Should I be listening for banjos?"

"This is Dunn's fishing cabin. Used to be my Great Uncle Waylon's place, and Dunn was his godson, so he inherited it. You can't see in the dark, but Bull Lake is out back and there's a big dock."

"Bull Lake," he repeated, staring at the cabin with his hands on his hips. "Because what this town needed was more bovines."

I came around the car to stand next to him. "Always."

He gave me a side-eyed glance. "And does Dunn know you're here?"

"Obviously."

In fact, after catching us in the Iveys' barn, Dunn had demanded the whole story, and I'd given it to him. It seemed I hadn't given my brother enough credit when I'd first gotten back to town. He was still as sweet and goofy as ever, but there was a new maturity about him I hadn't expected. More surprising than that, it turned out my brother was a sucker for romance, and he'd immediately pulled a key off his key ring and told me to make the most of my time with Mal.

He'd also given me a half-smile and said, "I miss you, Brooks. Don't be a stranger," which had made me feel pretty shitty for a minute. I'd convinced myself that going to New

York was the only option, but what if there'd been another way all along?

"So... you actually *planned* this?" Mal said.

"Duh. Was that not clear? Ava was the one who gave me the idea. She told me this morning she was going to prove what a good friend she was, and she did." I trailed a finger down his arm. "Even if fucking *Diesel* tried to mess it up."

"Poor Diesel," Mal said, grabbing my hand in both of his.

And you know what? *Yeah.* Poor Diesel was right. Because I was here right now, and he fucking wasn't.

I led him up the single step to the porch, unlocked the door, and flipped on the light. The room was the same as ever—double bed in the center, kitchenette tucked in one corner, table by the door, half bath off the back—but someone had clearly been here today, because the quilt looked clean and fresh, unlit jar candles were set on the few flat surfaces, and there were heaps of flower petals dropped at irregular intervals between the door and the bed.

Holy shit. I was *mortified.*

"I'd been expecting early modern plaid and antlers," Mal said wonderingly. "But it's a love shack. Did you do this?"

I shook my head. But the way the flower petals looked like they'd been dumped by childish hands gave me suspicions. "Gracie, I think. And Payton. My sister and niece. They clearly went a little overboard." Or a *lot* overboard.

"Wait, does she know about..."

"I guess?" I shrugged. "Maybe Dunn told her, or maybe we're not as sneaky as we thought."

Mal snorted. "True. Nobody's seemed particularly surprised by anything this week."

"Well, now, I wouldn't go that far." I stepped directly in front of him and stripped off his bow tie in one swift move. "I've been fucking astonished."

Mal grinned—a bright, shining thing—and pulled me down to kiss him.

The pieces of my suit and his tux went flying around the room like confetti, and before I knew it, I was groaning against Mal's mouth, both hands clutching his ass to pull him against me. The skin-on-skin of our chests touching was aching perfection, and after all of the teasing in the car, I was *primed*, when I'd promised myself that tonight I'd take my time and savor him.

I broke the kiss to coast my mouth down the side of his neck, and he shuddered against me, his hands grabbing at my hair as he tried to direct my mouth back to his. Instead, I stepped closer, forcing him to bend backward. I held him firmly at the waist and leaned down to lick his nipple.

Mal grabbed the footboard of the bed to brace himself. "Jesus, Brooks."

I took my time moving down his chest and abs, alternately licking and sucking and scraping him up with my teeth. He tasted seriously fucking good.

"Oh, fuck," he groaned. "You're gonna kill me. Suck me off, already!"

"Is this you begging for mercy?" I demanded, my voice hoarse with lust.

"What? Never."

I bit at the muscle just above his hip hard enough to leave a mark, and he cried out. "You will," I promised him. "Turn around."

He stared down at me like he'd lost his English vocabulary. "A-around?"

I would have smiled if I hadn't already been hard as a

fucking rock, but seeing him losing his control now just made it harder to maintain my own.

"Around," I repeated. I pushed lightly, and he bent over the side of the bed, exposing his gorgeous bubble butt.

Holy fuck.

I groaned as his piercing caught the light. Every once in a while, I managed to forget it was there, which made it exponentially hotter when I remembered, like a treasure I kept discovering. I couldn't hide how damn enthusiastic it made me to finally see it up close and personal.

I tugged gently at the tiny ring while I teased his opening with my tongue. And judging by Mal's garbled noises of ecstasy and how he rubbed himself against the bed in a way that made me fucking *envy* that old quilt, it seemed like he approved.

"Oh, that... oh, no... oh, mother... oh, my fuck... ohhhh yesssss," he cried into the quilt, and I was torn between laughter and orgasm, which was a whole new plane of existence for me.

I gave him one last lick and stood up shakily, thanking whatever deity had allowed the lube to move right next to Mal's hip, because my brain was so consumed with the need to be inside him. I could only think in one word phrases—Lube. Prep. Hot. Yes. Fuck. More. *Malachi*, and I just hoped that the sweet kisses I pressed into his skin conveyed all the shit I was unable to get out, like how hot he was. How special he was. How fucking *perfect* he was.

Mal writhed on the bed beneath me and cried out my name, and my dick literally throbbed against my stomach, I was so hard. I'd wanted to go slow, to tease both of us, to see what would happen if I played with the piercing while I gave him just the tip... but I couldn't do it. I wanted him too much.

Next time, I promised myself.

"Turn over?" I said. It was a plea, not a command. Mal was always ducking his head, hiding his eyes from me, but I wanted to watch the expression on his face as I took him apart. Wanted to commit it to memory. But I wanted him to want it too, and if he didn't...

Mal turned over without a protest, and it made my chest seize up, swamped by feelings that were way too big for a guy I'd known so short a time, but were so fucking real I couldn't deny them.

His hair was stuck to his face, sweaty tendrils across his forehead. I leaned over and brushed them away, and his eyes locked on mine, impossibly tender for a moment.

"Please, Brooks." He spread his legs wider, his blue eyes imploring.

I wanted to give him everything, promise him *everything*, but what we had right now was this. So I rolled a condom over myself, lined myself up, and pushed inside him, where both of us needed me to be.

It felt like coming home, which was fitting in a way, because Malachi Forrester was the guy who'd made Licking Thicket feel like home for the first time in my twenty-eight years.

"Move, baby," he begged.

I braced myself over him and thrust slowly, in tiny little nudges that didn't satisfy either of us. "Like this?"

"Fuck. *Fuck.* Fine. Mercy, okay? Mercy. I can't believe you actually made me say—*Oh* shit."

I pulled out all the way and slammed home, dragging my cock over his prostate.

"I never give up on a challenge, Malachi. You know me better than that," I said, repeating his earlier words. His sex-drunk eyes focused on mine for a single second, and I knew he got it—that everything I felt, he felt too.

He groaned and that sound... *Jesus, fuck.* Like spark to paper.

I fucked him harder, pushing his legs back so he was nearly bent in half, wanting to get as deep inside him as possible. His long cock bobbed against his abs with every thrust, leaving a sticky patch of precum. My eyes held his as I trailed a finger through the wetness and brought my finger to my mouth, and his own lips parted as he watched me taste him for the first time.

Fuck. I'd never experienced intensity like this, not ever. Every slap of my balls against his ass, every high, breathy moan he emitted just stoked the flames higher, and for once in my life, I had no desire to fight or control it.

Instead, I reached down and thumbed his taint, just above where our bodies joined, and tugged on the ring there. His face turned a shade redder, and his eyes rolled back in his head.

"Fuck, Brooks," he whimpered. "I need..."

"What, sweetness? What do you need?" Because by God, I would give it to him.

"You... more... *you.*"

I braced my hands by his shoulders and leaned down to kiss him deeply until both of us had to break for air. The air in the cabin was sweltering hot, and the air around us was even hotter, but I had never felt better or more alive. The look on Mal's face was pure desperation, and the knowledge I'd put it there was electrifying.

"You're gonna come for me," I told him, my voice wrecked. "You're gonna come so hard."

"Yes. *Yes.*"

"And I'm gonna fuck you through it. I want every last drop, Mal."

I did not talk like this. I did *not* growl like this. And I didn't get possessive like this either. Except, apparently I did. And it felt so damn right I would never question it. Not with Mal.

Our gazes locked and held as I reached between us to stroke him, gripping him just the way I knew—fucking *knew*—he liked it best. His back bowed and his neck arched back as he gasped in time to the rhythm of my hand, and I could feel my own orgasm tingling in my balls.

"Come on, Mal. Come with me. Come for me, sweetness."

"Oh, fuck, Brooks! *Fuck!*" His entire body jerked with the force of his orgasm, his hole clenching around me and his hands bunching the quilt beneath us like an anchor in a storm.

"I've got you. I've got you. I... God. *Malachi.*" I came a second later, my mouth frozen open and all my breath deserting me.

"Mother. Fucking. *Fuck,*" I said, panting with each syllable. My arms wobbled and I fell on top of Mal, forcing the breath from his lungs.

He didn't seem to mind too much, given the way he wrapped his arms around my shoulders. "It's like poetry," he teased breathlessly. "Brooks *Shakespeare* Johnson."

I snorted against his neck and pulled back just far enough to see that he was grinning though his eyes were shut tight. "I'll work on that," I promised, mostly joking. "I'll do better next time."

His beautiful eyes popped open to meet mine. "I don't think that's possible," he said, and there was so much warm sincerity in his gaze, I couldn't help but kiss him again.

Later, after I'd disposed of the condom and we'd cleaned up as best we could in the half bath, we climbed back on the bed with Mal sprawled out flat and me propped on my elbow beside him. I was close enough to trace the hollow of his ribs with my fingertips, but far enough for the cool night breeze to wash over us through the open windows while every bullfrog in the area serenaded us with their mating songs.

I trailed my fingers into the hollow of his abdomen and let out a breath, feeling my tired muscles and my brain relax completely for the first time in... ten years? No, maybe longer than that.

"Fuck, you're good at that," Mal groaned. His eyes had been closed so long, I'd wondered if he'd dozed off. Clearly not.

"What? Touching you?"

He nodded. "Kissing me. Fucking me. Talking to me. Fighting with me."

"Really?" I cleared my throat. The word had come out sounding seriously fucking needy. "I mean... I'm glad. Me too." I waited for him to make another joke about me being a poet or, worse, cheesy.

Mal's lips twitched and his gaze met mine. "Best ever," he said softly. His eyes tracked his fingers as he brushed a stray lock of hair off my temple, and he repeated, "Best... ever."

And maybe it was just my wishful thinking, but I felt like the *first* time he said it, he'd been talking about the past... and the second about the future.

I felt too thin-skinned suddenly, my tender underbelly literally exposed to the world, so I ducked my head and pressed a kiss to Mal's jaw in a total Mal move. I could sense his amusement, but he didn't call me on it. In fact, he pulled my head down to his chest and started mimicking my move-ments, drawing circles with his fingertips over my back.

I never wanted to move from this spot.

"Mr. Perfect is even a gold-medal cuddler," Mal teased, pressing a kiss to the top of my head.

"Am I? I'm a prodigy, then. I've never done it before," I admitted.

"Seriously? Never?"

I shook my head slightly against his shoulder. "Never wanted to, really. I..." I hesitated. "It's not a thing for casual hookups, you know? Wouldn't want anyone to get the wrong idea or think I wanted a repeat. And casual hookups are all I've ever had."

Mal held his breath, and I could almost hear the ques-tions he wasn't speaking aloud.

Does that mean you want a repeat? Does this mean we're not casual?

But when his hand resumed its motion and he finally spoke, he only said lightly, "Guess having a three-peat makes me special, hmm?"

"You are special," I agreed, tweaking his nipple. "*So* special."

"Well, if you're pondering a four-peat—"

"Is *four-peat* a thing?"

"Not if you keep interrupting me." He pinched me lightly, and I snorted. "But for the record, I liked the barn wall sex a *lot*—"

I yawned loudly, suddenly exhausted from a long day of putting out fires all over the damn place. Finally, now that I was with Mal, my brain felt like I could rest.

"Who doesn't like wall sex?" I grumbled sleepily. "That's like disliking blow jobs. Or chocolate chip cookies."

Mal pinched me again. "My *point* is that now that I've

tried it, I've discovered that I like love shack sex a hell of a lot too... Possibly even more." His hand swept down my naked back almost to the top of my crack, and my fatigue burned off like fog in the sunshine.

"Noted. And, um... what are your thoughts on under-the-bleachers sex?"

Mal fake-gasped. "Sex outdoors? In a semi-public place? Where we could get caught at any moment by busybody Thickatarians?" He pushed me onto my back and rolled on top of me, his half-hard dick showing just how horrified he truly was. "Just what kind of guy do you think I am, Brooks Johnson?"

But as he grinned down at me, I thought to myself that I knew perfectly well what kind of guy Malachi Forrester was.

He was the guy I couldn't get enough of. The guy I was falling for. The guy I wanted to be *mine*.

If I could just convince him that we could build something together.

Chapter Sixteen

Mal

I CAME AWAKE to the opening notes of "Mamma Mia" and damned near jumped out of my skin.

"Sorry," Brooks mumbled roughly into the skin of my shoulder. "My mom."

The reminder that I'd spent the night in bed with Brooks made me grin. I turned to look at him all sleep rumpled and sexy. He stretched to find his phone, exposing his bare back. Bands of muscle shifted under his pale skin marked with a few freckles here and there. Just as I reached out to trace them with a fingertip, Brooks yelped and shot out of bed.

"Fuck, fuck! It's already after eight. Fuck!"

I blinked at him in confusion. "What..."

He scrambled to put on his clothes. "The parade! The *parade.* Jesus. I'm supposed to be there to greet the General and then I have to ride in the final car with Ava, and there's no telling how Tammy is doing trying to wrangle the kids and the marching band. Fuck!"

I got up and started dressing, realizing belatedly that he

was my ride. "It's okay. The parade doesn't start until ten, right?"

He glanced over at me. "Yeah but..." He stopped and let out a breath before walking over to me and cupping my cheeks in his palms. "You're so fucking beautiful. Good morning, sweetness." He kissed me softly, taking me by surprise after his frantic flailing only a few seconds before. "I'm sorry to rush you. I hope you know that I want nothing more than to stay here in this bed naked with you all day."

I smiled up at him, feeling an expansion in my chest. "Yeah. Same. But that's okay. Sometimes Head Licker needs to man up and lick some head."

He rolled his eyes and grinned before turning away to look for his shoes. "You wish."

I so did. I wished really hard.

"Will I see you later?" Ugh, I hated sounding needy. "I only mean... whatever, it's fine. I'm sure I will." Okay, needy *and* bitchy. Great.

Brooks looked up at me from where he was slipping on his second shoe. "Of course. At the very least, I hope you'll save a dance for me tonight."

Oh. Well. Melt me into a puddle of goo and pour me into a Brooks-shaped mold. "Yeah. Good. I'd like that. Mm-hm."

Brooks got a twinkle in his eye at my feigned nonchalance. He winked at me. "And if I see you dance with Diesel, I will not be responsible for my actions."

I found my own shoes and slipped them on before following him to the front door. "If those actions are the good kind of actions, maybe it would be worth it. I've always fantasized about the jock and the bad, bad boy duking it out over me at the school dance."

Brooks barked out a laugh before turning to lock the cabin behind us. "I'll see what I can do."

The feeling of strange giddiness stayed with me all through the ride back to town when Brooks didn't let go of my hand, and halfway through breakfast at the Iveys' house where Ava seemed to be enjoying her own happy secrets. Mr. and Mrs. Ivey were discussing the Susie Dupree scandal which was apparently the most horrific story to hit the Thicket since TJ Calhoun and Bette Lander were caught loading the bingo cage with extra balls at the VFW.

"Brad, I just don't know about Partridge Pit..." Mrs. Ivey said, wringing her hands in front of her yellow apron.

"Monette, darlin', it'll be fine. I ate at the Pit in Nashville, and their meat damned near fell off the bone. I didn't want to say anything since everyone here is such a Susie devotee, but I actually—"

"Hush your mouth," Mrs. Ivey hissed.

I coughed to hide my surprised laughter. Ava's eyes twinkled across the table at me. "Don't mess with a Southerner's barbecue, Mal," she said calmly. "It can impact your marriage."

"Ava Marie," Mrs. Ivey chided. "Mind your business."

"Good thing I'm not getting married anytime soon, then," I teased. Mrs. Ivey sucked in a breath and clutched the front of her apron.

"Well, sometimes Malachi, dear, concessions need to be made. It might not be what we'd prefer, it might not be the person we'd hoped and dreamed of, but circumstances being what they are..." Her voice trailed off.

Ava and I stared at her.

"Marriage can give a person some much-needed stability," she continued. "And should be considered seriously in times when... a person might need that kind of... stability."

"Mother, I think love is more important than stability," Ava snapped.

I took a steadying breath, wondering if Ava's mom was suggesting anyone would be better than me. "You're right, Mrs. Ivey. It should be considered seriously. For instance, you should seriously consider more than a person's looks, their popularity, and their family. Make sure you're not with a person just because it makes everyone else happy instead of you," I added pointedly.

Ava relaxed and nodded, shooting me a small smile. "Exactly. Make sure it's someone who will do anything to make you happy. Who makes you their top priority."

She settled back into her daydreams of Paul while I thought back to the effort Brooks had gone to the night before to make our time more special than another stolen moment under the bleachers or in the barn. I remembered the way he'd traced lazy fingers across my skin and raked his teeth down my neck. The way he'd looked at me with tenderness and told me I was special. It made me drunk with possibility.

Was there even a future possible with someone like Brooks? And what would that look like?

"You two best be on your way if you want to get a decent parking spot," Mrs. Ivey said after we finished eating and cleared our dishes to the sink. There was still an hour to go before the parade, but since Ava was riding in it, she had to be there early.

"Come on," she said with a sigh. "If I have to squeeze into my cheerleading uniform, you have to at least wear a Licking Thicket shirt and represent."

I pictured a giant cartoon cow on the front with "Fighting Bovines" written over the top in obnoxious script, but when Ava set out the stack of shirts to choose from, one of them said "Licking Thicket Good" where all but the letters L-I-C-K-I and T were deliberately faded out to make it look like it said "Lick It Good."

I grabbed it and put it on before tossing my other shirt over my shoulder to leave in Ava's car in case I sweated my way through the Thicket one. August in Tennessee was no joke, and I didn't want to run into Brooks later smelling like an old locker room.

Ava's mom sent us on our way with a small soft-sided cooler filled with cold drinks and snacks which made me force myself to let go of the resentment I'd felt toward her over breakfast. I couldn't blame the woman for wanting a different match for her daughter, I just wished she'd spent more time getting to know me before declaring me unfit to be that match.

"You're being awfully quiet," Ava said on the way into town.

"Do you think if your parents knew that I was your best friend instead of your boyfriend, they might like me better? Maybe they'd feel less threatened by me?"

She thought about it for a minute while looking for a place to park. "Maybe. Do you care that much about my parents' opinion of you?"

I blew out a breath and ran my fingers through my hair. "If I was to move here—"

She didn't even let me say it before she screeched and nearly sideswiped a minivan. I grabbed for the handle at the top of the doorframe. "Oh my God! Are you thinking of moving here? For real?"

I waited until she'd found a parking spot and we were safely stopped. "No. I mean... maybe? I don't know. But I just wondered if—"

"Is this because of Brooks?" she asked, turning in her seat to face me.

"No," I said quickly. Too quickly. "Maybe? I mean... no. He lives in New York and—"

Ava was an interrupter. "But what if he moved back?"

"He won't." At least, I was pretty sure. But at least it would be easier to date long-distance if I lived halfway closer to him than California. And if I lived in the same place as his family and friends. Surely that would help, right?

I thought about how, before this week, he hadn't been back in the Thicket for ten years. Maybe I was being too optimistic.

Ava pressed her lips together before finally spitting it out. "You might be right. And anyway, you need to make this decision based on what you want, not based on him. Do you think you could be happy here? It doesn't have to be forever either, you know?"

I looked through the open car window at the small groups of happy families decked out in cow paraphernalia making their way to the parade route to get a good spot. The sun was shining, and the sky was a clear blue. Balloons were tied in bundles here and there, and colorful parade signage was posted showing people where to go, as if the main drag was so complicated, people needed arrows to find it.

The rich, smoky smell of barbecue already filled the air, and I could hear chatter and laughter from one of the groups of people walking by on their way past the car. I wondered if that would be Ava and Paul and their children one day, or someone other than Paul if things didn't work out between them. I knew regardless of what happened with him, Ava would land someone wonderful who would find it a joy and a privilege to raise her child alongside her.

I didn't want to miss it. And maybe, just maybe, Brooks would consider moving back here if Paul, Ava, and I were all making a home here.

"I think... yeah. I think I could maybe try it."

She squealed and leaned over to hug my neck, dropping a big smacking kiss on my cheek before pulling back with a wide grin. "I'm just excited you'd even consider it. I know it's a big decision, and I'll love you either way. But, God, Mal... I just... I want you to be in this baby's life. You're so important to me."

As we got out of the car and walked against the flow of traffic to find the staging area for parade participants, I daydreamed about what life in the Thicket would look like. Brooks had called me special. He'd cuddled with me and told me he didn't do that with casual hookups.

After leaving Ava at the staging tent, I wandered around in a happy daze, imagining what it would be like to live here with Brooks and Ava and even Paul. Trivia nights with the great group of friends I'd met the other night at the Tavern, incredible junk finds at Diesel's and first dibs on cool new stuff he got in, carrying Ava's son or daughter on my shoulders to future parades and helping them pick apples at the Lickin' Pickin'. It was an idyllic dream, but maybe, just maybe...

The sound of Brooks's familiar voice jacked up my heart rate. I knew he was probably really busy, but I at least wanted to say hi and wish him luck. I followed the sound of his voice until I came around the side of a building and saw him talking to a much older man in a narrow brick alleyway between a restaurant and a gift shop. This had to be General Partridge from everything Brooks had told me about the man.

I ducked back behind a tall decorative planter at the

corner of the building before Brooks could see me. The last thing I wanted to do was interrupt anything important with his hopefully new client.

"Yes, sir," Brooks said with a nod. "We can absolutely discuss that. I'll be back in the office on Monday morning. My flight leaves Nashville at 6:00 a.m., so we can plan a lunch meeting if that suits you?"

The General put his hand on Brooks's shoulder. "Why don't you and Paul join me on my plane so you don't have to get up quite so early? We're at the airfield just down the road in Presley. That way we can talk on the way and be ready to hit the ground running when we get into the office. I'd suggest meeting at my office in Nashville, but I have several other commitments in New York next week I can't miss."

"So do I, sir," Brooks said with a big smile. "New York works better for us as well. I'm looking forward to getting back there and setting things in motion. I just need to get this parade and the dance behind me, and then I'm all yours."

"There are a few things I'd like to knock out before then, if you don't mind, if only so I can get Parrish started on..."

The older man steered Brooks further away from me, closer to the parade route and the crowds, as they continued talking business.

I stared after them. New York. It wasn't like it was a surprise. The guy lived in New York. Of course he was going back. He had a good job, an apartment, a life.

In New York.

But the reality of it, hearing him talk excitedly about specific plans and how soon he was jetting out of Tennessee... God. It was just... a reality check. Kind of a slap in the face after the night we'd had last night. I'd thought at least he'd sound a little sadder to be leaving...

I blew out a breath and rubbed my hands over my face. Screw what I'd thought. I'd obviously thought wrong. He was looking forward to getting these last two pesky Lickin' commitments behind him so he could get back to his real life, the one he'd carefully created for himself somewhere else.

"Then I'll be all yours," he'd told the General, when I'd thought for a minute there that maybe he could be *mine*.

I let out a harsh laugh. Since when was I the kind of guy men changed their whole lives for? Did I really expect someone like Brooks Johnson to, what? Quit his job and move back to this town to date a welder?

I shook my head and got angry with myself.

An *artist*.

The fact I was already putting myself down was a huge red flag that I needed to cut the negative self-talk in the bud right now, and the only way to do that was to stop this thought process. I gritted my teeth and made my way toward the crowds to find a spot where I could watch the parade in peace and try to just... zone out or something. But as soon as I emerged from the narrow alleyway into the crowd, someone called my name.

"Mal! Over here! Come sit with us."

I glanced up to see Maureen and Latonya waving wildly at me with big smiles on their faces. They sat cross-legged on the sidewalk, and Maureen held a chubby-cheeked baby in her lap who had the same honey-brown eyes as Latonya.

"Hi," I said, squatting down to smile at the baby. Maybe this was a better distraction than being alone with my thoughts. "And who are you?"

Maureen puffed up with pride. "This is Mollie. She's ten months now, and her new favorite thing is blowing raspberries with her tongue. Beware when you're within strawberry distance."

Mollie's gummy smile was wide, and the tips of two bottom teeth flashed. I reached out to shake her little hand. "Nice to meet you, sweet girl. Aren't you a happy baby?"

Latonya handed me a bottle of water from their cooler. "Take this. You have to stay hydrated or you'll never make it in this sun. Here, have a seat." She leaned in and whispered. "We always spread out at first so when we see a friend, we can make room for them."

They shifted things around to make space for me, and I took a seat next to Latonya. When Maureen started talking to someone else, Mollie crawled across Latonya and into my lap to pat my cheeks. She was obviously not shy with strangers which made Latonya laugh. "Excuse you," she teased her daughter.

"It's no problem. I needed a good cuddle actually." I held her chubby body close and inhaled the baby scent of her, wondering what it would be like when I was holding Ava's baby like this. I'd never particularly liked babies all that much, but maybe it was true what they said about changing over time. It was hard not to notice the happiness these two women had with their daughter, and I knew Ava would be the same way.

The backs of my eyes stung as I flashed into the future. I did want this. I wanted to be part of Ava's and the baby's lives. But I needed to let go of the dream that it would include Brooks and a happy ever after for me too.

Latonya reached over and squeezed my arm. "You okay?"

I opened my eyes and glanced at her, feeling my face heat. "Just thinking."

She gave me a knowing look. "Sometimes holding a baby is a little bit like petting an animal. It's a kind of therapy. Gets you right in the heart, doesn't it?"

I nodded. "Who knew?"

Mollie tugged on the ends of my hair and said, "Bah-bah-bah!"

While we waited for the parade to start, I used my shirt to play a game of peekaboo with Mollie that earned me some belly laughs that lifted my spirits. I watched the people around me and tried to soak in the festive atmosphere to at least keep me steady until I could get somewhere private and throw myself a nice pity party about Brooks leaving.

It didn't work.

As the marching band and decorated floats began parading down the street and the crowd around me cheered and waved, I sank deeper and deeper into a funk. Not even the loads of candy being flung into the crowd could get through the mood I was in.

When the final car came down the road, I noticed the irony. Ava and Brooks rode on the back of a convertible classic Ford Fairlane Sunliner just like the one my landlord had back in California. The sun shone on the pristine pink and white paint, and I couldn't help but pull out my phone to snap some pictures for Neil since Mollie was safely back in her mother's arms.

Ava looked gorgeous in her cheerleading uniform, but I could hardly look at her long because sitting right next to her was Brooks Johnson in his football jersey. His arm was wrapped protectively around Ava's waist to keep her from falling backward out of the car. It was such a sweet gesture,

I almost wished I hadn't noticed it. I kind of wanted to hate him right now.

His face radiated happiness in a way completely different from the first night we'd met. Now, he looked more relaxed, as if he could see the light at the end of the tunnel and knew he was almost free to leave this place again. What if he didn't come back for another ten years?

He flexed his biceps and tossed out tiny plastic footballs to some of the young kids in the crowd who were yelling his name, and it was such a stark reminder of his quick retreat into chameleon mode. He was pretending to be the small-town hero, the jock, the smiling role model with the beautiful cheerleader on his arm. But that wasn't who he was. Or maybe it wasn't the only part of who he was.

I'd stupidly thought I had some innate ability to determine when he was being a chameleon and when he was being his true self. But what if I didn't? What if I'd been fooling myself and the man he was with me—the tender, caring one—was yet another one of the skins he slipped on?

"Excuse me," I murmured to Latonya and Maureen as I stood up. "Thanks for letting me hold Mollie."

The look on Latonya's face was kind and concerned, so I did my best to shoot her a reassuring smile. Her eyes widened and her forehead crinkled which led me to believe I'd failed. There was nothing I could do about it but simply walk away, weaving through the throngs of people until I found the narrow alleyway and could take a breath again.

So many destructive thoughts went through my head. I remembered the same feeling of uncertainty when I'd left Homer. Would my family fight to keep me there? Would any of my so-called friends care that I was leaving? The answer had turned out to be no on both accounts, and I was pretty sure I couldn't take that kind of rejection again.

No, it was much better to walk away on a high note and wonder what if, rather than wait around for the actual rejection and disappointment themselves.

I felt a vague numbness come over me as I made my way back to Ava's car to wait for her. Even though I still wanted to be there for her and the baby, I knew I needed to get the hell out of this town until Brooks was safely ensconced back in his big-city life. If I saw him again, or God forbid had time alone with him, I'd melt back into the puddle of Brooks goo, and this time I might not be able to recover.

When Ava finally got through the gauntlet of locals who wanted to talk to her, she was sweaty and red-faced but clearly happy.

"What did you think?" she asked. "Fun, huh?"

"Yeah. Very. Can we go?"

"What, now? But I thought we could wait for Paul and Brooks." She jerked a thumb behind her. "And Dr. Yates was interested in your reef piece. I could introduce you."

"No!" I blurted. Then, more calmly, I added, "Wouldn't it be even better if you waited to see Paul until tonight? A little absence to make his heart grow fonder?"

As much as I was dying to sell that reef piece, the thought of hanging around and making chitchat with Brooks was more than I could handle.

She frowned. "What happened?"

"I need space. From Brooks. Just for a minute. And besides, I want to hear everything about the parade. You looked great up there. Did you have fun?"

She chatted excitedly the entire drive back to the farm, telling me about old friends she'd run into and people she'd recognized in the crowd. I could see the spark of something new in her, something good. She really was making the right decision moving back here. It made me realize she'd probably only moved away in the first place because she couldn't handle the scandal of her breakup. But now that it was old news for the most part, she was able to be herself again. And herself thrived here in Licking Thicket. The locals loved her, and she seemed much more at home in her skin.

When we pulled into the driveway and got out of the car, she frowned at me. "Why are you being so quiet?"

"I want to go home."

There. I'd said it.

Ava looked around at the farmhouse, the barns in the distance, and the pathway leading back to the tree house. "We are home." She tilted her head at me in confusion.

"No. LA. I want to go home to California. Today. I can't... I can't..." I stopped talking before I turned into a mushy mess.

"Babe..." She took me by the hand and led me out back and up into the tree house. I sat down on the futon and buried my face in my hands. "Mal, what's going on? Did something happen with Brooks?"

I couldn't say anything at first, and she took my silence the wrong way.

"I'll fucking kill that bastard," she hissed. "Did he ditch you? What the fuck?"

I shook my head. "No. He didn't. It's just that..." I took a shaky breath. "He's going back to New York, and it just hit me that this isn't real. It's like a vacation fling and that's fine, but..."

The empathy on her face was sweet, but it only made me feel more fragile. I hated feeling fragile.

"You have feelings," she said softly. I nodded. "But, Mal, so does he. Anyone who looks at you the way Brooks does has to be having big feelings."

"I've seen pictures of the two of you from high school, Ava. Brooks looked at you the same way."

She paused for a minute before nodding slowly. "And he loved me. He did. Maybe it wasn't romantic love, but I know in my heart that Brooks loved me. I think he still does. I certainly still love him. For lots of reasons, but mainly because I have a history with him. He's kind and smart, funny and generous. He's very lovable."

"Fuck," I said, blowing out a breath and running my fingers through my hair. I stood up and paced in the tiny room. "Don't tell me how great Brooks Johnson is. I get it, okay? I do. That's the problem here. I need to go. Don't you see? If I stay here, I'll throw myself at him and beg him to leave everything he loves in New York. We've known each other a week. Less than a week. I don't want to be that guy."

"The guy who cares?"

"The needy guy who leads people into making bad decisions. The pathetic guy who falls for someone light-years above his league."

"Don't you dare imply that Brooks is better than you!" Ava reached out and slapped my leg. "Fuck you for even thinking that. You're the best man I know, and I know a lot of good men. You're worthy of the best man ever, better even than Brooks Johnson."

"He's a good man."

She sighed. "Yeah. He is."

"Fuck," I said again softly.

She let me stew for a minute before aiming the emotional dart gun at my heart and pulling the trigger. "You can't leave yet, though. I need you here. I'm telling my parents about the baby tomorrow. Please don't make me do it alone."

I looked up into the spiderwebbed rafters and let out a

frustrated sound. "Fine. Fine. Jesus. But I'm not going to the fucking dance."

She didn't say anything until I looked down and saw her giving me puppy dog eyes. "You can't expect me to walk in there alone after everything that happened the last time I went to this damned dance."

"Fuck," I said again. "Fuck, fuck, fuck."

She was right. I wasn't about to let her face this final demon on her own. I would go to the dance and keep my head down. Stay quiet and try not to look for Brooks in the crowd. And hopefully, if I was lucky, I could sneak out of there before he spotted me.

Because I knew that I was nowhere near strong enough to resist him if he asked for that dance I'd promised.

Chapter Seventeen

Brooks

THE FIRST TEXT Mal didn't answer hadn't bothered me.

The second had been a bit concerning, but I'd been sitting with Paul at my mom's kitchen table, finishing up the Partridge Pit presentation, so I'd let it go.

But when he'd also ignored my *third* text, that was when I'd finally broken down and refused to do any more work until Paul texted Ava to see what she and Mal were up to.

"Just to make sure they're okay! They could be in a *ditch*, Paul, and you'd never forgive yourself," I'd reminded him, which was such a Cindy Ann Johnson thing to say that I'd deserved every second of the pitying look he gave me.

Ava had texted back immediately. Spoiler: they were not in a ditch. In fact, they were in the Iveys' tree house—just a couple of acres from my mom's kitchen, and well within cell signal—discussing the logistics of Ava's move to the Thicket and the possibilities for her future. She told Paul they needed a little space and downtime, and she promised to fill him in on everything at the dance. She also sent him a dozen kiss-face emojis to tide him over until the next time she could kiss him again.

"That's nauseating," I told Paul crisply, reading the message over his shoulder as I paced the kitchen floor. He snorted in reply, obviously deeply concerned about my opinion.

Besides I wasn't even sure *what* was nauseating: the kisses Ava had sent... or the confirmation that Mal was leaving in thirty hours and instead of spending that time with me, he was pushing me away.

"At least they're not in a ditch," Paul said comfortingly.

I made a noncommittal noise. I mean... *yeah*. He was right. But at least if they were in a ditch, I could go and haul them out. I could bandage them up or call the paramedics. I could *fix* something. Instead, I was left with a whole lot of nothing, except my own tangled thoughts.

Well, that and half a gallon of my mom's sweet tea chugging through my bloodstream.

Things had felt so solid back in Dunn's cabin last night —the connection between us undeniable and the future as close as Mal's lean body next to mine on the double bed. I'd woken up starry-eyed, dreaming of a fairy-tale life where somehow Mal and I found a way to live together in the Thicket, were godfathers to Ava's baby and uncles to my nieces, worked every day at our incredibly successful and fulfilling careers, and came together each night to discuss every minor drama of our days before fucking like a pair of bunnies—one ridiculously insatiable bunny, and one lean, pierced, hot-as-fuck bunny. Not that I thought Mal was going to give up his amazing life in LA for *me*, of course, or that I could drop everything and move to Tennessee right away either, but someday, somehow, I'd find a way to make it happen, if he wanted it too.

Then, before the parade today, I'd talked to General Partridge about the concept Paul and I had put together.

The man had been really excited about our ideas, which amped up my own excitement exponentially. Instead of putting together meaningless eye candy, we'd taken the time to get to know the product and the people creating it, and the General saw it. Our Partridge Pit campaign was organic and genuine, and our limited testing suggested it resonated with consumers too. It was the way I'd thought marketing was supposed to work, back when I started, before my years at Storms Marketing had jaded me. In short, I was proud of the work we'd done... and I couldn't remember the last time I'd felt that way about a campaign. I wanted more of that feeling.

As I'd sat beside Ava in the parade, waving at all my old friends and neighbors, I'd seen a path shining before me that wasn't a path someone else had laid out, or a path that was *good enough*, but a path that was uniquely *mine* and worth having. A genuine life, with genuine relationships and genuine people, and no more faking my way through something that should feel right but didn't.

Which was why it was so fucking ironic that the second I'd come to this realization, it had all started slipping through my fingers.

"He needs *space*, Brooks. He's not breaking up with you."

I shot Paul a look across the table. "Who said I was thinking of... anyone?" I grabbed my iced tea glass and downed the rest of the liquid, then set the glass down with a *clack*.

"You just drew a bunch of hearts on our sales projections and then systematically drew a line through each one. Either you've really internalized losing the Lope the other day—"

I snorted.

"—or you're sad that Mal isn't texting you. Which is why I'm saying, one afternoon to process a whirlwind week is not saying he never wants to see you again. *He's not breaking up with you.*"

"But he doesn't have to break up with me, does he? Because he's not *with* me."

Paul sighed. "If you saw the way he looked at you, you wouldn't be freaking out over nothing."

"That's the trouble with this sudden-onset romance shit!" I said furiously. "How do I know it's nothing? I haven't had a single relationship to compare this to, and I've known Mal for six fucking days."

"Yes, which is why you need to let things settle. For both of you—"

"I didn't set out looking for this, you know! I was perfectly okay with my life in New York, and then my feelings fucking *accosted* me in the front hallway last Sunday, while the cows just *watched*." I pointed toward the offending area. "Next thing you know, chain reaction volcanic eruptions started going off, all *boom boom boom*, and now there are these *islands* where there used to be wide-open ocean, and all the people on the island are demanding voting rights and staging a fucking *coup* and taking over my life and it's scary as fuck." I threw myself into the chair, and it scraped against the wide pine floor.

"Shit, what is *in* this tea?" Paul demanded, picking up my glass and sniffing it.

I ran both hands over my face. The sugar and caffeine were sending my anxiety into overdrive. "You know what? I'm gonna take a walk. Too much sitting," I announced, jumping back to my feet. "Gimme an hour or so—"

"You're not going anywhere," Paul informed me, rising from his seat to block my exit. "They need *space*."

I folded my arms mulishly. "What makes you think I was going next door?"

I was totally going next door. I was going to find Malachi Forrester and throw him up against the first available barn wall, and fuck him witless... a strategy that had a one hundred percent success rate for getting him to answer my texts.

"Because I know you," Paul said. "For all that you're acting like a lunatic right now."

I wasn't sure when Paul had morphed from my inhaler-sucking junior colleague into my wise and patient BFF. I thought under other circumstances—non-cock-blocking circumstances—I'd kinda like it. Though obviously I'd never tell him that.

Paul's lips twitched like maybe he knew what I was thinking anyway. "Speaking of which, have I mentioned how much I like Lunatic Brooks?"

"Yeah? Great. Thank you. Your girlfriend likes it when I overthink. You like it when I'm insane. Mal likes when..." I broke off with a swallow. "I don't know how people tolerate me when I'm actually feeling *normal*."

"We do, we just like you best when you're human," Paul said. He grabbed me by the shoulders and pushed me into my chair. "Magic, perfect Brooks is cute and all, but he's harder to be friends with, you know? Intimidating."

I frowned. "For the eight billionth time, I have *never* been perfect or—"

"Oh, dude, I know." Paul snorted, pushing his glasses up his nose. "Believe me, I know. And I also know that when you're hell-bent on being the guy everyone counts on, you start to feel like you need to ride to the rescue and solve every problem. But you *can't*, Brooks. Not this time. If Mal needs space because Mal needs to process what's happening in Mal's own life, you literally *cannot* fix it."

"But what if—"

"*But what if* we get back to work, Big Daddy Brooks." Paul smacked my arm. "Come on now."

I knew Paul was right. I just had to hope Mal would tell me what was wrong so I could fix it later.

"Call me that again and I'll remind you who's the boss of this relationship, My Little Paul," I grumbled.

"Clutching my pearls here."

"I'll kiss you," I threatened. "In front of Ava. *With tongue.*"

Paul smiled. "You've met Ava, right? She'd probably love it. Then she'd kill you slowly and make sure they never found your body." He ran a hand over his thinning hair, and his eyes went dreamy behind his glasses. "I can't wait to introduce her to my mother."

I could only imagine. The question of what would happen when an unstoppable force met an immovable object would be answered once and for all.

Paul shook his head and hit a key to wake up his laptop. "But that's for later. Right now, we're finishing up this campaign, and then we're gonna talk about how I can convince Pamela to let me work remote from Tennessee after we nail the Partridge Pit contract." He grinned excitedly. "Ava's gonna cry when she hears."

Given how emotional Ava had been about corn dogs the other night, this seemed likely. "You haven't told her your plan yet? You waiting until you get it in writing from Pamela?"

He shook his head. "I thought about waiting, but nah. Truth is... I'll be moving here anyway, Brooks. *Soon.*" He held up a hand like he thought I was going to protest. "I know it's fast. I know there's a million reasons why it might not work. But I love Ava, and I really like this town too. So if things with Storms Marketing don't work out, I'll find a job in the Thicket. Maybe I'll create high-concept campaigns for local dairy farmers. Or maybe I'll learn to milk cows." He winked.

I stared at him, stunned. "You'd give up your career, Paul? Seriously?"

"No! The milking cows was a joke, dumbass. But I'm good at what I do, so I'll find a way to fit my career into my life, rather than the other way around. I'm gonna tell Ava tonight at the dinner dance. She's crazy nervous for some reason. This news will distract her."

I pushed the idea of Paul leaving New York out of my mind temporarily. "Makes sense, doesn't it? Last time we were at this dance, it was a shitshow. It's probably some kind of PTSD thing."

"Well, no one's breaking up with her this time," Paul said firmly. "So how bad could it possibly be?"

As it turned out, the answer was very, cataclysmically bad.

———

Me: *Mal. Sweetness. We just arrived and I'd really like to see you.*

I SENT off the message before Paul had even finished putting the car in Park in the gravel lot outside the town fairgrounds, but I sat there for a long minute after he'd gotten out and ditched me to find Ava, hoping against hope that the three little text dots would appear.

They did not.

Instead, while I was sitting there, my mother appeared next to the car in a floaty silver dress like a specter in the twilight... if a ghost were capable of knocking sharply on the passenger's side window and yelling loud enough for people in the next county to hear, "Brooks, honey! Stop hiding and come on out, now! The dance is about to start, and the Head Licker needs to officially open it!"

I snorted. I had a sense of déjà vu, recalling the hundreds of times she'd caught me reading or playing on my Nintendo in someone's laundry room when I was supposed to be hanging out with the other kids at a party. The more things changed...

The difference was, this time I actually couldn't wait to get inside the dance, if only to find Mal and figure out where his head was.

I pushed my door open and stood. "Mama! Don't you look beautiful! Don't let Dad see you in that dress. Who knows what it might do to his stent situation." I wiggled my eyebrows.

She blushed just a little, even as she rolled her eyes. "Your father's not even here yet. I came over early with the rest of the Beautification Corps to finish setting up, and he fell asleep in front of the television, poor man. I don't suppose you saw him on your way out?"

I shook my head. "The shower was on when I left."

"He *hates* to be late. Ah, well. The week's taken a lot out of him, even though you've taken the brunt of the work." She smoothed my already-smooth lapels and straightened my perfectly straight tie. "Have I mentioned how glad I am that you came home, sweetie?"

"I'm glad too," I told her sincerely as we started walking toward the barn, and she looped her arm around mine.

"And I'm planning to be home a lot more often from now on. Christmases, birthdays." Maybe more than that, but I didn't want to promise something I might not deliver.

"Wouldn't that be nice?" She smiled vaguely and patted my arm. "You know you're welcome any day, any hour, Brooks. You and Paul. Where'd he run off to, by the by?"

I winced. Right. Me and Paul. I'd been so consumed with Mal today I'd somehow sort of forgotten that whole fake-boyfriend thing. Paul, Ava, and I were going to have to come up with a really foolproof plan to get people accustomed to the idea of Paul being *Ava's* boyfriend with a minimum of fuss and bother, otherwise it would be a disaster. I thought maybe I should start laying the groundwork for that sooner than later.

"I'm sure he's around here somewhere, Mama. The thing is, Paul and I are... um..."

She turned to me with wide eyes as we passed through the open double doors into the barn. "Engaged?" she whispered.

"No. *No!* Jesus, no. I'm just not sure that he's... *the one,*" I hedged.

Her face fell. "Oh, Brooks, no! You're going to devastate him if you break up with him! And now he'll never come back to the Thicket! And Mrs. Rabinowitz started knitting him a sweater!"

Fuck. Okay, not my best effort.

"It's not that I don't think he'll be back, Mama," I insisted. "I think he and I are just going to be friends. He's, um..." Straight?

She pushed her lips together. "And here I was, ready to give him my sweet tea recipe and welcome him to the family."

"But—"

"I can't talk about this right now," she sniffed, holding up a hand. "I have to think about how I'm going to break the news to your father. Just please go backstage and see if Mr. Ivey and the others have finished setting up the electric for the band and the spotlights." She gestured toward the far side of the barn, with its wide, wooden stage.

"But, Mama—"

"Go, Brooks!" she insisted.

So I went, cursing whichever fool had come up with the idea of bringing a fake boyfriend to the Thicket, and knowing full well it was *me*.

The community barn had never, in my lifetime, held actual livestock. Even for the 4H awards, the cows and pigs were held in pens further down the grounds. Instead, this barn had been converted into a catchall function room a long time ago. Since the high school didn't have a theater, this was where school plays and Christmas concerts had been held for as long as I could remember. The stage was an enormous raised box in the center of the room, enclosed on three sides and open to the front. A red velvet curtain divided the front of the stage, where I'd stand while giving my remarks, from the rear of the stage, where the band's instruments would be set up, ready for the dance later.

While the stage area was permanent, the chairs and round tables for the audience could be rearranged according to need or broken down entirely. Tonight the tables were arranged in a large U shape to create a dance floor in the center. The whole room was decked out in flowers and fairy lights, and it was clear the Beautification Corps had worked their asses off.

The crowd of Thicketeers was already starting to stream through the doors. I saw my brother and sister and exchanged back-slapping hugs with a bunch of people who'd seen me just that morning. I kept my eyes peeled, but by the time I caught up to Mr. Ivey backstage a few minutes later, I still hadn't seen Mal or Paul or General Partridge anywhere.

"Ethan, you're sure you understand what you're meant to do?" Mr. Ivey was asking Ethan Howe when I stepped up beside them. "You sit up in the loft. When it's time for the band to come on, I'll wave my hand and you'll hit this green control to open the curtain. When you wanna move the spotlight onto whoever's talking, you use these arrows. Just make sure you center the light on whoever's speaking, okay? Brooks when he does the intro, or the band when they're playing, or the winners when they're announced, or whoever. Yeah?"

"Yes. Got it," Ethan said, accepting the remote control with two hands extended like it was an ancient relic of unimaginable power... or a bomb about to detonate.

"You're sure now?" Mr. Ivey looked doubtful.

"Positive, sir. Spotlight on whoever's talking. Curtains open when you wave. Easy peasy." He nodded once. "I'll be up in the hayloft if you need me."

Mr. Ivey and I exchanged a look as Ethan walked off. "That boy," he sighed.

"So I take it everything's worked out with the electronics, then? I can tell my mom and the rest of the Beautification Corps that things are going fine?"

He nodded and took out his handkerchief to mop his brow. "Every year there's a crisis at the last minute. Nothing ever goes quite according to plan."

I smiled. "But it comes right in the end, doesn't it? Everyone's happy?"

"I s'pose that's true, son." He patted me on the shoulder.

"Have you seen Ava or Paul... I mean—" I smiled nervously. "—not together, but separately?"

So subtle, Johnson.

"'Fraid not. Neither of 'em. But you can ask Ava's boyfriend." He nodded toward the darkest corner of the backstage area, where a bunch of fake plants and an over-sized cutout of a cow stood by the wall. There was move-ment near the cow's hindquarters, and I could just make out the profile of the man I was looking for.

"Thanks, Mr. Ivey."

"Sure, sure," he said, waving me off.

As I approached Mal, I noticed two things. One, he was hunched in on himself, looking more miserable than I'd ever seen him. And two, he had his phone open to our text conversation. This didn't seem like a good sign.

"You should reply," I said, coming up behind him. "That Brooks seems like a nice guy."

Mal startled so badly he nearly dropped his phone and shot me a glare over his shoulder. He slid his phone away. "I was thinking about what to say," he said defensively.

"Right," I said to cover the sound of my heart cracking just a little. "I can see how 'Can't wait to see you' would really throw you for a loop. What's wrong, sweetness? What's going on?"

His face flushed. "Can we just... not do this now?"

"This," I repeated. "Meaning what? Talking? Or being in the same room breathing the same air? Or—"

"Yes!" he cried, throwing his hands up. "Yes, that. All of it. You being so... *you*. It's impossible to think straight when you're around. I can't... I just... I need space, Brooks." He shouldered past me, heading for the stage.

"But what happened?" I demanded, ducking around props and rolls of electric wire so I could follow behind him.

I grabbed him by the shoulder and spun him around to face me. "Just please, tell me what I did, okay? Did I say something? Did I *forget* to say something? Is it... is it that I couldn't be with you at the parade? Or do you really hate being here in the Thicket? Or—"

"What? God, no. I love Licking Thicket." He snorted. "And there's a thing I never thought I'd say."

"Okay, so it *is* me, then."

Mal huffed out a breath, his blue eyes turbulent. "Not exactly—"

"Just tell me so I can fix it, Mal. Please," I begged. "Because you're leaving here Monday, and I have to go back to New York Monday too, and I was really hoping you and I could—"

"Could *what?*" he demanded. "Fuck one more time? Exchange addresses and promise to write? No—" He broke off and shook his head. "Look, this week has been fun, and we had a good time, but you can't fix everything, Brooks. You have a life in New York, and I have one in LA."

"But we could move!" I blurted with all the finesse of Miley Cyrus and her wrecking ball. So much for my ability to stay cool and articulate in a crisis. "Here. To the Thicket. Maybe. If you wanted to. Eventually. I mean—"

Mal looked stunned. "You and me? Move to the Thicket? Really? But... you ran from this place."

"Years ago. Things have changed!" I grabbed his hands, trying to force him to listen. "Paul's moving to the Thicket to be with Ava anyway. He says he's gonna do ads for farmers or learn to milk cows, and I didn't get it when he said it, but now I kinda do. He's happy to do it for Ava. And I'd do that for you—"

Mal bit his lip like he was really considering my words. "Brooks, you have no idea how tempting that is. God. But I just got this email from a gallery in Los Angeles about a showing, and I know you're waiting to talk to the General, and it's great that we're attracted to each other, but I can't see how we could make this work. My career has been the most important thing in my life for so long. My art gave me a purpose and a place to belong when I had nothing. I want to have faith in us, but moving here for you just seems so—"

"Brooks Johnson!" General Partridge called. His cane clomped on the floor behind me. "The man of the evening! You're a hard man to track down, but I told Parrish here that I couldn't wait to go over a couple of things tonight. You remember my nephew Parrish, don't you?"

Fuck. Talk about the worst timing ever.

"Sure," I said. "Yeah. Hey. Good to see you. And this is Mal. He's—"

"Going to go find Ava," Mal said. "But nice to meet you both."

"Same to you, son," the General said.

"No," I said firmly. "Mal, please don't go. I need to—"

"Talk to your clients," Mal said with a forced smile. "That's more important."

I couldn't disagree. It was important, especially since I'd already put the General off several times, but also because he'd swooped in and catered this entire event for free. I wasn't about to blow him off again because I was in the middle of a disagreement with a man I'd known for six days. No matter how much I wanted to.

My heart thundered hard in my chest. How was it possible it had only been so little time, when I already felt like a part of Mal was embedded in me the same way the license tag from the Thicket's first milk truck was embedded in the town sign? I knew as soon as this dance was over, I needed to find Mal and talk all of this out. I wasn't about to let him get away from me. But first, I had to give my clients my full attention.

"Yes, sir," I said, pasting on a smile. "Parrish, your uncle and I were talking about..." I fell back into ad exec mode, thanks to the years of work I'd put in at Storms Marketing. Mal's voice in the back of my head whispered about me being Mr. Perfect and wearing a polite mask, but for once, I didn't feel like it was true. I actually loved what we'd put together for Partridge Pit, and I enjoyed talking through some of the details with the General and his nephew in order to make sure our presentation Monday was the best it could be.

When we finally wrapped it up, my mom was there with her bright Welcome Wagon smile. "Brooks? Honey, it's time for your speech!"

I closed my eyes and expelled a breath toward the ceiling. *Jesus fucking Christ.* All I wanted to do was find Mal. I couldn't escape the feeling that I'd messed things up badly.

"Brooks?" Mama said.

I ran a hand over my face. "Yeah, coming."

"Don't forget to thank—"

"I know." Without another word, I moved past her and trudged up the stairs to the front of the stage. I gave the crowd a bright, fake smile. "Ladies and gentlemen! Thank you so much for coming here tonight, and thanks for another great Lickin'! First off, I'd love to thank everyone who made tonight possible! Thank you to General Beauregard Partridge and Partridge Pit for donating all of our food, and to the Licking Thicket Beautification Corps for these amazing flowers—"

I pointed toward my mother and her friends standing in the crowd, and Ethan swung a spotlight in their direction, which almost made me laugh despite wanting to punch something. Not quite what Mr. Ivey intended, but it was cute.

I paused for the applause to die down, and as I scanned the crowd, I saw Mal making his way toward the exit. *Fuck.* I needed him to stay.

"And thank you to Mal Forrester for his amazing Welcome to Licking Thicket sign. We are so very fortunate to have such a work of art in our town!"

Mal froze and turned toward me in disbelief, but I lifted a hand toward him like a game show hostess, and when Ethan put the spotlight on him and the whole town started clapping, Mal's quiet exit was foiled.

"A huge thanks to Mr. Ivey and his crew for helping to set up all the electronics for tonight." I pointed toward him in the crowd, and he waved his thanks...

And the velvet curtain started opening behind me.

I pressed my lips together, fighting a grin. Poor Ethan.

"I'd also like to thank—"

But then the crowd started muttering. My mother stared up at me with eyes wide as saucers. Mrs. Ivey screamed, "Oh my Jesus Lord!" And even Mal looked stunned.

I darted a look over my shoulder to see what the fuss was about... and found my ex-girlfriend caught in a deep-diving tonsil exploration with my fake boyfriend.

Well. *Fuck.*

"Ava Marie!" Mrs. Ivey yelled. "You get away from that boy!"

Paul and Ava finally seemed to realize their backstage hookup had become a front-stage spectacle, and they did move apart... but only slightly.

Ava grabbed Paul's hand and turned imploring eyes on her mother.

"No, Mama!" she cried, like a character in one of those TV movies I swear I only watched for market research. "I can't because I... I *love* him!"

Oh my God.

"But, Ava," Mrs. Ivey insisted, lifting a hand to block the glare when Ethan swung the spotlight at her. "You *can't* love him. You're... you know!"

"Presbyterian," Aunt Birdie explained.

"What? No," Mrs. Ivey said, confused. "We go to the same church as you, Birdie."

"Illegitimate?" Lurleen guessed.

"Absolutely not," Mr. Ivey said staunchly.

"Already shacked up with this hottie?" Alana jabbed an elbow into Mal's ribs, and Mal flinched but was too stunned to protest.

"Pregnant!" Mrs. Ivey blurted out. "She's pregnant!"

Ava gasped. "Oh, my God. How did you know?"

"Oh, Ava," Mrs. Ivey scoffed. "Honey, no one drinks that much tea."

"But..." Mr. Ivey looked from his wife to his daughter in confusion, and then his angry gaze narrowed on Mal. "*You!* After I let you use my workshop and everything?"

Mal's mouth opened and closed like a fish, and he looked to Ava for guidance. If I hadn't already thought he was incredible, I would have thought it then, because he looked like he was willing to let Mr. Ivey strangle him if that was what Ava wanted.

"No, Daddy!" Ava said. "Mal's not the father."

"Wait, he's not?" Mrs. Ivey demanded.

"No." Ava exhaled sharply. "He's my best friend, and he came here to provide moral support. But Mal's... gay."

"Gay! Oh, dear Lord, she done turned another one." Amos Nutter shook his head and made a *tsking* noise.

"Hey! She didn't *turn* anyone," I said hotly. "I was always gay, I just wasn't ready to come out in high school. Ava was an amazing girlfriend."

"Excuse *you*! You don't get to defend Ava!" Mal yelled from the crowd. "If you'd really cared about her, you wouldn't have made her fall in love with you and then run off and *left* her."

I gaped at him, shocked and hurt. Was that really what he thought? Was that really what I'd done?

"You broke her heart," Mal said, his voice cracking a little. I'd swear his blue eyes were shiny with tears... or maybe it was from Ethan and the death-ray spotlight he kept swinging at each person, like this was the world's most insane telenovela.

"Well, I mean, in retrospect it wasn't really broken—" Ava began from behind me.

"Malachi is *right*," my own mother said, striding forward to wrap an arm around Mal's shoulders. "You left and broke *all* of our hearts, Brooks!"

"Oh, God. Mama, please." Gracie covered her face with her hands and shook her head. "He did *not*."

"Has anyone seen my dad?" Dunn demanded, knowing my dad was the only one who could put the cork back in my mother's bottle. "Is he here yet?"

"And now, by failing to give your boyfriend the love he so desperately craved," my mother continued, undeterred, "you've driven him into Ava's arms!"

"Yeah!" Mal agreed. He paused and frowned, then shrugged like facts had ceased to be important. "What your mom said!"

I scowled down at him. "What the hell are you talking about? You know better!" I waved a hand in Paul's direction. "Tell them, Paul!"

"I mean, it's true that Brooks was never very emotionally available to me," Paul said sadly.

I turned and speared him with a look that promised endless painful retribution.

"But also, I'm straight," he admitted quickly.

"Wait, so now she turns the gay ones straight?" Amos Nutter demanded wonderingly. "Well, I'll be damned."

"She didn't turn him straight, Amos," Mr. Ivey scolded. "Biology doesn't work like that. But I'll tell you what else I know about biology. If Ava's pregnant, *somebody*'s gotta be the father." He glared at Paul. "Was it you, son?"

"Oh, God," Ava groaned. "No, Daddy, Paul's not—"

"I'm the father if Ava wants me to be," Paul said stoutly, adjusting his eyeglasses. "And the biological father of the child is Ava's business and absolutely *no one else's*." He glared at Mr. Ivey and then at the crowd in general, more commanding than I'd ever seen him, without a trace of his inhaler in sight.

The whole town let out a collective sigh. Even Lurleen nodded in approval.

"Hear, hear!" Diesel Church called out.

Ava's father nodded, and one side of his mouth quirked up. "Well, alright. All I've ever wanted for my girl is a partner who'd stand up for her. You'll do."

"But, Brad!" Mrs. Ivey wailed. "What if he moves her to New York?"

"Hush, Monette," he said, patting his wife on the back. "Still closer than Los Angeles. I'm satisfied."

I was really glad *somebody* around here was. But while the whole town was exclaiming over Ava, the guy I wanted was making a beeline for the door.

I jumped down from the stage and pushed through the crowd. "Mal! Stop, please!"

Mal whirled to face me. "We've said all there is to say. Please, Brooks—"

"But we haven't! We haven't. Mal, I—" *Love you* was on the tip of my tongue, but I couldn't bring myself to say it. Not here, not with all these people. Not when I wasn't sure how he felt. "I care about you. Please stay."

"If you care about me, Brooks, then do me this one favor, okay? Take care of Ava tonight. Make sure she's okay." Mal sniffled a little, and I wanted so badly to wrap my arms around him. "Be the friend she needed you to be ten years ago."

"And what about *you*?" I demanded. "Am I supposed to just let you walk away in the meantime?"

"Yes. I keep telling you, Brooks. There are some things you just can't fix." He pressed a kiss to my cheek and walked out the door.

I pressed a hand over the spot where his lips had hit my cheek and watched him go for half a minute, the need to go after him and the need to honor his wishes warring for dominance. But before I had a chance to commit one way or the other, Ava was behind me, laying a restraining hand on my arm.

"Let him go, Brooks."

"You know what happened to him before, Ava. He left his hometown, and not a single person went after him. I want him to know... to know that..."

Ava pulled me into a one-armed hug. "When Mal left his hometown, it wasn't his choice, Brooks. He *had* to leave. When he landed in LA, it was because he ran out of money." She smiled faintly. "There's not a lot in Mal's life that's really been his *choice*, you know? It's just been a string of reactions to other people's needs and wants. Including mine. Right now, he made a choice, and we have to respect that even if it's not the choice either of us wish he'd made. Respect the space he's asking you for."

"But he looked so damn *sad*—"

"He'll be okay, Brooks. I'll make sure of it."

I let out a shaky breath and admitted my true fear. "But what if he goes and—"

"And doesn't come back to Licking Thicket for, like, ten whole years? Or never comes back at all? Then I guess that's his choice too, isn't it?"

I glanced down at her. *Fuck.* It really was.

I'd spun out this whole fantasy life of me and Mal in the Thicket, and then I'd tried to show him how *perfect* it was...

Because that strategy had worked so well on *me* back in the day, right?

In the end, that life was *my* fantasy. Mal had made it pretty clear tonight that wasn't what he wanted. Our time together was done, and if I respected Mal at all, I had to respect his wishes about this.

After all that Mal had given me this week—his understanding, his humor, his passion, his insight into the Thicket that had finally made my hometown feel like my *home* town after all these years—I'd be a selfish bastard if I didn't.

And I had a sudden flash of insight into how Ava must've felt all those years ago, because it really was heartbreaking to be the person who got left behind.

Ava laid her head on my shoulder for a second, then sniffed and straightened. "Alright, enough. Come on back inside before Amos Nutter decides I've added you to my bisexual harem. And, ah... you might have a thing or two to explain to your mother."

"Yeah." Compared to Mal leaving, the rest of this shit-storm didn't seem too terrible.

"Strength in numbers," Ava said confidently, wrapping her hand around mine.

I remembered Mal teasing me for always trying to fix everything for everyone, for trying to be perfect. How ironic that the best way to make things right for the person who mattered most was to stand back and let him walk away from me.

Chapter Eighteen

Mal

I WAS BEING RIDICULOUS. I knew that. And quite frankly, it was nothing new. Echoes of "such a drama queen" bounced around my head in my mother's voice. It was as familiar to me as I'd imagine any lullaby would have been for a "normal" kid. Whatever normal meant.

But I also had a long enough and painful enough history to justify protecting my heart. And right now, I needed to get the fuck out of this place in order to do that. Regardless of how I felt about Brooks Johnson, I needed to focus on my career, and this gallery opportunity wasn't something I could pass up. I needed to get back to the Iveys' and pack.

Unfortunately, the fairgrounds were on the other side of Licking Thicket from the Iveys' farm, so I had to walk straight through the square and out by the highway on my way back. As I made my way through town, I tried not to notice the brick half wall where Brooks had sat and stared at my vendor booth when he thought I wasn't looking. I tried not to look at the tax office where he'd shoved me up against the wall and given me drunken heart eyes. And when I had to pass the back of the football stadium, I didn't dare look over at the metal bleachers.

But there was only so much emotion I could fight. When I arrived at the town sign, I stopped and stared. Someone had set up a new system of uplighting to display it to full advantage. The giant sculpture shone like a proud lion at the entrance to his lair. It was everything I'd wanted it to be: clean but well-used, classic but with a nod to modern technology, and whimsical without being cheesy.

I heard an older man's voice behind me. "You should be very proud of yourself, son."

I turned to see Red Johnson approaching from his parked truck. I'd been so distracted with the details of the sign and thinking about Brooks, I hadn't even heard him pull up.

I swallowed. "Thank you, sir. I'm happy with how it turned out."

Brooks's dad stepped up beside me and studied the sign with his hands in his pockets. "We've never had anything near this nice here, and I can't stop driving up and down this road just staring at it. It truly is a work of art, Mal. You're very talented."

His words shot right into my heart and bloomed into a wash of feelings I wasn't expecting. I wasn't sure I'd ever experienced paternal pride before. Another first here in the Thicket.

"Thank you," I said again in a bit of a whisper. His words were a kind of benediction of my decision to fly back to California and prepare for the gallery showing. I *was* talented. And I wasn't going to give that up for anyone.

Not that Brooks had asked me to, of course. He wouldn't do that. But the realization my self-doubt and second-guessing had come from my own internal bullshit was upsetting. Brooks was putting his own career first *as he should*. Why the hell had I contemplated letting my career take a back seat to this whirlwind romance, even for a minute?

Mr. Johnson looked over at me. "The Thicket could use more people like you. Entrepreneurs, artists... people who seem to get what we're all about. It's clear from this sign that you get us even though you've only been here a week. That's amazing."

I poked my toe at a rock in the dirt. "I grew up in a town like this. Well, not as great as this, but a small town where everyone knew everyone."

"They must miss you very much back there."

I bit back a laugh. "No, sir. Not a bit. Unfortunately, Homer isn't as accepting of people's differences as the Thicket is."

"Ahh." He looked back at the sign for a moment. "We weren't always this accepting either. I'm sure Brooks has told you about how uncomfortable he felt growing up. If he'd had friends like you back then, maybe he wouldn't have felt so alone."

I peered over at him in the darkness, lit only by the sign's uplighting. What did that mean? Did he know I was gay? Or did he just know I was different somehow? "Friends like me?"

"There's something about you that seems to relax him more than I ever saw before. At first I thought it was Paul, that maybe being in a relationship was what had caused the change, but then I remembered the night he arrived and how buttoned-up and stressed he still was. No, it wasn't until he started spending time with you and Ava that he calmed down. So then I thought it was Ava, that maybe he was back to feeling a connection with her somehow."

"Brooks is gay, sir," I couldn't help saying. "That's very real."

"I know it, son." He stopped talking for a bit and smiled softly at the sign. "Do you know what he did when he saw this sign for the first time?"

I shook my head. My heart was ka-thunking in my chest, and I was afraid to speak for fear it would fly out of my mouth.

"He crashed his car. He doesn't even know he did it. He yanked the car over to the side of the road and sideswiped the mirrors off Becky Dodd's jeep *and* Mr. Silverman's Buick in the process. They called me asking if he was having some kind of mental break. Becky said that he knelt down and ran his hands over this part here like it was the second coming of Christ." He crouched down and pointed to the 2010 Licking Lope trophy engraved with Brooks's name. Ava had given it to me from the shelf in her room where he'd apparently stuck it that day after winning it for her. The cow horn glinted in the cool light.

My throat felt too tight and my tongue too thick, so I stood there without speaking. If he so much as mentioned Brooks, I was going to burst into tears like an asshole. There was no solution to this problem. I lived and worked in LA. He lived and worked in New York. And his pipe dream about moving to the Thicket was just that. If he gave up his career for me, he'd resent me. And more than that? If I gave up my career for him, I'd resent him too. Especially if things didn't work out. That was way too much stress to put on a six-day relationship, no matter what my heart said.

Mr. Johnson stood up and put his hands back in his pockets, cool as can be. "Did you ever hear the story about how I stole Cindy Ann right out from under her parents' noses at the Blue Iris Debutante Ball?"

I wasn't in the mood for a folksy story, but I also wasn't about to be rude to Mr. Johnson. "No, sir."

He nodded. "You see, she was all set to get engaged to Daniel... aw, hell, I can't remember his last name now. Something stuck-up and Nashville snotty. Anyway, they'd been Mr. and Mrs. Perfect all through school, kind of like Brooks and Ava, you see?"

I bit my tongue to keep from giving him more of my thoughts on the topic than he'd bargained for.

"But I knew just because that pair looked good on paper, didn't mean it was the right thing. I'd met her several times before at events leading up to the ball. My cousin Brenda had asked me to be her escort for all of those fancy parties that summer in Nashville, and I'd gone to every single one of them. I'd like to have died at how boring those things were, and I'd never in my life had so much sweet tea and rubber chicken. But the afternoon of one of those stupid things, I'd looked up and seen this beautiful girl sitting by herself on a bench under a tree."

He sighed and smiled. Something about the gesture made my chest constrict. "She was wearing a little pout, and I wanted to see if I could piss her off and make her even madder." He laughed. "I don't even know why. Maybe because I'd gotten it into my head that most of those girls were spoiled princesses. Turned out, I couldn't have been further from the truth. When I went over there, she gave me a bunch of polite small talk while I kept pushing her. Finally, I saw one damned teardrop fall out of her eye."

I tried to picture perky, force-of-nature Mrs. Johnson crying all alone at a debutante soiree. The woman was a buzzy social bee, always in the middle of every conversation. It was strange to hear him describe her this way.

"Why was she crying?"

"Her daddy had died not three days before."

"You're kidding? And she was at a tea party?"

His jaw tightened. "Exactly. Her mama was even more insistent that Cindy Ann make a good marriage match now that they were left all alone. As soon as I learned that, I felt awful. I spent the rest of the afternoon trying desperately to atone for my atrocious actions and cheer her up. Her own date, Daniel Whatshisname, was nowhere to be found. After that, every time I saw her at one of those events, I made a point of keeping her company, getting to know her, trying to distract her. And I learned an important lesson that summer."

Here it was. The parental moral of the story.

I glanced at him. "Don't judge a debutante by her pout?"

He chuckled and nodded. "Damned right. Everybody is fighting a pain you don't know about. But that's not what I meant. I learned that it's possible to fall head over heels in love with someone in an instant. And I also learned that it can happen even when things seem impossible. Everyone knew she was promised to Daniel. But I didn't let that stop me. I kidnapped her right out of that ballroom and drove her all the way home to the Thicket."

My heart sped up. Did Brooks's dad know about the two of us? "What... what're you telling me this for?"

His smile was kind. Mr. Johnson's hand came up to squeeze my shoulder gently. "There are moments in our lives that define us. Moments where we have to make a choice that will change the path of our future. They come upon us suddenly, don't they?"

I thought about my decision to move with Ava or stay in California. "Yes, sir," I said weakly. "How do you know when you're making the right decision?"

"Well, son, I should probably tell you to follow your heart. But in my case, I followed my dick, and it hasn't steered me wrong yet."

I stared at him in shock for a few beats until the corner of his mouth curved up the tiniest bit.

"Malachi, if you weren't expecting a dick joke from a man named Red Johnson..." His eyes twinkled in the moonlight. "Then maybe you don't belong here in Licking Thicket after all."

A bark of laughter escaped me, and I clapped my hand over my mouth to keep from being rude. But Mr. Johnson's face was wide open with laughter, and he looked so much like his son, I couldn't hold back anymore. I laughed and cried like someone who'd come completely unhinged.

Mr. Johnson laughed with me until he realized I was crying too. Then he turned and pulled me into a giant bear hug, murmuring the kind of paternal reassurances I'd never heard from my own father. "It's gonna be okay, son. You're gonna be okay."

"I'm sorry," I sniffled when I finally caught my breath and pulled away. "I don't know what got into me."

"It's been a big week."

I snorted. "Yeah. I guess you could say that."

His big hands were still warm and solid on my shoulders as he leaned down to meet my eyes.

"You know, Dunn told me about you and Brooks."

I opened my mouth to sputter an explanation, although I wasn't at all sure what it would be, but he stopped me.

"Calm down," he said. "He only told me 'cause I had my suspicions and I asked him flat out. The boy's got no poker face whatsoever. He told me about Paul and Ava too, so I understand that puts a hitch in your giddyup. I just want you to know that regardless of what may or may not happen between Paul and Ava or you and Brooks or any combination of the four of you," he said, looking into my eyes with a kind of affectionate sincerity that nearly brought me to my knees, "I hope you'll consider spending more time here with us in the Thicket whether on a permanent basis or another good visit. We'd love to have you, and you'll be most welcome, with or without any of the rest of your crazy crew, including my son."

"Thank you, sir," I whispered.

He patted my shoulders before moving back toward his truck. "Now, hop in and let me give you a ride back to the Iveys' farm before you get bug-bit to death."

———

On the flight back to LA, I spent way too much money drowning my sorrows in mini bottles. It may have been a little too early for that much alcohol consumption, but that couldn't be helped. At one point, the older lady in the seat across the aisle from me shot me a judgmental look, and I muttered something about "the time change" as if I'd flown in from Rome where I'd left some kind of happy hour in full swing when I'd boarded the plane.

I'd held it together long enough to grasp Ava's hand Sunday morning over breakfast where she had a tearful but ultimately loving and understanding conversation with her parents about the pregnancy. I'd held it together long enough to accept the Mr. Licking Thicket crown I'd apparently won Saturday night in absentia. Mr. Ivey had placed it on my spot at the breakfast table and beamed at me. "You're an official Thicketeer now, Mal," he'd said.

The title had come with a T-shirt and a sash too, but I'd shoved them in my luggage without looking at them. There was no way I could face the guilt I had at not being there to accept such an honor in person. I must have looked like an ungrateful ass. Ava had told everyone that I'd had a work emergency come up which wasn't far from the truth.

When I'd stood in the corner at the dance and used my phone to keep from making eye contact with anyone, I'd noticed an email from one of the galleries back in LA. They wanted my reef sculpture for an upcoming show. The only catch was an incredibly tight turnaround. They wanted the piece installed within the coming week for the opening Friday night. It was the kind of break I'd waited years for. Acceptance into the official art scene meant legitimacy, connections, and future opportunities at other galleries.

So the drunken flight was the only pity party I allowed myself. As soon as I got back to the studio, I went straight to work. I used my headphones like a hair shirt and blasted some stupid fucking Spotify playlist called All The Feels which, honestly, had a decided lack of happy ones. So then I switched to a playlist called Happy Beats which literally had a song on it called "Pour The Milk" which made me fucking cry and think of Annabelle and her soft udder and warm brown eyes, and Jesus fucking Christ, now I was missing a cow.

There really should be a warning on Spotify. Something like... never press play if you've just walked away from the one you... like a lot.

I sighed and yanked the headphones off. This was fucking ridiculous. "He's just a guy. Nothing special," I told the smashed muffler flounder I was attaching to the base of a coral formation. The movers were coming in three days to crate the piece for transportation to the gallery, and I still had at least thirty hours of work left on it. "He doesn't even..." I tried to think of Brooks Johnson's shortcomings.

"He doesn't even..." I sighed. "Know who Milton Reeves is," I finally said to the flounder. I wasn't a hundred percent sure, but one could guess Brooks wouldn't know who the inventor of the muffler was. "So there. Imagine not knowing who Milton Reeves is. Pfft. You wouldn't even be here without him."

"Are you talking to a metal sproingy thing and his metal sproingy friends?" Ava asked, walking in with a giant iced coffee and a vanilla bean Frappuccino which was basically a milkshake dressed up to look like a fancy coffee drink.

"Those are struts, and if that coffee is for me, I will give you an extra foot rub later."

She grinned. "It is, but you would have given me the foot rub anyway."

I climbed down from the ladder and took the drink from her, groaning through the first sip. "True, but God, I could kiss you right now for this."

"Looks like you could use it. No offense, but you look like dog poop." She peered at the sculpture while she took a sip of her own drink. "How's it coming?"

I let out an internal sigh of relief that she wasn't bringing up the dreaded topic of a certain man from Tennessee. "Good. I'll probably spend a few more hours working on it tonight, but then I need to get some decent sleep since I have a teleconference with the gallery owner early in the morning. I don't want to look like dog shit on the call, you know?" I lifted an eyebrow at her.

"Good call. You might try some cucumbers on your eyes too. Or a cold compress if you don't have cukes. If I'd realized how bad it was, I could have brought—"

I held up a hand. "Stop it right there. I don't need a rundown on how bad I look or tips on how to fix it, okay?"

She tilted her head to study me. "This isn't just from

overworking yourself. You're spending time sniffling over Brooks, aren't you?"

So much for hoping she wouldn't bring it up.

"No idea what you're talking about," I said before setting down my drink and stepping back toward the ladder.

She let me go without arguing. When I peeked back down at her after drilling my next hole in the base of the strut, she was lying back in the overstuffed armchair and sipping her drink with a thoughtful look on her face. I went back to what I was doing.

Three minutes later, she broke the silence. "You know... I wasn't going to tell you this, but..." She stopped talking until I looked down at her again. I wondered if she had news of Brooks. Hell would freeze over before I asked her.

"But what?" I finally blurted.

"Paul decided to stay in New York. He said things were too unsettled between us. It wasn't worth the risk."

I blinked at her, completely unable to comprehend what she was saying. "What? What the fuck? What? Why? Brooks said Paul was moving to the Thicket. What?" I sounded like an idiot, but what could have possibly happened to turn a lovesick Paul Siegel into someone who'd walk away from Ava Ivey?

She shrugged and kept her eyes down on the hand she held protectively over her stomach. "I guess I don't deserve him."

"Bullshit," I snapped, climbing back down off the ladder and rushing over to crouch by her feet. "Maybe he's the one who doesn't deserve you." I thought about what a kind and sweet man he was and knew this couldn't be right. "He's just scared, honey. You need to talk to him. Tell him to get his head out of his ass. That man adores you. He worships the ground you walk on."

"But he lives in New York, and I'm going to be in Tennessee. How can I ask him to move to Licking Thicket and give up his career?"

"You won't be asking him to give up his career! He can have a career in Licking Thicket. Brooks said Paul would do local ad jobs or milk cows for you. There's no shame in that. If he loved you enough, he'd figure it the fuck out." I took her hands in mine. "Hell, Ava. You asked me to move there for you. Why can't you ask the man you care about to do the same?"

She finally looked up at me, and I saw the truth in her eyes. She'd been playing me.

"Paul's moving to the Thicket, isn't he?"

She nodded.

"Good. I didn't think he was dumb enough to walk away from the woman he loves."

"Then why did you walk away from Brooks?" she asked softly. "You care about him. You might even *love* him. Why didn't you tell him?"

I opened my mouth, then shut it again. "It's different with us," I finally said, getting back to my feet.

"Don't you *dare* tell lies like that in front of my baby, Malachi Forrester." Ava put her drink down so she could lay both palms against her perfectly flat stomach, like she was blocking the fetus's ears.

"Can babies that young even hear?" I demanded, sorting through the variety of smaller parts I'd laid out on the table earlier.

"Irrelevant. He can *sense* your lies."

I looked up at her. "Oh my God! Your baby has Jedi truth sense? Holy shit, who *was* that guy at Beyond Wonderland?"

"Mal."

I turned back to the sculpture. "And it's a boy? You're calling it right now?"

"Malachi."

"Because I'm picking *girl*, and I've never been wrong about this. Probably because I've never actually tried to guess before, but still..."

"Mal, turn around and look at me. All that shit you said to me applies to you too! How in the world do you think you don't deserve love? How can you possibly think what you have with Brooks isn't worth at least taking a risk to see if it could be more? He cares about you, you know."

"Of course I know." After that night in his brother's cabin, how could I not? "But he cared about you too, back in the day. And he cares about his family. He... he cares about a lot of things, Ava. Including his career in New York. And when it came time to pick between the things he cared about ten years ago, you know what he picked."

"But—"

I spun to face her. "Ava, babe. I've made up my mind. I won't do that to him *or* to myself. Reality is reality, and what happens in the Thicket stays in the Thicket."

She pushed her lips together unhappily but said nothing.

I knew she meant well. She loved me so much she couldn't imagine anyone *not* loving me. But I knew better.

Brooks and I had spent the last week in a Licking Thicket bubble—a human snow globe where everything was idyllic and sparkly bright and perfect. I'd fallen hard and fast, and I couldn't have stopped it if I'd tried. I couldn't even bring myself to regret it.

But no matter how tempting it was to listen to Ava, Brooks had been really clear about how important his career was and how happy it made him. I had no doubt that once he got back to his real life, he'd see how crazy the thought of moving to Tennessee permanently really was, if he hadn't already. He might miss me temporarily, but ultimately he'd be glad he hadn't tied himself down. God knew my own family seemed to get along without me just fine.

I would *never* allow myself to be Brooks's obligation, and I also wouldn't allow his career to take precedence over mine. Staying there any longer in hopes of some kind of happy ever after would not only have been a fool's errand, but it could also have cost me this incredible opportunity at the gallery.

"And what about you moving to the Thicket for *yourself?*" she asked softly. "It doesn't need to have anything to do with Brooks. The rent is cheaper there. Your niece or nephew will be there. *I'll* be there."

Except it *would* be about Brooks. Every blade of grass in every pasture in the town would make me think of him. If I ever managed to get my longing under control, I'd have to avoid him every time he came for a visit, or the addiction would come back stronger.

But then I thought about Brooks's dad, and how he said I was welcome no matter what, and how Dunn had called me his friend, and how the week I'd been forced to spend in that ridiculous town had been the best week of my life. Not *all* of that had been about Brooks. Not even half. If I made this choice for *me*, then I wouldn't be resentful. I just had to figure out what that would look like.

"I'll think about it," I told Ava. "But in the meantime, I'm going to finish this piece so I can sell it for a fortune and buy your Jedi baby a LEGO Death Star."

Chapter Nineteen

Brooks

"Partridge Pit is the real deal. It's small-town good," a smiling guy in a Gators hat said.

"You know I gotta add a couple little secret touches to make the sauce my own, right?" the middle-aged lady in the box braids said with a wink for the camera. "But I'd never start with anything else. Partridge Pit is small-town good."

"It's yummy!" a pair of redheaded twins in identical outfits sang in unison, sitting on the scrub grass in their backyard. Their mom leaned into the frame and added with a laugh, "And if these two will eat it, you *know* it's small-town good."

Even sitting in the ergonomic chairs in Storms Marketing's sleek glass-and-chrome conference room, I could feel the warmth as real people, *diverse* people, from hometowns across the country, filled the screen in a montage of squares that expanded out—what I liked to call Paul's *Love, Actually* montage—in a chorus of, "It's small-town good."

And then an older gentleman's face filled the screen, nodding as he told the audience, "You can believe me when I say... Partridge Pit is small-town good," in a manner so dignified and *sincere*, I'd have voted for him as president, let alone trusted his opinion on barbecue sauce.

The screen faded to black.

Holy. Shit.

We'd done it.

I caught Paul's eye across the table, and he nodded once, a little smile playing around his mouth that said he felt the same way I did. It was the best campaign we'd ever worked on. This was the proudest moment of my career.

General Partridge, who was seated next to Paul, whistled appreciatively. His nephew Parrish, who Paul and I had gotten to know better on the General's plane as he flew us from Tennessee to New York that morning, even slow-clapped while shaking his head and grinning. "Epic," he pronounced as someone turned the lights in the room back on.

To say this win felt good was an understatement, especially after the last couple of days.

They said it was better to have loved and lost, but I was not on board that bullshit train. Maybe I'd be able to find some silver linings later, after I'd laundered my shirts that still smelled like Mal's sandalwood fragrance, after I stopped looking for him in every room I entered and hoped to see his name on my phone every time it rang, after I stopped working on the project *he'd* spearheaded by tossing me the perfect tagline. Maybe once I stopped feeling like a stranger in the city that had been my home for ten years.

I remembered standing in my parents' backyard just over a week ago and feeling like a stranger, but the Thicket had sunk its claws into me, and now it was New York that felt weird. Too busy, too fast. Not a bovine or a crotchety old neighbor to be found.

No Mal. Not *home.*

Paul cleared his throat to catch my attention and subtly nodded toward Pamela.

Right. I snapped out of my reverie immediately. *Head in the game, Brooks.*

It took me a second to register that the silence from the other side of the table wasn't appreciative silence, but the silence of people who'd witnessed something embarrassing and weren't sure where to put their eyes. Pamela stared at the black wall screen and drummed her pink fingernails against the glass table thoughtfully. Kale watched me with a disdainful expression. Everyone else—my assistant Carlin and the members of Kale's "Team Fresh Blood"—studied the table like they might be tested on it later.

Shit.

The General waded into that silence fearlessly with a thump of his cane on the carpeted floor. "Well, Brooks, I take back everything I said about fancy New York advertisements. *That* is just what I want for my campaign. Ms. Storms, where do I sign?"

Pamela forced a smile. "General, I want you to understand, this is only one direction we can go in. Not even necessarily the best direction."

I frowned, and she cast me a look that probably would've made me quake in my bespoke suit a couple of weeks ago. I'd known she wouldn't be happy that I'd gone around her to share my ideas with the General. I'd had a fair idea she'd be displeased when I showed up to the office that morning *with* my client, without giving her a chance to preview the campaign. But I'd been confident she'd see the merit in what Paul and I had designed, be thrilled by the General's enthusiasm, and be too excited about nailing down a client to be truly angry.

I'd been wrong.

But I couldn't bring myself to care that I was disappointing her either. What was the point here? Pleasing *her*? Or pleasing the client?

General Partridge frowned. "I don't know how to be clearer than to say it flat out, Ms. Storms. I want that." He nodded to the empty screen. "Brooks got to the heart of what I wanted and served it up better'n I ever could."

"I'm sure," Pamela said blandly, with a cold smile that conveyed zero assurance. "But as marketing professionals, General Partridge, it's our job not just to give the customer what they want, but what they deserve. You wouldn't tell a brain surgeon how to operate, right? This campaign..." She shook her head sadly. "It's charming, but not particularly creative or even broadly appealing."

I clenched my hands into fists on my lap. Across the table, Paul's nostrils flared.

"Ms. Storms, I grew up in a town called Soddy Gulf. You ever been?"

"No," Pamela admitted.

"That's alright. Not a lot of people have." He waved the hand that wasn't holding the cane negligently. "I learned to cook barbecue on a repurposed oil drum, using the recipe my granddaddy passed to my mama and then to me. It's not real fancy or *creative*. I don't think it's even broadly appealing," he said with a chuckle. "But it's real and it's true and it's *good*. And I don't hold with overcomplicating things." He tapped his cane on the ground again like he'd said all he had to say on the subject and pushed himself to his feet. "Now. Brooks, how about you bring some contracts and let's sign 'em over lunch. I'm *starved*."

Everyone else darted a look at Pamela, who hadn't moved, then reluctantly got to their feet and headed back to their desks to post-mortem my downfall.

"Brooks. A minute of your time, please," Pamela called before I reached the door.

"Of course," I agreed smoothly, which was Brooks Johnson speak for, "Jesus Christ, Pamela, I just scored us a big client. I can't believe you're going to read me the fucking riot act." And then I caught myself.

How ridiculous. Turned out I wasn't any more "real" in New York than I'd been as a kid in the Thicket. I could hear Mal's voice in my head teasing me.

"Brooks, what the hell is going on?" Pamela demanded. "You were steady. Dependable. You were my rock."

I leaned back against the door and regarded her coolly. "I still am."

She shook her head. "You ran off in the middle of a proposal. You hardly returned my phone calls. You went behind my back to show General Partridge your designs—"

"Which he loved, and which are totally in line with his brand."

"But not with *our* brand. Brooks, you were the one who warned me that Storms Marketing had a reputation to protect—"

"That was back when you gave Kale the Partridge Pit campaign. And I was right. All he managed to do was piss the client off."

She shook her head like I was missing something crucial. "He might not have hit on precisely the right note, but he pushed the envelope. He innovated. You..." She shuddered delicately. "You put together an unironic, down-home, *junkyard* campaign that's like a hundred other campaigns out there—"

"That's like other things out there, but better. We repurposed old ideas and made them into something new. And for what it's worth, you can find lots of inspiration in junkyards."

She blinked. "Do you... do you even hear yourself? *Junkyarrrrds.* Since when do you have that accent? Are you having some kind of mental health... episode, or whatever? Is it because of what happened with your dad? Because we can arrange for some time off."

I almost laughed. I was miserable and homesick, but I felt like *myself* for the first time in maybe twenty-eight years.

"I'm fine, Pamela. The truth of the matter is, the General isn't going to accept another campaign—"

"He will if you convince him he's wrong. And you should, Brooks."

I understood the implication. What it meant for my job and my future. But... "I won't," I said, with no polite smile and no equivocation. And it felt *good.* It felt *great.*

It felt *right.*

Even though I wanted to vomit.

Pamela frowned. "Brooks, you're forcing my hand," she warned.

But I wasn't. I was forcing my own. And scary as it was to think about leaving everything I'd built for myself in New York, it was scarier still to think of living a life that wasn't anchored by anything real. I was done with faking my way through things. So it was clear what I needed to do.

I pushed away from the door, braced my hands on the table, and smiled. "You've taught me a lot, Pamela, and I can't thank you enough, but I quit."

———

"Son, I only wish I coulda seen the look on her face when you told her you were going back to Tennessee." General Partridge—or *Beau*, as he'd invited me to call him, since we'd become besties after he'd ordered a third round of Johnnie Walker—grinned at me, his cheeks pink behind his full, white beard.

I pushed my lips together and looked across the room to the bar, where Paul and Parrish Partridge chatted while waiting for another round of drinks.

"I'd rather I hadn't seen it," I said honestly, taking a sip of my *first* shot of whiskey since I was still dehydrated from all the Fuzzy Thickets last week.

Pamela hadn't taken the news well at all. She'd ranted and raved for a long while before realizing I was not going to change my mind. She'd said she was disappointed in me. She said I'd let her down. All the things I'd dreaded hearing all my life.

But in a strange way, I felt numb to it. Watching Mal walk away had been so gut-wrenching, other shit paled in comparison.

I downed the rest of my glass in one go.

"You did the right thing, Brooks. There are lines a man can't cross. Sounds silly, maybe, but I'm proud of you. And you're a man I'd like to do business with, once you start your own firm."

I laughed once. My own firm, with Paul as my partner. An ad company based in Tennessee. I wasn't sure why I hadn't put all the pieces together before today.

"Absolutely, Gener—ah, *Beau*. I'll let you know as soon as I have the paperwork drawn up."

The General nodded once and took another sip of his drink. He regarded me pensively. "You know, I can't help noticing you don't look like a man who's ready to celebrate."

"No, sir. Not what I expected to happen today. It's... terrifying," I admitted. "Good, but terrifying."

"Best things are." He watched me again. "Have you told your family and friends yet?"

"Not yet. My mama will be thrilled."

He nodded. "And will you be leaving behind a sweetheart here in the city?"

"I... no. No sweetheart." I swallowed and reached for another glass of whiskey.

"Ahhhh," he said, as though by saying nothing I'd nevertheless spilled my guts. "You know, my Marnie and I were childhood sweethearts. Married almost fourteen years this spring."

"Four...*teen?*" Quick math suggested the General had left childhood behind slightly longer than that.

"Yep. She was my first love. Everyone in town knew it. But I was smart, you see. I went off to the Army to make my fortune, so when I came back to marry her I'd be able to offer her the world... Only when I came back, she was already married with a baby on the way. Turned out, everyone knew I loved her except *her*, and I wasn't quite as smart as I thought."

My jaw dropped. "That's... awful."

"Oh, love's rarely perfect, Brooks. I left town again and said I'd never come back. But I did. For my fortieth high school reunion. By then, I'd really made something of myself, you understand. Married and divorced. Had my son and daughter. Built a whole flock of restaurants and bought a garage full of Cadillacs. I had this notion that I'd roll into Soddy Gulf and everyone would fall at my feet. Marnie'd see what she'd missed out on."

"Oh, Lord."

"Uh-huh." His mustache twitched as he laughed at the memory. "Proud as a peacock and twice as stupid."

"And did they not fall at your feet?"

"Oh, no, most of 'em did. But not my Marnie. She took one look at me and said it was pretty clear I drove a Cadillac 'cause it was the only car that would fit my ego. But she also said we could head to the Waffle House for coffee if I promised to leave my ego locked in the trunk. And the rest is history." His eyes twinkled. "Not gonna lie to ya, Brooks, havin' money's real nice, especially when you know what it's like to go without. But having a person who sees you for who you are and not who you're pretending to be? That's priceless."

"Yeah," I said tightly. "I'm glad it worked out for you." And then, because we were going to be working together and because I was *done* with projecting an image, I added, "Things didn't work out for me with the guy I met in the Thicket last week. Mal. He, uh... designed the Welcome to Licking Thicket sign. You might've seen it?"

He nodded and his face broke out in a grin. "An artist, then. Temperamental?"

"A little." I smiled. "So talented, though. And funny. Smart."

"Not too smart if he's put that look on your face."

I snorted. "He lives in Los Angeles." And as far as I knew, he was going to stay there. Ava told Paul that Mal had briefly considered moving to the Thicket, but then his work had been selected for a showing at a high-end gallery—the kind of thing he'd been wanting forever—and once everyone saw how amazing his art was, I couldn't imagine why he'd want to move to Tennessee. I was happy for him, though.

Or, you know, I was trying to be.

"Ah, well. If you've laid it out for him, and told him how

you feel, and asked him to take a chance on you, there's not much more you can do, son. Drink up."

I blinked. "I... I would *never* ask him to take a chance on me if it meant giving up his dreams."

The General looked at me like I was dim. "What's one thing got to do with the other? If you love the boy, you help him make his dreams happen, whether it's in Tennessee or Timbuktu."

I shook my head. "I'm trying to give him space. That's what he asked me to do. He doesn't feel the same way about me. And he liked visiting the Thicket, but he's not into small towns."

"The boy who made that sign?" He shook his head. "You'll never convince me he doesn't love that town. Sounds to me like he's running scared. Or you are. Or both of ya." He leaned toward me over the table. "So ask yourself this, Brooks. You willing to wait forty years to tell the man what you should've told him right now? What's the worst that could happen if you tell him how you feel in plain words? He sends you away again? What do you have to lose?"

My pride. The last scraps of my heart. Nothing that meant much at all.

The General nodded, though once again I hadn't said anything, and downed the last of his drink. "Exactly. My money's on you, Brooks."

Chapter Twenty

Mal

For some reason the tuxedo I'd worn in Licking Thicket only a week ago had fit better than the one I was stuck in now. Or maybe I'd just felt a little more comfortable in that one because I'd been relaxed and happy instead of nervous and nauseated, and feeling like something essential was missing.

I looked around the gallery's pristine white walls and sleek tracks of lighting, specifically designed to highlight the strengths of each piece they shined on. It boggled my mind that my piece was included among other LA up-and-comer sculptors. There were some incredible works displayed here, and I was shaking with a combination of anxiety and excitement. Ava had warned me against imposter syndrome, but it was impossible not to feel like this had all been some kind of misunderstanding. Surely they'd picked me by mistake.

My phone buzzed in my pocket.

Ava: Knock 'em dead. Sorry I can't be there, but I'm sending you love!

She'd also sent me flowers and chocolate this afternoon. I knew she felt terrible for missing the opening reception, but her closest friend at the day spa where she worked had asked Ava to be her maid of honor and the wedding was this weekend up in Napa. It had been planned for months, and even then, Ava had tried to beg off the rehearsal dinner so she could be here for me. I'd laughed and told her she could come to the next one.

As if there'd be more.

My hands shook as I texted her back.

Me: *It's no Licking Bachelor Auction, but it'll do.*

I sent her the selfie of me in a tux with my sculpture behind me that I'd taken earlier before the doors had opened to guests.

I tried to tell myself that I was fine. I'd made my way from Homer to LA years ago all by myself, so I could totally handle one showing, no matter how huge and intimidating it was, right? But I couldn't help wishing for a friendly face. Or maybe one *specific* face, even if it might not be so friendly after the way I'd left things.

After five days back in Los Angeles, I knew what I felt for Brooks wasn't temporary insanity. Even though the bubble around us had popped and I was back in my "real" life, my feelings hadn't lessened one bit, and ironically enough, nothing felt very real. I'd thrown myself into work to prepare for the show, but that hadn't stopped me from missing Brooks's wry humor, the way his eyes crinkled at the corners when he smiled, the way he wrapped his arms around me and made me feel like anything was possible... Hell, I even missed his over-thinking perfectionism. And his stupid eyebrow cowlick.

At night when I lay in my bed alone, I thought about the night we'd spent in Dunn's cabin—the moonlight filtering through the window and Brooks's warm breath against the back of my neck. I'd never felt safer or more loved than I did that night, even though we'd never used that word. My heart didn't seem to care that everything had happened way too fast; it knew what it wanted.

So why the hell had I walked away?

I'd thought I'd moved on from everything that happened back in Homer. It was pretty clear I *hadn't*, though, if I was still letting fear of rejection influence my decisions. I was not going to let them steal one more minute of my happiness. After this showing, I was going to New York to talk to Brooks. I didn't know how things would work for us long distance, or if I could handle living in New York, but I owed it to both of us to try.

As I slid the phone back into my pocket, the gallery owner walked up and slipped her arm through mine. "Come with me. I want you to meet a few people who are very interested in your work."

I looked over at Tabitha Turnbull, who was known for finding fresh talent. "Have I thanked you yet for this opportunity?"

Her smile was genuine and sweet. "Only a thousand times. Have I thanked you yet for sharing your talent with the world?"

I blew out a breath. "Is it always this nerve-racking?"

Her laugh was elegant but sincere, just like her personality. "Absolutely. I wish I could tell you it gets better, but Kimmer Sinclair was vomiting in the ladies' room only fifteen minutes ago."

The famous sculptor had been showing at galleries for

at least thirty years. "Shit," I muttered with a laugh. "Maybe this isn't for me."

"Nonsense. An artist spends 99 percent of their time creating and only 1 percent networking. You can do it. This is what pays for your materials and studio space, remember? Oh, there's Bill North and..."

My phone buzzed in my pocket, and I took a quick look at it, expecting a response from Ava.

Ava: Red Johnson just got rushed to ER for a suspected heart attack.
Me: Is he okay???
Ava: They don't know. He lost consciousness.

All the blood drained from my body, enough to make me feel suddenly faint. Not Red. I couldn't handle the idea of something happening to that sweet man, and the thought of Brooks hearing about it while he was so far away from home...

Tabitha gripped my arm. "Mal? Are you okay?"

I glanced at her. "Yeah, I just... no. Actually, no. I'm not okay." I swallowed and looked back at my phone before glancing up at her. "I have to go."

Her eyes widened. "But this is your grand opening. I have an entire lineup of people for you to meet."

"I know, but... there's an emergency at home. My... someone very important to me is in trouble. I'm so sorry. Please forgive me."

Home. It wasn't completely accurate, but it still felt truer than anything I'd ever said.

Tabitha's face softened into concern. "Oh, of course. I'm so sorry. Go be with your family. There will be other opening nights, Mal, but family comes first."

I stared at her while the words sank in. *Family.*

After bolting out of there and making my way straight to the airport, I bought a ticket to Nashville and used my phone to arrange for a rental car when I arrived. Ava was no longer answering my texts, most likely because of the wedding rehearsal, but not having any updates about Red's condition was making me frantic. Did Brooks know yet? Was he on his way home?

I wanted to call him, text him, anything at all, just to hear his voice and tell him I was there for him if he needed me. But I knew I was the last person he probably wanted to hear from, and I'd be damned if I distracted him from any updates he was probably getting from home.

The flight I'd found from LA to Nashville was leaving soon, and I raced through security, stopping only long enough to get wanded after all of my tuxedo studs and cuff-links set off the metal detector.

The TSA agent winked at me. "You didn't have to get dressed up for me, doll."

Smiling back at her was the first time I stopped to take a breath since getting the text. "My mama always told me to dress fancy for airplane travel. I guess I took it a little too far."

"Well, you're not the only one. You're the second person I've seen in a tux tonight. Must be a full moon or something."

"Nah. Just LA, right?" I teased. She laughed and waved me on.

I hurried to the gate and was relieved to find boarding hadn't started yet. Everyone was starting to line up, but I decided to pop into one of the gift shops nearby to grab a bottle of water and some snacks for the flight.

I turned around and almost tripped over another man in a tux.

A familiar man in a tux. He was a vision, an absolute hallucinated figment of my imagination. Not only was Brooks standing there at the Los Angeles airport, but he was wearing a tux like he'd just come from the gallery opening.

I blinked and shook my head, but he was still there. His forehead crinkled in confusion. "Mal?"

At the familiar sound of his voice, I burst into tears. Was I going to be the one to tell him about his dad? What if something happened to Red while Brooks was here in California? And, God, he looked so good, so steady and true. He looked like everything I'd ever wanted, and I'd fucked it all up.

"I'm sorry," I croaked.

He pulled me in for a hug. His arms were tight bands around me, and I never wanted him to let me go. "Baby, what are you doing here?"

When I finally caught my breath enough to speak, I pulled back and looked up at him. "Your dad..."

Brooks's eyebrows lifted. "You're here for my dad?"

"He's... he's... They think he..."

"Oh, God, no, I know." His hands cupped my face, and he swiped his thumbs under my eyes to brush the tears away. "He's okay. I just talked to my mom. They're pretty sure it's just the new heart meds causing a dangerous drop in blood pressure. They're going to keep him there until they get the doses right. I'm sure they'll do more tests to be sure."

I blinked at him while the words sank in. "Are you sure? He's okay?"

He nodded. "Yeah. He's okay."

I leaned forward and tucked my face into the warm,

cologne-scented skin of his neck. "I love you," I whispered as quietly as I could. If he heard it, I might have to die of mortification. It was too soon, too crazy, but it was the truth, and I knew it now the way I knew I was meant to work with my hands. It was a part of me I couldn't deny.

"I love you too," he said against my ear, making me shudder and igniting my face with heat. "So fucking much. I came to see your grand opening, but then I got the call from Mom."

I looked up at him. "You came for my gallery opening? Really?"

At least the tux made sense now.

Brooks brushed some of my hair off my forehead and leaned in to kiss me. The familiar taste and feel of him washed over me, but his words were what finally put me at ease. "I never want to miss a single important moment of your life, Malachi Forrester. Even if you're still upset with me and want space, that's fine. But I couldn't bear to miss seeing your first gallery opening."

I sighed. "Not upset. I was stupid. And scared. Too scared to take a chance on us, too scared to tell you how I really felt."

"Well, that makes two of us. But I'd rather be stupid and scared with you than stupid and scared alone in New York."

"I can move to New York," I blurted. "I mean, if that's—"

Brooks shook his head. "No, I know you need to be here in LA for your career, at least for a little while. I'm moving back to the Thicket. And if I can get things arranged the way I want, I'll be able to move here eventually. I just need you to be patient with me. Paul and I are starting an ad agency, and since he needs to be in Tennessee for Ava—"

I snorted out a sound of happiness and clapped my

hand over my mouth. Brooks's face lit up. "You didn't know Paul was moving to Licking Thicket to be with Ava?" he asked with a grin.

"No, I did, but..."

"You didn't know I was moving there too?"

"Well, no, but that's not why I'm so happy."

He leaned in and pressed a long kiss to my cheek. "Why are you so happy, sweetness?"

"Because I'm moving there too."

Suddenly, I knew it was the truth. Moving to the Thicket didn't mean giving up on my career. My art had been valued in the Thicket. I'd sold a commission and had a lead on another one right there in small-town Tennessee. There was no reason at all to think I couldn't thrive in the Thicket *and* be surrounded by everyone who meant anything to me.

Brooks let out a deep breath and tightened his arms around me. "Thank fuck."

I felt light and free in a way I hadn't felt for a very long time, if ever. Red was going to be okay. Ava and Paul were going to be a family. And Brooks Johnson loved me.

The boarding announcements began blaring overhead. Brooks grabbed my hand and towed me over toward the gate counter.

"Hi, my boyfriend and I would like to sit together, please," he said politely to the gate agent.

Boyfriend. I shouldn't have felt giddy hearing it, but I did.

After getting us all squared away, the gate agent pointed us to the boarding desk, and I realized the lines had gone way down. We made our way through the tunnel and found our seats.

Brooks helped me take off my tux jacket and tie.

"Better?" he asked after doing the same.

I leaned over and whispered, "Better would include the removal of many more items, sir."

He laughed and kissed me. "Soon. Unless..." His face turned serious. "You don't have to come back now if you want to stay and see how your gallery opening did. Dad's going to be okay."

"Don't be ridiculous," I said. "Your dad loves me. Seeing me will help him recover." I gave him a teasing grin.

Brooks smiled tenderly at me. "I can't believe you left your gallery opening to fly home without a second thought. Thank you."

I ran my hands up his chest, feeling the smooth fabric of his shirt beneath my fingers. I swallowed my nerves and claimed what I wanted. "I don't care about a gallery opening as much as I care about my family."

"Your family, huh?" he asked with a gentle smile.

I nodded. "If... if that's okay with you..."

Brooks's hands came up to cup my face again, and the look he gave me made my heart damn near skitter out of my chest. "I love you, Mal. And I would love to take you home as a part of my family. Forever, if you'll have me."

I blinked out another pair of tears, but this time they felt more like happy ones than sad ones. I felt like I had the whole world in my hands now that I was holding the person I cared about most.

"I'm sorry I ran," I admitted in a whisper.

"I'm sorry I let you," he said right back. And then he kissed me, and I knew I'd found what I'd been searching for when I left Homer all those years ago.

I'd finally found my home, and I was never leaving him.

I reached over to clasp his hand in mine. Somehow we'd ended up exactly where we were supposed to be: flying into our future *together*.

Epilogue

Brooks

One Year Later

MY PHONE RANG in the bedroom just as I finished shaving, and I debated running out to answer it.

See, Mal and I were running late—as in, really late. As in, *later* than late. As in, so late that Paul was on standby to run Mal's booth at the Lickin' Artists Fair when it opened in thirty minutes, because we might not make it. As in, so late my mom had called to inform us of our lateness *twice*, and I was pretty sure she would've come over to drag us both there by the ear already if Mal hadn't laid on the honey, cross-his-heart-promised her we'd be there in twenty minutes, and begged her, pretty-please, to bring some of her *delicious* leftover ham biscuits for his breakfast.

The way Mal understood my mother's compulsive need to help everyone (especially when they least needed it) might've surprised me a year ago, but now I knew it was just part of who he was—endlessly loving and understanding of the people he considered his family. Fortunately, my family had returned his love tenfold.

"You gonna answer that, Head Licker?" Mal teased, deliberately brushing against me on his way out of the bathroom. His shower-damp chest slid against my equally damp back in a way that made my well-satisfied cock twitch hopefully in my shorts, and the look in his blue eyes when our gazes met in the mirror was not the look of a man who'd already come twice that morning.

Head in the game, Brooks, I told myself, more out of habit than anything, but then I grinned, because I no longer had a game to get my head in. These days the only thing I really cared about winning was walking his bubble butt through our bedroom door.

I hastily wiped the remnants of shaving cream off my face, tossed my dirty towel in the hamper, and followed him, forgetting all about my phone for the moment.

"That's co-Head Licker," I reminded him.

It had been decided that since I was slammed at work and my dad was feeling much better, he and I would share the Head Licker title this year—or, as my mother liked to say, "Brooks and his daddy will be Head Licking together."

At this point I had to assume she said these things on purpose.

"You'll always be Head Licker in Chief to *me*, baby," Mal said, fluttering his eyelashes at me over his shoulder.

I snorted. "Just like you'll always be my Second Licker."

"We could skip it, you know." I caught Mal as he stood in front of our closet and wrapped my arms around his waist from behind. His deep chuckle said he knew I was joking— I'd never *really* let him miss the Artists Fair and a chance to show off his amazing work, but occasionally it was fun to pretend.

"Skip the Lickin'?" he gasped in a credible impression

of my mother. "Never. As long as there's been a Johnson in the Thicket, a Johnson's been licking head!"

I pinched the smooth skin on his flank, and he laughed out loud. "Ohhhh, wait. Did I misspeak? My bad."

I ignored his smart-assery and pulled him back against me more tightly, skin against skin. "We could be in Paris by nightfall. Oh, or *Miami*," I said, thinking of the work trip back in June when Mal, Ava, and the baby had traveled to Florida to see Paul and me win the Addy award for Best Regional Marketing Campaign for our work on Partridge Pit. "You liked Miami." And I'd loved spoiling him with fancy dinners and a room with a view.

"Mmm. I did like Miami." Mal leaned his head against my shoulder, and I buried my nose in the crook of his neck. He smelled like the coconut lime body wash in our shower and the pure sweet scent of Mal. "I liked being there with *you*. I liked watching you and Paul collect your Addy. I liked hanging at the pool with Ava and the baby. I really, *really* liked the way you used that balcony..."

"Did you?" I twisted a little so Mal's back was pressed against our closet door, and I started sinking to my knees. "Because I could show you how my skill at 'licking head' has improved since then..."

"But the thing I really liked best about Miami—" He halted my movement by pressing his lips to my chin. "—was coming *home*."

"Home," I repeated blankly.

"Uh-huh." Mal wrapped his arms around my neck, and I looked down at him in amusement. "To this beautiful old farmhouse we're renovating." He pressed a kiss to the hinge of my jaw. "In this crazy town." A kiss to my cheek. "Where we live." My temple. "With our friends." The tip of my nose. "And your family." The corner of my mouth. "Who're right now drawing straws." The other corner. "To see who comes to get us."

He kissed me full on the lips... but before I could deepen the kiss, he pushed me away, grabbed a shirt from the closet, and edged toward the door of the room.

"You know poor Dunn would be the one to draw the short straw, right?" Mal said conversationally, pulling the shirt over his head. "And he'd walk in here prepared to be traumatized like he was the time he walked into our barn unannounced back in the spring?"

"Please," I grumbled, folding my arms over my chest as I thought back to that March morning and the cock-blocking that had ensued. "*Poor Dunn*, my ass. That wasn't the first time he walked in on us, if you recall. There was the time in the Iveys' barn too. The man needs a hobby."

"Dunn doesn't need a hobby, he needs a date." Mal ran one tanned hand through his chin-length hair.

I frowned. I couldn't remember Dunn dating anyone in nearly a year. "Huh. You might be right."

"I always am." He took a step toward me and gave me a quick kiss... which turned into a longer one... and a longer one still... before he broke away. "Ugh, seriously. Hurry up or your mom's gonna hate me."

I stopped him with a hand on his waist. "True or false, my mother gave you her sweet tea recipe last Christmas, even though you've yet to make an honest man of me."

Mal's gorgeous lips quirked. "True," he said modestly.

"*And* she pulled out the last of her freezer stash of Susie Dupree's Deluxe sauce for your birthday dinner, which was basically like her offering you her life's blood."

Mama had tried to love Partridge Pit, especially after getting to know and love the General and his wife, but the habits of a lifetime were hard to break, and in her mind, nothing would ever be quite the same as Miss Susie's.

"Also true."

"Then I think it's safe to say she likes you just a little bit, baby."

"Yeah," he sighed happily.

But when my phone started to ring on my nightstand, Mal jumped and his eyes took on a fairly panicked look. "That's her. *Shit*."

"Go on," I instructed, only rolling my eyes a little. "Get the last couple things from your workshop into your truck, and I'll be down in two minutes, okay?"

I grabbed my special "co-Head Licker" T-shirt from the closet and tossed it on the bed, then grabbed my phone to appease my mother.

But it wasn't Mama calling; it was General Partridge.

"Mornin', Beau." I put the phone on speaker and set it on the dresser. "Y'all on your way to the festival?"

"Yep. The truck with the food got there almost an hour ago, and we'll be arriving any minute," he confirmed. He added in a lower voice, "Assuming this rig of Parrish's manages to get us there in one piece."

"You know I can hear you, right?" his nephew Parrish demanded in the background. "FYI, this *rig* is a cabernet-red 1987 Ford Mustang GT that I restored *myself*. It's a classic."

"'Course I know! And I'm very proud of you, Parrish!" But in the same totally audible whisper, he added, "I offered to buy the boy a decent car, but he wouldn't let me. Who doesn't accept a car, Brooks?"

"I can still hear you," Parrish called.

"Leave the boy alone, Beau, and state your business. Brooks hasn't got all day," a feminine voice commanded, and I grinned because Beau's wife, Marnie, had him wrapped around her finger as surely as Mal did me... and Beau didn't mind it any more than I did.

I shoved my wallet in my pocket and assessed myself quickly in the mirror. Hair done, T-shirt on, phone in hand. I needed just one more thing...

"I'm thinking that since your boyfriend kitted out all of my restaurants with those funky tables made out of tractors and the smokers made out of oil barrels, I'm ready to take things to the next level, as the kids say."

"Oh, yeah? Like what?"

"I'm thinkin' it's time to make a new location in the Thicket. Kind of a... whajermacallit, Parrish?"

"A flagship location," he supplied.

"Yep. That. A flagship. Something where Mal can display his pieces all the time, if he wants to. Other local artists too. We can have some bands from the area play and do some of that dancin' where they all stand in a line. What's that called?"

"Line dancing," Parrish said. "But, ah... let's not get ahead of ourselves, Uncle Beau."

"Right, right. But I think it might be fun. Like that whippersnapper in New York said, a man's got to contemplate his own immortality."

I opened my mouth to remind him that Kale's speech had mentioned *impotence* and *mortality*, then closed it again because I was smarter than that, and I liked the General's version better anyway. "Absolutely he does," I agreed. "So true."

"Gotta change things up. Make the good even better."

I pulled open my top drawer, dug under the pile of cow-inspired T-shirts I'd somehow acquired, and grabbed the little black box I'd stashed there. Just looking at it made my pulse pound with anticipation. Tonight, I was gonna ask Mal the question that had been on the tip of my tongue since we'd moved in together last September... and "make the good even better," for reals.

I clenched the box in my fingers. "I like your style, Beau."

"Knew you'd agree, Brooks," he said happily. "We'll see you in a little while, alright? And you remind Mal to bring that teddy bear sculpture he made me so I can give it to my favorite honorary great-grandbaby."

"Will do," I promised. "Baby Beau will love it."

I grinned as I disconnected the call. One of the best things about moving home to the Thicket and starting our business was that Paul and I had gotten to know Beau and Marnie a lot better—so much so that Paul and Ava had named their son after him, and the General was head over heels for the boy.

I slid the black box into my pocket and flew down the oak stairs and out the back door. At the rear of our property, Mal and I had built a triple-wide barn to serve as his workshop. He had the double doors thrown open and the tailgate down on his pickup, but the man himself was nowhere to be found.

I walked into the barn, blinking in the sudden darkness... and found my boyfriend talking to a cow for the *second* time in our relationship.

"Listen up, missy. *I* make the rules here, got it?" Mal blew at a strand of hair stuck to his forehead as he held the cow's udder with both hands. "I am gonna attach this clamp to your teat while I get my iron, and you *will* stay where I put you, or I'm gonna leave you tied up here until I get back from the fair and I will *not* let you come."

I leaned against the barn door watching him, feeling

that sweet tightness in my gut and peace in my soul that came over me whenever I looked at the man I loved.

"You are still *such* a sweet talker, baby," I said fervently. "I had no idea bovine dominants were a thing, but I'm here for it. Clamp those teats *good.*"

Mal whirled to face me, and his eyes narrowed. "Do you mind? Ethel and I were having a moment."

I pushed off the door and looked at the rusted metal cow with its compression-spring eyes and the pitchfork-tine blades of grass sticking out of its mouth. "Ethel, huh?"

"Yup. I finished her up yesterday after we brought all the other larger pieces over to the fairgrounds. I knocked off one of her udders when I was trying to get her in the truck just now."

I snickered. "Babe, I realize you're an udder newbie..."

"Brooks. Allen. Johnson. All this day needed was cow puns." He grabbed his soldering iron off a rolling metal cart and sighed. "Did you want something here, boyfriend?"

Yeah, I really, *really* wanted something here, more than I'd believed I could want anything, and I wanted it for the rest of our lives.

But what I said was, "You want help wrestling that udder? Or do you and Ethel need privacy?"

Mal shook his head and tried—really poorly, I might add —to hide his smile. "I just need two undistracted minutes. Can you grab the box of smaller sculptures on my work-bench? I forgot to bring them yesterday."

I saluted and made my way to the back of the barn, past all the junkyard treasures Mal found on his weekly trips to Diesel's place, and grabbed the box Mal had set on the bench. It was larger and heavier than I'd thought—proof that Mal had been pretty damn inspired the last few weeks, and I couldn't wait to see the crowd of visitors *ooh*ing and *ahh*ing over his work.

As I picked up the box, I noticed one last sculpture Mal had forgotten—an adorable little cow that looked like it was wearing a Fighting Bovines football uniform, complete with a helmet. It even wore my old number 10. I smiled as I put that on top of the others in the box and thought for a minute that I should really buy that one for myself just to have it on my desk.

"Ready when you are," I called to Mal as I set the box in the back seat.

"Two more minutes. You know, they just don't make car parts as sturdily as they used to."

"Are you going to lecture me about Milton Reeves again?" I demanded. "Because you know I love it when you get all stroppy about mufflers, but we've got a booth to open, Mr. Award-Winning Artist."

Mal blushed and rolled his eyes as he always did when I mentioned the awards his reef piece had won... just like he'd rolled his eyes when my mom framed the write-up in the *Tennessean* about the dragon sculpture made of recycled toys he'd donated to the Children's Hospital in Nashville last year... and the same way he'd rolled his eyes when Ava had made him her "bride's man" before she and Paul tied the knot at the Licking Thicket community church last Valentine's Day, but deep down I knew he liked it. More even than the awards, my man had needed a family and a town who celebrated his successes with him. And now he had us.

I helped him move Ethel onto the truck, and we headed down to the town square. We pulled in five minutes before it opened.

"Ha! Luck was on our side," I informed him... a second

before Diesel Church pulled in beside us and gave Mal a chin-lift through the window.

I bit back an annoyed growl. It wasn't that I thought the man had been lying in wait, or whatever... it was just that I wouldn't put it past him either.

Mal waved hello, then shifted the truck into Park, and looked over at me. Whatever expression I wore made him laugh out loud. He leaned over the console and grabbed my chin, pulling me in for a kiss. "Remember what I told you a year ago? There's only one grumpy giant I'm in love with, and it's not Diesel Church."

"There's always Paris," I reminded Mal as I took my seatbelt off. "Miami."

"*Home*," Mal repeated, tossing me a wink before he jumped down from the truck.

Diesel waited by the tailgate to help us unload the truck, and Mal greeted him with a big hug that was no doubt meant to show me where I could stow my attitude. But then, because he was Mal, as soon as he broke the hug, he wrapped his arm around my waist and stuck his hand in my back pocket in a subtly claiming gesture of his own that reminded me I would never, ever get bored with this man or doubt how important I was to him.

"Hey, what's that lump in your pocket?" Mal asked, frowning. "It feels like..."

Damn it.

"Wow, hey, let's unload the truck, huh?" I said, pulling away. "We are running *late*. My mom is gonna be so upset, gosh darn it!"

Mal was immediately distracted.

Diesel jumped up in the bed of the truck and helped lift Ethel down, and he and I carried her to Mal's tent while Mal followed with the box of smaller sculptures.

"Brooks!" Ava exclaimed, popping up seemingly out of nowhere to give me a fast, tight hug. She was dressed in a hot pink dress and carried a matching clipboard. "Where have you been? The Beautification Corps needs you to sign this to approve the flowers for the dance!" She shoved her clipboard at me and dragged me off to one side of the tent, then demanded in a whisper, "Is it done? Are you engaged?"

I glanced around, half expecting my mother to sneak out from behind the Biscuit Barn's tent and demand to know what we were talking about. Ava knew I'd bought Mal a ring a long time ago—before Christmas, even—but I hadn't told her I was planning to ask him today or even anytime soon. How the heck did she know?

"No, it's not *done*," I whispered. "You'll know. Mal will probably call you five minutes later."

She nodded once, blonde curls bouncing. "Damn straight, he will. But you could give me a clue. Is it going to be tonight? It *is*, isn't it?"

"What? No. What? Why would you think that?" I stammered.

"Mal told me, you know," she said smugly. "About you two hooking up under the bleachers last year. That's what I put my money on."

"Wait." I shook my head. "Money? Do *not* tell me people are betting on this."

"Duh. Of course we are. Don't tell Paul, but I put a hundred bucks down, and if I win I'm getting him this auto-graphed baseball thing he wants, so let me know if you need my help! I'm always happy to— Hey! Excuse me, Hiram Bassett! That T-shirt cannon is not a toy, young man! Where is your mama?" She strode off after the little boy, calling, "Be back, Brooks!" over her shoulder.

What the hell? Thicketeers were making book on my *engagement*? Fortunately, my plan for tonight had not involved the bleachers.

Mal's tent was already bustling with customers. Mal and Diesel were standing in the back, discussing wrenches, of all things. Paul was eagerly talking up the smaller pieces on the front table to a couple of buyers, while baby Beau cooed happily in his front pack.

"Hey, li'l buddy," I said, running a hand over little Beau's white-blond hair once Paul's last customer had moved on. "It's hard to say if you're looking more like your mama or your daddy today." Beau gnawed his own hand happily and blew spit-bubbles. "Oh, no, wait, definitely Daddy."

Paul rolled his eyes and looked down at his son with pure love in his expression. Then he licked his lips and darted a glance at Mal from behind his glasses. "Hey, Brooks? Let's go stand over across the way and look back at Mal's table, just to make sure we have the aesthetic right."

"The aesthetic," I repeated, letting him push me a few feet from the tent. "Who are you, Paul Siegel? Give a man one advertising award and suddenly he—"

"Is it gonna be tonight?" Paul interrupted in a low voice. "Look, I know your plans are a secret, blah blah, but I used to be your fake boyfriend and that's gotta count for something, right Big Daddy? Gimme the scoop."

"Huh?"

"Also, I *may* have put a hundred bucks down on the proposal happening tonight at the Tavern."

"A hundred— Wait, the Tavern? Are you out of your damn mind?"

"Yeah, maybe don't mention the hundred to Ava?" He rubbed the back of his neck. "I wanna buy her these fancy shoes for her birthday. And why *not* the Tavern? That's one hundred percent the place where you and Mal started falling for each other last year. The whole Thicket knows it. So in honor of the big event, I got Alana to add a couple extra questions to her Never Have I Ever game."

I blinked at him in confusion. "What questions?"

"Well, first she's gonna ask if anyone here has ever made out under the bleachers here in the Thicket, and this time you *and* Mal can say *yes*."

"Oh, Lord." I rubbed a hand over my forehead.

"And then she's gonna ask if anyone at this table has ever asked anyone to marry them before... and *that's* when you drop to one knee."

"On the manky-ass floor of the Tavern? Which probably hasn't been washed since the day it was installed? In front of all of you?"

"It's perfect!"

"You're delusional. Tell Daddy to get his money back," I advised baby Beau before brushing past Paul on my way back to Mal. I heard Paul sigh.

"Hey, big bro!" Dunn said, coming up behind me and slinging an arm over my shoulder, forcing me to walk in the opposite direction, away from my boyfriend.

I sighed. "Dunn, have you considered woodworking? Or macrame? Or paint by numbers? Or... finding a nice woman who likes fishing?"

He looked at me like *I* was the crazy one. "Why would I want a nice girl to fish with when I have Tucker? No, look, I just wanted to tell you I got the cabin *set* for you, m'kay? No need to worry."

"The cabin?" I scratched my head. "Set for what?"

"'For what?' he asks! For tonight, obviously, dumbass. The spirit of romance is dead with you, man. I pity poor

Mal. But don't sweat it, 'cause I got the flowers in place, I got the candles set up, I got the chocolate sauce ready. After what I witnessed in the barn, it doesn't seem like you two need much more than a wall, and I provided four of those, but I figured you might wanna get fancy just this once—"

"Are you kidding me right now?" I whispered hotly. I felt my cheeks burn as I pulled away from him. "Shut your damn mouth, Dunn Johnson!"

"Easy there, Brooks. No judgment, bro!" He held out his hands placatingly. "But it *is* gonna be tonight, right? You, taking a knee? Mal, getting a ring? Not that I'm looking for insider information or whatever, just that I put a hundred down on it happening tonight at the cabin, since we all know that's where you two had your epic *Brown Chicken Brown Cow* night of passion last year." He wiggled his eyebrows... and then he frowned. "The whole town knows it's gonna happen this week, 'cause you're a pair of romantic schlubs. But, like, if it's not gonna be tonight, I should probably find out if non-dairy whipped topping needs to be refrigerated."

"But why would... No, you know what? I don't even want to know. *No*," I said tightly. "It's not happening at the cabin. God."

Though I had definitely considered it, damn it. And now I was starting to get worried that someone might have actually guessed my plan.

How the *hell* had this happened?

I stalked back toward the tent with my hands clenched.

"Brooks!" a familiar voice called from behind me. I let out a deep breath and paused so my dad could catch me up because that was the polite thing to do. "Hey, son. You just get here?"

"A few minutes ago," I confirmed. "You already spoke a few words to the crowd?"

"Sure did." His smile was sunshine bright, and he was clearly in his element. "Just wanted to let you know, I'm handling the ice cream contest later. I missed the little tykes last year."

"Oh." I relaxed marginally when I realized at least *one* person in this town hadn't bet on me. "Yeah, that sounds great. I'll handle the football throw tomorrow morning."

"Well, you could," he agreed. "You definitely could. But, ah... you might be tired, don't you think? If you were, you know... planning something tonight? So I'm happy to take the football throw."

I gaped at him. *Et tu, Red Johnson?*

He shrugged good-naturedly. "I might've been inspired to put down a couple of bucks on the betting pool the young folks are running. 'Specially since I happen to know exactly where it's all gonna happen."

Do not ask. Do not ask.

"Where do you think it's happening?" I demanded.

"Out under the sign, of course." He grinned. "If it helps any, I got Amos to move his whole herd to the north pasture, so nobody'll be mooin' or passing gas while you're tryna be romantical."

I made a disbelieving noise, like the air being let out of a balloon, and he clapped me on the back.

"Good man, Brooks," he said as he walked away.

Holy shit. He'd guessed it. And if *he'd* guessed it, how many other people had? Damn it all.

I'd had this whole speech planned out and typed up on my phone. I had a *playlist*. The night was predicted to be clear and warm without a cloud in the sky, and after I asked him to marry me, I'd envisioned me and Mal dancing under the stars. But now it seemed like the only way to keep this proposal just between us would be to convince him to crawl under our bed with me so only the dust bunnies could witness it.

I kicked at a rock on the ground. Maybe it'd be better to wait until tomorrow night. One more night wouldn't really hurt, right?

I made my way back to Mal's tent. Diesel seemed to have disappeared and Mal was busy talking to a customer about Ethel, so I grabbed the box we'd brought from his workshop and started placing the smaller sculptures out on the table haphazardly. I noticed Paul avoided my gaze, and I was grimly satisfied. *Fuck the aesthetic. So there.*

"There's my great-grandbaby!" a voice shouted from twenty feet away, and I summoned a smile as Beau, Marnie, and Parrish arrived.

A few minutes later, the General was seated in a folding chair with Beau on his lap, and both of them looked perfectly pleased with this arrangement.

"So, Mal," Beau said slyly. "Did Brooks talk to you yet?"

"Good God," I exploded. "How many people know about this?"

Beau blinked and looked at Parrish, who shrugged. "Just the couple of us on the call this morning?"

Behind me, Mal laid a hand on my back and asked, "Brooks, baby, are you okay?"

I opened my mouth and shut it... then repeated the process. "You're talking about the flagship location," I finally realized.

"Yep," Beau agreed. "What else would I have been talking about?"

I closed my eyes and sighed. "Nothing. Never mind. No, I haven't had a chance to tell Mal. Baby, Beau wants to open a flagship Partridge Pit here in the Thicket. A restaurant with a market area, where local artisans can show their craft."

"That's amazing," Mal said. "What a cool idea."

"I hadn't seen much of your work before today," Parrish offered, "other than the tables at the restaurants. But I love it. I could use a piece like this for my office." He picked up a cow sculpture from the table and ran his finger over its tiny football jersey.

Shit. In my haste, I'd put out the sculpture I'd been hoping to buy, and now Parrish was going to grab it.

"Oh, no, wait!" Mal said, pushing past me and advancing on Parrish. "Not that one!"

Parrish instinctively took a step back from Mal just as Diesel wandered into the tent saying, "Mal. I've got the wrench you wanted—"

The two men collided with enough force to send Parrish to the ground with Diesel mostly on top of him.

"Shit!" Diesel said, pushing himself to his feet almost instantly and holding out a hand to haul Parrish to his feet. He brushed at the dirt on Parrish's shirt. "Sorry, man. I—"

"Nah, don't even worry," Parrish said, laughing as he dusted off his ass. "It was totally my—"

Both men broke off at the same instant and stared at each other with wide eyes and open mouths.

Parrish swallowed. "I—"

Diesel turned on his heel and left without a word, and Parrish's shoulders slumped as he watched him walk away.

Well, damn. Did they know each other somehow?

I looked at the General, but he seemed to be as mystified as I was.

Meanwhile, my boyfriend had dropped to his hands and knees on the ground at Parrish's feet. "Where is it?" he moaned, running his hands over the dirt. "Where, where, where?"

"Mal, baby?" I took a step toward him.

"Stay back, Brooks!" Mal insisted. "Don't come over here."

"Mal, I'm so sorry," Parrish said, cradling the football-cow sculpture protectively. "If it helps, I don't think anything came off! Just this little door-type thingy came loose."

Mal didn't even seem to hear him. "It's gotta be here. It's gotta—"

"Oh!" Parrish said, bending down behind Mal and picking up a tiny metal fragment from the ground. "Got it, Mal! Now let's see, where would a platinum ring fit on here?" He inspected the cow, turning it over in his hands. "Looks more like jewelry than junk metal," he mused. "It's even got a…" Parrish cleared his throat. "A little diamond in the center?"

Mal turned around slowly, still crouched on the ground, and looked up at Parrish in disbelief and then swung his gaze to me. He looked absolutely devastated, and my breathing hitched.

Marnie clapped her hands once and said, "Alrighty, then! Who wants some Biscuit Barn?"

"Yep! I sure do love me some Biscuit Barn," the General agreed, holding baby Beau protectively to his chest as he got to his feet. "Come on, Paul. First round of biscuits on me. Parrish, son… put down the cow now and come along."

Parrish stood frozen for a second, looking down at the ring and the cow sculpture, and then he set them down on the table. "I'm… my… *sorry*," he whispered before bolting from the tent after the others.

Mal sat back on his heels and squeezed his eyes shut. "Brooks?"

"Yeah, baby?"

"Did Parrish Partridge just find the engagement ring I hid in the cow sculpture I made for you?"

My stomach clenched at the disappointment in his voice. "Evidence suggests... he did."

"Thought so." Mal sighed and got to his feet. He picked the ring up off the table and buffed it against his shirt. "You know, I bought you this ring last fall, and I've been waiting for the perfect time to give it to you. I was thinking Miami, but... it wasn't right. I wanted to do it around here. Someplace we could come back to, year after year. Someplace special."

"Someplace *perfect*?" I teased gently. I pulled the ring box from my pocket, removed the gold-and-black band, and crossed the distance between us. "I think I might be rubbing off on you, because I had the same idea."

"No," Mal breathed, staring at the band in wonder. "Are you serious right now?"

"I was going to take you out to the sign and propose under the stars." My voice went hard. "But everyone and their brother—or at least *my brother*—have been laying bets on when and where I was going to ask you. I wouldn't put it past this bunch to jump out of the tree line right when you said yes."

The warm, teasing sparkle was back in Mal's blue eyes when they met mine. "So you were assuming I'd say yes, then?"

I laughed. "Not assuming, but hoping, yeah. After all, you were the one who taught me that my wildest dreams could come true."

He closed his eyes and swayed forward slightly, resting

his forehead against my chest. I bent to place a kiss against his hair.

Mal took a deep breath, and when he lifted his head, his smile was radiant. "Ask me, then."

"What, here and now? On the dirt floor, in a festival tent—"

"In this town that's our *home*, surrounded by these insane people who are our family, *yes*. Because you and I are never, ever going to be perfect people, baby, but this love between us? This is perfect. And the life we're building is pretty damn close to perfect too."

I smiled down at the man I loved, blinking back some weird moisture in my eyes I would never admit to noticing. "Malachi Forrester, I love you, and I want nothing more than to be your husband and to walk by your side forever. Wherever you are is my home. Will you marry me?"

Mal's eyes glowed with happiness. "Hell yes," he whispered. "Looks like there's gonna be another Johnson in the Thicket."

I pulled him closer and lowered my mouth to his.

"Oh my God!" Ava cried softly. "That was so beautiful."

"I'm so proud of my boys," my dad said, his voice choked with emotion.

"I *told you* it was gonna happen today!" my mom crowed. "Who said afternoon at the tent? That's right, *I did*. And I'm gonna use my winnings to throw them the best wedding ever! Ava, assemble an emergency meeting of the Beautification Corps, baby. Cindy Ann Johnson's got a wedding to plan!"

"You're sure about this?" I whispered against Mal's lips. "Last chance. Paris? Miami?"

"*Home*," he said with a soft laugh.

Mal stood on his tiptoes and kissed me without hesitation, sealing our bargain better than any rings or ceremony ever could, and I thought about how damn lucky I was to have been born in this town, even if it had taken me twenty-eight years to recognize it.

Because only in Licking Thicket could my ex-girlfriend's fake ex-boyfriend become the very *real* love of my life.

———

Want more Licking Thicket romance? Check out more hilarious reads set in the punniest small-town in America...
Flakes (Colin and Ryder)
Liars (Diesel and Parrish's story)
Fools (Dunn and Tucker)
Turkeys (Charlton and Hunter)
Peacocks (Lane and Jay)

Letter from Lucy & May

Dear Reader,

Thank you so much for reading *Fakers*! If this is your first book by one of us and you'd like to read more, we suggest you start with Lucy's *Borrowing Blue* and May's *The Date*.

We would love it if you would take a few minutes to review *Fakers* on Amazon, Goodreads, or BookBub. Reader reviews really do make a difference and we appreciate every single one of them.

We've been friends and fans of each other's work for a couple of years. Working together on *Fakers* was a dream come true and so much fun!

Since we both enjoy the fun and heart-warming hijinks of small-town romance, we decided to go all-in on some of these themes for our first collaboration. We ended up falling in love with the town and people of Licking Thicket so much that we decided to write more books in this world.

Check out the rest of the Licking Thicket series on Amazon
→ http://www.lucylennox.com/l/1444576

Our most recent cowritten series is set in another delightful small town and you can go here → https://readerlinks.com/l/3077980 to check out all the shenanigans in Honeybridge, Maine. And if you like to stay in the Thicket a little longer, check out our spin-off series, Champion Security here → https://readerlinks.com/l/4189908

Be sure to follow both of us on your favorite retailer site to be notified of new releases, and look for us on Facebook for sneak peeks of upcoming stories. You can also join both of us on Patreon for exclusive content and behind-the-scenes glimpses. Find Lucy here → https://readerlinks.com/l/4255454 and May here → https://readerlinks.com/l/4255455!

Feel free to sign up for our newsletters, stop by www.Lucy-Lennox.com, www.MayArcher.com, or visit Lucy's Lair and Club May on Facebook to stay in touch.

To see fun inspiration photos for this book, check out the Pinterest page for Fakers.

Happy reading!
Lucy & May

More From Lucy and May

Licking Thicket

Flakes

Fakers

Liars

Fools

Turkeys

Peacocks

Champion Security

Hijacked

Hitched

Hacked

Honeybridge

Firecracker

Mr. Important

About Lucy Lennox

Lucy Lennox is the USA Today bestselling author of over fifty gay romance titles including the GoodReads Hall of Fame winner Wilde Love. Born and raised in the southeast USA, she is finally putting good use to that English Lit degree she earned before the turn of the century.

Lucy enjoys naps, pizza, and procrastinating. She stays up way too late each night reading romance because it's simply the best.

For more information and to stay updated about future releases, sales and audio news and to grab some free and bonus reads, please sign up for Lucy's author newsletter on her website at LucyLennox.com or to stay in the know, join her exciting reader group, Lucy's Lair on Facebook.

facebook.com/lucylennoxmm

instagram.com/lucylennoxmm

amazon.com/Lucy-Lennox/e/Bo1NoIOYPT

bookbub.com/authors/lucy-lennox

patreon.com/lucylennox

pinterest.com/lucy_lennox

Also by Lucy Lennox

Find me online → https://linktr.ee/LucyLennox

Read my books:

Made Marian Series

Forever Wilde Series

Aster Valley Series

The Billionaire Brotherhood Series

After Oscar Series (with Molly Maddox)

Twist of Fate Series (with Sloane Kennedy)

Licking Thicket Series (with May Archer)

Champion Security Series (with May Archer)

Honeybridge Series (with May Archer)

Find a complete list of my stand alone romances and novellas at www.LucyLennox.com along with audio samples, freebies, suggested reading order, and more!

About May Archer

May is an M/M author who lives in Boston. She spends her days planning vacations, mainlining diet soda, avoiding the gym, reading M/M romance, and when all other forms of procrastination fail, writing it.

Visit her website at mayarcher.com to sign up for her newsletter to hear about sales and upcoming releases, freebies and behind the scenes info and more! Or join her Facebook group, Club May!

facebook.com/may.archer.author

instagram.com/mayarcherauthor

amazon.com/May-Archer/e/B075JQVGLX

patreon.com/MayArcherRomance

bookbub.com/authors/may-archer

Also by May Archer

Find me online → https://linktr.ee/mayarcherauthor

Love in O'Leary Series

Whispering Key Series

The Sunday Brothers Series

Copper County Series

The Way Home Series

Licking Thicket Series

(cowritten with Lucy Lennox)

Champion Security Series

(cowritten with Lucy Lennox)

Honeybridge Series

(cowritten with Lucy Lennox)

For a comprehensive list of titles, audio samples, freebies, suggested reading order, and more, visit my website at www.MayArcher.com!

www.ingramcontent.com/pod-product-compliance
Lightning Source LLC
Chambersburg PA
CBHW060646190726
48289CB00002B/294